# Northern Frights 5

# Northern Frights 5

Edited by Don Hutchison

Mosaic Press
Oakville, ON — Niagara Falls, NY

Canadian Cataloguing in Publication Data

Northern Frights 5

ISBN 0-88962-676-6

1. Horror tales, Canadian (English). 2. Canadian fiction (English) - 20th century.* I. Hutchison, Don

PS8S23.S3N665 1999   C813'.0873808054   C99-931838-1
PR9197.35.S33N66 1999

No part of this book may be reproduced or transmitted in any form, by any means, electronic or mechanical, including photocopying and recording information storage and retrieval systems, without permission in writing from the publisher, except by a reviewer who may quote brief passages in a review.

Published by MOSAIC PRESS, P.O. Box 1032, Oakville, Ontario, L56 5E9, Canada. Offices and warehouse at 1252 Speers Road, Units #1&2, Oakville, Ontario, L6L 5N9, Canada and Mosaic Press, 4500 Witmer Industrial Estates, PMB 145, Niagara Falls, NY 14305-1386

Mosaic Press acknowledges the assistance of the Canada Council, and the Department of Canadian Heritage for their support of our publishing programme. All stories copyright 1999 by the authors.

THE CANADA COUNCIL FOR THE ARTS SINCE 1957 | LE CONSEIL DES ARTS DU CANADA DEPUIS 1957

"Oak Island" was originally published in *Hong Kong Macabre,* 1994.
Copyright © 1999, The Authors
ISBN 0-88962-676-6
Printed and bound in Canada

MOSAIC PRESS, in Canada:
1252 Speers Road, Units #1&2,
Oakville, Ontario, L6L 5N9
Phone / Fax: 905-825-2130
cp507@freenet.toronto.on.ca

MOSAIC PRESS, in the USA:
4500 Witmer Industrial Estates
PMB 145, Niagara Falls, NY
14305-1386
Tel: 1-800-387-8992
cp507@freenet.toronto.on.ca

# Contents

| | | |
|---|---|---|
| *PREFACE* | Don Hutchison | vii |
| *A VOICE IN THE WILD* | Hugh B. Cave | 1 |
| *OAK ISLAND* | Rebecca Bradley | 11 |
| *THE BLESSING* | Scott Mackay | 45 |
| *TIME FLIES* | Gregory Ward | 63 |
| *SLOW COLD CHICK* | Nalo Hopkinson | 69 |
| *PET WORMS* | David Shtogryn | 81 |
| *THE EMPEROR'S OLD BONES* | Gemma Files | 87 |
| *CROSSING* | Andrew Weiner | 107 |
| *FLUSHED* | Dale L. Sproule | 125 |
| *PITTER PATTER* | Carol Weekes | 131 |
| *CAVE OF THE WINDS (poem)* | Carolyn Clink | 145 |
| *INSPIRITER* | Nancy Kilpatrick | 147 |
| *OYSTER LOVE* | Susan MacGregor | 155 |
| *THE RAT, PEERING OUT, SEES JUSTICE DONE* | Vincent Grant Perkins | 167 |
| *JANE'S HEAD* | James Powell | 185 |
| *DOING DRUGS* | Sally McBride | 203 |
| *NIGHT OF THE TAR BABY* | David Nickle | 217 |
| *PLATO'S MIRROR* | Robert Charles Wilson | 241 |

# Preface

Writers are often troubled by the question "Where do you get your ideas?" Similarly, we editors must face the daunting "What do you look for in choosing a story?" In reply I occasionally comment on style, theme, plot, characterization and other factors, but the truth is that an editor has less to fret about than the writer. Once he spots a well-written submission his main concern is whether he likes it, and whether the reader will too.

You never know where a good story will take you. With diversity as the rule, our *Northern Frights* tales have displayed a heady mix of differing themes and styles, many of them bordering on science fiction, mystery, mainstream, magic realism, or psychological thriller as well as outright horror and dark fantasy. And it's no secret that some of our more outrageous examples were meant to be funny — telling the dark jokes that make skulls grin.

Within the following pages are 17 stories, each distinctly different from the other but each an example of the kind of thing we like when we see it. No fanged Carpathian vampires here, no fog-shrouded ruins, chain-rattling spirits or forbidden eldritch tomes. Instead, we offer you contemporary journeys into the mysteries of human behavior and into the dark mazes of the mind as its own haunted castle, greater sources of fear than all the ghosts and hobgoblins that ever stalked Europe. But lest that sound too serious, we warn you that the following pages also feature a zombie cat, vengeful lake trout, flesh-eating worms, and a bathroom fixture that swallows humans — all viewed through the skewed mirror of imagination.

As we said, you never know where a good story will take you. Although there's no substitute for actually getting away from it all, you can go a long way with this book, a comfortable chair and a little imagination. So let us be your tour operators. Some of our landscapes are scary, but we think you'll enjoy the trip.

*Don Hutchison*

# A Voice in the Wild
## by Hugh B. Cave

*This latest story from one of the grandest of the Grand Masters of dark fantasy is based on a wilderness expedition into northern Ontario back in the days of the author's dominance as an icon of the pulp fiction era. Hugh writes: "It was a great adventure through what was then (in the mid-thirties) a real wilderness with no camps or campsites anywhere. For six weeks, living mostly on the fish we caught, we canoed north through a series of lakes (portaging over footpaths between them,) then turned around and came back down the Mississagi River. Even our Cree guides had never seen the Mississagi River falls before, and those falls seemed as high as Niagara and so loud we heard them from two or three miles away!"*

*Despite the foregoing, we should point out that the story is by no means autobiographical and that it has also provided the background for Hugh's latest book, an "end of the world" novel,* The Dawning, *soon to be published under the Leisure imprint.*

After the fourth bank robbery, in which they shot and killed a guard, the two of them drove north to Sudbury, then west on 17 along the north coast of Lake Huron. Their destination was a small town named Bridge from which Luke, before turning to a life of crime, had once embarked on a canoe trip into the wilderness with some adventurous pals.

Luke knew an outfitter in Bridge from whom they could rent wilderness gear and a canoe. Their car, which had not been used in the holdups and would not betray them, they could safely leave in his care. What they would do was hide out in the wilderness for a while, living off the land. Then when sufficient time had passed for the hue and cry to die down, they could return to civilization with money enough for a life of leisure.

All this had been planned out in detail a month or so before the robberies. What they had not planned on was getting drunk near Webbwood and raping a young woman when they found her and her boyfriend in a broken-down pickup truck beside the road at night. Emile had shot the boyfriend, then both of them had raped the girl. And then, of course, it had been necessary to kill her too, or she would have described them when questioned.

The outfitter said, "There's a feller here name of Charley you could use as a guide, if you like. He has a camp way back in there and is travelin' alone. You want to talk to him?"

"Why not?" Luke said, he and Emile agreeing it might be a good idea to have someone along who knew the lakes and portages, and could do the cooking. But Charley turned out to be a Cree Indian probably as old as the two of them put together, and they declined his services.

"Well," old Charley said with a shrug, "if you run into any trouble in there, I'll be pretty close behind you, I expect. Good luck, anyway."

They talked about that and other things their first night in the wilderness, with two lakes and two portages behind them. The outfitter had provided them with a lightweight tent, backpacks full of staples, fishing gear, and, of course, the canoe. Finding the canoe awkward at first, they had been forced to spell each other frequently over the portages. But each had quickly learned how to flip the craft upside down, lower it onto his shoulders, and stride along with it. Now with the tent up on the shore of the third lake and a cozy fire glowing in front of it, they finished their first wilderness meal of fresh-caught trout.

Trolling for fish while paddling, they had caught more than enough trout to know that with a whole string of such lakes in the wilderness ahead, they need not fear going hungry. While sharing the first of several bottles of whiskey they had brought along, they felt safe enough to reminisce.

"That girl," Luke said. "She was a bit of all right, eh? Told me her name was Michelle." Luke was twenty-seven and well over six feet, with dark hair that he had let grow long so that it framed his face. Not a bad-looking face unless you were turned off by thin lips, a sharp nose, and rather piercing dark eyes. "Michelle," he repeated, nodding. "Bit of an all-right name too, eh? Too bad their truck didn't break down closer to Bridge, or we might have figured out a way to bring her along for company."

Lifting his long-fingered hands to the back of his neck, Luke fumbled with the clasp of a gold necklace he had taken from the girl's dead body. After a moment of struggle he managed to get the clasp open and hold the prize out in front of him. Then, peering more closely at the heart-shaped golden locket dangling from it, he said with a frown, "Hey! You suppose this could be one of those with—"

Clutching the locket, he brought it closer to his dark eyes. And seeing for the first time that it was hinged, he employed a thumbnail to snap it open.

Inside was a tiny photograph of the girl and her boyfriend.

Luke turned it so his companion could see it. "Looka this, will you," he said with a grin. "We got somethin' to remember her by!"

Emile leaned forward to peer at the photo. A year younger than Luke, he was several inches shorter but larger around the middle, with close-cropped yellow hair and pale blue eyes. "Both of 'em, hey? Did she tell you what his name was?"

"Jeffrey. She said his name was Jeffrey and they were gonna be married in the fall."

"Michelle and Jeffrey, huh? And you're wearin' 'em 'round your neck. You think you oughta be doin' that, Luke?"

"Why not?" Luke shrugged. "You got his belt on."

Emile looked down at the leather band around his pudgy middle. True, he had taken it from Jeffrey's dead body after Luke shot the fellow. But it was the best brown belt he had ever seen, made of real leather but soft, with a handsome design carved or pressed into it. Why not, for God's sake? Jeffrey wouldn't be needing it any more.

Funny, he thought. Luke had shot the boyfriend and was wearing the girl's necklace. He, Emile, had shot the girl and was wearing the boyfriend's belt. Should be the other way round, huh?

A rustling sound behind him near the water's edge caught his attention and he jerked his head around. The sound came closer, as though someone or something were crawling through a clump of grass there. Frowning, he reached for the Beretta Model 70 that was never more than inches from his gun-hand. Each man carried one.

Taking aim, Emile squeezed the trigger.

The sound of the shot shattered the stillness and sent echoes bouncing over the lake. The brush stopped moving. Emile got to his feet and with the eight-shot automatic still clutched in his hand, went striding toward the water's edge. The light from the fire showed him what he had killed. With a whoop of triumph he snatched up and waved a small porcupine.

Striding back to the fire, he dropped his prize at Luke's feet. The bullet had all but taken its head off. "Some shot, hey?" he gloated.

"A real good one," Luke conceded.

"Even that old Cree Indian couldn't do better, I bet," said Emile, and kicked the dead porcupine aside before sitting down again.

Next day Emile and Luke used their auto pistols four more times as they crossed the third lake and walked their rented canoe and gear over the third portage to lake number four. There was no reason not to, they told each other. They had plenty of ammunition and were entitled to at least a little pleasure here in the wilderness.

From the canoe Emile shot a small otter that surfaced within range, hitting it squarely between the eyes. On the portage, while his companion trudged behind him with the canoe, he spotted a Canada owl on a dead branch overhanging the trail and sharpened his shooting skills on that. Then when Emile took over the canoe, Luke whooped with delight on knocking a hawk out of its nest — it fell behind them on the trail — and later in killing a skunk that waddled unsuspecting from the brush ahead of him.

Again that night they sat at a fire in front of their tent and talked about their careers. About the banks they had robbed, the guard they had killed, the girl named Michelle and her boyfriend, Jeffrey.

Again Luke removed the heart-shaped locket from his neck so they could look at the photo in it.

Again they bemoaned the fact — aloud — that they had not been able to bring Michelle into the wilderness with them.

"Geez," Luke said, pushing grimy fingers through his long dark hair while shaking his head. "With her along I wouldn't mind bein' stuck in here awhile."

"Me neither," agreed his pudgy companion. "But at least we didn't bring that old Indian along. Can you imagine havin' him in our hair every minute?"

They lived on the fish they caught, plus bannock, some packaged soups, powdered eggs and other basics with which the outfitter in Bridge had stuffed their backpacks. One day Luke managed to kill a small deer with his handgun, and they ate that for several meals. Another time Emile shot a duck and they ate that.

Other creatures they shot for amusement while telling each other it made sense to hone their skills whenever an opportunity presented itself.

Each new day brought such opportunities. An oversized turtle plodded into their camp one evening. A gray bit of fluff called a Canada jay betrayed its nesting site one afternoon by voicing its loud "Ka-whee!"

Luke shot the turtle and laughed when it flipped over on its back and struggled for two full minutes to right itself before dying.

Emile shot the jay and threw up his hands in self approval as it dropped onto the trail amid a flutter of soft gray feathers.

Then on the fifth day they came to a lake that pleased them, and after paddling across it and finding a likely campsite, decided to go no farther.

"To hell with more walkin'," Luke said. "This here's as good as we'll find, and far enough in for us to be safe. I say we set up a camp here, make real beds with pine boughs and stuff, and use some of these boulders for a decent fireplace. We already know the lake's full of fish."

The lake was indeed alive with fish. Caught by trolling as they had paddled across it, eleven large trout lay in the bottom of the canoe at that moment. To celebrate their decision Emile raised his Beretta, took aim at a large green frog that watched them from a nearby lily-pad, and squeezed the trigger. The frog burst into fragments.

By nightfall they had settled in and were seated around a fire with another bottle of the whiskey they had brought along. And when drunk enough they talked again of their accomplishments.

Of the banks they had robbed.

Of the guard they had killed.

Of the young woman, Michelle, and her fiancé, Jeffrey.

"Let's see that locket again," Emile said, putting a hand out. "Lookin' at her in the photo ain't as good as havin' her here, o' course, but it's better'n nothin'."

Luke took off the necklace and opened the locket, helping himself to a long look at the photo before handing it over. "What the hell," he said then. "Let's have a look at what you got from those two. I never did really look at it."

Emile unbuckled the belt and passed it over. "I ain't swappin'," he warned. "It may be a bit snug on me, but that's the best belt I ever owned."

After a while they ran out of memories and, being too drunk to talk any more, turned in.

Most of the following day they spent sleeping off hangovers, though late in the afternoon they devoted an hour or so to fishing. As the day waned, Luke carried a collapsible canvas bucket down to the shore for some water and, while scooping it full, saw a canoe on the lake. Wide-eyed with astonishment, he straightened up and watched it glide toward him for a moment, then shouted for Emile, who came running.

The man so skillfully wielding the paddle was the Cree they had been introduced to by the outfitter in Bridge. As he stepped ashore and drew his craft up on the sand, he frowned at them. He was no threat to their safety, of course. Even without the weapons they carried, they could have handled with ease anyone that old.

"You been followin' us?" Standing tall, with arms folded across his big chest, Luke made the question a challenge.

"Following you?" The old fellow seemed puzzled. "There is only one way through these lakes, friend. All of us must use the same portages." He peered past them at the camp they had set up. "But you are planning to remain here awhile, no?"

"That's right," said Emile, adding pointedly, "and we got here first, mister."

"Charley. My name is Charley, and I will not trouble you." The Cree lifted his aged shoulders in a shrug. "For tonight only will I be stopping here, then with break of day I will be on my way again.ö He turned as though to look across the lake at the way he had come. "I knew you were ahead of me, of course. You left your mark on every portage. Dead things, everywhere." Bending over his canoe to lift out a lightweight one-man tent, he muttered something else that sounded to Luke like "God's creatures."

"What?" Luke snarled. "What's that you said?"

The Cree glanced up over a shoulder. "I said good night," he replied with a shrug. Then after turning his canoe over on the sand, so in the event of rain it would not collect water, he swung the tent onto one shoulder, picked up a backpack, and walked away, evidently in search of a suitable place to spend the night.

Luke and Emile returned to their campfire and prepared an evening meal of trout. When finished, they carried their soiled tin plates and cooking utensils down to the lake to clean them. Dusk had descended. As they squatted side by side at the water's edge, scrubbing the gear with sand, they heard a sound that caused them to stop work and look to their left along the shore.

Their unwelcome guest, Charley Cree, was singing. Or was it chanting? He was doing something with his vocal chords, at any rate. With night coming down, the sound knifed eerily through the stillness.

It was still doing that when they finished their cleaning up and returned to their fire. As their talked turned again to the deeds they were so proud of, the chanting became an intrusion that could not be tolerated.

"Come on," Luke said angrily. "We gotta shut him up!"

Together the tall dark man and the short blond one descended to the lake again and made their way along the shore toward the glow of Charley Cree's fire. Reaching it, they found him seated cross-legged on a dark blanket beside it, his arms folded on his chest, his upper body swaying back and forth as the chant poured from his aged lips.

"You!" Luke snarled. "What are you doin', for God's sake? Tryin' to wake up the whole of creation?"

The chanting ceased, and the Cree looked up at them in silence.

"How the hell you expect anyone to sleep around here with all that racket goin' on?" Emile demanded. "What's it for, anyways?"

In a voice not nearly as loud, the Indian replied with a shrug, "I talk with the spirits."

"What spirits?" Luke asked in anger.

"Those of my people. We—my people—always talk with them when we have problems."

"Well, not tonight you don't," Luke snarled. "Not with us needin' our sleep. You keep it up and you'll get an answer from this, see? And nobody way the hell back in here will ever know what happened to you." Reaching into his pocket, he produced the Beretta automatic with which he had killed the bank guard and Jeffrey. "You got that, old man? You hearin' me good?"

Charley Cree gazed at the weapon in silence for a few seconds, then moved his grizzled head slowly up and down. "I am finished, anyway," he said.

"All right," Luke said. And to Emile, "Come on, let's get out of here. This guy gives me the creeps."

There was no more chanting. The only intrusive sound after that was made by Luke himself when, seeing what he thought was an eagle above the treetops, he lay flat on his back by their fire, took careful aim with his Beretta, and tried to shoot it down. He either hit it or badly startled it, for while it did not plummet to earth as he hoped, it did stagger in flight and drop a few feet before recovering and soaring away.

"Shit," Luke said. "I'm losin' my touch."

"Can't win 'em all," said his companion. "Come on now. We oughta hit the hay if we're gonna try for some fish in the mornin'."

Charley Cree appeared to be gone when they went down to the lake in the morning. At least, his canoe was gone from where he had left it. They could not see his campsite from that stretch of shore to know whether the tent, too, had disappeared.

"We trollin', or should we cut some poles?" Emile asked. The outfitter in Bridge, probably guessing they were not sportsmen, had not provided them with fly-rods, only with lines and hooks, plus a few lures in case they were unable to find bait at times.

"Trollin's easier," said Luke. "But wait'll we're out a ways."

With the short one in the bow and the tall one in the stern, they paddled out onto the lake. The sun was just coming up. On the opposite shore, tall evergreens stood black as etchings against a crimson sky. When he felt the water was deep enough, Luke tied one end of his line to a thwart, fastened a lure to the other end, and dropped the lure into the water. Emile did the same. In a moment both lines were taut as the canoe continued more slowly on course with only a gentle gurgling sound to disturb the morning stillness.

Nothing happened.

Bored, Luke began a conversation. The usual conversation. About the accomplishments they were so proud of. About the bank robberies, and their encounter with the young couple in the disabled pickup truck. About what a shame it was that they had been forced to kill the young woman rather than bring her here into the wilderness with them.

"Damn it, we should've brought her," Luke said. "It would've been worth the risk."

Suddenly the line he had fastened to his thwart tightened with a jerk and began vibrating like a plucked guitar string. Then Emile's, in the bow, did the same. The talk ceased, and each man eagerly became an angler.

But as they reached for their lines to haul in what was causing the twitching, their outstretched arms abruptly froze.

"What the—" The fishing forgotten, Luke began clawing with both hands at his neck, where the necklace he had taken from the dead girl had suddenly come alive.

"Hey!" shouted Emile, dropping his line to claw with both his hands at the belt he had taken from the girl's dead boyfriend.

It, too, had suddenly begun to tighten.

Luke let out a yell, too, and then had no breath left for yelling as the necklace tightened like a hangman's noose about his throat. It shouldn't have been strong enough to do that, he told himself as panic gripped him. It was only a thin band of gold and should be a cinch to break. But he couldn't break it. The band was already so tight around his neck, there was no way he could even get his clawing fingers behind it. Every second it became tighter.

Now it was like a ring of steel, seemingly determined to cut his head off. Struggling with it in vain, his arms, hands and head going through a pantomime of contortions, he was so short of breath he could not even cry out.

In the bow of the canoe, the performance was being duplicated, except that Emile struggled with the band about his middle. The belt. The handsome, soft-leather belt he had taken from the body of the dead girl's dead fiancé. It had been a bit constrictive about his pudgy waist from the start, with no flap to spare, no extra holes. Now it was becoming tighter every second.

"My God, Luke, what's happenin'?" he screamed at his companion.

Luke had no breath with which to respond. Luke was no longer even struggling. His mouth was open as though gasping in vain for air. The necklace was so deeply buried in his throat, it was all but invisible. Even the locket containing the two miniature photographs seemed about to disappear into an ever deepening fissure of flesh.

Meanwhile the lines continued to jerk, though perhaps, like the necklace, they too should have broken under such stress, and now there was a kind of rhythm or synchronization in the way they were jerking. As though the two fish on the ends of them were working as a team to turn the canoe over.

Neither Luke nor Emile noticed. In the stern, Luke's face was turning purple as the golden noose about his throat became ever more tight. In the bow, a flap of leather with four empty holes in it now dangled from the belt tightening about Emile's tortured middle. Both men struggled feebly in silence, having no breath left with which to cry out.

Suddenly the two lines quivered in a climactic tug, and the canoe turned over with a convulsive gurgle.

The craft was still upside down and obviously empty moments later when a second canoe, with Charley Cree paddling, appeared around a wooded bend of shore and came gliding out into a blaze of golden sunlight. It continued to jerk and twitch, however, as the hooked trout that had overturned it struggled to free themselves.

Coming alongside the overturned craft, the Cree leaned sideways to put a hand on it, then lifted his grizzled head and gazed up at the sky. "Thank you," he murmured. "Thank you for answering this humble one's prayer."

He felt the jerking then. Guessing what was causing it, he investigated, and after a moment of maneuvering located the twitching lines. Very gently he drew the two hooked fish to the surface.

"As for you," he said as he released them, "you did well, though I think those two were disposed of anyway and drowning them was probably not necessary. Go now, and be content."

# Oak Island

## by Rebecca Bradley

*Rebecca Bradley was born in Vancouver and grew up largely in Calgary, but her archaeological studies (she earned a Ph.D. at Cambridge) took her to Egypt and the Sudan and eventually to Hong Kong, where she began writing fiction full time. She is the author of six books, an outstanding fantasy trilogy published by Gollancz in London as well as a vampire novel and two short story collections produced in Hong Kong. True to her peripatetic background, the following story is set in Ireland but was written during Rebecca's Hong Kong sojourn. She is now back home in Calgary, where she lives with her phonetician husband and their children.*

I

Nobody goes to Oak Island. Who in his right mind would want to or dare? Flattened, scarred, matted with new growth feeding off the ashes of the old, it is the sole blemish on the lough's otherwise fair and photogenic face. Navigation markers, pied red and white, stud its shallows to warn the little boats to keep away. Recent guidebooks on the amenities and antiquities of the Ulster loughs accord it only two or three lines, attesting to its lack of both. The tourists pass it by. The locals, knowing its history, could not be paid to go near it.

This was not always so. Older guidebooks would mention a path to the highest point of the island, where "rock carvings of an unusual nature, unique in Irish archaeology" were once to be found. A paragraph would usually be devoted to historical connections with the neighbouring island of Devenish, and with Devenish's long monastic history; reference might be made to exorcisms performed on Oak Island's crest in the fourteenth and seventeenth centuries. And, assuming these academic attractions were not enough, the island's one jetty was said to afford excellent fishing.

Captain H. Magill, retired lifeboat master for Lough Erne, will tell you that the first signs of trouble were brought to his attention in June of a year in the early 1970's, a time when Ulster's sad troubles were on the rise. The tourist season had only just opened, but rented cabin cruisers were already menacing the waterways of the lough and competing for moorage at the public jetties. The summer promised to be a good one, the marinas reported full bookings, and Captain Magill expected nothing worse than a busy few months pulling grounded landlubbers off the sand-bars, or making the odd rescue in the lower lough when the winds were high. He admits to having felt a certain skepticism when Mr. Mervyn Boyd of Belfast staggered into the Enniskillen office one morning, just as Magill thought of closing for lunch.

Mr. Boyd was obviously respectable, with one of those florid, round-jowled faces that abound in the Presbyterian churches of Northern Ireland; but Captain Magill's first impression was that the gentleman was drunk. Despite the cool of the morning, his bright summer shirt was soaked with sweat on the back and under the arms. Gibbering, white-eyed, stabbing the air with an urgent forefinger, he had the look of a man well on in the day's delirium tremens; but when the Captain pieced his broken story together, he reached decisively into his bottom drawer for the bottle of Bushmills, and poured them both a dram. Then he asked for the story again.

Mr. Boyd was an ordinary and rather prosperous dealer in furniture in one of the better shopping districts in Belfast. For the past three summers he had brought his wife and three young children to Fermanagh for a week of cruising and fishing, and he flattered himself that he was becoming a fair sailor, at least under those undemanding circumstances. This year, the family had arrived on the previous Friday, taken possession of the boat, and spent two pleasant and unremarkable days among the islands of the the upper lough. On the previous morning, Mr. Boyd had gone through the lock below Enniskillen and cruised directly to the jetty at Oak Island, intending to fish all day and barbecue his catch in the evening. On arriving at the jetty, he was slightly disappointed to see two other cruisers tied up already, for the previous year they had had the island to themselves. There were, however, no signs of their co-inhabitants.

"That's odd," he remarked to his wife as the children leaped onto the jetty to secure the ropes. "It's gone half-ten already, and the boats yonder aren't up."

"They'll be on the island, so they will, or off out in their dinghies. Mind out for the wean!" returned his very practical wife, adroitly preventing their youngest from leaping into the water fully clothed. The feeling of oddness dissipated under the pressures of parenthood; but when the parents rambled up the path to the antiquities, they could see that the island truly was deserted, nor were there any dinghies in the vicinity of the shore. Furthermore, both of the elder Boyds noticed how peculiarly quiet the island was: no birds, notably, and no splashing of fish in the shallows, which Boyd had remembered with hope, pleasure and high optimism from the previous summer. The only sound came from the jetty, where their children were noisily splashing in the shallow water, and from some farmer's tractor on a distant hill on the mainland.

"Let's go back. I'm afraid the weans will be waking up those poor people in the other boats with their shrieking," said Mrs. Boyd as they turned away from the ancient rock carvings. "Wee devils! Will you listen to the racket they're making?"

Mervyn Boyd listened. There was that in his children's voices which suddenly seemed to be deeper and more desperate than sibling warfare routinely involved. There was, it seemed to him, real terror. He raced down the slippery grass in the direction of the jetty with his startled wife close behind, and burst puffing through the trees to the extraordinary sight of his two elder children, their faces convulsed, hauling the youngest up the path towards him, rigid as a plank. As he reached them, he saw with relief that the child was not dead, but apparently paralyzed with fear, and the sight of his parents relaxed him to the point where he could scream instead. As the adults attempted to calm the children, Boyd watched the bay with growing anxiety; whatever had happened to plunge his offspring into this state of dread was not apparent, but suddenly he did not like the look of the jetty, with its three gently rocking cruisers. Nor, when he turned around to survey the island, did he like the oppressive quiet, the shadows pooled around the unnaturally still trees, the dark undisturbed waters that lay against the tiny beach.

"Mammy," the little boy gasped when he became capable of speech, "it touched me! The mud...it TOUCHED me..."

"You silly wee doat," his mother said tenderly. "For sure, the lake's wild shallow at the jetty, and you touched the slimy bottom..."

"No, Mammy, it touched ME!" he cried, and stiffened into another bout of hysteria. The girl and elder boy, affected by their brother's wails, joined him; and it was with terrible difficulty that the senior Boyds calmed them again.

Mervyn Boyd, despairing of his children's reason, carried the youngest to the edge of the jetty. His wife followed behind with the others clutching her skirt. According to Boyd's account, it required the greatest firmness, almost amounting to brute force, to get the children onto the jetty and into the cruiser, and every small, rare lapping of ripples against the piles threatened to send them into fresh panic. While Mrs. Boyd soothed them in the cabin, Mervyn cast off the mooring ropes and took the boat into the channel, turning north towards the big marinas on the mainland.

At that point, he told Captain Magill, he was in something of a quandary; like a good citizen, he felt the urge to report something to the proper authorities, but was uncertain of what it was he had to report. Panic on the part of his children, for no reason but the touch of a slimy lake bottom, did not seem the sort of crisis to interest the Tourist Board. He thought it was likely they would recommend a good psychiatrist, if not for the children, then for himself. At bottom, he was afraid of making a fool of himself.

He glanced back at the island as it slid behind another, and was disturbed to see a cruiser approaching the jetty he had just left. He wrestled briefly with the idea of going back to warn its inhabitants, but again could not think of what to say. In the end, he settled for mooring at the busy rental marina at Kesh, an hour's cruise to the north, and saying nothing at all. The children soon revived, and showed little reluctance to jump into the lake with the horde of others at the dock. Mervyn Boyd did not recover so easily.

The next morning, after a distressed night, he decided to return to Oak Island to set his conscience at rest, leaving Mrs. Boyd and the children at Kesh. Mrs. Boyd agreed, but with obvious reluctance. "Don't you be long, mind!" she shouted after him as he pulled away from the jetty. He could see fear on her face as the gap widened between them, and he shouted back something reassuring; but he was more than a little afraid himself.

As he approached the island, he was relieved to see three boats tied up already at the jetty. This relief darkened when he recognized two as those which had been there the previous morning, and the third probably as the one which he'd seen arriving. Furthermore, there were still no signs of life, despite it being close on eleven o'clock. When he cut the engine and leapt onto the jetty to tie up, the eerie unbroken silence which had oppressed him before still lay over the island, somehow deepened by his solitude.

"Hello? Hello? Is anybody there?" he called, and immediately regretted it. He felt foolish, primarily, his stolid Ulster sense telling him he was waking up three cruisers full of sleeping tourists, who would not thank him for the service. Something deeper, atavistic, made him wonder what else he ran the risk of waking up. In any case, there was no reaction from the boats, and none from the lake except a slight rising of the swell. Mervyn looked out across the water to see if another cruiser might be approaching, but the lake was empty.

Feeling a complex of foolishness and chill, he walked up the jetty to the path, and on up to the rock carvings. As he'd expected, there was nobody there, and no sound of birds or small creatures. He was a little reassured to see several boats in the channel on the other side of the island, moving steadily towards Devenish, one with a small bikini-clad female on the foredeck. It was pleasantly normal.

Mervyn Boyd jogged back down to the jetty, trying to decide whether to pursue matters further, or just leave be; presumably plenty of people on holiday liked to sleep in. Still — three boatloads at once, and one at least with children on it, judging by the small life-jackets draped over the bow. Perhaps they were sick, needing help. He hovered on the end of the jetty for a few moments, still fearful of embarrassing himself, then turned back and half-heartedly rapped on the cabin window of the cruiser nearest the shore.

There was no answer, no movement inside the cabin. He stood irresolutely for a moment, and moved on to the second. This time as he bent over to tap, he found himself peering through a small chink in the curtains, down into the dimness of the main cabin. The fold-down berth in the table area was still made up, although the counterpane was thrown back to reveal dark-colored sheets and pillows, on one of which was a curiously shaped object like a boot with a jagged top. He called out cautiously. There was no reply. Thoroughly intrigued now, he pushed a finger through the open inch at the top of the window to twitch the curtain aside.

In the augmented light, he could see that the dark color of the sheets was an ugly brown, not uniform, but dappled and splattered; and that portions of the sheet were white. Moreover, the boot-like object was not a boot, but a bare foot, truncated, stained the same ugly brown as the pillowcase, and with a shattered tip of gray bone protruding from the ankle. Beyond it was a ragged chunk of white-skinned meat.

For a few seconds, Mervyn Boyd felt himself tranquilly observing these details, and taking additional note of a half-full cup of coffee balanced beside the berth. In the end, it was the cup of coffee that jolted him out of his calm observant trance; in that context, it was too jarringly *normal.* He shrieked out loud and twisted his body around, stumbling on the edge of the boat and nearly falling between that and the side of the jetty. There was a roar in his ears, and a naked feeling at his back; he ran tripping and sobbing to his own cruiser, and hastily untied the mooring lines before leaping aboard.

Then he stopped short. On the clean white hull was an shiny greenish trail, as if something large and deliquescent had hauled itself up over the edge of his cruiser. From the bow back toward the bridge was a small river of the stuff, turning a revolting brown around the edges as it dried. Mervyn shrieked again and took a step backwards, feeling as he did so a motion in the jetty too extreme to be of his making. He turned, and not ten feet away, saw an amorphous green member reaching up from the water and scrabbling for purchase on the timbers of the dock. He watched in shock as it found a handhold, and a large wet green shape began to follow it out of the murky water. Mervyn could not tell Captain Magill just what happened then, for his next clear memory was of vomiting copiously over the wheel of the cruiser, a hundred yards out into the channel. When he looked back, the jetty and the three cruisers were deserted.

He cruised aimlessly about the channel for a few minutes, trying to recover his breath and the control of his stomach. He had no doubts about his own sanity and his perceptions; he had enormous doubts about what to do, what to say, and whom to say it to. Eventually he turned the cruiser south towards the lock and Enniskillen, where he knew he could find some sort of official ear. The operator of the lock was sympathetic, and referred him to Captain Magill's office, only a few minutes away. And that, the Captain saw, was that.

## II

By the time Mervyn Boyd had finished his story twice over, it was well after two o'clock, and the secretary had returned from her lunch. Captain Magill sat regarding Mervyn Boyd, who sat regarding him back with a hopeful you-can-handle-it-from-here look on his face. Magill himself felt no such confidence; in fact, he was not even sure that he believed Boyd's story, for all that the man was a respectable Belfast furniture salesman, and as solid as one of his own sitting-room suites. And, if the scene were as he described, and the cruiser a charnel-house — who was to say that Mervyn Boyd had not run amok, and done the deed himself? To the best of the Captain's knowledge, large slimy green bodies did not abound in the waters of Lough Erne.

After a few moments of this mutual contemplation, Magill picked up the telephone and rang down to the government jetty, telling his officer on duty to get the launch ready for a short jaunt. He looked across the desk at Mervyn Boyd.

"You'll be coming with us, I hope?" he said. Boyd's palpitations, soothed by the shot of Bushmills, began to shake him again.

"N-no thankyou, sir," he stammered. "I'd best be getting back to the wife and weans, for she'll be walking the walls for me already, so she will."

"Ah," said the Captain, "but Oak Island is on your way back to her. And don't you be worrying, you won't be alone this time. Nor unprotected."

As Boyd watched, Magill put the whisky bottle back in the drawer, and took from the same place a medium-sized revolver, with the look of being well cared for but not often used. This he tucked into an inner pocket, and the two men set off for the lakeside, taking with them the Captain's clerk and an off-duty inspector of fisheries who had stopped by to pick up his cheque. From the quay, on a belated impulse, Magill rang up the constabulary and asked for an constable to join the expedition. With each addition to the party, Mervyn Boyd visibly breathed easier.

They passed in convoy through the lock, the launch leading and Boyd's cruiser following, with the constable keeping Mervyn Boyd company. As they rounded the point of Devenish Island, dominated by the tall round finger of the ruined monastery tower, Captain Magill looked keenly towards the hump of Oak Island. It looked peaceful, pretty, as harmless as a summer's afternoon.

He glanced back at the cruiser, where the constable hunched beside the unhappy figure of Mervyn Boyd. The constable didn't look happy either — the cruiser smelled bad. Much vomit in the cockpit, as Boyd had described; hasty swabbing had removed the worst of it, but not the stench. Worse yet, the cruiser's deck was indeed befouled with some kind of revolting greenish matter, now dried in the sun, and a few buckets of lakewater sloshed over it only seemed to release its stink more efficiently. This did not, however, prove anything more to Magill than that Mervyn Boyd had a weak stomach and did not keep a clean boat. As for the rest of the story, well — Magill was inclined to reserve his verdict.

But when they approached the jetty on Oak Island, angling in from the open channel, he saw that matters there were also much as Boyd had described. There were the three cruisers, festooned with towels and life-jackets; the jetty quiet and deserted, the smooth waters by the shore innocent of fish. Above all, there was the strange poised silence, in which the chugging of their engines seemed ominously magnified. Captain Magill did not like it. He did not like it at all.

There was just room enough for the two craft to tie up prow to stern on the projecting end of the jetty. The party climbed warily down onto the boards and moved as one man to the nearest of the cruisers. There was a faint odour of decay in the air.

"Is this the one you looked into?" asked the Captain. It annoyed him to find his own voice hushed.

Mervyn Boyd shook his head and pointed at the middle craft. Followed by the policeman, the Captain clambered aboard and moved gingerly around to the cockpit, and down into the well. The cabin door was closed. Captain Magill put his hand on the revolver and cautiously swung the door open. Then he gagged and stumbled back, colliding with the policeman behind him; the smell, faint outdoors, was an overwhelming stench in the confined space below.

"Can you see anything?" asked the policeman. Magill knew him well, and knew him moreover for a strong unimaginative man with a stomach of lead-lined cast iron; but even so, there was a quaver in the constable's voice. Without answering, Magill put his handkerchief over his nose and entered the cabin.

A glance at the berth sufficed to place Mervyn Boyd's veracity beyond question, though he'd fallen far short of a full catalogue of the cabin's horrors. Scraps of bone, of tufted scalp, of twisted offal, littered the floor and the berth, even clung to the walls and ceiling as if glued there. Spatters of brown, and of sticky brownish-green, lay everywhere.

The policeman at Magill's heels retched and reeled to the tiny sink to throw up, but leapt backward with a cry. Magill pushed him aside to look. From the sink, glistening, a single eye stared back at him, unblinking even when a drip of water plopped onto it from the tap above. Beside it was a stack of dirty plates, laden with blood-spattered congealed grease. Mechanically, Magill reached forward and tightened the tap.

The normalcy of this gesture, like Boyd's view of the coffee cup, served to shake Magill from acceptance into horror. He took a quick look into the forward cabin, retched, and led the green-faced policeman up through the well and into the open. Together they leaned over the low railing, pulling great gasps of air into their lungs while the small group on the jetty watched in silence.

Magill's nausea began to pass first. Gradually, he focussed on his reflection in the water, a shocked face with wide eyes and a slack, trembling jaw. Beside him, the policeman heaved and vomited, breaking the glassy surface. Magill, staring past his fragmented reflection into the depths, saw movement under the surface, not like a fish, not catching the light on scales and tail and fins, but moving darkly and ponderously like the slow surge of a submarine tide. Then it was gone, but the cruiser rocked violently; the policeman lost his balance and pitched over the railing into the turbid depths.

The launch pilot cried out and poised himself for a dive, but Captain

Magill shouted to him to wait, his eyes fixed on the water. "There's something down there...!" he began. Something had closed over the policeman's body, something more opaquely green than the muddy greenness of the lake, and then a darker cloud had mushroomed up towards the surface from an unseen source below. A second passed, and the policeman's arm, in its olive uniform sleeve, broke the surface. The rest of him did not follow.

Captain Magill, with a deliberation born of barely suppressed panic, aimed his revolver at the centre of the dark cloud blood, he thought and fired until the gun was empty. The shadow behind the cloud moved, was gone, and he looked around in confusion. The boat jerked again.

"I think I hit it!" he cried to the others, turning to the jetty. He froze. Behind the four men on the jetty, a wet, green, man-form had hauled itself half out of the water and was reaching stealthily across the boards with an arm the thickness of a child's body. Magill shouted too late. The fisheries man was jerked backwards into the water and pulled under, disappearing into the centre of an expanding ring of ripples. If there was a struggle, no sign reached the surface until the tell-tale dark cloud appeared.

The Captain swore, but did not stand still to do so, and nor did his surviving companions. With a few energetic leaps they were all aboard the launch, and in seconds the craft was speeding into the channel. There, to Boyd's dismay, Captain Magill ordered the launch to stop.

"You're crazy, man," Boyd cried. "We've got to get out of this!" But the Captain looked thoughtfully back at the jetty, now with four silent cruisers moored to its pilings.

"We've got to warn people off until something can be done," he muttered. "Strewth! If another boat should come, there'll be more people dead from that...whatever on God's earth it is."

He looked across at the Devenish jetty, where two cruisers were tied up. He'd commandeer one to take them back to Enniskillen, and leave the launch at a safe distance from Oak Island to steer other cruisers away from danger. Beyond that, he could hardly think. What he had just seen, what he had to do next both were unthinkable. He ordered the launch to Devenish.

## III

Thirty-seven hours later, Captain Magill hunched over a cup of hot coffee from his thermos, feeling remarkably unhappy. It was not that he regretted the godless time of the morning, though he was a man who valued his sleep; nor that he had not had a decent meal in two days, though he valued his feed even more than his sleep. Since returning from Oak Island, the Captain had felt very little attraction to food anyway, and (though he'd be reluctant to admit it) a certain disinclination for the dark and the possibility of dreams.

He stared over the bows of the peculiar vessel towards the island, just gathering color in the limpid early dawn. The helmeted heads below him bobbled as the soldiers craned to see over the high sides of the boat. It was a bit like a ferry barge, broad and flat-bottomed, and its twin sister chugged placidly to starboard with an equal cargo of uniformed men. Twenty altogether in the reconnaissance force, the commander had enthused, plus Magill and himself and the crews of the two boats. The Captain's launch still kept its vigil, but it had moved away to stand off the point of Devenish. Captain Magill heartily wished himself aboard her.

Still, positive action felt good — relatively speaking. For nearly a day it had seemed that the higher-ups were only willing to clamp a tight lid of silence on all witnesses, and hope the problem would take itself away. It didn't. In the afternoon, a blood-stained dinghy with a few grisly shreds of humanity in the bottom was found drifting in the channel west of the island; a few hours later, a woman's head washed up on the mainland opposite Devenish. Magill doubled his patrol and waited feverishly for orders. Late in the evening, the orders came — and the result was this early morning expedition, which seemed like a step in the right direction. The only trouble, in Magill's view, was the hearty British officer who seemed to view the operation as quaint Irish lunacy compounded with a lovely opportunity to exercise his boys.

The boats proceeded side by side, not to the jetty, but to the small shingle beach about twenty yards beyond it, scarred with the rings of old campfires. The silence would have been uncanny but for the whispers rustling through the ranks of soldiers. Somebody laughed just below Magill, and Major Hacker barked a sharp word of reproof — much too loudly, in Magill's opinion. Oak Island seemed, in some indefinable and undesirable way, to wake up to their approach. Magill shivered.

The boat's squat bows grated against the shingle of the beach. "First groups off," barked Major Hacker. His voice echoed off the silent trees.

Five soldiers scrambled over the side and moved cautiously upwards the path, while the second five trotted with more confidence onto the jetty. Did they not feel the menace, wondered the Captain. To his ears, the soft susurration as their wake reached the shingle was as loud as surf crashing in a storm. He glanced at Hacker, found him calmly loading a pipe.

"The second boat will stay in reserve for the moment. Now, let's have a look at this bloody abattoir of yours."

Reluctantly, Magill followed the officer onto the beach and then the jetty. The four cruisers butted gently against the pilings, as innocently tranquil as any human habitation when its occupants are sleeping in. One of the soldiers stooped to pick up a towel that had blown off a railing, and threw it awkwardly onto the deck.

"Looks shipshape from here," commented Hacker briskly. "None of your Irish bogles up yet, eh, Captain Magill?"

Magill bit back something unprintable. Let the English eejit see for himself. "Look below," he said flatly.

"Right! Hopkins — got your camera at ready, for the record? Follow me, gentlemen." The six military men pulled themselves smartly aboard, edged around the stern to the bridge, and disappeared down the well into the cabin. Magill hung back — he had seen enough already on the adjacent cruiser. Moments later, one of the soldiers stumbled green-faced up the steps, gagging and coughing, and hung his head over the side of the boat.

"No!" shouted Magill. "Back from the edge!" He scrambled onto the boat and pulled the boy by the scruff of his battledress, back around the stern and onto the jetty, and propped him against the butt of a piling. From inside the cruiser, Magill could hear Hacker giving orders in a subdued tone. The voices of the reconnoitering squad floated thinly down from the crest of the island.

Magill waited impatiently, trying to watch the water in all directions at once. After about five minutes, Hacker reappeared, moving slightly unsteadily up the stairs. He breathed deeply and gratefully as he stepped down onto the jetty.

"You all right?" he asked the boy, who was slowly regaining some color. "I don't blame you, lad, felt a bit queasy myself down there. Well, Captain, it's obvious we've got a maniac on the loose."

"No. A maniac would be human. Sure, whatever I saw wasn't human."

"Now, Captain, I've read your report. I can see how the... the situation inside the boats might well turn your head. But you can't expect the rest to be taken seriously."

"And the two men I saw taken with my own eyes?"

"*Thought* you saw. Were they good swimmers?"

Magill's lips tightened. The man was more of a fool than God made him.

"At any rate, Captain," continued the officer, "we've got to treat the enemy as human. I'm sending the other boat around the island, to do a recce of the far side; between them and the lot already searching, we're bound to flush the bugger out, eh?" He strolled back to the shingled beach.

Magill flinched as the lake rose murmurously against the jetty and set the cruisers into light rhythmic motion. It was all too familiar. He looked down into the murky water, expecting darker green shadows to uncoil slowly in its depths and reach up towards him. Nothing moved.

He watched the second landing craft waddle sedately towards the curve of the island. Then his eyes narrowed. He blinked and looked again. Surely something was trailing behind the boat, something green and glistening like a floe of lakeweed caught on a projection of her keel. He pointed it out to the young soldier, who was woozily pulling himself upright beside the piling. The boy shook his head. When Magill looked again, straining his eyes, the mass was gone.

Hacker had set up a scratch command post on the beach, and was leisuredly pouring himself a cup of tea from a thermos when Magill reached him. "Ah, Magill," he said, proffering the thermos, "I think we've got things under control now. As soon the camera detail finishes inside the boats, I want to send the film back for processing. And then, maybe you can make arrangements to have the cruisers moved so the forensics chaps can take over. This really is police business, you know; bit of a waste to bring the military in."

Magill's answer was cut off by a staccato outburst of gunfire in the near distance. Both men leapt to their feet. The echoes, rattling off the islands and the mainland, confused the direction of the source. The gunfire crashed again, longer, mingled this time with a medley of shrieks.

"It's the second boat!" cried Magill. "Just around the point — that way!"

The soldiers from the hill appeared at a run down the path, alert, but confused at seeing no enemy. Hacker started leading them down the beach towards the point, but stopped when he saw the way barred by a swampy tract of bulrushes and reeds. "The boat," he cried, "on the double. And call the lot off the cruiser, I want every man we've got!"

The soldiers feverishly scrambled into the landing craft and pushed off, Magill among them. In the rush, and the initial clatter of the boat's engine, it was several long seconds before Magill noticed that the island was otherwise silent again. No shrieks, no guns. He glanced at Hacker at the same instant as that realization dawned on the officer's face.

"Can't this bloody tub go any faster," Hacker muttered, craning anxiously over the gunwale. "I say," he shouted at the pilot, "get a move on!" Magill shook his head sombrely in the tense cluster of soldiers. He had a feeling that speed no longer mattered.

It was fully five minutes after the first gunshot before the clumsy boat rounded the point. The second boat was about thirty yards off, idling stolidly towards a shallow-water buoy in the centre of a little cove. No one was visible on the tiny bridge. As they watched, the boat's keel caught on the bottom, and it slewed lazily around till its blunt bows faced them.

"Hoy!" shouted Hacker. "Hoy! What's going on there? Baker!"

There was no reply. The only sound from the boat, apart from its idling engine, was a curious bumping noise as it rocked in its own wash, as if numbers of bowling balls were rolling about in its bottom.

"Closer," Hacker called up to the pilot.

"We can't get too close," cautioned Magill, "or we'll run aground too. And I wouldn't advise putting the raft down."

"We'll get as close as we can, then. I say, what's that?"

Something had risen in the stricken boat, something green and shapeless, vaguely rounded, shining wetly where the sun caught it. It rose higher, thickening as more of it appeared. Magill had a confused impression of massive shoulders, sloping down from a bulbous, neckless, faceless head, then the thing rolled itself over the side and disappeared into the water without a splash. It had been in view for no more than a few seconds.

Hacker shouted an order that Magill could not make out, but the soldiers leaped to the bow with their rifles trained on the spot where the thing had sunk. They fired in volleys, again and again, raising miniature fountains where the bullets ploughed into the water. Magill saw a line of perforations appear in the hull of the other boat where some bullets went wild, well above the water-line. As the craft tilted again, pivoting on the point where it was aground, a dark liquid gushed from the holes.

Magill swore. Ignoring the commotion of the soldiers, he grabbed Hacker's binoculars and focussed them on the bow of the other boat. The liquid was dark red. It looked as if the boat was bleeding from its wounds. The flow slowed to a trickle as the vessel shifted again.

"Whatever it was, we must have hit it!" said Hacker exultantly at his side. "I'm taking the raft over to check out Baker's squad."

"I hit it at least six times the other day, Major, and it replied by taking another poor soul into the lough with it. The raft isn't safe. I doubt if this boat is, either."

Hacker looked at him with contempt. "I take it you don't want to accompany us." Magill realised with horror that Hacker was enjoying himself.

"No, I'll not be coming with you," he cried. "It's suicide, so it is. And it's murder to take others with you."

The officer turned his back on Magill. The rubber raft had already been broken out, inflated and put over the side. Hacker climbed awkwardly over the gunwale into it, followed by two soldiers carrying oars. Helplessly, Magill watched them cross the expanse of still water.

He saw Hacker stand up precariously, grab the gunwale with both hands, and peer over into the boat. The officer stood there for a long moment, frozen; then the boat began to swing again, and he lost his balance, shoving the raft away with his feet while still clinging desperately to the larger boat. It was almost comical, a slice from a slapstick film — except for the expression on Hacker's face. One of the soldiers back-paddled frantically to close the gap.

Suddenly, the raft overturned — not, as Magill instinctively expected, to the side where Hacker's weight was pushing it down, but to the other side, and with great force. Hacker was left dangling from the gunwale of the landing craft, while the two soldiers spilled into the lake. One surfaced at once, and started to hoist himself aboard the up-turned raft. Of the other, there was no sign.

Hacker let himself drop into the water, and struck out strongly for the raft. Abruptly, he swerved and made for Magill's boat instead. His mouth was working soundlessly. In the same instant, the remaining soldier shrieked and tried to twist his body further onto the raft, sobbing and scrabbling at the slippery rubber.

A soldier beside Magill cursed and threw a leg over the side of the boat. Magill grabbed him, and held him while he struggled. "There's nothing to be done," he said quietly. "Just get the boathook ready to help the Major aboard."

"But there's Matthews...!" the soldier cried.

"He's already dead." Magill looked back and saw the soldier, sprawled across the raft, convulse in a final agonised spasm, then slide quietly over the side. The water around the raft visibly darkened. Hacker, almost to the boat, cried out for help. He grabbed the end of the boathook and was hauled aboard, and collapsed into a corner inert with shock.

Magill glanced around the horrified faces of his companions. They were still in danger — and himself with them. "Head for deeper water!" he shouted to the pilot, praying fervently it was not too late already. Even as the engine spluttered into life, he saw a surge of darker water pass under the bow of the craft, and felt a hesitant bumping on the keel. Then the boat took off, jerking forward as the pilot strained the engines.

Magill took a deep breath. Had they shaken the thing off? He waited for an extra vibration in the keel, the muffled grapplings of something working its way up the hull, the first appearance of a green and formless horror over the gunwale — but the boat went on, shuddering only from the unaccustomed stress on its engines. He moved to the stern and peered back at the stranded boat, just in time to see it heave as a dark mass hauled itself up the side and dropped out of sight into the interior.

"We're safe, now," he remarked to no one in particular. "Unless, of course, there's two of them." He felt blankness, not relief. The problem remained.

Hacker was stirring in his corner. Magill crouched down beside him and helped him gently to a sitting position.

"What did you see in the boat?" he asked softly. "They're all dead, aren't they?"

Hacker shivered. "Not just dead, Magill. Torn to pieces. All of them. A bloodbath..." He broke off as another deep shudder shook his body. "Torn to pieces, Magill! What was left of them was in the bottom of the boat — arms, legs, heads, guts — and the guns, twisted into knots. Sloshing about knee-deep in blood..."

Ten armed men plus two crew. Dead and dismembered in minutes. Magill shifted as a soldier brought blankets to wrap around Hacker, but the officer caught his jacket with one shaking hand and pulled him closer.

"That's not all," he choked. "It touched me. Brushed my foot underwater, that's why I left poor Matthews on the raft and swam for the boat. I deserted him, Magill, but I... I can't describe how it felt. It was evil..."

"Hush, Major. Rest quietly now," Magill said. No wonder the Boyd child had thrown fits — Hacker, a patently stupid and unimaginative man, was on the point of doing the same.

The Captain rose and went aft to gaze at the island as it disappeared behind Devenish. He pounded his fist on the gunwale, suddenly seething with hatred. "We'll get you. Somehow, we'll get you," he muttered. In the corner, Hacker began to cry.

## IV

The cock-up theory of history notwithstanding, military solutions can be simple and direct. Within a couple of hours of Hacker's surviving party limping home, after due lip service was paid to the ecology, the tourists, the fish, local sensibilities, and a duty to preserve the phenomenon for scientific study, the decision was taken to blow Oak Island off the face of the earth.

The first step was to clear the area. By four o'clock in the afternoon, launches were scouring the islands in the south end of lower Lough Erne, ordering all civilian boats north to Kesh or south to the upper lough, on the pretext of a bomb threat from an unspecified paramilitary group. Magill himself was frenziedly busy, busy enough to keep from remembering more than he needed to, supervising the evacuation and reassuring nervous tourists that the army knew what it was doing — something he was not entirely sure of himself. By nine o'clock of a perfect summer's evening, the evacuation was far enough advanced that Magill felt free to return to his office in Enniskillen. The operation was set for five the next morning, and it had been made clear to Magill that no civilians were invited.

The office was deserted — even his secretary, working overtime for the third evening straight, had been shifted to the army's temporary command post. After the chaos of the day, Magill welcomed a bit of peace. He made himself a cup of coffee and sat down in front of the mountain of papers on his desk.

Two new reports were on top of the pile. He shook his head bitterly as he skimmed them. They were lists from the rental marinas that owned the cruisers still desolately moored to the Oak Island jetty. Kesh Rentals listed four young businessmen in the Egret, and a retired couple from London in the Tern. The Arbuth Admiral had carried a family of six, including four children ranging in age from seven to twelve, plus a spaniel dog. A dozen human souls and a dog, a hundred stones or more of flesh, blood and bone, copious amounts of which remained in memoriam. Plus, of course, the constable and the fisheries man, twelve soldiers and two sailors, and perhaps a few more that they didn't know about yet. And fortunate it was, Magill reflected, that the toll wasn't even higher.

There was a firm knock on the door. Magill grunted. He had left word of his whereabouts with the command post, but he was not expecting visitors. Nor did he welcome any. "Who is it?" he growled. His mood did not improve when the door swung open, and the caller entered the room.

The man was probably a shade over five feet tall, and draped in a brown cassock belted with rope. His pate was bald, though the skin around his eyes, visible at the edges of his bottle-end spectacles, was fresh and unlined. Magill judged him to be an absurd figure of a man.

"Captain Magill? I'm Father Devlin," he said politely. His voice was soft and breathy, like that of a man from the south, but his accent was more suggestive of Chicago than Cork. Without waiting for an invitation, he sat down across from the Captain and pulled a oversized leather briefcase into his lap. He opened it and rummaged inside while he talked.

"I won't waste any time, Captain. I'm prepared to go ahead as soon as you give the word. Tonight, if need be." He pulled a sheaf of papers out of the briefcase, frowned at it, and thrust it back.

Magill, taken by surprise, felt his face go tight. "Begging your pardon, Father, but..."

"Hang on a second... here we are." Father Devlin leafed through the papers in his hand, nodding thoughtfully. "Yes, I think it's all here. Mythological background, historical and archaeological references, textual analysis, and list of expenses." He peered at Magill over the top of the papers. "There's no chance, I suppose, of the government covering the costs?"

"Costs?"

"Well, it doesn't really matter, there aren't many. The sheep, of course, but most of the equipment was already held by the Order." Devlin paused. "You seem confused, Captain Magill. Did you not read the summary report I sent?"

Magill stared at him for a moment, then rested his forehead in his hands. "I'm swimming in reports, Father. And if it's fund-raising you're after, this is not the best time."

"Fund-raising be damned," said the priest. "I'm talking about Oak Island."

The Captain slowly lifted his head from his hands and met Devlin's eyes. So much for the affair being top secret. "What do you know about Oak Island?" he asked.

"Just about everything. Anyway, more than you know. The Order's traditions go back thirteen cycles. We're now at the end of the fourteenth."

"Cycles?" Magill repeated warily.

The priest settled back in his chair. "Dear, dear, you should have read my report. Three-hundred-year cycles, which is how long the evil needs to gather itself together again and assume a form that is dangerous in this world.

Since the last occurrence was in the seventeenth century, we'd been expecting something to happen soon — although to be honest, we didn't expect it until the mid-eighties."

"Oh aye." A gold-plated nutter. Magill rubbed his eyes, wondering how soon he could be rid of him.

"I see," said Father Devlin serenely, "that you think I may be touched in the head. Here, have a look at this." He extracted a sheet from the pile of papers in his hand, and pushed it across the desk.

It was a photocopy of a primitive-looking drawing. Magill gave it a cursory glance and began to push it back, but then grunted and picked it up. He had seen that shape before that domed, neckless head set on lumpen shoulders, branching down into thick unjointed arms — but here there was a face, or at least a mouth, and the suggestion of stumpy legs at the nether end of the body. In the foreground was a tangle of human figures, or portions of them. Heads, legs, arms, trunks, separate and contorted, bringing Hacker's description of what he saw in the landing craft back to Magill's mind. The technique was crude but vivid; Magill's stomach turned over.

"Where did you get this?"

"It's a facsimile of the rock drawing on the top point of Oak Island. Early Bronze Age, or thereabouts. Do you recognize the subject matter?"

"Only too well. And when was the Bronze Age?"

"We've dated the drawing to about 2,000 BC."

"Strewth. Away back then." Magill blinked his eyes against the first throb of a headache. "And you're telling me it was another of the same sort...?"

"The identical one, as far as we know."

Magill gave him a very hard look, which the priest softly returned. "All right, then," said Magill. "And what do you say it is?"

"It's called the Ulk, the Evil. Have you never wondered, Captain Magill, why the place is called Oak Island when there's not a single oak on it?"

"No. I have not."

"It's an anglicized version of Inish Ulk — Old Erse for the Island of the Evil."

"Oh aye," said the Captain, only because Devlin seemed to expect a comment.

Devlin smoothed his hand over his bald pate, and his voice dropped.

"It's been around forever, Captain Magill. The Milesians knew of it, and the Tuatha De Danaan. The Fir Bolg, the Fir Gaileoin, the Fir Domnann, the Peoples of Nemed and Partholon — as far back as you go, you find it as legend, even among those that are legend now themselves. It's older than the banshees, older than the leprechauns. Even the Fomorians feared it, and they were almost the vilest creatures the Devil ever spawned. And they all agreed on one thing: that it's impossible to kill. You can dissolve its form, drive it away, push it back into that other world — but it always returns. Three hundred years later, give or take a few."

Magill gave him a longer, harder look, and then reached into his bottom drawer for the bottle of Bushmills. He hadn't dared to drink for the past three days; he had been afraid that once he got started, he'd never stop. Father Devlin, however, seemed worth a dram of the right stuff. Magill poured out a tot for them each, and watched as Devlin downed his at a single pull.

"I think I should tell you, Father," he said cautiously, "that the matter you speak of is well in hand."

Devlin snorted and held out his glass for more. "You mean the military's firecrackers and pop-guns? I'm glad you brought that up. They must be stopped — and if they can't be stopped, then we must get in there ahead of them."

"And why is that?"

"First, because that approach will not work. Second, because it will make things worse. Once it takes shape, the Ulk cannot be dismissed in that way. The body it's clothed in, formed of the slime from the bottom of the lake that can be destroyed, but the Ulk will only gather itself another. There's plenty of slime on the lake bottom, heaven knows. And meantime, it will have gained strength from the energies those fools want to throw at it."

Magill did not answer immediately. He refilled the priest's glass, and took a first sip from his own. "What you're telling me," he said at last, "is that if the military blows up Oak Island, the...Ulk will just get stronger."

"That's right." Devlin downed his second drink.

"How do you know?"

"Remember that we've studied its nature for a long time. Anyway, the Tuatha de Danaan tried something of the sort, using fire and hot metal in catapults. The concept was away ahead of its time, but it didn't work. That cycle, the Evil was harder to drive away than ever before or after. Heaven only knows what the effect of modern explosives might be."

"What's your suggestion then, Father?"

The priest stood and leaned across the desk to put his papers into Magill's hands. "Better if you read this, Captain, and then you'll know. I'll leave you to it there are things I need to do." He pulled back the sleeve of his cassock to expose a thin Swiss watch. "It's half-ten now. I'll be back in about an hour."

"Father Devlin," Magill said as the priest opened the door. "You realize I'm far from being convinced about this. I don't even know why I let you talk to me about it. The higher-ups would have my head."

A smile of great sweetness and certainty spread across Devlin's face. "Read what I've given you, Captain," he said, sounding fully Irish for the first time. The door closed behind him. The Captain looked from the papers in his hand to the stack of official reports on his desk, sighed heavily, and pushed the reports to one side. Settling back in his chair, he took another sip of Bushmills and began to read.

## V

When Magill finished the last of Devlin's papers, he set it carefully down on the desk and walked to the window to stretch his cramped legs.

He pulled the curtain open a couple of inches. It was just before midnight, and most of Enniskillen was dark except for streetlights and the odd prowling vehicle. Downhill, across a dim carpark, the narrow neck of the lake flowed like a black silken ribbon in the direction of the lock — and Oak Island. There was no sign of the priest.

Priest! And what kind of priest would be mixed up in unholiness of the likes of this? Exorcism was one thing — Magill had seen it done, all right and proper, when he was a boy in Ballynalee and Finoula Cassidy had fancied herself possessed. His parents and the other Protestant stalwarts of the town had denounced the proceedings as heathenish papist tomfoolery, and there had been a fair stink raised. What, then, would they make of Devlin? And of the dark pagan diablerie which he proposed to carry out on the topmost point of Oak Island?

Aye, Devlin was a funny kind of priest. Who could believe the claims in his report — that his Order, now wearing the protective coloration of the Roman church, traced itself back to the Druids, and beyond them to the shamans of Nemed and Partholon? That the most esoteric lore of the Celts and shadowy pre-Celts reposed in their shaven heads? That the bloodthirsty horror infesting Oak Island was something they had dealt with before, and could deal with again? The military would hardly believe them, that was for sure. Which no doubt explained, Magill reflected sourly, why Devlin had approached *him*.

A gentle rapping made him jump. Devlin pushed the door open and smiled at Magill. He had thrown a hooded cloak over his cassock, and was carrying two large plastic shopping bags in place of his briefcase. "Well now, Captain," he said.

"Well now, Father."

"Did you read my report?"

"Oh aye, I read it." Magill deliberately settled himself in his chair behind the desk. "And but for one thing, Father Devlin, I'd think you were certifiable."

Devlin pushed his hood back and perched comfortably on the edge of the desk. "And what is that one thing, Captain Magill?"

"The thing itself. The Ulk. I've seen it. I've seen what it can do. It's not to be easily believed, and yet I know it's for real. After that, Father Devlin, I think I could believe anything."

The priest nodded benignly. "I knew we'd picked the right man. Now — do you see any point in approaching the military?"

"None at all. They'd lock us both up."

"When are they attacking the island?"

"Five o'clock this morning. Helicopters, and mortars set up on the mainland."

"Will you help me get to the island before then?"

Magill grimaced. "Heaven forgive me, but I'll lend you my own dinghy. There's a wee inlet on the mainland about a half mile from Oak Island where you can set off without being noticed, and you should have no trouble avoiding the patrol boats if you don't use the motor. And if anything happens to you, I'll never have another night's sleep in this world."

The priest looked mildly troubled. "You'll be coming with me, surely?"

"Do I look crazy? I'll help you launch the dinghy."

"You don't understand. I need you. I have incantations to perform while we're approaching the island."

"Sure, if it's just your mouth you're using, you can spare your hands for the oars. I've been twice more often to that damned island than is wise, and I won't test my luck again."

Devlin nibbled on his lower lip. "It won't work, Magill," he said finally. "If you won't go, will you find me another man to manage the boat?"

"No. You want to go, and on your head be it. But I'll not have another soul on my conscience." Magill thought bitterly of the constable and the fisheries inspector.

"But that leaves me in an impossible position."

Magill shrugged. "Can you not get another of your own Order to help you?" He paused, suddenly suspicious. "For that matter, why have they sent you alone?"

"It's the way it's always been. The Ulk versus a champion from the Order, plus one man of the people. It's in the report I gave you."

"Aye, so it is. But..."

Devlin stood up and walked around the desk. He put his hands on Magill's shoulders and looked steadily into his eyes through the thick spectacles. "Captain Magill, you believe me far enough to lend me your boat. Can you not trust me that little bit farther? I can promise that no harm will come to you."

For a little bald man in fancy dress, he exuded a disproportionate assurance and authority. Magill felt a flash of recognition deep in his mind, a stir of instinctual awe, as if some racial memory lodged in the backmost whorls of his brain were struggling to be recalled. Wonder floated toward the surface — and with it terror, primitive and pagan. Magill's good Protestant soul recoiled from them both.

"No," he said shakily. "And it's not just that I'm afraid, it's that I want no dealings with you or with yonder heathenish thing. This is the twentieth century, and I am a Christian man..."

"So you are. I understand your revulsion, Magill, I do indeed. But you've seen what the Ulk can do — think about what you've seen."

Helplessly, Magill did just that. Pictures rose in his mind. Coiled tubes. The boat bleeding from its wounds. One eye glistening in the befouled sink, the constable's arm breaking the surface of a ripple of blood. The forward cabin, the one where the children had been sleeping...

"Well? Does it make you angry?" Devlin whispered.

"Aye," said Magill. "But..."

"You can help to stop it."

"It's unnatural. It's against everything I've ever done."

"Of course it's bloody unnatural! It's an evil monstrous thing, and it's your duty to help me stop it."

Magill was silent. Devlin's hands tightened on his shoulders.

"It's your chance, Captain. Your chance to strike a blow at the thing yourself. How many dead?"

"That's enough," Magill said slowly. "I'll go. God love me, but I'll go."

The priest released his shoulders and sat back on the desk. He pushed his glasses up on his nose. "I've left the sheep outside," he said.

## VI

Grimly, Magill launched the dinghy, pulled the outboard clear of the water and unshipped the oars. Fifty-two years old, he grumbled to himself, and reduced to playing nautical hide-and-seek with his military colleagues, in his own bailiwick, at half-two in the morning; and, as if that weren't enough, he had a cowled lunatic in the bow of his boat, and a live ewe trussed in the stern.

In the bow, Devlin stood up. "Get you down, Father!" Magill whispered fiercely. "Do you want to turn us over?"

Ignoring him, Devlin produced an object like a censer from one of the plastic bags and began to weave an elaborate pattern with it in the air around his own head. A fine powder followed it like a vapour trail, and Magill caught a strong odour, pungent like musk but tinged with the stink of the grave. He bit back a protest when Devlin crawled aft and shook the powder over Magill's head and shoulders, and over the tarpaulin covering the sheep, and then laid a thin track of powder along the gunwales. "The first line of defence," the priest whispered.

Magill settled himself morosely on the thwart and started to row. Defence, was it? Well, it was obvious that guns were no use, but somehow the priest's idea of an arsenal was no great improvement. When he looked back over his shoulder, Devlin was standing upright in the bow with his arms outstretched, looking like a dwarf in a Disney cartoon, swaying back and forth and chanting in a low voice. Magill tried to pick out the words, but only the cadences were familiar, touching again that pocket of ancient memory deep in Magill's subconscious. He shivered, and pushed the memory away.

As he rowed, he could see activity on the mainland at the foot of McLaren's farm — floodlights, army trucks, and little dark knots of men moving back and forth hauling what Magill supposed were the big guns. The sound of orders carried crisply across the water; Magill felt exposed. The moon was rising, its light strengthening every moment. He listened anxiously for the return of the circling patrol boats from the far side of the island.

When he looked over his shoulder again, he was astonished at the nearness of the jetty. He swivelled the boat to manoeuvre past the blind black ports of the cabin cruisers at a distance of a dozen yards or so, wrinkling his nose at the stench of death that hung around them. The early morning was cold, but he was sweating — less from exertion than from his consciousness of the water a bare half-inch below his feet. The brute power that had twisted army rifles into knots and torn heads from necks would have no trouble with a fibreglass hull, he thought. And what had the priest done to protect them, after all his promises? A sprinkle of smelly powder, a mumble of nonsense words. For the fiftieth time in two hours, Magill cursed himself for coming, and Devlin for talking him into it.

He rounded the end of the jetty and made for the little shingle beach. Was it his imagination, or was the rowing harder than it had been, as if the oars were pushing through syrup? Or as if hands below the water were pulling at them, slowing them, dragging them counter to the force of Magill's arms? By the time the keel pushed sluggishly up onto the shingle, his shoulders were on fire.

"We're here, Father," he whispered. The priest took no notice. Nervously, Magill stood up and studied the smooth water, the dark queue of cruisers, the motionless bushes crowding the beach. The moon passed through a cloud, shifting the shadows; small waves slapped the pilings in the cavernous dark beneath the jetty. Magill pulled his jacket tighter.

A fish splashed in the shallows nearby. No, he remembered, the fish were all gone. Nothing was visible, although sequins of moonlight flashed from disturbed waters about twenty feet offshore. He looked at Devlin, who had stopped chanting, but appeared to be meditating with his hands high in the air. The boat began to roll slowly on its grounded keel. What in the name of heaven was the priest waiting for? Magill opened his mouth to speak, but a sensation of being watched oozed over his body. He turned lakeward again and froze.

It was just disappearing. Water closed over the hump of its head, and the rippling surface gave no clue to its direction. "Devlin, it's come!" he hissed. No reaction. Swearing, Magill reached for an oar and braced himself. He waited. At the far end of the jetty, the cruisers ground gently together, and a towel flapped in a sudden gust. On his neck, Magill felt a few cold droplets of rain.

He raised a hand to brush them away. It was not raining. Something was poised above his head, a thick blunt arm dripping water, weaving back and forth like a blind worm. Magill whirled, gasping. The Ulk was rooted in the shallows beside the dinghy, its featureless face inches from his, sunk between its great humped shoulders. Magill squawked and lurched sideways towards the bow.

"Stay in the boat!" Devlin was suddenly beside him, holding him to the spot with unexpected strength. The Ulk's head shifted minutely, and the terrible arms fell to its side. Abruptly, without a sound, it was gone, cutting into the shallow water leaving only ripples behind it.

"In God's name...!" Magill began explosively, but Devlin shook his head.

"Hardly that, Captain," he said. "Anyway, forget about the Ulk for a moment. It's time to move."

"But it was right there! Why didn't it go for us?"

"The spell, the spell. Do you think I've been chanting for my own amusement? Listen, Magill. When I've lit the lamps, get the sheep and the bags onto dry land, and start up the path. I'll be right behind you." He poked into one of the shopping bags and brought out two lamps like ornate storm-lanterns. Magill, his heart pounding in syncopated rhythms, pulled the tarpaulin off the ewe and cut her hobbles. A match struck behind him, a light flared, and the smell of musk-and-death thickened. When he turned again, hauling at the sheep, Devlin was waiting impatiently with a lamp swinging from each hand.

They moved cautiously off the boat and up the path, holding together in a tight cluster. The malodorous smoke from the lamps swirled around them and mingled with the mist hanging above the undergrowth. Magill muttered under his breath as he pulled the sheep along. The short climb to the top of the island seemed to stretch into miles, and he was clammy with cold sweat when at last they broke into the clearing around the carven stone.

Magill held the sheep in the centre while the priest went to work, looking like a busy black beetle in his ludicrous cloak. He was chanting again, outlandish unnatural sounds that shivered in Magill's ears. Devlin placed the lamps at opposite ends of the clearing, and set about tracing a circle of powder around the central stone, with a complex pattern of lines radiating from it. Magill crouched on the stone, half-watching him, half-watching the bushes around the clearing. Every slight breeze that stirred them seemed to cover an advance of shadow; every shadow, a coil of brute malice poised for the spring.

Devlin touched him on the shoulder. "Ready," he said. "Stay where you are." He pulled the ewe outside the circle and tethered her to a stake which he had driven into the ground. The animal bleated questioningly. Devlin patted her head, and poured a line of oily liquid along her back from a small vial. Then he joined Magill on his rock, pulled a pack of Dunhills from under his cloak, and lit up.

Magill watched this with confusion. "What's happening, Father?" he said. "What do we do now?"

"We wait," Devlin said.

"Wait?"

"That's right."

Magill digested this. "It will come to us?"

"It will come to the sheep. Don't worry, we're safe inside the circle."

"And then what?"

"You'll see, Captain. Whatever happens, stay inside the circle until I tell you to go. Then run like fury for the boat and get ready to cast off. Understand?"

"Right you are. But Father..."

"Yes?"

"It's a quarter past three. At five o'clock sharp, the military is going to pulverize this place."

"Don't worry, my son. There's plenty of time."

"Don't call me your son." Magill hunched on the rock and resumed his fearful study of the bushes around the clearing.

## VII

By four-fifteen even Devlin was getting restive, while Magill felt himself sliding into a kind of twitchy fatalism. The ewe had long since gone back to sleep. It was windier, and the moon struck solidly into the clearing from the open sky on the east, highlighting the near leaves of the thicket against a tossing umber background. "So where's your Ulk, then?" asked Magill as he struck the latest in a long series of matches and peered at his watch.

Devlin expelled his breath slowly. "It's coming. It always comes."

"Perhaps it won't, this time. The fourteenth cycle, did you say? Perhaps it learned something from the first thirteen."

"That's a daft idea."

"This is a daft affair. Is it possible?"

There was silence behind Devlin's latest cigarette. "I don't know," he said finally. "I suppose anything's possible. I don't know that it's ever delayed this long before."

"Well, if it doesn't come soon, it'll win by default. We'll have to leave or be blown to bits, and the Ulk..."

"...will soak up all that lovely energy I know, I know." Devlin threw his fag end to the ground, and lit another.

Magill watched with disapproval. "Shouldn't you be doing something? Chanting, or meditating, or whatever it is you do?"

"No, not really. Whenever the Ulk comes, I'm ready for it."

"And what if it doesn't take the bait? Is there not something more you can do to fetch it?"

"No! Anyway, the sheep isn't exactly bait. She's been blessed and anointed, she's a sacrifice. The Ulk will doom itself by killing her."

"Oh, aye. And then what's meant to happen?"

"And then you leave. The rest of the banishment is for no outsider's eyes." Devlin's voice was firm.

"Have it your way." Magill surveyed the silent clearing again. Nothing moved that wasn't traceable to the wind. Out on the water, he could see two launches mounted with floodlights sheer away from the island and turn south towards Devenish at a spanking pace. "Devlin," he said.

"What?"

"The army launches are already pulling out. Maybe we should try and get to the military after all. Maybe it's not too late to delay the bombardment."

The priest hesitated. He started to nod thoughtfully. Then the cigarette snapped between his fingers.

"I think we've been spared that decision."

"What do you mean?" Even as he spoke, Magill heard it too — a stirring in the bushes, not the wind. It was just the kind of stir that a weighty wet thing might make, oozing over the ground without crackling the deadwood. He scanned the thickets. Nothing was visible.

Devlin was digging into one of the plastic bags. As Magill turned to him, he stood up, cruciform, with what looked like a rope stretched between his hands and trailing down on both sides. Magill bit off the question that was rising to his lips. Something was happening to Devlin; he no longer looked ridiculous. Something was being shed like a cloak, and what was left was pure shaman. Magill felt invisible, irrelevant. He backed away, then remembered the limits of the circle and crouched down in the lee of the stone.

Abruptly the Ulk was there, rearing up over the ewe. It was even larger than he remembered, a nasty shiny green in the moonlight, and the stink of water and slime pushed Magill's belly close to revolt. Its arms hung almost to the ground, and seemed boneless — as they reached for the ewe, they uncoiled in a smooth rippling curve like a snake striking in slow motion.

Beside Magill, Devlin's voice rose in a harsh measured chant.

The Ulk paid no notice. It rolled the ewe over, and lifted her off the ground by her hind legs as she awoke and began to bleat in terror. A twist, and the animal fell two-legged to the ground. She flopped onto her belly and scrabbled with her front legs, but the Ulk scooped her up again and held her against its chest. The ewe squealed and convulsed. Darkness fountained from her mouth and spattered across the clearing — Magill felt it on his cheek, warm and wet. A voice in his ear was urging him to go, go now, but he was mesmerized. Something ballooned from the ewe's mouth, and between the stumps of her hind legs; there was a fusillade of moist snapping noises from inside her body. A hand was shaking Magill's shoulder. The Ulk threw down the sack of wet wool and buried the ends of its blunt arms in it. They reappeared after a sound of tearing silk, trailing loops of glistening gut. "Go, go, go!" A shove sent Magill spinning out of the circle and into the bushes at the edge of the clearing.

He landed on all fours, already moving. It was not clear to him where he was going, it mattered only that he was in motion. Then he remembered. The dinghy. But which way was it? He stopped to yank at a branch snagged in his jacket, and glanced back at the clearing to get his bearings.

The Ulk appeared to have lost interest in whatever rags were left of the ewe. It stood fully upright, and the intensity of its concentration upon the centre of the clearing made it easy for Magill to imagine eyes in the blank horror of its head. The priest looked like a child in front of it, still holding the rope in outstretched arms, with the moon flashing off his glasses. But not quite like a child — a curious pale nimbus of light was growing around his head and spreading across the clearing; there were holes in it, Magill thought, as if shadows stood in a protective circle around the priest along the line of the powder. Then Devlin cast the rope upwards and Magill saw that a net played out after it, filmy and glittering with its own radiance. It sailed over the Ulk's head and wrapped itself around the lumpish body. The Ulk roared. Magill, freed from this second trance, ripped his way through the bushes and emerged with glad surprise onto the path.

The dinghy was just as they had left it. Magill pushed its nose off the shingle and waded out knee-deep with the painter in his hand, ready to leap in at the first sight of Devlin. The noises from the crest were strange;

they sounded too far away, and too various to be accounted for by Devlin and the Ulk alone. He could pick out Devlin's voice clearly, but whose were those that were answering him? Magill strained his ears to hear.

Thunder from the mainland. Before he could turn, a stone wall slammed into him from behind and knocked him face-down into the water. He struggled to his feet under a shower of shivered wood and fibreglass and chunks of metal. He looked back. The end of the jetty was on fire, half-hidden under a roiling black mass which blocked out the stars to the east. As he watched, one of the cruisers exploded in a geyser of water and flame.

Magill's mouth fell open. "Those army eejits..." he hissed, then he turned and tore for the path, falling flat when another boom from the mainland presaged another explosion on the jetty. He pressed his face into the moss as a shell burst on the shore, far too close. Over the roar of the flames, he could hear the helicopters approaching. On his watch, just visible in the fire from the jetty, the time was half past four.

Behind him, the beach vanished in a blast of pebbles. Above him, the strange lambency still played over the crest of the island. Voices were miraculously audible, thin and high. *Christ*, he thought, *Devlin*. Two more shells burst to the right of him, and the branches above the path began to burn. He veered off to the left and floundered up through the dense undergrowth, keeping his eyes on the clearing. There was a shout from Devlin, echoed, it seemed, by a dozen others and then a giant fist knocked Magill backwards down the hill and into a brief soothing dimness. When he groggily shook himself awake, the crest of the island was on fire.

Sobbing, Magill staggered to his feet and plunged south. The bombs were falling there too, for the helicopters were laying a systematic grid of destruction over the entire island, but the chief areas of focus still seemed to be the jetty, the path, and the clearing. Magill reached the waterside in one piece and struck out weakly for Devenish. Halfway there, in the middle of the channel, an army launch picked him up.

# VIII

"It's the uncertainty," Captain Magill will say. He'll pour you out a mug of tea, or a shot glass of Bushmills if you catch him in the right mood, and direct your gaze across the channel to the scarred ruin of Oak Island. If it's a wet day, he'll entertain you inside his tidy little caravan at the foot of MacLaren's farm; if fine, at a table outside the door, a few feet from the edge of the lough. In either case, there will be a pair of binoculars at his elbow. Should a craft of any sort seem to be approaching Oak Island, the Captain will break off what he is saying and watch through the glasses, muttering, until the boat moves on. His hands shake much of the time. He has strange eyes.

"There was no trace of the Ulk, of course," he'll say. "Not that you'd expect any, seeing as the thing was nothing but lake slime held together by the sheer force of evil. There was no trace of Devlin either — he was blown to bits, and the bits were blown to atoms. No one ever came asking after him."

He'll lean forward and fix you with his bright Ancient Mariner eyes. "They told me I was concussed. They told me Devlin never existed. They retired me. They cut Oak Island off, and closed the file. They're sure it's over. But I'm not."

You'll recoil from his Bushmills breath. His voice will rise. "How can I know if Devlin finished the spell — or if the bombs fell before the Ulk could be banished? How can I know if it's not still there, under the surface, gathering itself together again, and stronger than before?"

His old face will be haunted. "How can I know? How can I know?" Then he'll pick up the binoculars and scan the island again, back and forth, shore to crest, until at last you realize you've been dismissed, and rise to go.

# The Blessing
## by Scott Mackay

*Recent short stories by Scott Mackay have appeared in **Science Fiction Age**, **Ellery Queen Mystery**, and **Tesseracts 6**. 1998 saw publication of his two new books: a science fiction novel, **Outpost** (Tor Books, New York) and a crime novel, **Cold Comfort** (Carroll & Graf, New York). Like Scott's previous **Northern Frights** tale, "Reasons Unknown," this ones is again set in Ontario's Lambton County, leading this reader to wonder if there might be something just a little unusual about the region.*

I'm in a hospital room late at night with my fifty-one-year-old wife, Dianne. She's lying in bed, her skin is yellow, her lungs clutch for breath, and her body is so wasted she can hardly move. She has cancer. As the rain beats against the window, I watch morphine drip into Dianne's arm from an overhead bag. I rub my hand over her bald scalp, every so often glancing at the clock. We're home now. After thirty-three years we've finally moved back to Lambton County. This is where Dianne wants to die. This is where she wants to be buried.

I know how cancer works. Dianne has a frozen pelvis. Everything from her waist down has turned to tumour. She hasn't eaten solid foods for three weeks, she keeps inhaling her own saliva, and she has an infection the doctors don't see much point in treating. Her condition is end-stage terminal, so why treat an infection?

You shake your head. This is depressing. Why begin this way, you ask? This isn't what you expect when you read Dennis Connel. When you read Dennis Connel, you expect the usual upbeat opening. You expect escape. You expect a happy ending. I know you've read too many cancer stories, and that the last thing you need is another, but I promise, this one's different. I can't offer an upbeat opening. I can't offer escape. And as for the ending...well, you'll have to read and find out. But please, let me break the mold just this once. Let me write this. I think once you get started, you're going to want to read it. How do I know? One simple reason: Howard Hampton.

Home for both Dianne and I is Clearwater, Lambton County, near Lake Huron. We settled in a forty-year-old ranch-style among huge oaks not two blocks from the lake. We installed a hospital bed. We hired a live-in nurse, Violet Brewer, and implemented round-the-clock care.

One evening in early summer, when the air was thick with the scent of lilac, I ran into Howard Hampton, an old friend of my father's. He was a contemporary of my father's, should have been well over eighty, but to my great astonishment, even to my utter bewilderment, he didn't look much past forty. His reddish hair had only a few strands of grey, his freckled face was smooth and firm, and his body was as vigorous and upright as a young man's. How could this be? I wasn't mistaking him, I knew it had to be Howard Hampton, not just somebody who resembled him. I recognized him plainly. But how could he look and move like a forty-year-old when he was, in fact, an octogenarian?

"Mr. Hampton?" I said.

His eyes narrowed. He was trying to place me. "The name is Abernathy," he said.

I paused. Was he joking? He was so obviously Howard Hampton I couldn't begin to guess why he would call himself Abernathy.

"It's me, Dennis Connel," I said. "Jack's son."

"I don't know any Connel," he said.

Despite his denial, I knew this had to be my father's good friend. I remembered him well. Years ago, he always took my brothers and I to Murphy Beach whenever the mercury broke eighty. So why did he deny it now?

Before I could ask, he hurried away. I stared after him. I watched him disappear behind a hedge of bridal lace, wondering why he refused to acknowledge me.

As I pace in front of my wife, Violet Brewer comes into the hospital room with two cups of vending machine coffee.

"How's she doing?" asks Violet.

Before I can answer, Dianne sits up and gazes around the room. "Dennis?" she says. "Dennis, are you here?"

I put my hand on her shoulder. "I'm here, Dianne," I say.

She looks at me but she doesn't see me. The cancer has metastasized to her optic nerves. She's blind now. "Have you called Lorna?" she asks.

Lorna is her boss. Dianne hasn't been to the office in over a year. I glance at Violet Brewer. "Yes," I say, playing along, "I called her."

"Because those overlays are all wrong," she says. "They have to be done again."

Violet calls the nurse and the nurse administers five milligrams of Ativan. Dianne settles down. Her eyes close and she resumes her tortured inhalations.

I wonder if I've put this to you convincingly enough. Violet gives me my coffee. Howard Hampton looked and moved like a forty-year-old. Not bad for a man born on the day of the European Armistice in 1919. Thunder peals somewhere out over the lake and rains pelts against the window. His youthfulness is a miracle. How has he stayed young so long? My wife is dying, old before her time. I want her to be young again. Is it any wonder that on the night I met Howard Hampton I began to think that he might help Dianne, that he might, with the secret of his eternal youth, indeed make her young again?

Let me tell you about the photographs and the painting. Then you might better understand what I mean when I say this cancer story is different.

I hurried back to the ranch-style on the night I met Howard Hampton in the street, my mind filled with hopeful conjectures. Violet Brewer glanced up from her romance novel. "Try and be quiet," she said. "Your wife is sleeping."

I hardly heard her. I went to my den and searched through unpacked boxes. I found my oldest photograph album. I flipped it open and looked for photographs of Howard Hampton.

The first photograph was from 1953. I stood in the foreground. I was nine years old. In the background the Indians of the Chippewa Reservation performed a traditional rain dance at their annual summer pow-wow. Howard Hampton sat in a lawn chair beside me, his legs crossed, a cigarette poised between his fingers, smiling because my face was covered with ice cream. He looked about thirty-seven in this picture. The next photograph was from 1964. I was eighteen. I was in cut-offs and a T-shirt, had a brush cut, and held a big soapy sponge in my hand. I stood in front of Howard Hampton's brand-new Pontiac Strato-Chief, a car I adored. I'd just washed it, and Howard Hampton was giving me a two-dollar bill. Howard looked about thirty-seven in this picture as well.

You see what I mean? How could he look thirty-seven in 1953, and thirty-seven in 1964? Eleven years had passed, but physiologically he hadn't aged at all.

Finally, there was a Polaroid Instamatic shot taken in 1972. I was twenty-six, had hair down to my shoulders, wore yellow bell-bottoms and platform shoes with silver stars. Howard Hampton, his own hair a bit longer, stood next to me outside the Shoreham Inn near Murphy Beach. Dianne was there too, in her own bell-bottoms, wearing big square sunglasses. Howard looked maybe thirty-nine. Time was rushing by for the rest of us, but for Howard Hampton it was standing still.

There were more photographs. I was asked by the Clearwater Public Library to read from my latest novel. I don't know who told them I was in town, but Violet thought it would be a good idea, a way to get me out of the house for an afternoon, and to alleviate, at least for a short while, the strain of looking after Dianne. So I did my reading, sold some books, and a young woman from the *Clearwater Observer* asked a few questions and took my picture. Afterwards, I looked through the library. I hadn't been to the Clearwater Public Library in years. That week in the display cabinet the librarian was show-casing photographs of historical Clearwater. My hands went cold when I saw the photograph of Howard Hampton. He was standing with the Lodge Brothers of the

THE BLESSING

Independent Order of Odd Fellows; the photograph was dated 1902. I peered more closely at the group shot. No doubt about it, there he was, second from the left, wearing a starched collar, a worsted suit, and a bow-tie. Howard Hampton. In 1902. Looking about thirty-seven.

"Could you tell me who owns this photograph?" I asked the librarian.

"It belongs to a Mr. Abernathy," she said.

That same afternoon I visited the Clearwater Historical Society Museum. The museum is generously supported by the Colbourne family and has a substantial collection of early lithographs, antique photographs, and historical documents, all pertaining to the Clearwater area. I went through the photographs first. I found a print of the Lodge Brothers of the Independent Order of Odd Fellows, dated 1902, the same photograph I'd seen in the library, and made a copy. I also found an 1880 photograph of well-to-do guests at the Lombardy Hotel. They posed among garden furniture, the women in bustle dresses, the gentlemen in top hats and bow-ties. Howard Hampton, the only man not wearing a hat, stood off to the side with a croquet mallet in his hands. An 1861 photograph showed a garden party at the Colbourne mansion on Murphy Beach. Many of the men wore military uniforms. The caption beneath said the occasion was a prize-giving for the Fifth Militia District Rifle Association. The women wore crinoline skirts and bonnets. A young officer wore a Scottish uniform — cap, kilt, and riding crop — and stood under a spreading oak, stiff to attention. This young officer was none other than Howard Hampton. In 1861. No mistake about it. He was a little younger in this photograph, maybe thirty.

Then I discovered the painting. Or rather a print of a painted portrait dated 1814. The man in the portrait looked as if he had just stepped from the pages of *Pride and Prejudice*. I read the caption: "Colonel Howard William Hampton led troops against Colonel Beacom's American forces at Fort Erie in June, 1812."

I asked the curator if he knew anything about Colonel Howard William Hampton.

"Only that he was well-liked by his troops," said the curator. "He once carried a wounded soldier five miles through dense bush to the field hospital. Saved the man's life." The curator nodded sagely. "The colonel always looked after his men."

49

You see what I mean when I say this cancer story is different?

I don't know why I assumed Howard Hampton would live in the same house I remembered him living in all those years ago when I'd been a kid. He didn't. A woman of fifty opened the door. I caught her at a bad time. She held her hands up in small claws. Her fingers were covered with flour. I saw a half-made pie-crust sitting under a rolling pin on the kitchen table. A cigarette dangled from her lips.

"Yes?" she said.

I glanced into the living room. "Is this not the Hampton residence?" I asked.

Her eyes widened. "No," she said. She looked me up and down. "Howard Hampton died years ago." The cigarette bobbed between her lips. "Some time in the mid-seventies." She peered at me more closely. "Were you a friend?" she asked.

I stared at her, knowing she had to be wrong. Howard Hampton couldn't be dead. I'd seen him just the other night around the corner from my ranch-style on Lakeshore Road.

"My father and Mr. Hampton were old friends," I said.

The woman's features softened. "Oh," she said. "Well, I'm afraid he's...I'm surprised you didn't know."

"I've been away over thirty years," I explained. "Any idea how he died?"

"A boating accident out on the lake," she said. "My husband and I bought this place power-of-sale back in '76, after he died. I never met the man, but I read about his death in the *Observer*."

I apologized to the woman and walked back to my car. In my car I opened my briefcase and looked at my mimeographed copies, half expecting to discover that the man in the photographs bore no resemblance to Howard Hampton, that the colonel from the War of 1812 wasn't really my father's friend after all. But my eyes hadn't deceived me. Howard Hampton was there, in all my photographs, and in that painting. And if he didn't live here, he had to live somewhere else, and I had to find him. My wife's life depended on it.

A minute with the slender Clearwater telephone book unearthed Mr. Abernathy's current place of residence easily enough. I sat in my car watching Howard Hampton's house that night, a two-storey brick one with black shutters, a black roof, and ivy climbing the sides. As clouds gathered above the oak trees in the front yard, a man drove up in a blue Chevrolet van. *H. W. Abernathy, General Contracting. We Specialize in Basements*, was painted along the side. Howard Hampton got out. I clutched my mimeographed copies, left my car, and hurried up the drive.

"Mr. Hampton?" I called. Howard Hampton turned and stared. His initial surprise gave way to resignation. As I reached him, I said, "Mr. Hampton, please, you've got to help me."

"Mister, I already told you, my name is Abernathy."

I nodded, trying to defy as amiably as I could his flat denial. "I'm Dennis Connel," I said. "You must remember me. I delivered the *Observer* to you when I was a boy. I'm Jack's son. Dennis Connel."

He pushed the van door shut. "I think you got the wrong guy, Mr. Connel," he said.

I looked at him closely. I was certain this was Howard Hampton. I proffered my mimeographed sheets, first the Lodge Brothers. "Look at this," I said. "That's you. The librarian says you own this photograph." He lifted his chin and looked at the photograph. "That was taken in 1902," I said. "And this one, at the Lombardy Hotel, in 1880. And this one at Murphy Beach in 1861. You're the man in the kilt."

He took the copies and looked at them. And then he grinned.

"Isn't that something?" he said. He was amused. The resemblance was just a coincidence to him. He looked up at me. "But I'm afraid I've never seen these photographs before. And I certainly don't own them."

"Look at this," I said, pressing on. "It's a painting of you. You can see the date down there, 1814. Please, Mr. Hampton, don't deny it. How do you do it? How can you be in all these photographs? There must be something keeping you alive. And I need that, Mr. Hampton. My wife's dying, and I need it. You remember Dianne, don't you? Dianne Sloan? We got married in 1969 in the Congregationalist Church on Cathcart Boulevard, and you were master of ceremonies, and you were wearing that white top hat, and you — "

"Mister, I don't know what you're talking about." He shoved the mimeographed copies back at me. "I'm sorry about your wife, I really am, but I..." He raised his eyebrows, exasperated. "If that were me," he said, tapping the print of the painting, "I'd be over two hundred years old." He put his van keys in his pocket. "And I don't think that's possible." He tried smiling, but his lips managed only a weak twist. "Why don't you go home?" he said. "You look tired. I've had a long hard day and I want to go inside and get some supper."

When I got home, Dianne was worse.

"I phoned Dr. Kwant," said Violet. "He says we should take her to Emergency."

As we lifted Dianne into her wheelchair her head jerked back and forth, her eyelashes fluttered, and she insisted she had to go to the office, seemed to have forgotten that she would never be going to the office again.
She started to cry. "Dennis, I'm scared," she said. "This is it, isn't it?"

She actually fought Violet and I as we helped her into the car, hit me with a weak fist, bit Violet on the wrist. I thought it must be the morphine. Morphine makes people do crazy things. Or maybe it was the Prednisone. Or possibly the Decadron. She was full of drugs.

When we finally got her settled, Violet turned to me. "You all right?" she asked.

I backed down the drive. "I wish my brothers were here," I said.

She looked sorry for me. "Have you looked up any of your old Clearwater friends?" she asked.

I glanced at her as I clutched the wheel. "I don't have any Clearwater friends, Violet," I said.

When we got Dianne to the hospital, Dr. Kwant told me it wasn't the morphine, it was the calcium.

"Her cancer's metastasized to her bones," he said. "It's breaking up the calcium and the calcium's settling in her brain.

That's why she's so confused." He looked away. "I think you should prepare yourself, Mr. Connel."

So here we are. Violet and me. With our vending machine coffee. Waiting for Dianne to die. I have no one. My mother and father are dead. Dianne and I don't have any children. She's always had something wrong with her ovaries and I guess it finally turned into cancer. One of my brothers has disappeared, last known whereabouts, New Mexico. The other one is stationed with the Armed Forces in Bosnia. I need someone to help me. And not just anyone. I need someone to give me a last-minute life-saving miracle that will finally rescue Dianne from her killer disease. I need someone who knows the secret of eternal youth.

"Violet," I say, getting up, "I've got to go."

I pound on Howard Hampton's door as the rain thrashes sideways in the wind, trying one last time. Colonel Howard William Hampton always looks after his men, and now I want him to look after me. I want him to tell me the secret of his eternal youth so I can give it to Dianne. This time I have the photograph of the Chippewa pow-wow. I have the photographs of the 1964 Strato-Chief and the Shoreham Inn. I clutch them like talismans. It's well past eleven. I pound and pound and finally the porch light comes on. Howard Hampton opens the door.

When he sees me, his face squeezes into a few wrinkles, and he shakes his head. "Look, mister, I don't know who you are, or why you — "

"Please, Mr. Hampton," I say, holding up the photographs. "Just look at these. These are you. This one here, in front of the Shoreham Inn in 1972. You don't look much younger than you do now. And this one from 1964, your new car, the same thing. And look at this. From 1953. The Chippewa pow-wow? Remember? That's you in that picture. And that's me when I was kid. Please. Dianne's in the hospital and she's dying."

He looks at the floor. Am I wrong about this? He lifts his chin and stares out at the rain. Has the strain of Dianne's slow death at last made me delusional? Howard Hampton shifts his gaze, looks directly at me, and I see pity in his pale blue eyes. Maybe he isn't Howard Hampton after all. Maybe he's who he says he is. Maybe he's really H. W. Abernathy, and his specialty is basements. I think he's going to slam the door in my face, but he sighs instead.

"You're getting wet," he says. "Come in and get dry." I follow him into the kitchen. He tosses a tea towel to me, takes a bottle of scotch from the cupboard, and pours two generous drinks. "Sit down," he says.

I sink into one of the wicker chairs. He sits in the chair opposite. He takes a sip of scotch, lifts the photos, and looks at each in turn. He lingers longest over the one of Dianne at the Shoreham Inn.

"Denny..." he says. I feel something jump inside. I haven't been called Denny in forty years. "Denny, I'm sorry about Dianne." He takes another sip of his drink. "I'm telling you this, and I know I can trust you because if you turned out anything like your dad...well, me and your dad...it's the least I can do for Jack. Please try and understand my situation. I like Clearwater, I keep living here, I consider this my home." He rubs his hands together and takes a deep breath. "But every so often I'm forced to leave. I'll leave for thirty or forty years, until I'm reasonably sure everybody I know is gone, and then I'll come back and build a new life for myself. It's not easy. People get suspicious. Not so much now. But when I first moved here, superstition was a lot stronger. I keep more to myself now. You see why I have to be careful. Anybody like me is bound to raise suspicion."

He takes another sip of scotch. I stare. So I'm not wrong? My conjectures are true after all? He *is* over two hundred years old? He grows silent, brooding. He looks at me, and I realize that, as youthful as he appears, his eyes are immensely old, weighted with untold years of experience. This isn't just Mr. Hampton any more. This is Colonel Howard William Hampton. This is the man who fought Colonel Beacom's American forces at Fort Erie in 1812.

"I've always been honest, Denny," he says. "And I've always been blunt. And I'll tell you right now, I can't give you what you want. There's nothing I can do for Dianne."

He lets that sink in. I don't want to believe him. "But there must be something you can do for her," I say.

"Do you have any relatives staying with you?" he asks.

"I have no relatives," I say. "When Dianne's gone, I'm alone."

He thinks about that, glances out the window as some passing headlights brighten the speckles of rain on the glass. "Do you have any friends?" he asks. "What about Ken Hastings? Wasn't he your friend?"

"I haven't seen Ken in over thirty years," I say.

"Because the best I can offer you right now, Denny, is friendship." He stares at me. "I can't believe how much you look like your dad."

"I have to go back to the hospital now," I say sullenly. "Dianne's dying."    "I'll come with you."

"You don't have to."

"Denny, don't be like that," he says. "You were one of my favorite kids. You tried, that's about the best anybody can do, but there's really nothing I can do for her."

"Why not?"

He sighs, leans forward, and picks up the photograph of the Chippewa pow-pow. "You remember how I was always taking you to these things?"

"I remember."

"I can't count how many of these things I've been to, and I've never told anyone the real reason why I go. At least no one besides your father. But it has to do with the way I am, with what I've become. That painting you showed me of Colonel Howard William Hampton. That's me, I admit it. The caption says I fought Colonel Beacom's American forces at Fort Erie in 1812. That's also true. But that's not the only fighting I did. I was at Fort Sutton for a while, before Fort Erie. Fort Sutton's just up the lake here, at least it was. There's nothing left of it. It's just cottages up there now." He slips the photograph of the Chippewa pow-wow back on the table. His eyes grow pensive. "We had a running feud with the Chippewa back then," he says. "They harassed our settlers, even killed a few. My company commander sent us to retaliate." I stare at him. I can hardly believe I'm hearing this. Is this true? I glance at the photographs. It must be. "It feels strange telling you this," he says. "I never talk about the past with anyone. I don't want to be hounded out of town, or taken for the devil's right-hand man." He pulls his cigarettes out of his shirt pocket and puts them on the table. "But you're Jack's son, and I feel I can trust you." He gives me a pointed look. "Can I?"

I'm startled by his directness. "Sure..." I say. "Sure, I — "

"You're a writer," he says. "You've done newspaper work."

"Don't worry," I say.

He continues to stare at me, like a wolf with its fur up, but then his shoulders relax, and he sinks into his chair. "Not that I really care," he says. "I just want you to believe me. I don't want you blaming me later on. I don't want you telling me I made the whole thing up as a way to get you off my back about Dianne. Because if there were any way I could help her, Denny, I would."

I stare at him. The air is thick, seems to resonate with the depth and length of his unique experience. "Okay," I say, feeling as if I've just stepped off a cliff. "Okay, go ahead."

Howard Hampton takes a deep breath. "Well..." He collects his thoughts. "We followed these Chippewa all the way to Georgian Bay." He nods at the memory. "Of course there were no roads in those days, and that was a hard trek for us because it was all bush. Our tempers were short by the time we got there. We found these Chippewa camped on the French River, fifteen tee-pees in all. Men, women, and children. We weren't even sure if these were the ones who had killed our settlers, but by then we didn't care."

His lips tighten, he lifts his scotch glass, stares at the amber liquid, and his pensive look turns to one of regret. He glances at me doubtfully. He's still not sure if I believe him. He's like a man who's been abducted by aliens, possessed by the devil, or haunted by a ghost, wary of telling his tale, afraid he'll be taken for a fool, or worse yet, of being feared and hated.

"I believe you," I say, reassuring him.

He glances up. "So did Jack."

"You talked to him about it?"

"Jack's the only one I ever told." He taps his package of cigarettes a few times, as if he's resisting the urge to light up. "He's the only one I could trust." He finally gives in to his urge, sticks a cigarette in his mouth, lights it, gets up, and walks to the window, sliding his hands into the pockets of his workman's coveralls as he looks out at the rain. "To make a long story short, we found them on the French River, and we burned the whole place down," he says. He rocks on his heels. "I don't know how many Chippewa we killed. Twenty or thirty, at least. I personally didn't kill any. I couldn't. All I saw was a bunch of innocent people getting slaughtered." He scissors his cigarette between his fingers and pulls it from his mouth. "I ran around trying to stop it all."

# THE BLESSING

"What does this have to do with your longevity?" I ask.

"I saw a mother killed," he says, as if he hasn't heard me.

"She was in a tee-pee. She had a baby strapped to her back. The soldier who killed her...oh, now, what was his name..." He puts his fingers to his brow, squints, tries to recall the soldier's name, but gives up. "I guess it doesn't matter." He turns around and looks at me. "But he killed her, and he left the baby strapped to her back, and he lit her tee-pee on fire. It went up like a torch. Those skins they had over those poles were as dry as tinder. I knew I couldn't let that baby die. So I rushed into the tee-pee, took the baby, and ran into the forest with it. I got as far away from the rest of the soldiers as I could because I didn't want any of them to kill it. I ran and ran, and I wasn't sure which direction I was going, but I finally came out of the woods downstream, where I saw some other Chippewa trying to get away in canoes." He walks back to the table, flicks his ash in the ashtray, takes a sip of his scotch, and sits in his wicker chair. "I carried that Chippewa baby a long way, Denny, longer than I could really manage. All I wanted to do was get that child back to its tribe, but I could hardly keep up. I must have walked twenty or thirty miles through dense bush trying to catch them. I called to them, but they were too far away, and the wind was strong, and it broke my voice apart before it could travel any reasonable distance, so I had no choice, I had to keep following them. I knew I was risking a court martial, deserting like that, but I didn't care. I was doing the right thing."

I think of the other story about the colonel, how he carried a wounded man through dense bush five miles to safety.

"Were you able to catch up with them?" I ask.

"After a while I did," he says. "I followed the canoes for twelve hours." He shakes his head at the reminiscence, staring at the gray ribbon of smoke twisting from the end of his cigarette. "By the time I caught up with them, I was so exhausted I fell to my knees at the edge of their camp. The warriors were on their feet in seconds, ready to spear me. But an older tribesman said something to them, an order, I guess, and they stopped. I offered the child to this older man, raising it in my arms. He was dressed in beads and feathers, and he had a few raven heads tied to his belt. I knew enough about Indian ways to know he was their medicine man. He approached me. He looked me up and down. My uniform was in tatters and I was covered with dirt, and he could see I'd had a rough journey. He looked at the child. The child was smiling, playing with my collar. I remember that distinctly. The old man cracked this strange grin." Howard Hampton leans forward, puts his elbows on the table, and stares at me, his eyes narrowing. "And that's when it happened, Denny." He nods, but it's a bewildered nod. "That's when I became what I am." A rain squall lashes the window. "The old man tapped his head a few times, outlined a crescent moon on his chest, and drew a similar crescent moon on my own chest. He said an Indian word. *Pekitawsit.* He said it three times quickly." Howard Hampton leans back, shrugging wearily. "Like I was telling you before, superstition was a lot stronger back then. I knew a curse when I saw one."

I stare at him. I'm not sure I'm getting this. "You were cursed?" I say. I'm so distraught I don't know what to believe. He looks out the window where the rain comes down harder. He neither confirms nor denies the curse. He simply continues with his story.

"I went back to the fort," he says. He takes another pull on his cigarette and lets the smoke drift out his mouth. "What else could I do?" He shakes his head. He looks tired now. "Everyone was surprised to see me. They thought I was dead. My commanding officer gave me a reprimand, but there was never any court martial. We were too short-handed. I spent a night in the stockade and that was it. I told a few of the soldiers about the curse, and they scoffed, said I shouldn't be concerned about a flea-bitten old savage. But I couldn't stop thinking about the curse. I thought something bad was going to happen to me." He again taps ash into the ashtray. "But nothing ever did." The grin comes back to his face. "After five or six years I forgot about the curse. At least until everybody started telling me how young I looked. I turned fifty. I looked twenty-five. I turned sixty. I still looked twenty-five. I started having dreams about the old man. I heard his voice in my head. *Pekitawsit.* That same word, over and over again. I had no idea what it meant. On my hundredth birthday I decided I had to find out. People were getting suspicious of me. They thought all sorts of weird things. I was nearly lynched once. So I moved away. And then I came back. I came back because I wanted to find a descendent of that original Chippewa tribe we massacred, someone who might tell me what *pekitawsit* meant."

Thunder growls over the lake. "What does it mean?" I ask.

"Actually, it's not a Chippewa word at all," he says. "That's where I went wrong. I can't count how many years I spent pestering every Chippewa tribe between hear and Kenora looking for the meaning of that word. I didn't find out the meaning till 1962. By that time I'd checked every Chippewa-English dictionary ever printed. I was up in Rouyn-Noranda on business, and I met the son of the local Ojibwe band-leader up there. He was a student at the University of Minnesota taking Native American Studies. He was the one who told me *pekitawsit* wasn't a Chippewa word. It's a Micmac word. It means live a long life. He told me it wasn't a curse. It was a blessing. It was the old man's way of thanking me for saving the baby's life." Howard Hampton peers at me quizzically. "Do you know anything about the Micmac?"

I shrug. "Not really."

"They're mainly from Nova Scotia," he says.

"So you went down there?" I ask.

"I sure did." He smiles. "After my boating accident. My Chippewa medicine man picked up a Micmac blessing somehow, and he used it on me. I flew to Halifax and talked to some of the band leaders along the south shore there. They said there was nothing they could do for me. They told me that my medicine man was one of the Old Ones and that all the Old Ones had died out long ago. They said the blessing was irreversible, that I was stuck with it whether I liked it or not."

I raise my eyebrows. "Why wouldn't you like it?" I ask. "You're going to live for hundreds of years."

He frowns. "After the first two centuries you begin to see it's really not much of a blessing."

I sigh, fighting with the hopelessness of my situation. "And there's really nothing you can do for Dianne?" I ask.

"No," he says. "I wish I could, Denny, I really do, but I can't." I sag into the wicker chair, devastated with disappointment. He puts his hand on my knee and shakes his head. "Every so often I get someone like you on my doorstep," he says, "begging me. Someone who's found out, who's put it all together. And you come to me expecting the impossible. You want Dianne to live forever. I don't want to lecture you, Denny. I always liked you. I always knew you were special. I've read all your books. But about the only thing I can do for you now is..." He lifts his hand from my knee and nods. "You're not alone any more, Denny." He nods again. "You've got me." He forces a grin to his face. "And at least that's something."

When we get back to the hospital, Dianne lays in her bed with her mouth open, her eyes closed, her respirations coming once every three to five seconds. I thought I wasn't going to make it. I thought when I got back she would already be dead. I'm glad she's not. I'm glad I can be here with her at the end.

Violet glances past my shoulder at Howard Hampton. I mumble an introduction. "This is...this is Howard Abernathy," I say.

"He's an old family friend." I turn to Howard. "This is Violet Brewer, our private nurse."

The two shake hands. We settle in the hard hospital chairs for our late-night vigil.

Dianne's last breath leaves her lungs at precisely 2:32 in the morning. I look around the hospital room. I am numb. I'm in shock. I don't know what to do. Howard puts his hand on my shoulder. Dianne lays there, skeletal in her thinness, her face pale and cold. She will never move again. She will never speak. She will never smile.

I told you this cancer story was different. Howard Hampton is as different as different gets.

As I walk along the shore of Lake Huron gazing out at the waves, I try to reconcile myself with what's happened. Dianne's dead. Dianne's buried. Is that a blessing? After all her suffering, I sometimes think it is. Sometimes it takes a while to know exactly what a blessing is. Howard and I have become good friends. He sits on a piece of driftwood smoking a cigarette, staring out at the lake. He's the only smoker in the world who doesn't have to worry about cancer. I find a flat rock and skip it over the waves. He tells me how he fought in the War of 1812, yes, of course he does, and he tells me about his endless skirmishing with the Chippewa. He tells me how he homesteaded in Alberta in 1878, how he lost all his money in the Crash of '29, how he staged his own boating death in the 1970s when people again got suspicious of him. He tells me about the Lodge Brothers of 1902, about flying biplanes in World War One, about his 1908 Pierce Arrow, the best car he ever owned, even better than his 1964 Pontiac Strato-Chief. He tells me about his family. He's had several families over the years. And he's watched them all grow old and die. So he knows about death.

He gets up, comes over, his deck shoes sinking into the sand, and puts his hand on my shoulder. The mercury's topped eighty, and, like in the old days, he's taken Denny Connel to Murphy Beach. "Isn't this great?" he says, waving his hand at the lake. "I bet you wonder why you ever left. And you know what? This lake is how you should think of Dianne. Attach her to something that lasts forever, Denny. It's always worked for me. Think of her as those small waves. Think of her as this sky. You're always going to have these things, Denny, just like you'll always have Dianne."

I'm not sure what he means. But as I stare at the thin line where sky touches water, I begin to understand. I can't see where the lake ends and the sky begins. The line shimmers invisibly. I can't see it, but I know it's there. I think of Dianne as that line between lake and sky. I can't see her, but I know she's here. I turn to Howard. He lets his hand fall from my shoulder.

"Now, why don't we go to the Shoreham Inn for a pitcher of draft and a basket of wings?" he says. "My treat."

I nod gratefully. The colonel, having had years of battle experience, has always looked after his men. We walk up the sandy hill to Murphy Road. In the distance I see the Shoreham Inn, a quaint beach motel of white stucco with a red tile roof, the place where I first met Dianne Sloan all those many years ago, when the world was a difference place, and when our lives still held so much promise. I've never been abducted by aliens. I've never been possessed by the devil. And I've never seen a ghost. But I think I can say I've felt one. Dianne, standing in front of the Shoreham Inn, in bell bottoms and big square sunglasses. I feel her right now. I remember Howard's words, how I should attach her to something that lasts forever. And I think I finally understand. I make the adjustment. Like finding out the Chippewa word you've struggled all your life to understand is really a Micmac word. Comprehension sinks in. I see it clearly now. She is here. She is like those small waves out on the lake. She is like this sky. She is, and always will be, my eternal blessing.

# Time Flies
## by Gregory Ward

*Gregory Ward's first two novels, The **Carpet King** and **Water Damage**, were published to critical acclaim, both shortlisted for national prizes. A new novel, **Kondor**, was published in September 1997, while a film version of **Water Damage** has just finished shooting in Toronto, starring Daniel Baldwin.*

*Trained as an actor at the Birmingham School of Dramatic Art, Mr. Ward performs regularly in the role of narrator with regional orchestras. He has appeared often on Canadian radio and television, most recently as Writer In Residence with the CBC national television program, **What On Earth**. He is currently at work on another thriller.*

Fishman waited alone in the gas chamber at San Quentin prison, watching the fly on his knee responding to its movements with slight spasms in his long pale fingers. The fly ranged energetically across his narrow thigh, riding the switchbacks of gathered denim, no doubt looking for some speck of filth to eat or lay its eggs in.

The fly stopped. Motionless, it looked like the magnetized kind that people bought in joke shops to brighten their lives, along with their plastic turds and plastic vomit.

There were two flies now. He bent slightly forward so that he could see the furred bodies through their wings, like looking through a grimy window pane. But such demurely folded wings; and now the fly on the left was washing its legs with that prissy thoroughness. A feast of excrement, and then this obsessive toilet. Fishman ground his teeth, his hand itching to slap it to paste for its hypocrisy.

His thin fingers walked with slow stealth along the metal chair-arms, both hands creeping into place, a spider for each fly, until he felt the canvas straps clutch his wrists.

His rage was instant and overwhelming, a flash fire consuming the dry tinder of his soul.

"McLellan!" he shrieked, but the only reply was a glimpse of an echo from the close steel walls around him.

"McLellan!"

Fishman struggled in the chair, screaming obscenities, hurling himself against the restraints until he slumped back, hoarse and exhausted.

Through smoldering, lidded eyes, he looked through the gas chamber's oval window at the institutional electric clock on the wall of the observation room. It gave him two minutes past the hour. A thin shaft of sunlight slanted from an upper window, bisecting the clock face vertically, through the twelve and the six. He couldn't see the window now, but he had glanced up at it when McLellan escorted him into the chamber, had seen the crooked black fingers of a winter tree holding a small, watery sun.

Why was the observation room still empty? Where were the vultures?

They had been long minutes since McLelland and the examining doctor left, closing the rivet-studded door behind them. Fishman's scalp still crawled from that last human contact, the doctor's soft hand on his head, the whispered reassurances, the humane final instructions...screw and quack settling their consciences. And now, hypocrisy of hypocrisies, they were making him wait like this. While Fishman was in no particular hurry to sniff the eggs (he had long marveled at the trenchancy of prison jargon), he had always valued punctuality and neatness in his own work, had conducted it with chronological and surgical precision. His departure had been scheduled on the hour, so what was the problem?

The two flies had taken off at the onset of Fishman's tantrum, but they were back now. Three. Four of them on his left knee. His mouth began to secrete saliva, the old phobia. It had been a long time since flies had made him physically sick, since the days of mosquito netting and bee-keeper's veils. He could more or less control it now, encouraged the flow of saliva which he stored, then spat with maximum velocity at the flies on his leg. The spray was thin and harmless, but one of the flies sruck an overhand of denim as it took off, and flipped over onto its back.

It required only a slight movement of his legs to deepen the fissure of cloth. Fishman gazed steadily at the fly as it struggled and fizzed, clearing his throat deeply and repeatedly. For a moment he held back, disgusted and fascinated by the tiny, sensual vibrations just discernible through the denim, and then he opened the fissure and spat a second time, substantially and accurately.

The fly struggled in slow motion, its legs paddling the glue of phlegm. Fishman's heart beat fast while it drowned, a poignant reminder of happier times, the long afternoons in his locked bedroom, the experiments that had brought him the earliest whispers of his vocation. The mountains he had made of their legs and wings, so much like the mountains of shoes and spectacles in his scrap book; his expertise with needles, his magnifying glass by the window to muster his own tiny, terrible incinerator. Later, there had been a regular bounty of mice and hamsters, cats when he could get them.

His apprenticeship.

Fishman emerged from his brief daydream with a start. There were more flies on his legs now. A lot more. Eight. Nine. And several more spinning around his head. Flies seemed to be arriving every few seconds, more than he could count.

He called out again to his executioners, but there was no response, nothing to interrupt the buzzing which was building to an alarming level.

"McLellan!"

Fishman twisted from side to side in the metal chair in a vain attempt to increase his field of vision, cursing the straps that held his wrists and ankles. The flies must be coming from somewhere behind him, from some kind of vent.

"McLellan!" he screamed again.

No reply, but the old, too-familiar edge of panic in his voice sobered him. Even as one fly, then another, bumped against his face, he forced himself to relax against the chair-back, to breathe deeply and steadily, which was what the doctor had advised.

"Breathe deeply and you won't suffer."

But what if he cheated a little and held his breath? As long as the flies weren't immune to the effects of hydrocyanic gas, maybe he would have the satisfaction of watching them drop...like flies!

Julian Fishman managed a pale smile. He wasn't afraid of death. Death had been his stock in trade, his life's work. He looked on his execution as nothing more — or less — than the golden handshake at the end of a hugely satisfying career. In fact he applauded the state of California for having retained the death penalty for him.

His whole body jolted as a fly tickled up the side of his face and into his hair. He shook his head wildly, but then it was on his nose. A fly howled into his right ear so that his head whipped sideways in an involuntary spasm, crashing his cheekbone against the steel chairback. He screamed, and with the intake of breath inhaled a fly. Fishman made garberator noises as the thing scrabbled in his throat. He smacked his head against the steel rest, raked bloody furrows into his tongue with his front teeth, spat his own blood along with the debris of legs and wings.

For several minutes he raged, until his head rang like a fire alarm and his body trembled out of control, hardly able to believe it when, quite suddenly, all sound of buzzing ceased in the chamber.

Fishman held his breath until he was sure of the silence, then let it out in a slow hiss of relief. His head was on fire, his mouth and throat a raw agony, but there were no flies on his face any more, none on his pants. No flies on Fishman!

He smiled again. His elation, like his terrible anger, was manic.

Someone was coming. That was the answer. The flies had disappeared into their vent the way animals melted into the jungle at the approach of a predator.

"McLellan!" he roared for the fifth time, encouragingly. He glanced again at the observation room clock, ready with a good-natured rebuke for McLellan for his thoughtlessness, until he realized that the black hands still stood at exactly two minutes past the hour. Typical San Quentin, underfunded and run down — he was more than thankful to be leaving it. It couldn't be a power failure because the hard bare bulbs inside the chamber were still burning, making his eyes smart.

For a brief second of weakness, he found himself regretting his decision not to see the priest, the anxious young chaplain who had tried so hard during the night, who had used every trick in his ridiculous book, a bad loser unable to admit he was powerless against the single, simple truth that Fishman regretted nothing.

"And do you also fear nothing? You're pale, Julian. Why?"

"The last supper, father." He grinned. "Chicken *cordon bleu*. Too rich. Given me the shits."

"I've one more card to play, you know."

"I've seen your hand. It's too low."

"But the stakes are so very high."

"Not in my game."

"Alright then," the chaplain said. "Just for match sticks I'll tell you about hell, and I'll do it in less than ten seconds of your precious time. But it'll be a highly accurate description, I guarantee that. Ten seconds. Interested?"

Fishman shrugged, bored.

"It's as simple as this," said the bad loser priest: "Whatever you most dread, that will be your private hell. Forever, Julian. And ever. I'm on call all night if you hit on something and want to talk again."

He had listened to the priest's light footsteps echoing away along death row. He could hear them now, this morning, but he knew it was only a trick of his imagination. There was no one coming. Nothing moved in the empty observation room behind the oval window, not the hands of the clock which still stood at exactly two minutes past the hour. Not even the shaft of winter sunlight that still bisected the clock's face straight down through the twelve and six.

Fishman blinked. He looked away, refocused, looked again. He watched, scarcely breathing, waiting for his eyes to work properly.

He was an intelligent man; of course the light beam had moved; it must have moved. Sundials didn't break down or run out of power.

He stared until his eyes watered. Every time the line of light seemed to move away from the twelve or six, he sweated with excitement. Every time he realized that it had not moved, that his eyes had merely gratified his desire, he sweated with anxiety.

After an hour, he wore his prison denims like a soaking skin, but the shaft of sunlight haven't moved one millimeter.

After twelve hours, which he had no way of measuring, Fishman still hadn't quite let go of hope. He had almost managed to convince himself that he had called the priest back in an act of contrition.

He had also done a passable job of forgetting the thing he had "hit on" in the early hours of the morning—that most dreaded thing that was supposed to become his private hell.

Forever.

As if to job his memory, a fly landed on his hand.

# Slow Cold Chick

## by Nalo Hopkinson

*Nalo Hopkinson was born in Jamaica and grew up in Jamaica, Trinidad, and Guyana before moving to Canada in 1977 at the age of 16. Like her highly regarded novel* **Brown Girl in the Ring** *(winner of the Warner Aspect First Novel Contest) "Slow Cold Chick" employs Afro-Caribbean culture, language, and sensibilities within the northern setting of the author's adopted home of Toronto. It is an understatement to say that she is a fresh voice in the field of dark fantasy.*

They'd cut off the phone. Blaise slammed the receiver back into its cradle. "Oonuh couldn't wait just a little more?" she asked resentfully of the silent phone. "I get paid Friday, you know." Now she couldn't ask her mother if to put milk or water in the cornbread. Chuh. Blaise flounced into the kitchen and scowled at the mixing bowl on the counter.

Mummy used milk, she was almost sure of it. Blaise poured milk and oil, remembering her mother's home-made cornbread, yellow-warm smelling, hot from the oven, with butter melting more yellow into it. Yes, Mummy used milk.

And eggs. And Blaise didn't have any. "Damn." It was almost a week until pay day. She made a sucking sound of irritation. Frustration burned deep in her chest.

A movement through her kitchen window caught her eye. From her main floor apartment, Blaise could easily see the Venus-built lady in the next door garden. The Venus-built lady's cottage always gave the appearance of having just popped into existence, unexpected and anachronistic as Doctor Who's call box.

Chocolate-dark limbs peeking out of her plush white dressing gown, the Venus-built lady waded indolently through rioting ivy, swollen red roses, nasturtiums that pursed into succulent lips. Blaise had often thought to ask the beautiful woman what her name was. But to meet the eyes of someone so self-possessed, much less speak to her...

Branches laden, an otaheite tree bobbed tumescent maroon fruit, so low that the lady could have plucked them with her mouth. Blaise's mother sometimes sent her otaheite apples from Jamaica, but how did the tropical tree flourish in this northern climate?

As ever, the Venus-built lady's gingered brown hair flung itself in crinkled dreadknots down her back, tangled as lovers' fingers. Blaise had chemically straightened all the kinks out of her own hair.

The Venus-built lady was laying a circle of conch shells around a bed of bleeding hearts. She reached out to caress the plants' pink flowers. At her touch, they shivered delicately. Blaise looked down at her own dull brown hands. The Venus-built lady's skin had the glow of full-fat chocolate.

The woman bent and straightened, bent and straightened, leaving a pouting conch shell behind her each time, until pink echoed pink in a circle around the bleeding hearts. Blaise thought of the shells singing as the wind blew past their lips.

The lady turned away from the flower bed and swayed amply up her garden path. As her foot touched the first step of the cottage, a fat, velvet-petalled rose leaned beseechingly towards her. She tugged the rose from its stem and *ate* it. Then she opened her gingerbread door and sashayed inside.

*Weird.* Blaise imagined a spineless green grub squirming voluptuously in the heart of the overblown rose. And an avid mouth descending towards it. She shuddered. *I don't want to eat the worm.*

It had gotten hot in the apartment. The fridge burped. Distractedly, Blaise opened it.

# SLOW COLD CHICK

There was an egg huddling in one of the little cups inside the fridge door. Where had that come from? Exactly what she needed. She was reaching eagerly for it when a stench from deep inside the fridge slid into her nostrils; a poisonous, vinegary tang. The scotch bonnet pepper sauce she'd made, last year sometime? was rotting in its glass jar. The pepper crusting the jar's lid had begun to corrode the metal. A vile greenness bloomed on the surface of the red liquid. Blaise kissed her teeth in disgust and dumped the mouldering sauce into the sink.

Cornbread now.

The egg was a little too big for its cradle, a little rounder than eggs usually were. Blaise picked it up. Its cold, mercurial weight shifted in her palm, sucking warmth from her hand. She cracked it into the bowl. With a hollow *clomp!* a mass disappeared below the surface of the liquid.

A sulphur-rot stench filled the kitchen. "Backside!" Blaise swallowed a wave of anger. A bubble of foetid air popped from the depths of the bowl. Blaise grimaced and began to pour the swampy goop down the drain. The tainted milk and oil mingled with the pepper sauce.

Something rubbery thumped into the mouth of the drain and lay there. It was small and grey and jointed. A naked, fully formed chicken foetus. Blaise's gorge rose. When the thing moved, wallowing in the pepper sauce remaining in the sink, she nearly spewed the coffee she'd drunk that morning.

"Urrrr..." rattled the cold-grown chick. Slowly, slowly, it extended a peeled head on a wobbly neck. Its tiny beak was thin as nail parings. Its eyes creaked open, stretching a red film of pepper sauce from lid to lid. It shrieked tinnily as the pepper made contact with its eyes. Frantically it shook its head. Its pimply grey body contorted in agony. It shrieked again. Fighting revulsion, Blaise grabbed a cooking spoon and scooped it up.

"Shh, shh." She wadded a tea towel in her free hand and deposited the bird into it. It wailed and stropped its own head against the tea towel. Its cartilaginous body writhed against her palm. Her skin crawled.

"Arr..." the chick complained. Blaise filled the cooking spoon with water and trickled it over the grey, bald head. The bird fought and spluttered. Reddened eyes glared accusingly at Blaise.

"Make up your mind," she flared. "You want fire in your eyes, or cool water?" The chick tried to peck. Blaise hissed angrily, "Well here, then, take that!"

She scooped some drops of pepper sauce from the sink with her fingers and flicked it at the bird's head. It yowped in indignation. Then, worm-blind, a tiny grey tongue snaked out of its mouth and licked some of the pepper sauce off its beak. "Urrrr...." This time it didn't seem to mind the taste of the pepper. It licked it off, then blinked its burned eyes clear.

Its body a blur, it shook the water off. It sat up straight in her palm, staring alertly at her. It seemed a little bigger. It did have a few feathers after all, Blaise must have just not noticed them before.

Her anger cooled. She'd let loose the heat of her temper on such a little thing.

The chick opened its mouth wide; Blaise nearly dropped it in alarm. Its hungry red maw looked bigger than its head.

Well, it had seemed to like the pepper, after all. Blaise scraped stringy threads of it out of the sink and dangled them in front of the cold chick's beak. It gaped even wider, begging to be fed. She let slimy tendrils fall. Red threads wriggled down the bird's throat. Ugh.

The chick swallowed, withdrew its pinny head into its ugly neck, and closed its eyes.

"That do you for now?" Blaise asked it.

The chick purred, a low, rattling sound. It radiated heat into her hand. It wasn't so ugly, really. She tucked its warmth close to her breast.

Someone knocked at the door. Blaise gasped, jolted out of her peaceful moment. She dumped the chick into a soup bowl. It squawked and toppled, legs kicking at the air. "Stay there," she hissed, and went to answer the knock.

It was the guy next door, lanky and pimply in a frowsty leather jacket. "Hi there, Blaise," he leered. "Whatcha up to?"

The red tongues of his construction boots hung loose and floppy. He was gnawing on the gooey tag end of a cheap chocolate bar, curled wrapper ends wilting from his fist.

"Nothing much," Blaise replied.

Tethered by a leash through its studded leather collar, the guy's ferret humped around and around in sad circles at his feet. Something about its furtive slinkiness brought to mind a furry penis with teeth.

The guy took a hopeful step closer. "Want some company?"

Not this again. "Um, maybe another time." She remained blocking the doorway, hoping he'd get the point. The ferret sneezed and rubbed fretfully at its snout. Oh, goody: the guy next door's ferret had a head cold. Gooseflesh rose on Blaise's arms.

"What, like this evening, maybe?" asked the guy. His eyes roamed eagerly over her face and body. The familiar steam of stifled anger bubbled through Blaise. Why couldn't he ever take a hint? She wished he'd just dry up and fly away.

There was a thump from the kitchen. The ferret arched sinuously up onto its hind legs, its fur bristling. Blaise turned; her blood froze cold. A creature something between a chicken and an eagle was stalking menacingly out of her kitchen. It was the cold chick, grown to the size of a spaniel. Its down-feathered neck wove its raptor's head in a serpentine dance. Its feet had become cruel, ringed claws. It stared at her with a fierce intelligence.

The guy goggled. "What the...?"

At the sound, the chick's fiery-red comb went erect. Nictitating membranes slid clear of its eyes, which glowed red. Blaise felt a peppery warmth flood her body briefly. Frightened, she stepped aside. The chick turned its gaze full on the guy. It hissed, a sound like steam escaping. The guy next door looked down at it, and seemed immediately held by its stare. He whimpered softly. Heat danced between the chick and the guy next door, then he just, well, *vaporized*. In a second, all that was left of him was a grey smear of ash on the hallway carpet, and a faint whiff of cheap chocolate.

"Oh, my God," Blaise said, feeling frantically for the open doorway.

The ferret growled. The chick pounced. Blaise leapt out of the way. Jesus, now they were between her and the way out.

The ferret wound itself around the creature. The chick's beak slashed. The ferret yipped, sneezed. Drops of ferret blood and mucus flew. The cold chick flexed a meaty thigh to slice a talon through the ferret's middle. The ferret arched and writhed in extremis. Knots of bloody intestine trailed from its belly. The cold chick twisted its head between the cruel tines of its beak. Blaise heard the ferret's neck snap. Holding it down with its claws, the cold chick began to devour the ferret with a wet crunching sound. Blaise could hear her own panicked sobbing.

The chick sucked up looped coils of gut with little chirps of pleasure.

Then it *blurred*. When Blaise could see it clearly again, it was the size of a rotweiler. Its feathers had sprouted into rich burgundy and green plumes. It snapped up the rest of the ferret, then crouched in the doorway. It looked at her, and Blaise knew it would burn her to death. A keening sound came from her mouth. Heat washed over her, but then the membranes slid down over the chick's open eyes. Blaise could still see its piercing stare, slightly opaqued.

"Mmrraow?" it enquired fondly. It had a satisfied look on its beaky face.

It wasn't going to eat her. It had done this to please her, and now the guy next door was really dried up and gone. "That isn't what I meant," Blaise wailed. The chick cocked its head adoringly at the sound of her voice.

Blaise sat down heavily in her tattered armchair, trying to figure out what to do next. The chick groomed, rattling its beak through its jewel-coloured feathers. Its meal was still altering its body. It blurred again, it morphed. Four clawed, furred front legs sprouted to replace its chicken feet. The chick cockatrice looked down at its own body, stomped around experimentally on its new limbs. It made a chuckling noise. Would it have stayed a slow, cold chick if it hadn't eaten the ferret? Or the burning pepper sauce?

It belched, spat up a slimy black thread; the ferret's leash. It pounced on the leash and started worrying at it. Sunlight danced motes of colour through its plumage. It was very beautiful. And it would probably need to feed again soon.

*I not going to be second course,* Blaise thought. She moved to the door. Happily torturing the leash, the cockatrice ignored her. She grabbed her jacket from its peg and locked her door behind her. She left the apartment.

The clean fall air cleared her mind a little. The animal shelter, yeah, they'd come and take the beast away.

She had to pass the Venus-built lady's garden on the way. There was a man in the yard with his back to her: a slim, bald man with a wiry strength to his build. Shirtless, he was digging beside the otaheite tree. His tanned shoulders made a "v" with the narrowness of his waist. With each thrust of the shovel, corded muscles flexed like cables in his arms and back. Blaise slowed to admire him. He pumped the shovel smoothly into the earth with one bare, sturdy foot, but something stopped it from sinking any further. He went down on one knee and began tenderly pulling up clods of dirt, crumbling them between his fingers. Blaise crept closer to the gate and craned her neck to see better. The man sniffed at the dark soil in his hands and poured a handful of it down his throat. His adam's apple jumped when he swallowed.

Was everybody eating something strange today? All Blaise had wanted was cornbread.

The man looked round, saw her, and grinned. It was a friendly expression; there were well-worn smile lines pared into his cheeks. She grinned back. His lean face had the rough texture of chipped rock. Not handsome, but striking.

He reached into the womb of soil again and tugged out the rock that had stopped his shovel. His fingers flexed. He crushed the rock between them like a sugar cube and reverently licked up the powdery bits.

The cottage door opened, letting the Venus-built lady out. She had changed into a sweater and close-fitting jeans that made her hips heart-shaped. She had a basket slung over one shoulder. A smile broke onto the man's face the way the stone had cracked between his fingers. He offered a stone-powdered palm. "It's sweet," he said in a voice like gravel being ground underfoot. "The fruit will be sweet too."

The Venus-built lady smiled back. Then she looked at Blaise. "So come and help us then, nuh?" she asked in a warm alto that sang of the tropics, "instead of standing there staring?"

Blaise felt heat warming her face.

But what about the cockatrice?

The problem was too big for her to deal with for the moment. With an "Um, okay," she chose denial. She let herself into the garden, trying shyly to avoid eye contact with either of them. "What you doing?"

"Getting the otaheite tree ready for winter," the man replied. "It won't last out in the open like this."

"I bury it in the soil every winter," the Venus-built lady told her. "Then I dig it up in summer, and it blooms for me by the fall."

"And that works?"

"It works, yes," the Venus-built lady replied. "It bears, and it feeds my soul. Is a flavour of home. You going to help me pick, or you want to help Johnny dig?"

Standing this close to her neighbour, Blaise could taste the warm rose spice of her breath. Even her skin had the scent of the roses she ate. Blaise looked at Johnny. He was resting comfortably on the shovel, watching both of them. He grinned, jade eyes bright.

Who to help? Who to work close beside? "I will help you pick for now," she told the Venus-built lady. "But when Johnny get tired, I could help him dig."

Johnny nodded. "The more, the merrier." He returned to his task.

The otaheite apples seemed to leap joyfully from their stems into the Venus-built lady's hands. She and Blaise picked all the fruit, ate their fill of maroon-skinned sweetness and melting white flesh, fed some to sweaty Johnny as he dug. The woman owned a flower shop over in Cabbagetown. "Is called Rose of Sharon," she laughed. "Sharon is my name." Blaise inhaled her flower-breathed words.

Johnny was a metalworker. He pointed proudly at Sharon's wrought iron railings. "Made those."

His ruddiness came from facing down fire every day. Blaise imagined him shirtless at the forge, forming the molten iron into beautiful shapes.

"I need help at the shop," Sharon told her. "You don't like the job you have now, and you have a gentle hand with that fruit you picking. You want to come by Monday and talk to me about it?"

Blaise thought she might like to work amongst flowers, coaxing blooms to fullness. "Okay. Monday evening," she replied.

She and Johnny dug out most of the soil from around the tree's roots while Sharon steadied its trunk. Then all three of them laid the tree in its winter bed, clipped its branches and covered it with soil.

"Goodnight, my darling," whispered Sharon. "See you soon." The bleeding hearts quivered daintily. The roses dipped their weighty heads.

The sun was lowering by the time they were done. The shelter would be closed, but probably the cockatrice was asleep by now. Blaise stood with Sharon and Johnny beside the giant's grave that held the otaheite tree. She ached from all the picking and digging; a good hurt. Johnny put a hand lightly on her shoulder. She felt the heat of it through the fabric. He smelt of sweat and fire and earth. On Johnny's other side, Sharon took his free hand. She and Johnny kissed, slowly. They looked into each other's eyes and smiled. Sharon slid an arm around Blaise's waist. Blaise relaxed into the touch, then caught herself. Ears burning, she eased away, stood apart from the warmth of the two.

"I should go now," she said.

Sharon replied, "Johnny likes to take earth into himself. Soil and rock and iron."

"What?"

"It's what I crave," Johnny told her helpfully. "And plants nourish Sharon. What do you eat?"

"How you mean? I don't understand."

Sharon said, "You must know the things that nourish you. Sometimes you have to reach out for them."

No, that couldn't be right. The bird birthed of the heat of Blaise's anger had eaten as it pleased, and it had turned into a monster.

"Um, I really have to go now. Things to take care of."

"Something we can do?" Johnny asked. Both his face and Sharon's held concern.

Blaise looked at this man who ingested the ore he forged, and the woman to whom flowers gave themselves to be supped. She took a deep breath and told them the story of the cockatrice.

Blaise's hallway still had the oily smell of cheap chocolate, burnt. She stepped guiltily around the ash smear on the carpet. "This is my place."

"Careful as you go in," Sharon warned.

The apartment was close and hot. It reeked of sulphur. Blaise flicked on the light.

The tv had been gutted. It lay crumpled on its side, a stove-in, smoking box.

"Holy," Johnny growled. The couch was in shreds, the plants steamed and wilting. The casing of the telephone was melted, adding its own acrid smell to the reek.

Blaise could feel the tears filling her eyes. Sharon put an arm around her shoulders. Blaise leaned into the comfort of Sharon's petal-soft body and sobbed, a part of her still aware of Sharon's rosiness and duskiness.

A bereft screech; a flurry of feathers and fur and heat; a stinking hiss of pepper and rotten eggs. The cockatrice rammed full weight into Blaise and Sharon, bearing them to the floor. Sharon rolled out, but the cockatrice sat on

Blaise's chest. Its wordless howl carried all the anguish of *Mummy gone and leave me,* and the rage of *Oh, so she come back now? Well, I going show her.*

Blaise cringed. The cockatrice spat a thick red gobbet at her face. It burned her cheek. The drool smelled like rotting pepper sauce. Blaise went cold with horror.

Suddenly the creature's weight was lifted off her. Johnny was holding the cockatrice aloft by its thick, writhing neck. Blaise scrabbled along the floor, putting Johnny between herself and the monster. Johnny's biceps bulged; the rock-crushing fingers flexed; the cockatrice's furred hindquarters kicked and clawed. It spat. Johnny didn't budge. Fire had met stone.

"Kill it for me, Johnny, do." Blaise shoved herself to her feet.

"Oh God, Johnny; you all right?" Sharon asked.

"Yes," he muttered, all his concentration on the struggle. But his voice rang flat, a hammer on flawed steel.

The cockatrice thrashed. Blaise's belly squirmed in response. The animal made a choking sound. It was dying. Blaise felt warmth begin to drain from her body. Her heat, her fire was dying.

"You have to go," Blaise whispered at it. "You can't do as you want, lash out at anything you don't like."

Sharon gripped Blaise's shoulder. Where was the softness? Sharon's hand was knotted and tough as ironwood. "You want to kill your every desire dead?" she asked.

The cockatrice sobbed. It turned a hooded look of sorrow and rage on Blaise. Then it glowered at Johnny. Blaise saw the membranes slide back from its eyes. She lunged at it.

Too late. The heat of its glare was full on. The air sizzled, and Johnny was caught. Sharon screamed. Johnny *glowed,* red as the iron in his forge fires.

But he didn't melt or burn. Yet. Blaise could see him straining to break the pull of the cockatrice's glare, see him weakening. Her beast would kill this man.

"Bloodfire!" Furious, she charged the cockatrice, dragged it out of Johnny's grasp. She heard Johnny crash to the floor.

The cockatrice glared at her. Hot, hot. She was burning up with heat, with the bellyfires of anger, of wanting, of hunger.

"Talk to it," Sharon told her. "Tell it what you want."

Blaise took a step towards the cockatrice. Bird-like, it cocked its head. It mewed a question.

"I *want,*" she said, her voice quaking out the unfamiliar word, "to be able to talk what I feel." God, fever-hot. "I want to be able to say, *you hurt me.*" The cockatrice hissed. "*Or I'm not interested.*" The cockatrice chortled wickedly. "Or," Blaise hesitated, took in a burning breath, "*I like you.*"

The cockatrice sighed. It leapt into her arms, its dog-heavy weight nearly buckling her knees. Its claws scratched her and its breath was rank, but somehow she held it, feeling its strength flex against her. She held the heat of its needing body tight.

Suddenly, it shoved its beak between her lips. Blaise choked, tried to drop the beast, but its flexed claws held her tightly. Impossibly, it crammed its whole head into her mouth. Blaise gagged. She could feel its beak sliding down her throat. It would sear her, like a hot poker. She fought, looking imploringly at Sharon and Johnny, but they just sat on the floor, watching.

Blaise tried to vomit the beast out, but it kept pushing more of itself inside her. How, how? It was unbelievable. Her mouth was stretched open so wide, she thought it would tear. Heat filled her, her ribs would crack apart. The beast's head and neck snaked down towards her belly. Its wings beat against her teeth, her tongue. Her throat, it was in her throat, stopping her air! Terrified, she pulled at the cockatrice's legs. It clawed her hands away. With a great heave, its whole bulk slid into her stomach. She could feel its muscly writhing, its fire that now came from her core. She could breathe, and she was angry enough to spit fire.

"What oonuh were thinking!" she raged at them. "Why you didn't help me!"

Johnny only said, "I bet you feel good now."

*Oh.* She did. Strong, sure of herself. Oh.

Sharon leaned over Johnny and blew cool, aloe-scented breath on his blisters. Blaise admired the way that the position emphasized the fullness of her body. Johnny's burns healed as Blaise watched. "I enjoyed your company this afternoon," she said to them both. Simple, risky words to say with this new-found warmth in her voice.

Sharon smiled. "You must come and visit again soon, then."

Blaise giggled. She reached a hand to either of them, feeling the blood heat of her palms flexing against theirs.

# Pet Worms

## by David Shtogryn

*David Shtogryn lives in Scarborough, Ontario, with his wife and a powder puff German Shepherd called Rambo. He has had over thirty stories published in a wide variety of magazines and genres, science fiction, fantasy, horror and mainstream. He says that the idea for the following story originated from a graveyard illustration. "For several days I pondered that there must be a unique approach to such a subject as inspiration for a story. Eventually, I came up with worms as pets."*

Ronnie Grenfeld, the proprietor of Handy Butcher, died horribly only minutes after he spoke to me on the telephone. Though our conversation was bizarre, I can honestly say that he gave no hint of what he planned to do.

Had he not been an old high school acquaintance, it's unlikely that I would even have spoken to him, as most of my law practice is now handled by junior partners. Three years ago I had processed his divorce and had not heard from him in the interim, until this. I would have paid more attention to Ronnie and his ranting about his pet worms at that time, but a distracting smell of smoked meat followed him everywhere and my queasy stomach forced me to cut our meetings short.

The homicide detective who was first called to the death scene telephoned me immediately. He stated that my name and number were found on a piece of paper beside the body. After he assured me that Ronnie's death was considered suicide, I briefed him on that last, strange conversation between Ronnie and myself.

"Pet worms," I said.

"What?"

"He wanted me to take care of his pet worms, should anything happen to him." I could visualize the officer's face screwing up as I spoke.

"Hm," he grunted. "I'll stop by. Got an envelope for you."

I shrugged, checked my appointment book, and agreed to see him in an hour. I walked across the street for a quick lunch at Marty's Diner. When I returned, he was sitting in my reception office.

"Detective Morrow," he rose, not offering his hand.

He was someone new on the force whom I had not seen before. His relaxed bearing and sardonic glance did not present the respectful attitude I was used to. He handed me a thick brown envelope that held a hint of Ronnie's nauseating smell and had my name printed on the face.

"Blood all over the place," he described with relish.

"Oh?" I tore the end off the envelope.

"Yep. Took the safety guard off the big meat slicer. Took his thumb and index finger off right up to the wrist. Blood everywhere."

I waved the detective into my office and dumped the contents of the envelope on my desk.

"Passerby," his voice never changed tone or rhythm, "saw blood spraying on the front window. Didn't hear any screams or anything. Just splattering blood. Called the emergency number from a pay phone. Too late."

I scanned the several documents and realized that Ronnie had made me executor of his will, which shockingly left everything he owned to me. There was also a deed to a grave plot in Seven Acres. Funny, I was sure that unkempt cemetery on the other side of the conservation area had been full for years. Obviously not.

I gave Detective Morrow a quick glance. He was in no hurry to leave. "Have the coroner contact me when the body is released," I finally said brusquely, and turned away. Morrow took the hint and let himself out.

I found a small piece of brown paper, buried in the stack of documents. On it were Ronnie's hastily scrawled instructions about his worms. They were to be fed only oatmeal and released in November, one month from now, no sooner. The intrusive meat smell was now stronger and my stomach twitched.

"Mrs. Seams," I called into the intercom. "Send Sparrow in here."

Sparrow was one of the new junior partners. I would have him handle the legal data pertaining to Ronnie's estate and see what he could do about cleaning out the supplies in the butcher shop. A quick distribution to a food bank would get me some good publicity.

"Also," I had almost forgotten. "Go to the butcher shop yourself and look around for some worms." Sparrow looked at me oddly. "And get rid of them."

"Get rid of some worms? What kind of worms?"

"Pet worms. You'll know when you find them."

"Tomorrow okay for that?"

"Yep."

The coroner did a quick autopsy on Ronnie's body the next morning, and I then contacted White's Funeral Home. The use of Seven Acres startled them as well, but a call confirmed that the place was still in business, so to speak. Ronnie was buried a day later.

Daniel Sparrow died that evening at the Handy Butcher shop. Detective Morrow had no qualms about giving me the gory details while standing in the change room of my exercise club.

"Had holes all over his body." Morrow was watching me intently, his mouth set in a tight slit. "Worm holes, we think. His flesh ..."

I hated his dramatizing.

"... had been sucked dry. Pulled back from blood vessels, cartilage, fingernails. We hoped you might have some further information. Might help us." His lips were moist.

Shaking, I stepped over to a steamy mirror to fix my tie. "Grenfeld had pet worms. I told you that before, and that's all I know," I stated with finality.

Morrow left.

That night, in spite of an extra measure of cognac before bed, I had horrible visions as I wavered in and out of sleep. I saw Sparrow knocking over the huge container of worms. I saw his body full of gaping holes, mouth and eyes open wide. He sat up and pointed at me. Then came the worms, thousands of tiny segmented serpents twisting along the walls of the main sewer system. The stench of death surrounded them, overriding the rankness of untreated feces. They moved as a team, almost in military formation, slotted mouths with needle teeth snapping open and closed. The undulating mass slowly turned and funneled up into a small pipe, then poured over the lip of a toilet bowl. I screamed and woke up.

Morrow was on my doorstep as the sun rose that morning. I knew what he had come for.

"Two more people dead. Over on Magdel street." A bead of perspiration slipped off his upper lip as he spoke. "Same thing. Worm holes. Flesh withered."

I responded in my usual blunt manner. After all, what did I really know?

Morrow squinted at me thoughtfully, then turned and left. He stayed parked in front of my house for a long time before driving away.

I went to the office early and pulled Ronnie's divorce file. Maybe his ex wife could tell me something. She answered the phone after one ring. The news of Ronnie's death did not seem to cause her undue grief.

"Of course," she sighed impatiently when I asked about the worms, "they were his life, those worms, literally. Ronnie said they were his key to immortality. They were supposed to bring him back to life someday, but needed to mature, or something." She laughed. "Living with Ronnie was so much fun."

I thanked her and hung up. I got Mrs. Seams to get me a city road map. With a pencil and ruler, I drew a line connecting the Handy Butcher shop and Seven Acres. The line crossed Magdel street. Genius was not required to figure out that the worms were on their way to Ronnie's grave. So, someone must be there when they arrived, ready to destroy them.

Once again, the vision of Sparrow's mangled corpse flashed through my mind. If I had gotten rid of the worms myself, Sparrow and the others would still be alive. So now it was up to me to do it right. I never considered the possibility of failure, yet I was terrified by the thought of what I would find at the cemetery. I contemplated for a moment calling Morrow to come along and help. Then I remembered his cynical, hard-boiled attitude and imagined his reception of a "killer worm" theory. I reconsidered. I hated to be laughed at.

I punched the intercom on the desk. "Mrs. Seams?"

"Yes sir."

"Order me in some lunch, and cancel any bookings I've got for today and tomorrow."

I looked up the scale on the street map and did some quick calculating. The worms should reach Ronnie's grave early tonight. I drove home and changed into old boots and clothes, then stuffed a shovel and the gasoline container from the garden shed into the back of my station wagon. A packet of matches from the kitchen cupboard, and I was ready.

My car's tires crunched over the leaf-covered road to Seven Acres as the day dulled into twilight. The iron entrance gate to the isolated cemetery appeared slightly ajar, but I drove by it and parked the car beside a narrow gap in the surrounding spiked fence. Lowering the tailgate, I picked up the shovel and the can of gasoline, then squeezed through the opening into the graveyard.

Grass and weeds grew knee high. Close trees were barren of leaves and the dying daylight cast eerie shadows over everything. I passed by old, untended gravestones and a dilapidated mausoleum. The freshly turned earth of Ronnie's grave was easy to find.

My plan was simple. Digging to or just above the level of the casket should be easy in the unpacked earth. I would dump the gasoline and torch the whole business, worms and all. They had to be here by now.

The absolute silence was broken by the whisper of my shovel slicing through the soft soil. I hit something almost immediately and stepped back as the earth began to heave.

Terror! A hideous hand of withered flesh dotted with small worm craters rose out of the soil. Another hand with two fingers missing, exploded upwards beside it.

The shovel tumbled from my grip as I scrambled from the grave and grabbed the gasoline can. Ronnie's arms were thrashing upwards and his head broke through the earth's surface. A skeletal face, unrecognizable, buzzing with countless segmented worms, looked at me and uttered a soundless threat.

I began to spray gasoline everywhere in a panic. Ronnie's hand struck out to grasp my leg, but I was just beyond his reach. The gasoline fumes gave me urgently needed confidence. Ronnie had now struggled out up to his waist. His worm-riddled torso was exposed through shreds of torn clothing. His movements were frantic, erratic.

I threw the emptied gasoline can at him but missed, and pulled the matches from my pocket. Ronnie was fully out now, staring at me through hollow eye sockets. One strike, and I tossed the little yellow flame through the air. The gasoline exploded. Ronnie, enveloped in flames, continued to stumble towards me.

I could see the worms, slotted mouths smiling, withdrawing into the safety of Ronnie's inner body. The fire suddenly dwindled, and Ronnie lunged. I froze and screamed as a smoking hand dug into my shoulder. Then someone grasped my arms and yanked me backwards.

Detective Morrow stood behind me.

"Follow me!" he yelled.

Ronnie kept coming. The worms slowly reappeared as the smoke from his flesh dissipated.

I ran after Morrow. A police van was parked just outside the gate. Morrow swung open the rear doors and started unlatching huge crates. He threw back the crate doors and ducked as birds swooped out, pigeons, countless pigeons.

"From my Aviary group," Morrow bellowed. "Passengers and racing. Hobby. Didn't feed them today. Wanted them hungry."

The birds swarmed over Ronnie, knocking him to the ground. They pecked at his flesh, pulling the worms out, ripping and swallowing. Ronnie shook in death spasms, then suddenly lay still under the pounding of the birds' wings.

The air filled with the putrid smell of rotted, smoked meat.

"My babies sure like eating worms," Morrow smirked.

# The Emperor's Old Bones

## by Gemma Files

*Gemma Files' first professional fiction sale was to Northern Frights 2, but since then she has sold numerous stories to both small press magazines and mainstream anthologies. The quality of her work can be measured by the fact that she has received an honorable mention in every volume of Ellen Datlow's Year's Best Fantasy and Horror anthology since 1993. In addition, a number of her stories have been adapted for television and produced for The Hunger, a half-hour anthology series under the aegis of well-known filmmakers Tony and Ridley Scott.*

*The author had this to say about her story: "'The Emperor's Old Bones' is a for-real dish, inexplicable as it may seem — although I've never heard of anybody but a fish falling victim to it. What I was aiming for here falls somewhere between bittersweet nostalgia and that cold, sinking feeling you get from realizing your personal morality is even more porous than you originally suspected it might be. That, and really grossing a few people out. I hope I've succeeded in at least one of these aims."*

**Oh, buying and selling...you know...life.**
—*Tom Stoppard, after J.G. Ballard.*

One day in 1941, not long after the fall of Shanghai, my amah (our live-in Chinese maid of all work, who often doubled as my nurse) left me sleeping alone in the abandoned hulk of what had once been my family's home, went out, and never came back...a turn of events which didn't actually surprise me all that much, since my parents had done something rather similar only a few brief weeks before. I woke up without light or food, surrounded by useless luxury—the discarded detritus of Empire and family alike. And fifteen more days of boredom and starvation were to pass before I saw another living soul.

I was ten years old.

After the war was over, I learned that my parents had managed to bribe their way as far as the harbor, where they became separated in the crush while trying to board a ship back "Home". My mother died of dysentery in a camp outside of Hangkow; the ship went down halfway to Hong Kong, taking my father with it. What happened to my amah, I honestly don't know — though I do feel it only fair to mention that I never really tried to find out, either.

The house and I, meanwhile, stayed right where we were — uncared for, unclaimed — until Ellis Iseland broke in, and took everything she could carry.

Including me.

"So what's your handle, *tai pan*?" She asked, back at the dockside garage she'd been squatting in, as she went through the pockets of my school uniform.

(It would be twenty more years before I realized that her own endlessly evocative name was just another bad joke — one some immigration official had played on her family, perhaps.)

"Timothy Darbersmere," I replied, weakly. Over her shoulder, I could see the frying pan still sitting on the table, steaming slightly, clogged with burnt rice. At that moment in time, I would have gladly drunk my own urine in order to be allowed to lick it out, no matter how badly I might hurt my tongue and fingers in doing so.

Her eyes followed mine — a calm flick of a glance, contemptuously knowing, arched eyebrows barely sketched in cinnamon.

"Not yet, kid," she said.

"I'm really very hungry, Ellis."

"I really believe you, Tim. But not yet." She took a pack of cigarettes from her sleeve, tapped one out, lit it. Sat back. Looked a me again, eyes narrowing contemplatively. The plume of smoke she blew was exactly the same non color as her slant, level, heavy-lidded gaze.

"Just to save time, by the way, here's the house rules," she said. "Long as you're with me, I eat first. Always."

"That's not fair."

"Probably not. But that's the way it's gonna be, 'cause I'm thinking for two, and I can't afford to be listening to my stomach instead of my gut." She took another drag. "Besides which, I'm bigger than you."

"My father says adults who threaten children are bullies."

"Yeah, well, that's some pretty impressive moralizing, coming from a mook who dumped his own kid to get out of Shanghai alive."

I couldn't say she wasn't right, and she knew it, so I just stared at her. She was exoticism personified—the first full-blown Yank I'd ever met, the first adult (Caucasian) woman I'd ever seen wearing trousers. Her flat, Midwestern accent lent a certain fascination to everything she said, however repulsive.

"People will do exactly whatever they think they can get away with, Tim," she told me, "for as long as they think they can get away with it. That's human nature. So don't get all high-hat about it, use it. Everything's got its uses—everything, and everybody."

"Even you, Ellis?"

"Especially me, Tim. As you will see."

It was Ellis, my diffident ally—the only person I have ever met who seemed capable of flourishing in any given situation—who taught me the basic rules of commerce: to always first assess things at their true value, then gauge exactly how much extra a person in desperate circumstances would be willing to pay for them. And her lessons have stood me in good stead, during all these intervening years. At the age of 66, I remain not only still alive, but a rather rich man, to boot—import/export, antiques, some minor drug smuggling intermittently punctuated (on the more creative side) by the publication of a string of slim, speculative novels. These last items have apparently garnered me some kind of cult following amongst fans of such fiction, most specifically—ironically enough—in the United States of America.

But time is an onion, as my third wife used to say: The more of it you peel away, searching for the hidden connections between action and reaction, the more it gives you something to cry over.

So now, thanks to the established temporal conventions of literature, we will slip fluidly from 1941 to 1999—to St. Louis, Missouri, and the middle leg of my first-ever Stateside visit, as part of a tour in support of my recently-published childhood memoirs.

The last book signing was at four. Three hours later, I was already firmly ensconced in my comfortable suite at the downtown Four Seasons Hotel. Huang came by around eight, along with my room service trolley. He had a briefcase full of files and a sly, shy grin, which lit up his usually impassive face from somewhere deep inside.

"Racked up a lotta time on this one, Mr. Darbersmere," he said, in his second-generation Cockney growl. "Spent a lotta your money, too."

"Mmm." I uncapped the tray. "Good thing my publisher gave me that advance, then, isn't it?"

"Yeah, good fing. But it don't matter much now."

He threw the files down on the table between us. I opened the top one and leafed delicately through, between mouthfuls. There were schedules, marriage and citizenship certificates, medical records. Police records, going back to 1953, with charges ranging from fraud to trafficking in stolen goods, and listed under several different aliases. Plus a sheaf of photos, all taken from a safe distance.

I tapped one.

"Is this her?"

Huang shrugged. "You tell me—you're the one 'oo knew 'er."

I took another bite, nodding absently. Thinking: *Did I? Really? Ever?*

As much as anyone, I suppose.

To get us out of Shanghai, Ellis traded a can of petrol for a spot on a farmer's truck coming back from the market—then cut our unlucky savior's throat with her straight razor outside the city limits, and sold his truck for a load of cigarettes, lipstick and nylons. This got us shelter on a floating whorehouse off the banks of the Yangtze, where she eventually hooked us up with a pirate trawler full of U.S. deserters and other assorted scum, whose captain proved to be some slippery variety of old friend.

The trawler took us up and down-river, dodging the Japanese and preying on the weak, then trading the resultant loot to anyone else we came in contact with. We sold opium and penicillin to the warlords, maps and passports to the D.P.s, motor oil and dynamite to the Kuomintang, Allied and Japanese spies to each other. But our most profitable commodity, as ever, remained people — mainly because those we dealt with were always so endlessly eager to help set their own price.

I look at myself in the bathroom mirror now, tall and silver-haired — features still cleanly cut, yet somehow fragile, like Sir Laurence Olivier after the medical bills set in. At this morning's signing, a pale young woman with a bolt through her septum told me: "No offense, Mr. Darbersmere, but you're — like — a real babe. For an old guy."

I smiled, gently. And told her: "You should have seen me when I was twelve, my dear."

That was back in 1943, the year that Ellis sold me for the first time — or rented me out, rather, to the mayor of some tiny port village, who threatened to keep us docked until the next Japanese inspection. Ellis had done her best to convince him that we were just another boatload of Brits fleeing internment, even shucking her habitual male drag to reveal a surprisingly lush female figure and donning one of my mother's old dresses instead, much as it obviously disgusted her to do so. But all to no avail.

"You know I'd do it, Tim," she told me, impatiently pacing the trawler's deck, as a passing group of her crewmates whistled appreciatively from shore. "Christ knows I've tried. But the fact is, he doesn't want me. He wants you."

I frowned. "Wants me?"

"To go with him, Tim. You know — grown-up stuff."

"Like you and Ho Tseng, last week, after the dance at Sister Chin's?"

"Yeah, sorta like that."

She plumped herself down on a tarpaulined crate full of dynamite — clearly labeled, in Cantonese, as "dried fruit" — and kicked off one of her borrowed high-heeled shoes, rubbing her foot morosely. Her cinnamon hair hung loose in the stinking wind, back-lit to a fine fever.

I felt her appraising stare play up and down me like a fine gray mist, and shivered.

"If I do this, will you owe me, Ellis?"

"You bet I will, kid."

"Always take me with you?"

There had been some brief talk of replacing me with Brian Thompson-Greenaway, another refugee, after I had mishandled a particularly choice assignment — protecting Ellis's private stash of American currency from fellow scavengers while she recuperated from a beating inflicted by an irate Japanese officer, into whom she'd accidentally bumped while ashore. Though she wisely put up no resistance — one of Ellis's more admirable skills involved her always knowing when it was in her best interest *not* to defend herself — the damage left her pissing blood for a week, and she had not been happy to discover her money gone once she was recovered enough to look for it.

She lit a new cigarette, shading her eyes against the flame of her Ronson.

"'Course," she said, sucking in smoke.

"Never leave me?"

"Sure, kid. Why not?"

I learned to love duplicity from Ellis, to distrust everyone except those who have no loyalty and play no favorites. Lie to me, however badly, and you are virtually guaranteed my fullest attention.

I don't remember if I really believed her promises, even then. But I did what she asked anyway, without qualm or regret. She must have understood that I would do anything for her, no matter how morally suspect, if she only asked me politely enough.

In this one way, at least, I was still definitively British.

Afterward, I was ill for a long time — some sort of psychosomatic reaction to the visceral shock of my deflowering, I suppose. I lay in a bath of sweat on Ellis's hammock, under the trawler's one intact mosquito net. Sometimes I felt her sponge me with a rag dipped in rice wine, while singing to me — softly, along with the radio:

*A faded postcard from exotic places...a cigarette that's marked with lipstick traces...oh, how the ghost of you clings...*

And did I merely dream that once, at the very height of my sickness, she held me on her hip and hugged me close? That she actually slipped her jacket open and offered me her breast, so paradoxically soft and firm, its nipple almost as pale as the rest of her night-dweller's flesh?

That sweet swoon of ecstasy. That first hot stab of infantile desire.

That unwitting link between recent childish violation and a desperate longing for adult consummation. I was far too young to know what I was doing, but she did. She had to. And since it served her purposes, she simply chose not to care.

Such complete amorality: It fascinates me. Looking back, I see it always has — like everything else about her, fetishized over the years into an inescapable pattern of hopeless attraction and inevitable abandonment.

My first wife's family fled the former Yugoslavia shortly before the end of the war; she had high cheekbones and pale eyes, set at a Baltic slant. My second wife had a wealth of long, slightly coarse hair, the color of unground cloves. My third wife told stories — ineptly, compulsively. All of them were, on average, at least five years my elder.

And sooner or later, all of them left me.

Oh, Ellis, I sometimes wonder whether anyone else alive remembers you as I do — or remembers you at all, given your well-cultivated talent for blending in, for getting by, for rendering yourself unremarkable. And I really don't know what I'll do if this woman Huang has found for me turns out not to be you. There's not much time left in which to start over, after all.

For either of us.

Last night, I called the number Huang's father gave me before I left London. The man on the other end of the line identified himself as the master chef of the Precious Dragon Shrine restaurant.

"Oh yes, *tai pan* Darbersmere," he said, when I mentioned my name. "I was indeed informed, by that respected personage who we both know, that you might honor my unworthiest of businesses with the request for some small service."

"One such as only your estimable self could provide."

"The *tai pan* flatters, as is his right. Which is the dish he wishes to order?"

"The Emperor's Old Bones."

A pause ensued — fairly long, as such things go. I could hear a Cantopop ballad filtering in, perhaps from somewhere in the kitchen, duelling for precedence with the more classical strains of a wailing *erhu*. The Precious Dragon

Shrine's master chef drew a single long, low breath.

"*Tai Pan,*" he said, finally, "for such a meal...one must provide the meat oneself."

"Believe me, Grandfather, I am well aware of such considerations. You may be assured that the meat will be available, whenever you are ready to begin its cooking."

Another breath — shorter, this time. Calmer.

"Realizing that it has probably been a long time since anyone has requested this dish," I continued, "I am, of course, more than willing to raise the price our mutual friend has already set."

"Oh, no, *tai pan.*"

"For your trouble."

"*Tai pan,* please. It is not necessary to insult me."

"I must assure you, Grandfather, that no such insult was intended."

A burst of scolding rose from the kitchen, silencing the ballad in mid-ecstatic lament. The master chef paused again. Then said:

"I will need at least three days' notice to prepare my staff."

I smiled. Replying, with a confidence which — I hoped — at least sounded genuine:

"Three days should be more than sufficient."

The very old woman (89, at least) who may or may not have once called herself Ellis Iseland now lives quietly in a genteelly shabby area of St. Louis, officially registered under the far less interesting name of Mrs. Munro. Huang's pictures show a figure held carefully erect, yet helplessly shrunken in on itself — its once-straight spine softened by the onslaught of osteoporosis. Her face has gone loose around the jawline, skin powdery, hair a short, stiff gray crown of marcelled waves.

She dresses drably. Shapeless feminine weeds, widow-black. Her arthritic feet are wedged into Chinese slippers — a small touch of nostalgic irony? Both her snubbed cat's nose and the half-sneering set of her wrinkled mouth seem familiar, but her slanted eyes — the most important giveaway, their original non-color — are kept hidden beneath a thick-lensed pair of bifocal sunglasses, essential protection for someone whose sight may

# THE EMPOROR'S OLD BONES

not last the rest of the year.

And though her medical files indicate that she is in the preliminary stages of lung and throat cancer, her trip a day to the local corner store always includes the purchase of at least one pack of cigarettes, the brand apparently unimportant, as long as it contains a sufficient portion of nicotine. She lights one right outside the front door, and has almost finished it by the time she rounds the corner of her block.

Her neighbors seen to think well of her. Their children wave as she goes by, cane in one hand, cigarette in the other. She nods acknowledgment, but does not wave back.

This familiar arrogance, seeping up unchecked through her last, most perfect disguise: the mask of age, which bestows a kind of retroactive innocence on even its most experienced victims. I have recently begun to take advantage of its charms myself, whenever it suits my fancy to do so.

I look at these pictures, again and again. I study her face, searching in vain for even the ruin of that cool, smooth, inventively untrustworthy operator who once held both my fortune and my heart in the palm of her mannishly large hand.

It was Ellis who first told me about The Emperor's Old Bones — and she is still the only person in the world with whom I would ever care to share that terrible meal, no matter what doing so might cost me.

If, indeed, I ever end up eating it at all.

"Yeah, I saw it done down in Hong Kong," Ellis told us, gesturing with her chopsticks. We sat behind a lacquered screen at the back of Sister Chin's, two nights before our scheduled rendezvous with the warlord Wao Ruyen, from whom Ellis had already accepted some mysteriously unspecified commission. I watched her eat — waiting my turn, as ever — while Brian Thompson-Greenaway (also present, much to my annoyance) sat in the corner and watched us both, openly ravenous.

"They take a carp, right — you know, those big fish some rich Chinks keep in fancy pools, out in the garden? Supposed to live hundreds of years, if you believe all that 'Confucius says' hooey. So they take this carp and they fillet it, all over, so the flesh is hanging off it in strips. But they do it so well, so carefully, they keep the carp alive through the whole thing. It's sittin' there on a plate, twitching, eyes rollin' around. Get close enough, you can look right in through the ribcage and see the heart still beating."

She popped another piece of Mu Shu pork in her mouth, and smiled down at Brian, who gulped — apparently suddenly too queasy to either resent or envy her proximity to the food.

"Then they bring out this big pot full of boiling oil," she continued, "and they run hooks through the fish's gills and tail. so they can pick it up at both ends. And while it's floppin' around, tryin' to get free, they dip all those hangin' pieces of flesh in the oil — one side first, then the other, all nice and neat. Fish is probably in so much pain already it doesn't even notice. So it's still alive when they put it back down...alive, and cooked, and ready to eat."

"And then — they eat it."

"Sure do, Tim."

"*Alive*, I mean."

Brian now looked distinctly green. Ellis shot him another glance, openly amused by his lack of stamina, then turned back to me.

"Well yeah, that's kinda the whole point of the exercise. You keep the carp alive until you've eaten it, and all that long life just sorta transfers over to you."

"Like magic," I said. She nodded.

"Exactly. 'Cause that's exactly what it is."

I considered her statement for a moment.

"My father," I commented, at last, "always told us that magic was a load of bunk."

Ellis snorted. "And why does this not surprise me?" She asked, of nobody in particular. Then: "Fine, I'll bite. What do you think?"

"I think..." I said, slowly, "...that if it works...then who cares?"

She looked at me. Snorted again. And then — she actually laughed, an infectious, unmalicious laugh that seemed to belong to someone far younger, far less complicated. It made me gape to hear it. Using her chopsticks, she plucked the last piece of pork deftly from her plate, and popped it into my open mouth.

"Tim," she said, "for a spoiled Limey brat, sometimes you're okay."

I swallowed the pork, without really tasting it. Before I could stop myself, I had already blurted out:

"I wish we were the same age, Ellis."

This time she stared. I felt a sudden blush turn my whole face crimson. Now it was Brian's turn to gape, amazed by my idiotic effrontery.

"Yeah, well, not me," she said. "I like it just fine with you bein' the kid, and me not."

"Why?"

She looked at me again. I blushed even more deeply, heat prickling at my hairline. Amazingly, however, no explosion followed. Ellis simply took another sip of her tea, and replied:

"'Cause the fact is, Tim, if you were my age — good-lookin' like you are, smart like you're gonna be — I could probably do some pretty stupid things over you."

Magic. Some might say it's become my stock in trade — as a writer, at least. Though the humble craft of buying and selling also involves a kind of legerdemain, as Ellis knew so well; sleight of hand, or price, depending on your product...and your clientele.

But true magic? Here, now, at the end of the twentieth century, in this brave new world of 100-slot CD players and incessant afternoon talk shows?

I have seen so many things in my long life, most of which I would have thought impossible, had they not taken place right in front of me. From the bank of the Yangtze river, I saw the bright white smoke of an atomic bomb go up over Nagasaki, like a tear in the fabric of the horizon. In Chungking harbor, I saw two grown men stab each other to death over the corpse of a dog because one wanted to bury it, while the other wanted to eat it. And just beyond the Shanghai city limits, I saw Ellis cut that farmer's throat with one quick twist of her wrist, so close to me that the spurt of his severed jugular misted my cheek with red.

But as I grow ever closer to my own personal twilight, the thing I remember most vividly is watching — through the window of a Franco-Vietnamese arms-dealer's car, on my way to a cool white house in Saigon, where I would wait out the final days of the war in relative comfort and safety — as a pair of barefoot coolies pulled the denuded skeleton of Brian Thompson-Greenaway from a culvert full of malaria-laden water. I knew it was him, because even after Wao Ruyen's court had consumed the rest of his pathetic little body, they had left his face nearly untouched—there not being quite enough flesh on a child's skull, apparently, to be worth the extra effort of filleting...let alone of cooking.

And I remember, with almost comparable vividness, when—just a year ago—I saw the former warlord Wao, Huang's most respected father, sitting in a Limehouse nightclub with his Number One and Number Two wife at either elbow. Looking half the age he did when I first met him, in that endless last July of 1945, before black science altered our world forever. Before Ellis sold him Brian instead of me, and then fled for the Manchurian border, leaving me to fend for myself in the wake of her departure.

After all this, should the idea of true magic seem so very difficult to swallow? I think not.

No stranger than the empty shell of Hiroshima, cupped around Ground Zero, its citizenry reduced to shadows in the wake of the blast's last terrible glare. And certainly no stranger than the fact that I should think a woman so palpably incapable of loving anyone might nevertheless be capable of loving me, simply because—at the last moment—she suddenly decided not to let a rich criminal regain his youth and prolong his days by eating me alive, in accordance with the ancient and terrible ritual of the Emperor's Old Bones.

This morning, I told my publicist that I was far too ill to sign any books today—a particularly swift and virulent touch of the twenty-four-hour flu, no doubt. She said she understood completely. An hour later, I sat in Huang's car across the street from the corner store, watching "Mrs. Munro" make her slow way down the street to pick up her daily dose of slow, coughing death.

On her way back, I rolled down the car window and yelled: "*Lai gen wo ma, wai guai*!"

(*Come with me, white ghost!* An insulting little Mandarin phrase, occasionally used by passing Kuomintang jeep drivers to alert certain long-nosed Barbarian smugglers to the possibility that their dealings might soon be interrupted by an approaching group of Japanese soldiers.)

Huang glanced up from his copy of *Rolling Stone*'s Hot List, impressed. "Pretty good accent," he commented.

But my eyes were on "Mrs. Munro", who had also heard—and stopped in mid-step, swinging her half-blind gray head toward the sound, more as though scenting than scanning. I saw my own face leering back at me in miniature from the lenses of her prescription sunglasses, doubled and distorted by the distance between us. I saw her raise one palm to shade her eyes even further against the sun, the wrinkles across her nose contracting as she squinted her hidden eyes.

And then I saw her slip her glasses off to reveal those eyes: still slant, still gray. Still empty.

I turned to Huang.

"It's her," I told him.

Huang nodded. "Fought so. When you want me to do it?"

"Tonight?"

"Whatever you say, Mr D."

Very early on the morning before Ellis left me behind, I woke to find her sitting next to me in the red half-darkness of the ship's hold.

"Kid," she said, "I got a little job lined up for you today."

I felt myself go cold. "What kind of job, Ellis?" I asked, faintly — though I already had a fairly good idea. Quietly, she replied:

"The grown-up kind."

"Who?"

"French guy, up from Saigon, with enough jade and rifles to buy us over the border. He's rich, educated; not bad company, either. For a fruit."

"That's reassuring," I muttered, and turned on my side, studying the wall. Behind me, I heard her lighter click open, then catch and spark — felt the faint lick of her breath as she exhaled, transmuting nicotine into smoke and ash. The steady pressure of her attention itched like an insect crawling on my skin: Fiercely concentrated, alien almost to the point of vague disgust, infinitely patient.

"War's on its last legs," she told me. "That's what I keep hearing. You got the Communists comin' up on one side, with maybe the Russians slipping in behind 'em, and the good old U.S. of A. everywhere else. Phillippines are already down for the count, now Tokyo's in bombing range. Pretty soon, our little oufit is gonna be so long gone, we won't even remember what it looked like. My educated opinion? It's sink or swim, and we need all the life-jackets that money can buy." She paused. "You listening to me? Kid?"

I shut my eyes again, marshaling my heart-rate.

"Kid?" Ellis repeated.

Still without answering — or opening my eyes — I pulled the mosquito net aside, and let gravity roll me free of the hammock's sweaty clasp. I was fourteen years old now, white-blonde and deeply tanned from the river-reflected sun; almost her height, even in my permanently bare feet. Looking up, I found I could finally meet her gray gaze head-on.

"'Us'," I said. "'We'. As in you and I?"

"Yeah, sure. You and me."

I nodded at Brian, who lay nearby, deep asleep and snoring. "And what about him?"

Ellis shrugged.

"I don't know, Tim," she said. "What *about* him?"

I looked back down at Brian, who hadn't shifted position, not even when my shadow fell over his face. Idly, I inquired:

"You'll still be there when I get back, won't you, Ellis?"

Outside, through the porthole, I could see that the rising sun had just cracked the horizon; she turned, haloed against it. Blew some more smoke. Asking:

"Why the hell wouldn't I be?"

"I don't know. But you wouldn't use my being away on this job as a good excuse to leave me behind, though — would you?"

She looked at me. Exhaled again. And said, evenly:

"You know, Tim, I'm gettin' pretty goddamn sick of you asking me that question. So gimme one good reason not to, or let it lie."

Lightly, quickly — too quickly even for my own well-honed sense of self-preservation to prevent me — I laid my hands on either side of her face and pulled her to me, hard. Our breath met, mingled, in sudden intimacy; hers tasted of equal parts tobacco and surprise. My daring had brought me just close enough to smell her own personal scent, under the shell of everyday decay we all stank of: a cool, intoxicating rush of non-fragrance, firm and acrid as an unearthed tuber. It burned my nose.

"We should always stay together," I said, "because I *love* you, Ellis."

I crushed my mouth down on hers, forcing it open. I stuck my tongue inside her mouth as far as it would go and ran it around, just like the mayor of that first tiny port village had once done with me. I fastened my teeth deep into the inner flesh of her lower lip, and bit down until I felt her knees give way with the shock of it. Felt myself rear up, hard and jerking, against her soft underbelly. Felt *her* feel it.

It was the first and only time I ever saw her eyes widen in anything but anger.

With barely a moment's pause, she punched me right in the face, so hard I felt my jaw crack. I fell at her feet, coughing blood.

"Eh—!" I began, amazed. But her eyes froze me in mid-syllable—so gray, so cold.

"Get it straight, *tai pan*," she said, "'cause I'm only gonna say it once. I don't buy. I *sell*."

Then she kicked me in the stomach with one steel-toed army boot, and leant over me as I lay there, gasping and hugging myself tight—my chest contracting, eyes dimming. Her eyes pouring over me like liquid ice. Like sleet. Swelling her voice like some great Arctic river, as she spoke the last words I ever heard her say:

"So don't you even *try* to play me like a trick, and think I'll let you get away with it."

Was Ellis evil? Am I? I've never thought so, though earlier this week I did give one of those legendary American Welfare mothers $25,000 in cash to sell me her least-loved child. He's in the next room right now, playing Nintendo. Huang is watching him. I think he likes Huang. He probably likes me, for that matter, We are the first English people he has ever met, and our accents fascinate him. Last night, we ordered in pizza; he ate until he was sick, then ate more, and fell asleep in front of an HBO basketball game. If I let him stay with me another week, he might become sated enough to convince himself he loves me.

The master chef at the Precious Dragon Shrine tells me that the Emperor's Old Bones bestows upon its consumer as much life-force as its consumee would have eventually gone through, had he or she been permitted to live out the rest of their days unchecked—and since the child I bought claims to be roughly ten years old (a highly significant age, in retrospect), this translates to perhaps an additional sixty years of life for every person who participates, whether the dish is eaten alone or shared. Which only makes sense, really. It's an act of magic, after all.

And this is good news for me, since the relative experiential gap between a man in his upper twenties and a woman in her upper thirties — especially compared to that between a boy of fourteen and a woman of twenty-eight — is almost insignificant.

Looking back, I don't know if I've ever loved anyone but Ellis — if I'm even capable of loving anyone else. But finally, after all these wasted years, I do know what I want. And who.

And how to get them both.

It's a terrible thing I'm doing, and an even worse thing I'm going to do. But when it's done, I'll have what I want, and everything else — all doubts, all fears, all piddling, queasy little notions of goodness, and decency, and basic human kinship — all that useless lot can just go hang, and twist and rot in the wind while they're at it. I've lived much too long with my own unsatisfied desire to simply hold my aching parts — whatever best applies, be it stomach or otherwise — and congratulate myself on my forbearance anymore. I'm not mad, or sick, or even yearning after a long-lost love that I can never regain, and never really had in the first place. I'm just hungry, and I want to *eat*.

And morality...has nothing to do with it.

Because if there's one single thing you taught me, Ellis — one lesson I've retained throughout every twist and turn of this snaky thing I call my life — it's that hunger has no moral structure.

Huang came back late this morning, limping and cursing, after a brief detour to the office of an understanding doctor who his father keeps on international retainer. I am obscurely pleased to discover that Ellis can still defend herself; even after Huang's first roundhouse put her on the pavement, she still somehow managed to slip her razor open without him noticing, then slide it shallowly across the back of his Achilles tendon. More painful than debilitating, but rather well done nevertheless, for a woman who can no longer wear shoes which require her to tie her own laces.

I am almost as pleased, however, to hear that nothing Ellis may have done actually succeeded in preventing Huang from completing his mission — and beating her, with methodical skill, to within an inch of her corrupt and dreadful old life.

I have already told my publicist that witnessed the whole awful scene, and asked her to find out which hospital poor Mrs. Munro has been taken to. I myself, meanwhile, will drive the boy to the kitchen of the Precious Dragon Shrine restaurant, where I am sure the master chef and his staff will do their best to keep him entertained until later tonight. Huang has lent him his pocket Gameboy, which should help.

Ah. That must be the phone now, ringing.

The woman in bed 37 of the Morleigh Memorial Hospital's charity wing, one of the few left operating in St. Louis — in America, possibly — opens her swollen left eye a crack, just far enough to reveal a slit of red-tinged white and a wandering, dilated pupil, barely rimmed in gray.

"Hello, Ellis," I say.

I sit by her bedside, as I have done for the last six hours. The screens enshrouding us from the rest of the ward, with its rustlings and moans, reduce all movement outside this tiny area to a play of flickering shadows — much like the visions one might glimpse in passing through a double haze of fever and mosquito net, after suffering a violent shock to one's fragile sense of physical and moral integrity.

*...and oh, how the ghost of you clings...*

She clears her throat, wetly. Tells me, without even a flicker of hesitation:

"Nuh...Ellis. Muh num iss...Munro."

She peers up at me, straining to lift her bruise-stung lids. I wait, patiently.

"Tuh—"

"That's a good start."

I see her bare broken teeth at my patronizing tone, perhaps reflexively. Pause. And then, after a long moment:

"Tim."

"Good show, Ellis. Got it in one."

Movement at the bottom of the bed: Huang, stepping through the gap between the screens. Ellis sees him, and stiffens. I nod in his direction, without turning.

"I believe you and Mr. Huang have already met," I say. "Mr. Wao Huang, that is; you'll remember his father, the former warlord Wao Ruyen. He certainly remembers you — and with some gratitude, or so he told me."

Huang takes his customary place at my elbow. Ellis' eyes move with him, helplessly — and I recall how my own eyes used to follow her about in a similarly fascinated manner, breathless and attentive on her briefest word, her smallest motion.

"I see you can still take quite a beating, Ellis," I observe, lightly. "Unfortunately for you, however, it's not going to be quite so easy to recover from this particular melee as it once was, is it? Old age, and all that." To Huang: "Have the doctors reached any conclusion yet, as regards Mrs. Munro's long-term prognosis?"

"Wouldn't say as 'ow there was one, *tai pan*."

"Well, yes. Quite."

I glance back, only to find that Ellis' eyes have turned to me at last. And I can read them so clearly, now — like clean, black text through gray rice-paper, lit from behind by a cold and colorless flame. No distance. No mystery at all.

When her mouth opens again, I know exactly what word she's struggling to shape.

"Duh...deal?"

Oh, yes.

I rise, slowly, as Huang pulls the chair back for me. Some statements, I find, need room in which to be delivered properly — or perhaps I'm simply being facetious. My writer's over-developed sense of the dramatic, working double-time.

I wrote this speech out last night, and rehearsed it several times in front of the bathroom mirror. I wonder if it sounds rehearsed. Does calculated artifice fall into the same general category as outright deception? If so, Ellis ought to be able to hear it in my voice. But I don't suppose she's really apt to be listening for such fine distinctions, given the stress of this mutually culminative moment.

"I won't say you've nothing I want, Ellis, even now. But what I really want—what I've always wanted—is to be the seller, for once, and not the sold. To be the only one who has what you want desperately, and to set my price wherever I think it fair."

Adding, with the arch of a significant brow: " — or know it to be unfair."

I study her battered face. The bruises form a new mask, impenetrable as any of the others she's worn. The irony is palpable: Just as Ellis' nature abhors emotional accessibility, so nature—seemingly—reshapes itself at will to keep her motivations securely hidden.

"I've arranged for a meal," I tell her. "The menu consists of a single dish, one with which I believe we're both equally familiar. The name of that dish is the Emperor's Old Bones, and my staff will begin to cook it whenever I give the word. Now, you and I may share this meal, or we may not. We may regain our youth, and double our lives, and be together for at least as long as we've been apart—or we may not. But I promise you this, Ellis: No matter what I eventually end up doing, the extent of your participation in the matter will be exactly defined by how much you are willing to pay me for the privilege."

I gesture to Huang, who slips a pack of cigarettes from his coat pocket. I tap one out. I light it, take a drag. Savor the sensation.

Ellis just watches.

"So here's the deal, then: If you promise to be very, very nice to me—and never, ever leave me again—for the rest of our extremely long

partnership-"

I pause. Blow out the smoke. Wait.

And conclude, finally:

"—then you can eat first."

I offer Ellis the cigarette, slowly. Slowly, she takes it from me, holding it delicately between two splinted fingers. She raises it to her torn and grimacing mouth. Inhales. Exhales those familiar twin plumes of smoke, expertly, through her crushed and broken nose. Is that a tear at the corner of her eye, or just an upwelling of rheum? Or neither?

"Juss like...ahways," she says.

And gives me an awful parody of my own smile. Which I—return.

With interest.

Later, as Huang helps Ellis out of bed and into the hospital's service elevator, I sit in the car, waiting. I take out my cellular phone. The master chef of the Precious Dragon Shrine restaurant answers on the first ring.

"How is...the boy?" I ask him.

"Fine, *tai pan.*"

There is a pause, during which I once more hear music filtering in from the other end of the line — the tinny little song of a video game in progress, intermittently punctuated by the clatter of kitchen implement. Laughter, both adult and child.

"Do you wish to cancel your order, *tai pan* Darbersmere?" The master chef asks me, delicately.

Through the hospital's back doors, I can see the service elevator's lights crawling steadily downward — the floors reeling themselves off, numeral by numeral. Fifth. Fourth. Third.

"*Tai pan?*"

Second. First.

"No. I do not."

The elevator doors are opening. I can see Huang guiding Ellis out, puppeting her deftly along with her own crutches. Those miraculously-trained hands of his, able to open or salve wounds with equal expertise.

"Then I may begin cooking," the master chef says. Not really meaning it as a question.

Huang holds the door open. Ellis steps through. I listen to the Gameboy's idiot song, and know that I have spent every minute of every day of my life preparing to make this decision, ever since that last morning on the Yangtze. That I have made it so many times already, in fact, that nothing I do or say now can ever stop it from being made. Any more than I can bring back the child Brian Thompson-Greenaway was, before he went up the hill to Wao Ruyen's fortress, hand in stupidly trusting hand with Ellis — or the child I was, before Ellis broke into my parents' house and saved me from one particular fate worse than death, only to show me how many, many others there were to choose from.

Or the child that Ellis must have been, once upon a very distant time, before whatever happened to make her as she now is — then set her loose to move at will through an unsuspecting world, preying on other lost children.

*...these foolish things...remind me of you.*

"Yes," I say. "You may."

# Crossing
## by Andrew Weiner

*Andrew Weiner has published over fifty short stories in magazines and anthologies in Canada, the United States, the United Kingdom, France, Italy, Poland, and the Czech Republic. His most recent collection,* **This is the Year Zero***, reprints "The Map," a story we were proud to publish in the first of the* **Northern Frights** *volumes. Like his previous story, "Crossing" is a clever blending of the mystery genre with that of dark fantasy.*

1

Wagman woke suddenly, as if from a bad dream, as the train jolted to a halt. His head flew back, his eyes jerked open. He looked out of the window of the carriage, but could see only a thick darkness. He leaned forward to press his face up against the cold glass, but still he could see nothing.

He felt a nameless dread.

"Border," said the fat man on the seat across from him. "We're at the border."

The fat man's head had been shaved down to a stubble. Although the lights in the compartment had been dimmed, he was wearing shades: their small, round, black lenses made his face appear owl-like.

"Might as well go back to sleep," he said. "Gonna be a while until they come around."

"Come around?"

"To check your papers."

The fat man talked to Wagman in a familiar way, as though he knew him. Perhaps he did, although Wagman had no idea how.

"My papers?" he echoed. "What about yours?"

"Mine? Oh, sure. Mine too."

"Where are you heading?" Wagman asked.

"Barcelona. How 'bout you?"

"I'm not sure," Wagman said, after a moment. "I'm really not sure."

It was hard, trying to think about where he was going and why. It made him feel a dull, leaden tiredness. His eyelids felt heavy as he stared back at the fat man, and he allowed them to close.

Later he thought he heard gunshots, some distance away. But he could not stir himself to wake up.

It must have been a dream in any case, only a dream, like the fat man, like the train compartment, a dream within a dream.

2

He woke up as the bus crept across the interstate border, a sign by the side of the road promising tourist information ahead. It was dark out, but Wagman could see that it had been raining. The road was slick, reflecting the neon of the all-night restaurant up ahead. A police car was parked outside the restaurant, lights flashing. A state trooper stood, hands on hips, watching the traffic.

Wagman wondered if the trooper was watching for him. It was possible that they had already circulated his description, that they were already watching the highways and the railway stations and the airports. But the trooper stood motionless as the bus passed by.

He leaned back in his seat.

"Wet out," said his seatmate. "Cars slipping all over the dammed place."

His seatmate was an older man, grey-haired, wearing checked pants, a green wool sweater, a blue down vest, a white painter's cap. In his lap he held a copy of *Satellite TV Guide*.

"Wet," Wagman agreed. "Sure is."

It had been pouring back in the city, he remembered now. He had parked a block away from Parker's building and got soaked through by the time he reached the entrance. His clothes were still damp even now.

Parker had been sitting on the couch in front of the TV, his hands folded in his lap, a neat hole in his forehead, a look of mild surprise on his face. He had been dead only a few minutes. The TV was tuned to one of the news channels.

"Soon be snow," Wagman's seatmate said. "You'll see."

"Yeah," Wagman said. "I will."

He saw snow in his mind, miles of snow, saw himself trudging through it towards a ever-receding horizon. And he felt cold, icy cold, chilled right through. His teeth chattered.

*Going to catch my death,* he thought. *In these wet clothes.*

3

There was a hotel around the corner from the bus station, an older building, somewhat rundown.

"Welcome to the crossroads," said the desk clerk.

"Crossroads?"

"Crossroads Inn and Apartment Hotel."

He registered as Rick Nevada, paying cash in advance.

"Do you have any baggage, Mr. Nevada?"

"No," he said. "I don't believe I do."

His room was small, with faded wallpaper and drab floral curtains. There was an ancient TV set with a rabbit's ears that picked up only two stations: one was playing the news and the other some kind of soap opera.

There was a clock on the wall. It was not as late as he had thought. Or else it was much later.

Although it was possible that the clock was wrong. Momentarily, it seemed to him to have stopped. But even as he stared at it, he saw the second hand lurch forward a notch, then another one. The clock was still working, after a fashion, but it was moving much too slowly.

Wagman tore his eyes away from the clock. He lay down fully-clothed on the frayed bedspread covering the hard, uncomfortable bed and closed his eyes. He felt exhausted, completely wrung-out, as though he could sleep for a thousand years. But he could not sleep. He saw Parker's face staring back at him, the bullet-hole in his forehead glowing green, like a third eye. And he felt himself falling. And he opened his eyes and sat up in bed.

In the drawer in the table beside the bed he found a Bible, a Book of Science and Health, a Book of Mormon, a Tibetan Book of the Dead.

He closed the drawer and went for a walk.

## 4

Wagman wandered the streets, walking aimlessly until he came to a rundownwn movie theatre a few streets away from his hotel. The movie had already started, but he went in anyway.

The theatre was almost empty. Wagman sat down about halfway towards the screen and tried to make sense of what was happening on the screen. But the movie made no sense to him at all. There was much violence, mostly erupting unmotivated, and maybe some religious symbolism, too. It was familiar to Wagman, somehow, and yet he was sure he had never seen it.

Afterwards, unaccountably, he managed to get lost on the way back to his hotel, arriving at the entrance to a park instead. He retraced his footsteps, only to find himself back at the park. He stood in confusion, looking around him.

"It's trickier than it looks."

It was a woman's voice, coming from across the street. She was wearing a raincoat with the collar turned up, and a scarf over her hair.

"Trickier?"

"Finding your way." She crossed the street towards him. "This town, it's small but complex."

"I'm looking for the hotel. The one next to the bus station."

"It's that way." She pointed. "I'll walk you there if you like."

"Thank you."

"Enjoy the movie?" she asked.

"Not much. How do you know I was at a movie?"

"I was there, too. A few rows behind you. What kind of movies *do* you like?"

"Oh, I don't know," he said. "Anything with Gregory Peck, James Stewart, Dick Powell, Robert Mitchum. Westerns, mysteries, gangster pictures, movies set in prison camps or submarines. How about you?"

She took the scarf off her head and shook out her thick dark hair. "Let's go get a drink, and I'll tell you."

With her hair down, she looked oddly familiar to him, but he couldn't figure out how.

Maybe she reminded him of Vicki. Except that Vicki had been blonde, and her hair had been shorter. And Vicki was dead.

Parker had hired him to find her, and he had done that. But he had been careless. And now she was dead.

"Sure," he said. "Why not?"

## 5

It was dark in the bar, and it seemed like everyone was smoking. Clouds of tobacco smoke hung in the air, thick enough to touch.

Wagman was smoking too. It seemed to him that he hadn't smoked in a long time, but when the woman had offered him a cigarette he had taken it without hesitation and sucked on it greedily, like a long-lost teat.

"I like movies with fog," the woman told him. "Lots of fog. And people lost in small boats. Airplanes that can't land, circling endlessly. People moving through crowded streets, against the flow, with an urgent goal in mind. People searching for what is lost, and what is not. People pacing in empty apartments, trapped in elevators, looking down from the mountain to the city below. People standing at a crossroads, figuring out which way to go. People arriving and departing, appearing and disappearing. Those are the movies I like."

Wagman coughed. "You don't care about the plot?"

"Plot is overrated. No one remembers plot."

It was hot in the bar. Sweat was trickling down Wagman's neck. He took a sip of his drink, but it tasted foul.

He tried to remember whether he had given up drinking.

He too another drag on his cigarette, then stubbed it out. It was hard enough to breathe as it was. He loosened his collar.

"Staying long?" the woman asked him.

"A day or two."

"Business?"

"That's right," he said. "I've got some business here."

"What kind of business?"

He sat back in his chair and looked at her appraisingly. Was she just making conversation? Or had someone sent her to spy on him?

"I'd like to tell you. But I can't right now."

She shrugged. "Whatever."

As she looked back at him, her features seemed to shift, to melt, to morph, as if lights were playing upon them. For a moment she was Vicki, dead in her bathtub, face bloated, eyes lifeless, and for another moment she was Vicki radiant with life. And then she was herself again.

"Who are you?" he asked.

"Anyone you want me to be."

The room was getting smaller, the walls closer. Wagman was finding it harder and harder to breathe. He wiped his brow with the sleeve of his jacket. He gasped for air.

"Your name. What's your name?"

"Would it make any difference?"

"Do I know you?" he asked. "Did I know you before?"

"Before what?"

"Before tonight."

"Why? Are you having trouble remembering things?"

The truth of it was, he was remembering things all too well.

Vomit rose up at the back of his throat. He struggled to his feet.

"I've got to get out of here," he said. "I've really got to go."

He turned and fled from the bar.

## 6

The phone call woke him from a confused dream in which was back in his own apartment, walking restlessly backwards and forwards between the kitchen and the living room, backwards and forwards, backwards and forwards.

He glanced at the clock radio. It was 6.00 am.

"Wagman," said the voice. "How the hell are you?"

The voice sounded distant, scratchy. But he recognized it immediately.

"Kelsey," he said.

"None other. I hope I'm not calling too early. I'm not much of a sleeper these days. I happened to be passing through, so I thought I would look you up."

"I just got here myself. How did you know I was here?"

"I'm surprised you would ask me that, Bobby. Knowing things, that's what I do best."

Kelsey had been one of Wagman's best informants, back when he had been on the police force. Even after he had quit to become a PI, he would still consult Kelsey on occasion. But he had not seen Kelsey in years.

"I thought you retired."

"You don't stop knowing things, Bobby. Although you may stop telling them."

"Actually," Wagman said, remembering, "I thought I heard that you were . . ."

"Dead?" Kelsey asked. "I heard that too. Isn't it strange, the way these stories go around? I've been hearing about you, Bobby. I hear you're in trouble. But maybe I can lend a hand."

"They're looking for me, aren't they?" Wagman asked. "The cops. They think I killed Parker. And the woman, too. If you found me, they can't be far behind."

"Meet me in the diner behind the hotel," Kelsey said. "In half an hour. Oh, one thing: Don't use the elevator."

"Why not?"

"Elevators can be a problem. I'll be seeing you."

He cut the connection.

ANDREW WEINER

## 7

It was still dark out, and the street was deserted. Wagman could see the diner as he turned the corner, light blazing from the big front window.

Inside, Kelsey was sitting at the counter. He was wearing a brown raincoat and a grey trilby hat. A counterman in a white shirt and apron was pouring him coffee. Apart from Kelsey and the counterman, the diner was empty.

"Still early, I guess," Wagman said to the counterman, as he took the stool next to Kelsey.

"Whatever you say," the counterman said. He was tall and gaunt, with Gary hair sticking out from under a white hat. "Coffee?"

"Sure."

The counterman poured him a coffee.

"Something to eat?"

Wagman considered. He could not remember when he had last eaten. But he did not feel hungry. "Maybe later."

The counterman moved away from them, and Wagman turned to Kelsey.

"Long time," he said, offering his hand to shake.

"Long," Kelsey agreed. His grip was cool but firm.

Kelsey did not seem to have aged. He looked the same as ever: the tobacco-stained teeth, the plump rosy cheeks, the tiny, glittering eyes.

"You've been dreaming," Kelsey said, without preamble. "Strange dreams."

"All dreams are strange."

"You know what a dream is, Bobby? It's a story we tell ourselves to try to make sense of what we're dreaming. Except that some things don't ever make sense."

"You're wrong about that," Wagman said. "Everything makes sense eventually."

"You're on the run," Kelsey said.

"I'm working on a case."

"You're on the run. What else would you be doing here, a hundred miles from nowhere?"

"Finding the killer. The cops think *I* killed them. I have to prove differently."

Kelsey nodded. "Of course," he said. "Of course you do."

"That's why I came here. I came because . . ." He frowned. Why *had* he come here? Then he remembered. "I'm looking for Parker's backers. His silent partners. This is where they hang out."

He nodded to himself, remembering how it had been.

He had gone out to meet Parker at the offices of his software company, in a new industrial mall on the outskirts of town. He remembered it all, now, Parker's limp handshake, the smell of expensive cologne, the view from the window of the shopping mall across the highway, and beyond that the miles of flat, dead, abandoned farmland waiting to be concreted-over.

"The woman, Vicki, used to work for Parker," he told Kelsey. "She was the financial controller. They became lovers. But they had a big fight and she ran away. Disappeared from sight. Parker hired me to find her. He told me he loved her, he couldn't live without her . . ."

"You weren't convinced?"

"To tell you the truth, no, not entirely. He was a cold fish, Parker. There was no passion in it, the way he talked about her, it was like he was playacting. But it didn't matter to me why he wanted her found. And I needed the work." He shook his head, sadly. "It was a set-up, Kelsey."

"A set-up?"

"He didn't care about the girl, only about what she took with her when she went away. Something he had been working on, something new and hot. He needed it back in the worst way. Because without it, his partners were going to kill him."

"What kind of partners would do that?"

"The only kind he could find. The company was in big trouble. Parker had pinned everything on this new product, but development was way behind schedule, the bank was about to call his loan. He had no other choices. Vicki told me all about it, how it went down."

"So you found her?"

"Oh, I found her. And she told me how it really was between her and Parker, how he promised to leave his wife for her, how he strung her along . . . how she took the program to spite him."

"Not to sell it?" Kelsey asked. "You don't think she was planning to sell it?"

"What if she was? They were partners, Kelsey. That's how she saw it, anyhow. That at least half of it was hers."

"You fell for her," Kelsey said.

"Hard," Wagman agreed. "I don't know how . . . One minute, I'm getting ready to take her back to Parker. The next I'm telling her how I'm going to help her get away from him. So yeah, I fell hard, Kelsey. Hard enough to give up everything for her. To run with her wherever she wanted to go."

"This is a hell of a story," Kelsey said. "I'm on the edge of my seat."

"So, like I told you, I found her. It wasn't easy, it took a lot of effort and a lot of skill, but I tracked her down. And I led them right to her. They must have been following me all along, Parker's friends. I just stepped out for a moment, to get us Chinese food, and when I came back she was dead. They took the program, and they killed her. We were together only a couple of days, but it was like a lifetime. And then they killed her."

"Tough break," Kelsey murmured.

"Then they went back to the city and killed Parker, because he knew about them killing the woman, and because they didn't need him anymore. Now I've got to find them." Unconsciously, he patted his jacket where his gun was hidden.

"You think you know where to look?"

Wagman fumbled in his pocket, produced a matchbook. "This was on Parker's coffee table. From some place called the Pink Parakeet."

"Out on Highway 80," Kelsey said. He held up the matchbook and stared at it for a moment. He shook his head. "Give it up, Bobby."

"I have to find the people who did this."

"It doesn't matter who did it. It never mattered." Kelsey pushed his coffee cup away from him, still full to the brim. "Can't you see that?"

"I thought you were going to help me."

"I am trying to help you, Bobby. But first you have to stop running."

Outside, the sun was coming up. Kelsey took off his hat and ran his hand through the stubble on his head. He took a pair of shades out of the pocket of his raincoat and put them on. He put his hat back on and stood up.

"I'll be seeing you," he said. The small, round lenses of his shades gave his face a beatific expression. "Sooner or later."

8

According to the clerk at the rental car office, it was a half hour's drive out to the Pink Parakeet. But it seemed to Wagman he had been driving much longer than that, past rolling fields and dense evergreen woods. It seemed like it had been hours. The clock on the dashboard said it had been only minutes, but the clock, like all the clocks in this town, was slow.

He had bought a package of cigarettes before he left town, unfiltered, high tar. He shook one out now, one-handed, then tried to light it with a match from Parker's matchbook, but the match was damp and would not light and so he used the lighter from the dashboard instead. He inhaled deeply, then started coughing. The cigarette tasted stale. He flipped it out of the window.

At last he saw the sign for the Pink Parakeet: "A Touch Of Paradise. Exit 12A, 3M ahead."

He took the exit road, then the long driveway that led up to the Pink Parakeet itself. It was housed in a colonial-style mansion, with ornate white pillars holding up the roof of the porch and carved stone lions guarding the doorway.

He pushed on the door, but it did not open. He rang the bell. A panel in the door slid back, and a pair of eyes appeared.

"Yes?" asked a woman's voice.

"You open?"

"Always."

"Then let me in."

The eyes stared out at him, unblinking, for a moment. "Oh yeah," she said. "I know you."

The panel closed, and the door swung open. Wagman stepped through into a large, dimly lit room. Armchairs and couches were scattered around the room. Perhaps a dozen women were sitting around on these armchairs and couches, talking amongst themselves, or drinking, or watching the news on the TV mounted over the bar. Some of the women were fully dressed, others were wearing only undergarments, a few were completely naked.

"Your choice," said the woman who had let him in, a tall black woman in an African dress with close-cropped grey hair.

But then a woman with thick dark hair got up from the couch and walked towards him. "He's here to see me," she said.

It was the woman he had met after the movie. She was wearing dark blue leggings, and a low-cut turquoise top.

"This way," she said. She took his hand and led him up the oak staircase. They climbed two flights, emerging into a corridor with doors leading to rooms on either side. She chose one apparently at random. Inside was a four-poster, and a bureau with a TV on it. Wagman crossed to the TV and flipped it on. A news show was playing.

The woman pulled off her top. Her breasts were large and pendulous and somehow familiar. She stood there, hands by her sides, in apparent expectation.

"I didn't know you were a hooker," he said. "Maybe I should have figured it out, but I've been so tired, you know, and there's been a lot on my mind... Anyway, you're very attractive, but that's not why I came here, and I'm really not in the mood, being so weary and rundown and all."

"Maybe you should see a doctor," she said. "Take some tests."

"Maybe I should."

He paced back and forth in the room, agitated. He picked up the TV remote and flipped through the channels. News, news, news, news, news.

"What's with all the news? Don't they show anything else?"

"Maybe you need to hear the news, Bobby."

"How did you know my name?"

"You told me."

"I don't think so."

She lifted up her heavy dark hair, and pulled it of her head. Underneath the wig, her hair was blonde and cut short.

"You told me before."

"Vicki," he said.

"Yes."

"I thought you were dead."

"I *am* dead," she said. "Now that you mention it. Someone drowned me in my bathtub."

He shook his head. "This is crazy. This is some kind of hallucination."

"Who was it, Bobby? Who drowned me?"

"It was Parker's partners. His mobster buddies. I came here to find them."

"You sure about that, Bobby? You sure it wasn't you?"

"Me? Why would I want to do that? I loved you, Vicki."

"But maybe I didn't love you. Maybe I told you to get lost. And maybe you didn't want to hear that. Maybe you got so angry you didn't know what you were doing..."

"They killed you to get Parker's program."

"What program, Bobby? I don't remember any program."

"Stop it," he said, backing away from her. "Stop fucking with my mind." He pulled out his gun from his pocket.

"Or what? You'll kill me again?"

He turned and fled the room. He ran down the stairs two at a time, almost falling headlong down the final flight.

"You look like you saw a ghost," said the tall black woman who had let him in.

"Maybe I did," he said.

"Then we have something in common."


9

Kelsey was sitting in the passenger seat of the rental car holding a sandwich, turning it over and over. He had not bitten into it, and now he offered it to Wagman.

"Tuna?" he said.

"I'm not hungry."

"You lose your appetite," Kelsey said. "You think you want to eat, but really you don't. It's just force of habit."

"What are you talking about, Kelsey?"

"I'm talking about you, Bobby. *Your* habits. Running around, investigating stuff. Making connections. Looking for patterns."

"That's what I do, Kelsey. That's who I am."

"It's what you used to do." Kelsey nodded back towards the big white-painted house. "So what did you find? Any clues?"

"I found Vicki," he said, his voice dropping to a whisper. "At least, I thought it was her."

"Except that's not possible."

"No," Wagman agreed, "no it isn't. Unless I was wrong, thinking she was dead. Or unless this woman was faking me out, pretending to be Vicki. Messing with my mind."

"Why would she do that?"

"Because it's a cover-up. They killed Vicki and then they killed Parker. Now they're trying to make me think I did it."

"But what if you did, Bobby? What then?"

"Get out," Wagman said. He reached into his jacket and took out the gun. "Get out of this car."

"Like I said, force of habit." Kelsey sighed heavily, then opened the door and got out. "I'll be seeing you," he said. He slammed the door shut.

## 10

Wagman drove. He drove until he was all the way out of the state, and then he kept on driving. The miles kept accumulating on the car's odometer, but the clock was still barely moving.

It began to get dark. His eyes were burning, he felt like he hadn't slept in a week, but he kept on driving. He punched the radio on, searching for a music station to help him stay awake, but all he could find were news broadcasts.

"... police reported no further leads in the death of private investigator Robert Wagman, found dead in his apartment three days ago by a client, well-known software developer Jason Parker. Parker had employed

Wagman to locate a missing employee, Vicki Benson. According to Parker, Wagman had asked him to meet him at the apartment, claiming to have solved the case..."

He flipped off the radio.

## 11

He stopped at the next service centre. The car needed gas, and he needed a cup of coffee. He sat the counter of a fast-food restaurant and lifted the Styrofoam cup to his lips. But he could not make himself drink it.

*You lose your appetite,* Kelsey had said.

He needed to think through what was happening to him. But he was just so tired, so very tired...

A tall man in a dark overcoat came out of the bathroom and walked through the restaurant's seating area, stopping at the news-stand near the exist. As he turned into profile, Wagman recognized him.

"Parker," he said, standing up.

But Parker was already out the door, taking long strides towards the parking lot.

Wagman followed. "Hey," he called, as he emerged from the restaurant. "Parker."

Parker stopped halfway down a row of parked cars and turned towards him.

"Wagman," he said. He stood there waiting, as Wagman closed the distance between them.

"Now," Wagman said, pulling out his gun and pointing it at Parker. "I want some answers right now."

Parker shook his head from side to side. "Stop it, Wagman. You have to try and stop this."

"I want to know who killed Vicki, and who killed you. And why you didn't stay dead."

"I never was dead, Wagman. Actually, it's just the opposite."

He turned and continued walking down the row of parked cars.

"Come back," Wagman called. "Come back here or I'll shoot."

Parker kept walking. Wagman's fingers closed on the trigger, but he could not make the gun fire. Parker turned a corner in the aisles of cars and kept on walking. Wagman tossed the gun aside and ran after him.

He caught sight of Parker at the edge of the lot, disappearing through the door of a featureless low-rise building. Wagman followed. The building was a shell, empty to the bare concrete-block walls. A narrow flight of stairs led down. After a moment's hesitation, Wagman began to descend.

The stairs ended at the entrance to a dimly lit, narrow, metal-roofed tunnel carved into a rock face. What is this, he wondered. Some kind of mine?

He stood and listened for a moment, but he could hear no footsteps ahead. Nonetheless, he began to jog down the tunnel. He had come too far to turn back now.

## 12

The tunnel came to an end, finally, opening out into a cavern with a domed roof. There was an elevator on the other side of the cavern, the doors standing open. There was no other exit he could see.

*Elevators can be a problem*, Kelsey had told him.

He got into the elevator and the doors closed behind him.

He looked around for a control panel, but there was none.

The elevator shuddered, and began to move. Not up, not down. Sideways.

"Enough," Wagman said, to himself. "No more."

## 13

In his dream, his last dream, he was standing on an escalator, going up. The sides of the escalator shaft were closing around him, tighter and tighter. Ahead of him, the passageway looked impossibly narrow.

And then he felt himself shooting through, head first.

## 14

The interior of the train was lit up by a soft reddish light. The far man sitting across from him took off his shades to polish them on a tissue. Wagman recognized his old acquaintance, Kelsey.

"How much longer?" Wagman asked.

"Not long now. You ready, Bobby?"

Wagman nodded. "Yeah," he said. "Now I'm ready."

The train jolted forward, across the border.

# Flushed

## by Dale L. Sproule

*Dale L. Sproule has over 30 published stories, including two in previous **Northern Frights** volumes. With his wife, Sally McBride, he founded **TransVersions**, a magazine of fantastic literature. He is also a professional artist who most recently illustrated **Poking the Gun**, a chapbook by poet John Grey.*

T he toilet bowl was less than six inches in circumference above the trap and it funneled even narrower into a four inch sewer pipe, and yet Lawrence had seen his wife getting sucked down. Had touched her.

How could he go to the police or even call a plumber about this? Hearing such a story second hand, he himself would not have believed it. But he had heard the shriek from the bathroom; and the flushing, screaming and gurgling as he tried to break down the heavy oak door with his shoulder before running for the crowbar.

The wood cracked like gunshots, door popping open just in time for Lawrence to see Christine's arm reach up out of the toilet, grabbing the rim with whitened fingers. He stood gaping in disbelief, spurred to action only when he spotted the wedding ring on her finger. The implications of what was happening sank in. At the very instant she lost her grip, he reached out, catching her by fingertips which wriggled and clawed at the palm of his hand, then finally, slippery with the residue of cheap toilet cleanser, oozed from his desperate grasp.

The blue water in the bowl burbled, then chugged repeatedly. An unbearable stench rose from its depths and the water turned purple before congealing to a thick, rusty brown. Something pink broke the surface. Lawrence fished it out with the pole end of the plunger, washing the slime off in the sink to find Christine's sock, the one with the hula-bears around the rim.

Spending the next ten minutes dragging and plunging the toilet to no avail, he pulled the lid from the toilet tank and heaved it into the bathtub, but could see nothing inside to help him figure out what had happened or what he could do to get his wife back.

Running to the roll top desk in the kitchen, Lawrence sat down at his computer and hammered on the keys, making several attempts before successfully logging onto *The Psychic Explorers Hotline*.

"Emergency! Anyone ever heard of disappearances involving toilets or waterclosets? Esp. supernatural. Need help in Pacific northwest, BC lower mainland area. E-mail or phone response. (604) 380-7150. Reward offered for any information. ASAP. Ask for Lawrence."

Then, he went down to the basement to see what he could see.

Half way between the floor and ceiling, the sewer pipe bulged out around the object it was digesting.

"Christine!"

Had the metal somehow softened? Lawrence tried to sink his fingers in, then tapped, and ultimately whacked at the swollen surface of the pipe with a crescent wrench, but it was as thick and strong as ever. He ran to his workbench, found an axe and contemplated it for a moment before spotting the hacksaw, which had no blade. His eyes lit on the blowtorch before he realized that any attempt to cut the pipe would heat it up, thus poaching his wife.

The phone rang and Lawrence ran to answer it. Glancing back at the pipe from the top of the stairs, he saw the bulge sinking into the floor. The concrete seemed to have become elastic around the base of the pipe, because it didn't break or buckle.

On the line was a man with a uncannily deep, yet squeaky voice. Like Mickey Mouse on steroids. "Mon nom est Monsieur Clarrisse. I am responding to your electronic admonishment."

"You know something about disappearances of this nature?"

"Mais, oui. I have encountered them before."

"No, I don't think you quite grasp ...I'm saying that...I mean..." He decided to just come out with it. "The toilet *ate* my wife."

"Hers was not the first such disappearance, Monsieur Lawrence. Was she, par chance, a cheerleader?"

Lawrence gasped so hard he choked. "How could you...possibly...?"

"I share not only your area code, but your prefix. It seems I am nearby. And eager to investigate this phenomenon. But my knowledge is not the sort which can be dispensed over the telephone."

Hesitantly, Lawrence divulged his address, wondering the whole time whether this was some sort of elaborate scam to get appointments for vacuum cleaner demonstrations.

The gaunt, goateed man with the hypnotic gaze who showed up at Lawrence's door was dressed like a plumber, but looked as absurd in his crisp, clean blue coverall as God in a tutu.

"I am M. Clarrisse," he said, holding up a box. "Et voila, this is my snake, Maximillian."

He named his plumbing snake? Lawrence wondered again if it had been a good idea, inviting this man into his home. But then, what choice did he have?

As Lawrence ushered the man to the washroom, Clarrisse explained how he knew so much, "You see Monsieur Lawrence, my own wife, Trixie was an earlier victim. She was employed by the franchise de la Dallas Cowboys, eh? The police were determined to charge me with murder, but no evidence could be found. After one year, they allowed me to depart. For four more years, I studied with mystics in Nepal and the Phillipines and learned to project my consciousness into the body of Maximillian."

"But during my absence, Trixie's brother, Ace had built an apartment block where my house had been, changing the whole sewer system in the process. The trail was lost. But perhaps now, we have discovered another route, n'est ce pas?"

As he lowered the snake into the thick, brown water of the toilet bowl, M. Clarrisse instructed Lawrence sibilantly, "I warn you, do not disturb me when I am one with Maximillian. Such interferance would be disastrous and tragic. Just listen and I will describe whatever I see or touch or smell."

The python's head creased the water's slimy surface, long, silver body arcing up as it dove and its disappearance left a dimple.

"Merde," muttered Clarrisse.

As Lawrence stood beside Clarrisse, watching Maximillian slide like a strand of spaghetti into porcelain lips, he reflected upon how lucky he had been to find M. Clarrisse so quickly.

Clarrisse, meanwhile, appeared to be in some sort of trance. His voice provided a droning commentary, "Maximillian has reached the sewer main without encountering any major obstacles. Wait. He's being channelled off, sucked down and down and now...he is emerging into a pool...a fountain, surrounded by cherubs and angels with gargoyle faces. A fountain of excrement. The walls are ornate, pebbled with tiny bones, trimmed with skulls, human and otherwise. Heavy trellises of big bones form gothic archways. Most of the bones on the floor of the chamber are human and recent, some still with strips of flesh and sinew attached.

"There's something dark and...massive. A monster so large that the air in the chamber gets thin when it inhales. And whistles out in a fetid hurricane.

"And, Tabernacle! There they are. Women. Dozens of beautiful young women, half naked, their hands blossoming with human entrails. One of them is Trixie. Ma belle, I have found you at last!"

"Does one of them have red hair?" Lawrence asked anxiously. "A gorgeous mane of bright red hair?"

But instead of answering his question, the snakeman said, "The monster looks at the women hungrily with each of its thousand eyes."

Lawrence grabbed Clarrisse's arm and shook it excitedly. "Is Christine there? Can you do anything to save her? You must save her!"

Clarrisse turned and stared at him with beady snake eyes. "You idiot! You have broken the connection! Because of you, Maximillian is now trapped in the same netherworld as my beloved Trixie!" The man turned purple with rage. Grabbing the soap-on-a-rope from the bathtub caddy, he whipped it at Lawrence's head, catching him across the temple.

Lawrence fell heavily, smacking his forehead against the rim of the toilet bowl. Groggily, he clung to consciousness, his ear pressed against the cold porcelain which conducted the sounds from the unspeakable depths. In the instant before Lawrence was beaten insensible with an economy sized shampoo bottle, he heard sounds that would be imprinted in his memory forever: the ululating chant of the cheerleaders, ripe with terror and despair — drowned out by the roar of the monstrous crowd that filled the subterranean chambers like aural sewage.

# Pitter Patter
## by Carol Weekes

*Carol Weekes made her first fiction sale in 1995 and has been published regularly since. She is editor-in-chief of the science fiction, fantasy and horror magazine **Northern Fusion**, to which she contributes a regular column, occasional interviews and book reviews. Carol lives in a 100 year old farmhouse in Ingleside, Ontario with her husband Rick, their two children, two cats, and a bat named Bernice.*

Tanya Elizabeth Patterson kept her collection of skeletons neatly arranged on the top level of her bookshelf. The bookshelf sat parallel to her bedroom door so that the soft light from the hallway lamp threw a band of gold into the room every evening when she lay in bed waiting to fall asleep. It tarnished the bones in copper streaks, highlighting ribcages, each notch and nugget of spine, tiny beaks and teeth.

Most of the animals had come from the woods which ran north to south behind the Patterson's house. She'd find their bodies during the autumn, frozen snarls poking out from damp leaves and fallen logs, as if this were a dying time for everything. They were always messy, sometimes having been dead since summer where worms, caterpillars, and the birds of the woods had picked off the most succulent strips of flesh... leaving only the papery decay of skin and waxy sinew behind.

She'd roll them about in both hands, animating limp limbs, watching pale bone grate against equally pale sockets and wonder what was death? These things had skittered with the wind in their fur, had guarded their routes tentatively for the fleeting shadow of a hawk's passing wings had felt the whisper of a beating heart, only a short while ago.

In their broken bodies lay the fragile shells of forgotten things, and this bothered her enough to bring them home and care for them.

"It's a disgusting habit," Tanya's mother told her. "You could pick up parasites or disease from those things." She'd turned to Tanya's father, her brow knit. "Jeff, tell her to get rid of them. Back me up on this."

But Tanya's father had only laughed. "Take it easy, hon. She's a curious kid, and she probably has a natural inkling towards science. Heck, back in my high school days we dissected enough frogs, guinea pigs, worms to jeopardize the continuation of those species." He grinned. "Okay, only kidding. Maybe several dozen over my four years there. It's no big deal. Just make sure you wash your hands after you handle them, punkin."

"Yes, Dad."

Her mother glared at her father.

"No big deal," he repeated. He threw Tanya a wink.

The skeletons stayed.

October 28th, and cold. Fresh flurries blew up against the side of the house, granule and driven, prying at the shingles and shutters and the warmth of inner light spilling from windows along the ground. Tanya had let their house cat, Mr. Toodles, outside during the afternoon. On a hobby farm in central Ontario, and surrounded by acres of alfalfa field and rambling trees, traffic was sparse and danger minimal to a domestic cat. He always came in at night. Well, almost always. Before Mr. Toodles had been neutered he'd once stayed out for the better part of a summer week pursuing a queen in heat. Maybe he'd gotten lucky, too. They didn't know, but his luck ran out a week later when Dad had taken Mr. Toodles to the vet's. Ever since then Toodles had returned to the house faithfully by dusk each evening.

Tonight he didn't heed her call.

"Toodles. Toooodddlllleesss!" She cupped both hands to her mouth, squinting against a sudden shriek of wind. Snow blew into the kitchen. She couldn't see beyond the edge of the wire fencing. In the distance the woods shimmered in ashy shadow against a growing storm. If there had been any trace of his footsteps earlier, they'd long since been filled in with gathering frozen precipitation.

By nine o'clock Toodles still hadn't returned.

"He has probably sought shelter under someone's porch until the storm blows over," Dad told her. "Don't worry, punkin. He'll come home when things die down a bit."

"What if he dies?"

"He won't die. He'll be fine. Brush your teeth and get to bed."

The night passed. She woke up to the sound of her older brother, Scott, brushing his teeth. Toodles wasn't on her bed, nor was there any trace of his fur to indicate that he'd been there.

She swung her legs out of bed, and in the movement caught sight of the skeletons lined up like soldiers along the shelf. Cavernous eye sockets watched impassively. They seemed to grin. She had a fleeting thought about what Mr. Toodles might look like beneath the luxury of his thick, tabby coat, except she couldn't accept this happening to him. She dressed and hurried downstairs to where Scott and her parents sat at the kitchen table. Scott was busily pushing bloated cornflakes around the rim of his bowl. He ignored her. Her mother mashed frozen orange jiuce into water with a wooden spoon.

"Did Mr. Toodles come home yet?" she asked them. The room went stiller than it had been. Scott stopped stirring. Her mother paused and turned to look over her shoulder at her. Even her father lowered his newspaper.

"I don't think so," said her mother. "Jeff?"

"I didn't let him in."

Scott shook his head. "Stupid cat," he said. "Who would want to stay out in that?"

"He isn't stupid!" Tanya shot back.

"Take it easy," her father assured her. "He'll probably come nosing around for food soon. He'll be cold and hungry, but I'm sure he must be fine, punkin. Don't worry about him. By the time you get home from school today, why...I'll bet you find he's taken over your bed for you!"

"I hope so," she said. She ate her breakfast, then got up to find her jacket, hat, and mittens. None of them seemed to notice the sound of the front door opening. She stood on the porch looking over the mounds of blue-white snow twinkling like sequins. He was out there, somewhere, and she hadn't a clue where to begin to look. If he'd gone and died on her, where would he likely be? She walked to the side of the house, kicking powdery snow with the toes of her boots and came to a stop to regard the stark woods silhouetted against a sky as pale as the land. She had found all of her dead things in there. It would be a likely place to begin.

It was as she thought it would be: she'd returned from school, and no Toodles.

"He may be lost in this weather," her mother told her and Scott. "The snow has probably wiped away the scents of the house for him."

"Can we look for him? Please?"

Her mother drew a tense hand through her hair. "All right. We'll take a look around and see if we can find him, but in weather like this I don't know how much luck we'll have. Tanya..." her eyes strained, her mouth working with words difficult to say. "If something has happened to Mr. Toodles — I just want you to be prepared for the worst...in case he's frozen somewhere out there. I know it's a terrible thought, but it's not impossible."

"No!" She stood back, angry.

Her mother let out a weary sigh. "I don't want to lose him either, but this is unusual for him, Tanya. Okay. We'll go looking for him."

Scott frowned. "Can't I stay home?"

"Scott, an extra pair of eyes might help right about now."

He dressed reluctantly. Toodles had always been her cat, as far as he was concerned.

They began their search in the front yard. They got down on hands and knees to peer along a flashlight beam directed beneath the front porch. Damp leaves, a forgotten soccer ball, and a moldy mitten caught the light. No cat. They stood up and walked over to the shed where they parked the car. It's folding door was firmly closed and locked, the side door also shut. They went inside and called for the cat anyway. No luck again.

"I don't know," Tanya's mother began. "I could call a few of the neighbors to ask them to check their properties."

"Maybe we should look in the woods," Tanya said, thinking of tiny decayed snouts thrust up through dark soil and damp leaves; miniscule teeth looking like rows of tainted pearls. Would Toodles eyes be filled with snow, the sticky gaze undirected as ice worked its way between his open lips?

Not her cat, no...not something she'd loved so much. She hadn't known the others along her shelf.

They stared in the direction of the woods waiting less than a quarter of a mile away.

"I don't see why he'd want to go in there during a storm," their mother said. "I suppose it doesn't hurt to look along the first bits of trail."

The woods smelled musty with the sweet decay of wet leaves, frost-bitten mosses, rotting bark. Wet ground padded the whisper of their boots, the hush of movement so gentle, as if their very passage through this winter sanctuary remained sacrilege. For the first time even Scott refrained from complaining. They stood with heads canted slightly back, observing the weight of snow upon the branches, a slash of black trunk here, withered green blade there. A gentle slap of melting snow kissing the ground made them gasp.

"I don't see him anywhere," Scott finally broke the silence.

"Toodles!" Tanya shot out. More snow fell and from somewhere behind them a branch popped. They whirled to see a cloud of grackles fly shrieking against the sky, protesting their presence.

She bent and began to root between the hollows of tree trunks and the scrabble of fallen branches. Dusk set in, throwing long, ropey fingers of purple shadow along the ground.

"I think we'd better get back home before it gets too dark out here. Dad will wonder where we are."

"I have to find my cat!" Tanya protested.

"He isn't here!"

They stared at one another. Her mother's cheeks had gone a rusty red, partly with the cold and maybe with the fire of her welling emotions. Her eyes shone. A gust of wind picked up again, biting at their skin and tugging at their clothing.

Her mother and Scott turned back along the trail of muddled footprints, towards the direction of their house now a dark, hazy square in the dying light. Trees seemed to close in around them. Shadows hovered, quivering in the wind, criss-crossing, growing closer. To their right a large deadfall, spidery branches black against the snow.

Spidery branches which seemed to curl around a darker nugget of rock or fallen log, except...

...except for the cant of a tiny head, one ear flattened into whiteness, the other peaked towards the night sky.

Toodles.

As apathetic as the lifeless creatures she'd stumbled across so often in the past, as if this place was meant for this sort of thing, a haven of cradled mystery waiting to be discovered.

They lay his frozen body in the shed, in an open cardboard box half-filled with newspapers, the only warmth from their tears as they bent over him.

"Dad will take him to the vet." Her mother wiped at both cheeks, her breath a cloud of silver in the air.

"Why?" Scott asked. He hadn't cried. Instead, he'd been the one to lift Toodles' body from the ground, front paws first. Toodles had come away from the frost with a horrid, sucking sound of wet cardboard being ripped apart. "He can't do anything for him now."

"He'll dispose of the body for us," Mom answered. "The ground has frozen and we won't be able to bury him ourselves. We can't keep him in here until spring. God, what ever made him want to go into those woods? Why didn't he come home when the snow started?"

Tanya stared at the wet, stink of what remained of Mr. Toodles. Half a tail hung out of the box, no flicker of life in it any longer. Where was he and what was this clotted, leaf-ridden mess he'd left behind?

"Let's get inside." Mother hearded them both towards the house and shut the shed door behind her. She didn't look back at the dark window of the door leading into the shed. Only Tanya did.

"Where is he now?"

Dad reached out with the fingers of his right hand and tenderly touched her hair. "I don't know, angel. No one knows for certain what happens to us when we die."

"But I miss him. Can't I keep him with me?"

Her father was the one to start now. "If you're asking to keep him the way you have those animals in your room? No, princess, I'm sorry. He was a part of our family, not just something you found out in the woods. A pile of bones isn't a pet cat anymore, Tanya. Keep a part of him close to your heart. That's how he'll live forever. I know this is hard. I miss Toodles, too. We all have to get through this"

She reflected on his words.

"Go get ready for bed and try to get some sleep. Tomorrow I'll take him to Dr. Jordan's. It's all we can do, punkin." He kissed her forehead and looked down into her eyes. "Maybe you should think about getting rid of those skeletons¼..perhaps they aren't the best things to have around at a time like this."

"If I keep a part of him close to my heart, will he really be all right?"

Dad smiled. "I think he'd like that, punkin. He'll know you're thinking of him."

She lay with her hands behind her head, listening to Scott brush his teeth again. Mom had gone into the bedroom after supper and they'd listened silently as she'd cried over Toodles.

"Stupid cat," Scott had mumbled, but even his eyes had shone as he'd said it.

The snow had died down and a half moon threw a milky glaze over the room and the skeletons on the shelf. They seemed to regard her with their eyeless sockets and mirthless grins. Bury them or toss them out? They weren't what they'd been, were they? If she were to do that to Mr. Toodles she'd have to keep it a secret, and for what? A quick, papery pat of cold bone hidden in the back of a closet, just for old times sake?

Then it occured to her. *Keep a part of him alive in you...close to your heart.*

A part of him.

She hadn't done that with the others. She hadn't known them the way she'd known Toodles. She'd lovingly cleaned them of their decomposition and had set the brittle hollows of tiny legs and vertibrae to rest, more a curious hobby than a longing passion.

But what part to keep? She sat up in bed, gripping the covers. Did it matter which part? If she didn't try this idea tonight, tomorrow would be too late. Dad would bring Toodles in to see Dr. Jordan, to dispose of Toodles' body. Why didn't Dad do this himself, if he missed Toodles as much as he said he did; as much as they all did?

A sterile click of a lamp set the house to darkness an hour later. Soon the sounds of steady breathing came along the hall. Tanya got up and dressed in a sweat suit, boots without socks, her winter jacket. She felt her way along the corridor to the stairs and along the stairs to the back door leading out of the kitchen.

In the moonlight the shed shone silver, the window of its side door a dark channel.

A moment later she stood over Toodles with the flashlight. His tail hadn't moved. It still hung halfway out of the damp cardboard box like a broken snake. A piece of dry grass clung to him.

What part indeed? What would be the easiest way to take a bit of Toodles close to her heart?

She stooped down on each knee and propped the flashlight against an empty oil drum. It smelled of gasoline, old newspapers, and the woods in here. Toodles smelled of the woods.

Tanya reached out carefully and trailed her finger tips across his head, running the course of his ear, feeling the viscid surface of one eye. Cold, all of him.

She suddenly plucked at a tuff of loose fur near his neck and raised her hand in the watery flood of light to examine it. Here was a part of her cat, a gentle reminder.

She opened her mouth and lay the wad of fur on her tongue. It tasted of dust, of soil. Her heart pounded and her mouth began to salivate. She gagged and forced herself to swallow the fur, forcing him down, closer to her heart...to the steady beating of her hope for him, as her father had explained things to her.

"I miss you," she told Toodles. "Please, come home for me. Please."

She leaned forward and kissed the matted head, hating the ball-bearing roll of his neck and the smell of dampness permeating him. She picked up the flashlight and stepped away from the box, from the broken snake tail with its blade of dead grass, and backed towards the shed door. This time she didn't shut it all the way. She propped a brick behind the frame to keep the door open a few inches, then she fled back to the house. Before she went upstairs to bed she did one other thing she'd become accustomed to through habit; Toodles had always enjoyed sitting in one of the windows above the living room hearth. She cranked the window open four inches, ignoring the frosty bite of wind pushing through the room.

She went upstairs to bed and lay beneath the covers, the wad of fur no longer traceable in her larynx. She believed it must be deeper in her now, closer to her heart. She lay her hand across her chest, feeling the minute pulse of the skin, and waited for him.

A pitter patter of something soft moving quickly over carpet brought her out of a half-sleep. It was still night and the hall beyond her open doorway sat bathed in shadow. A scuttling up the stairs came followed by a pause, and then twin globes of green caught the moonlight and ascended onto her bed. Toodles landed with his full weight, making the mattress shake.

She sat straight up, frightened and overjoyed at the same time. It had worked! She could have kissed her father for letting her know what to do.

"You're okay!" she whispered and leaned forward to touch Toodles. He smelled of the outside and the shed. He didn't back away from her hand, but his eyes locked with hers. He didn't purr like he used to.

She petted his head, rolling her fingers over the slant of his ears and coming away with more bits of grass. Her hand stunk of the woods and its mosses. He propped himself back on his haunches and began to groom himself, one leg thrust up into the air. His breath came in quick, sharp bursts. It didn't matter. He was alive, he'd come home again. She placed her hand over her heart, certain the wad of fur lay close by, linking them forever.

"What the hell?" Her father's mug slipped to the floor and exploded in a vortex of black coffee and glass shards. Tanya stood in the kitchen doorway holding Toodles in her arms. Toodles sprung away from her and rubbed against the refrigerator, waiting to be fed.

"I went out to see him," she explained. "I wanted to keep a part of him close to my heart. He woke up again." She couldn't understand the confusion.

Scott gripped the edge of the table, his face a rictus of horror. Her mother's hand had flown over her mouth.

"Well, if this doesn't take the cake," her father exclaimed, glancing around the room at them. He approached Toodles carefully, one hand extended out towards the cat. Toodles sniffed at his fingers, then backed away. "I've heard of the cold slowing a heart beat right down to minimal activity," he continued. "He seemed as good as dead when I saw him. Maybe the shed being warmer than the outdoors revived him again." He shook his head. "The doc is going to hear a good story this morning. I think Toodles will need a thorough check up, make sure he hasn't suffered too badly from frost bite. Geez, I would have never believed anything could come back out of that kind of a state!"

"Stupid cat," Scott said, but a smile broke over his lips. "It's good to see you again...even if you do stink."

Dr. Jordan said Toodles' heart sounded slow for a cat's but at least he was still alive. He'd suffered frostbite to his extremities but nothing severe enough to warrant amputation.

"This is one lucky cat. I'd say bathe him, keep an eye on his appetite, keep him warm. Perhaps his pulse will pick up as he gathers strength again." They brought him home wrapped in a blanket. They bathed him and blew his fur with a hair dryer. He still smelled faintly of moss, and something else which they couldn't quite put their finger on.

"It's as if he'd begun to decay," Dad said sheepishly, "but he hasn't. He looks fine." A strangely sweet odor clung to Toodles.

Tanya sat with him on her bed. She stroked his fur with one hand, and placed the open palm of her left hand on Toodles side to feel the gentle murmur of his pulse. She lay her right hand over her own heart. They both beat in unison, hers the proper rate for a seven year old girl's, his unusually slow for a cat's. It didn't matter. He was back, on her bed.

In their lives.

The phone call came several weeks later, during another storm. Dad answered the telephone and his face went grey.

"Take it easy," he spoke into the receiver. "Dad, I'll be right there. Don't go out, don't do anything else. Give me ten minutes." He hung up. "Grandma took a heart attack trying to clear snow away from the back of their car...she's dead. That was Dad who called. I have to get there right away."

Mom began to cry. "Oh my God, Jeff — you can't do this alone. When did it happen?"

"Just a few minutes ago. He tried to revive her and couldn't...I think an ambulance is on the way. I don't want the kids to see her this way."

Tanya stood in the kitchen doorway listening. "What's a heart attack, Daddy?"

They whirled and she saw that Dad's eyes were wet like Mom's had been last month, over Toodles.

"Tanya, geezus..." He explained what had happened and that she wouldn't be able to see Grandma again.

"I'll call you from the house after the ambulance arrives," he told them and left for what had once been his home.

They sat in Grandma's old living room that evening, watching the snow fall in big, quarter-sized flakes. Grandpa wept and Dad consoled him. People had come to the house; Dad's two brothers, Grandma's younger sister, an array of cousins and friends and neighbors. They'd brought their condolensces, prepared dishes, flowers, cards. So sorry, she'll be missed, always a part of your memories.

Grandma was gone. Tanya walked into her grandmother's old bedroom, the one where Grandpa had slept beside his wife for years and stood looking at the patchwork quilt, the polished rosewood furniture. A clock ticked gently by what had been her side of the bed. Potpouri in a clear crystal jar on a woman's bureau threw a scent of distant gardens into the room. She lay somewhere far from here, her mother had said. Grandma was sleeping they all told her. Sleeping in a building blocks away from her home.

She'd never seen her father cry before today, or her grandfather.

"Can't you keep her alive, close to your heart?" she'd asked them.

Dad had wiped his eyes. "I think we all have to try to do that, punkin."

But no one seemed to be doing anything except crying, talking, eating food, whispering.

"She's holding up remarkably well for a child," Grandpa finally commented to Tanya's father.

"Yes. I wish I had her strength," he whispered.

She walked through the house, wondering how to keep a part of Grandma close to her heart. The woman who had always held her to her bosom, who always smelled faintly of lilac, whose kisses were furry with fine white hair sprouting from the base of her chin, was gone before Tanya had ever been able to see her again.

She was too late, wasn't she? They'd arrived after the ambulance had taken Dad and Grandpa to the hospital.

Tanya walked back to her grandmother's bedroom and got up on her grandmother's bed. She lay quietly in the faint glow of the lamp, thinking of Mr. Toodles now. He still didn't purr when you petted him, and no number of baths could ever seem to remove that whisper of the woodland mosses caught in his fur. Still, he was with them, and everybody had seemed so pleased to have him back.

She re-adusted the pillow behind her head and that's when she noticed the silver lamé hair brush on Grandma's bureau. It matched a silver and ivory comb, and the two sat side by side between the perfume bottles, the potpouri, and an assortment of bath products.

Tanya got up and walked over to the brush, her heart beating faster.

Fine white hair...how long Grandma's hair had always been, clung to the bristles of the brush.

It would take only one hair, close to the heart.

She made herself swallow, washing the hair down with water from the bathroom. Then she went back to lay down in her grandmother's room.

How embracing her bosom, how furry the hair along her chin. She would smell faintly of lilac, Tanya supposed. She hoped that's all Grandma would smell like, but she supposed a scent of mosses or winter was something they could live with.

She waited in the dark for the pitter patter of an old woman's step upon the porch, wondering how Grandma's broken heart might pulsate to the beat of her own? How pleased Daddy and Grandpa would be to see her again.

She got up in the dark of her grandparents sleeping house and unlocked the front door.

Soon after, she was not disapointed.

# Cave of the Winds
## by Carolyn Clink

Mist, breath of ancient
tears, beaded on yellow
slickers over
rolled-up jeans, feet wet in felt
slippers, our hoods pulled down low

The red wood walkway
is rebuilt in spring, each post,
each step placed by heart
then torn up and stowed away
in fall to sleep under deep snow

Algae covered boulders
shimmer as we climb — a rainbow
caught, suspended
by the sound of potential
energy, hurricane

CAROLYN CLINK

Guides tell the story —
why the tour no longer goes
behind the falling
curtain high above, point
to where the cave used to be

Hanging back against
the rail, cameras flash
with memory — a tour
trapped in the cave when earth weakened
by water, time collapsed

Bridal Veil wept
as wind and cave were both blown
out. White water flows
compulsively down, trying
to wash the ghosts away

# Inspiriter
## by Nancy Kilpatrick

*One of Canada's premier horror writers, Nancy Kilpatrick has appeared with stories in each our previous* **Northern Frights** *voloumes. Her most recently published books are* Reborn, *the third novel in her vampire series* **Power of the Blood,** *and* **In The Shadow of the Gargoyle,** *an anthology co-edited with Thomas Roche. The tow are about to edit another project for Ace-Berkley,* **Grotesques: A Bestiary.**

*About her current story, Nancy writes: "Meeting the muse can be the best thing that ever happens to a creative person, or the worst. Concretized in artwork, in artwork, it's often the best. Seeing the muse in another person usually leads to trouble."*

Paul spotted her the Saturday after he arrived at the farm. Unrelenting sunshine had bleached her quaint straw hat titanium, as white as her waist-length hair. Under the cloud-studded cerulean sky, hair and hat glowed brilliant as white gold. Pale arms at her sides, she headed north at an easy pace through the corn fields toward what he'd learned was 'the Jacobs place'.

Paul opened the screen door and called out, "Hi there!" imitating the locals.

She should have heard him. A crow protecting raspberry bushes across the road screeched. The warning vibrated through the fresh air, startling him, but she didn't seem to notice.

He inhaled. Sweet hay. Sweet and sour manure. Rich earth. Basic scents untainted by the worship of product. He was sick of the city, the twisted values that substituted racing into the future for life in the present, annihilating process en route. More, he was sick of himself. Life no longer reverberated with passionate mystery, constantly unfolding. His days had become predictable hysteria, people busy stereotypes, and worse—he concretised that frantic banality in highly commercial art that sold so well in Toronto, Montreal and Vancouver. The bleakness of his empty existence had driven him out here for the summer, to Odessa, small-town Ontario. Maybe, if he could just slow down, catch the moment, he could unearth his *anima*. What the classical artist had called soul.

Her slim body, in loose purple nightshade pants and a daffodil shirt, glided easily through the young corn. She stopped to pick and husk an ear and eat the raw kernels straight from the cob.

When she started walking again, her movements struck him as animal grace imprisoned in human form. Primitive within the socialised. He wondered what she was seeing. And thinking. Although he had abandoned the bulk of his materials in Toronto, he fantasised about painting her and absently reached for the sketchbook and charcoal on the porch swing. If he had his acrylics, he would layer thin washes to create shading and capture that repressed wildness. Or better yet air-brushing, although he had not brought that equipment with him either. As the fields of corn engulfed her, an outline formed unconsciously on the page.

Snap out of it! he told himself. He was helping form devour content. Fantasy annihilate reality. The medium suck the life out of the message. He threw the sketchbook onto the swing and ran across the lawn to the dirt road. She was already out of sight but he jogged after her, determined to make human contact.

As he rounded the curve, a startlingly modern farmhouse came into view. It was at the dead end of the road and Paul noticed the stainless-steel mailbox with 'Jacobs' precisely stencilled on the side.

On his first shopping trip in the town, the man at the hardware store had mentioned Jacobs. "Moved up here some five years ago," he'd said. "Claims he's from down in the Caribbean. White man from the Caribbean. Imagine that."

Paul learned more about Jacobs than he wanted to know — produced a super yield insect-resistant corn that he refused to sell locally — the entire crop exported back to where he came from... The store owner warned that Jacobs wasn't friendly; he had also confided, "Pays cash for everything, and has plenty of it."

The girl was nowhere in sight. A large man, mid-fifties, with ruddy cheeks and midnight hair that trapped sunlight carried an aluminum pan toward lethargic hens inside a wired yard. He wore crisp overalls, and the requisite Wellingtons, all spotless. As Paul passed between the shiny viridian pickup — even the tires were clean — and the pristine house, he peered through a window and saw an empty kitchen. No sign of her. Near the chicken coop lay a neat vegetable patch, mature plants meticulously staked and tied, not a weed in sight. Five corn cribs loaded with the early crop stood at the edge of the closest field; beyond, the fields sparkled, dense with emerald stalks.

The man scattered a meagre amount of corn meal through the chicken wire. Seven hens jerked toward the grain like animated puppets. The man turned on a hose and aimed it at a water dish. "Hi there." Paul spoke louder. "Mr. Jacobs?"

Before the hens could get to the food, water flailed them, chasing them into the coop, soaking the grain and the ground. The man then carefully rewound the hose and returned it to its hook. When he turned, Paul was shocked to see the pocked skin, gouged with down-turned lines and dabbed with white scars. His thin lips seemed incapable of either offering or taking. From this hideous mask, hooded obsidian eyes glared into Paul's — vulture assessing potential carrion.

Paul stuck out his hand reluctantly. "Hi. I'm Paul Williams. I'm renting the old Knowlton place. Next door." His hand was ignored so he lowered it. "I was just out for a walk. Thought I'd meet my neighbours. I saw your daughter, or a young lady wearing a straw hat coming this way, and..."

"I own this property, and everything on it. Get off it while you still can." The man turned his back on Paul, crossed the clipped yard and walked up the back steps and into the house, his movements as efficient and economic as his words. The screen door slammed behind him.

Once Paul got out of sight of Jacobs' place, he realised his shoulders were tense. He knew men like Jacobs in the city. Gallery owners. Masters at the game of control. The end rationalised the means. Product was the god that granted money, power and prestige. Paul rotated his head slowly, feeling the calcium deposits between the vertebra in his neck crack. The anger loosened its grip.

Split-rail fences ran along both sides of the road. Every fifty feet Jacobs had posted 'Trespassers Will Be Prosecuted' signs. Master of all the corn he surveys, Paul thought. The idea of Jacobs staking out territory infuriated him again. He climbed over a fence and fearlessly walked between the stalks planted north-south. Blue cornflowers lined the path. The air smelled verdant and sun kneaded his back muscles, but he still felt irritated. Jacobs reeked of death and power. And barely controlled sadism. Paul wondered if the girl was a relative, or a friend, not that he could imagine Jacobs having any of the latter. Maybe she didn't even live there. But that was the last farm on the road before the lake. A woman so delicate, sensitive, yet earthy — she couldn't be with a gargoyle like Jacobs by choice...

White glinted ahead. Two rows over. He saw her reach out and pluck an ear from a stalk. She didn't seem to hear him approach from behind and he was afraid he'd frighten her. He rustled leaves and cleared his throat twice, then said "Hi!" but she still didn't turn. Maybe she's deaf, he thought, or, like Jacobs — doesn't want to hear.

He stepped around to face her. She had stripped the cob, exposing kernels even whiter than her hair. He wondered if this was a hybrid Jacobs had brought with him from the Caribbean. The only corn Paul remembered seeing even remotely like it was the starchy 'white corn' his dad fed the pigs back in Brandon, but that was yellow compared to what this girl held.

She dug out one kernel, put it in her mouth and swallowed without chewing. He watched her eat two more. When she still didn't look up, he tapped her arm; the heat of the day had not penetrated her skin. Her eyes followed his hand, as though waiting for signals. She *is* deaf, he realized. He moved his hand to his face, and smiled to reassure her.

Her eyes reminded him of Jessie's, the depressed life-drawing model at art school who most of the time had been drugged to the hilt on heavy-duty anti-depressants. The irises were ash. Matte. No luster at all, as though the liquid had dried up leaving circles of powdery grey tempera behind. He knew this girl wasn't blind, because she'd followed his hand, but she stared blankly, unseeing.

He pointed at his chest. "Paul. Your new neighbour."

Her skin was calcimine, smooth, lineless flesh that the big hat did an extraordinary job of protecting. Set against it were brows as black as her widow's-peek was white—India ink on bleached paper. Where her generous lips didn't quite meet in the centre, the space between them formed a tiny 'o', as if caught in perpetual surprise. His energy galvanised. The esthetics of perfection enthralled the artist; her bizarrely controlled wildness taunted the man. The thought crossed his mind: she might be the most repressed woman I've ever seen, but, God help me, what's under that?

She had not blinked once. In fact, she seemed to be barely breathing. He considered that she might be mentally impaired, and that what he was about to do could be construed as politically incorrect, to say the least. But the urge to draw her was overwhelming. Now. And there was more. He didn't understand it, but he needed to be near her. To smell her. To touch her skin.

"Hot day. Come over for a cool drink. We'll get to know each other." When she didn't answer, he took her hand and she followed obediently.

What am I doing? he asked himself, leading her up the porch steps. But the sensation of the small cool hand within his merged with the penetration of the sun, the clarity of the air and the unpretentious perfume of the soil.

He placed a glass of lemonade on the table and sat next to her on the porch swing. She picked at the corn cob she still held, continuing to eat the chalk-white kernels. Paul put one in his mouth and bit down. Sour mould coated his tongue. He spat the kernel out. As she ate, she watched without really seeing him. For some reason he could accept that.

He picked up the charcoal and sketchbook and drew her heart-shaped face, then the maize yellow shirt, open at the throat, exposing her delicate collar bone. Hands damaged from rough work had collapsed around the cob in her lap and he smudged the coal lines to capture them. It had been years since he'd drawn a human being and her eyes challenged him. Behind the grey flatness were sparks. Pain. Terror. Anger. And something ephemeral. It called to him, awakening a feeling crushed by the weight of passionless glass and chrome. He heard the whisper of life buried in burnt umber soil. Writhing. Undulating. Hot.

His hand moved faster—he felt driven to recreate that primitiveness, to possess it, to bring her darkness into the light.

Hours passed in silence. She had not moved. He could not remember a model as patient as his 'muse'.

Paul filled two sketchbooks, one with black charcoal, the other using oil pastels, cursing himself for the lack of better materials. Gradually he geared down to her stillness. He felt his heart beat and touched the inside of her cool wrist, hoping they were in sync, but couldn't find a pulse. Her essence was near, though, within reach. He longed to stroke the unknown lingering behind the fortress, to meld with the concealed.

A noise jarred him.

Jacobs' half ton plowed the lawn and screeched to a stop feet from the bottom step. He jumped out, leaving the door open, and in two steps reached the porch.

The girl only noticed him when he yanked her to her feet. Her face remained expressionless.

Jacobs glared first at her, then Paul. His eyes bulged like a bird-of-prey on the attack.

"Look," Paul stood, "she just came over for a lemonade..."

"Come near her again and I'll kill you!"

Jacobs dragged her down the steps and shoved her into the pickup before Paul could stop him. The vehicle door slammed. The truck reversed, then barrelled across the lawn. It accelerated. Paul raced to the road, using his body as a roadblock. Jacobs bore down on him. In a split second Paul hurtled himself into a ditch, gasping in pain as his ankle twisted. The truck missed hitting him. Just.

He crawled to his feet, ankle smarting, and stared down the dust-enshrouded road. Twilight and silence pressed into the empty space within him where she had lived. That emptiness ached but behind that feeling loomed blind fury.

It wasn't until he stood peering through the side window of Jacobs' farmhouse that Paul realized what he was doing.

The girl, emotionless, ladled thick white liquid from a pot into a porcelain bowl. She carried the bowl to the table where Jacobs was tearing into roast chicken and mashed potatoes. The girl sat quietly, facing Paul. If she saw him, she didn't let on.

Blank-eyed, she brought a steaming spoonful of soup to her lips and swallowed it, disregarding the temperature. Despite himself, he saw an Alex Colville painting: Window split into four panes; beautiful, silent farm girl eating soup; hurricane lantern on sideboard. Jacobs was the flaw on this canvas.

Paul stood at the window until the sky turned raven and crickets screeched. He watched her waiting on Jacobs, hand-and-foot. Jacobs had her paralysed with fear, that was obvious; Paul's blood seared his veins.

After dinner — after she had washed the dishes, thoroughly cleaned the already spotless kitchen and taken him a beer — Jacobs went into another room, out of sight. He yelled, 'Mira.' Immediately, as if she were mechanical and a switch had been turned on, she stopped what she was doing and lighted the hurricane lamp. She carried it with her out of the room. Paul moved to the back of the house.

A small part of his brain flashed a warning: *this is not your business.* But when Jacobs pulled her roughly onto the bed and tore open the buttons of the yellow blouse...

Her eyes got to Paul. A helpless animal. Trapped by a manipulative power. An animal that had given up struggling. As Paul burst into the bedroom, he was vaguely aware that the irrationality of his act did not matter to him.

Before Jacobs could get up, Paul's hands clamped around his throat. "You treat her like a slave. Your own personal whore."

Jacobs' fist smashed against his ribs. Paul gripped the windpipe tighter. Strong hands grabbed his wrists, nearly crushing them.

"She's not your wife or your daughter, is she?" Paul screamed.

Jacobs gasped, "You don't know what she is."

"I know what *you* are!" Suddenly Paul saw his thumbs crushing the vulnerable air passage. Jacobs face had become a hideous crimson bust.

Paul pulled away. Mira, the front of her shirt torn open, stood beside the bed like a marble statue. The plea for freedom in those dimmed eyes tore open his heart. "She's not happy. Not with you." He took her hand and turned toward the door.

He heard a sound behind him and let go of Mira for a second. Only a second. Too many things happened at once. Glass shattered near his head and hot lamp oil scalded his cheek. Darkness overwhelmed light. Something slammed into Paul's stomach. He struggled with it and then, inexplicably, it was gone. Jacobs' scream split the black air. The curtains ignited and at the same instant, flames licked the sheets. Jacobs became human fire.

Paul couldn't find Mira. Smoke forced him out of the blazing bedroom. He shouted her name and searched the house, but the fire had already spread to other rooms.

He staggered outside coughing and finally found her at the edge of a field, as if protecting the corn. The full moon illuminated her face, her naked breasts, her hair, giving her a silver, other-worldly hue. For a moment her dull eyes appeared to shine like white light, the absence of all color. But Paul had no time to study them. He grabbed her and ran.

They swayed together on the porch swing, as they did each day and night, through sunrise and sunset, munching raw corn. Corn that before — how long ago was it? — had tasted bitter to him, and been impossible to swallow. The last moon of the harvest reflected off her ghostly face, as pale as his limp hands. Her cold ash eyes rested too easily on his. The sketchbook lay abandoned on the table.

His longing to capture her had evaporated, dispersing like the image in a cloud. He felt no need to touch her. Or even to speak with her. And why should he? Her essence wove through him now, a single memory eternally forming, decomposing, reforming. Undying. Undiminishing. Forever.

# Oyster Love
## by Susan MacGregor

*Susan MacGregor has been writing for a number of years and is a co-editor of* **On Spec** *magazine. She also edited the anthology* **Divine Realms** *(Turnstone Press, 1998), a collection of speculative fiction stories with spiritual themes featuring 17 short stories from writers across Canada and the U.S. "Oyster Love" is her second attempt at horror, the first of which, "About Face," appeared in* **On Spec**'s *Fall 1995 issue and received Honorable Mention in Ellen Datlow's* **Year's Best Fantasy and Horror**.

There is something clinically beautiful about a freshly cut oyster tin, the metal all coppery on one side and white on the other, the edges tricky in the fingers, as likely to slice open a palm as not if I'm not careful. Sometimes I like to kiss it, to let my tongue stray to the edge just to take my chances. I'm very good at it, and in a sense, oysters are only my secondary pleasure.

In fact, I tried raw oysters once, but the experience wasn't the same. They were too slimy, too manipulative, slipping inside my mouth as if they had a sense of their own. No, I much prefer my oysters smoked and polite, waiting until I'm ready for them, and then sometimes, mingling with my own red mistakes, having them drop down my throat, dismembered and docile.

Whenever I watch the hemoglobin fall, it reminds me of oysters. It makes the work seem a little less dull, a little less boring.

"I'm supposed to ask you this. You've not given blood in the last two months, have not been ill in any way, including a cold, you've not had your ears pierced or any other body part within the last six months, you're not allergic to anything, you've taken no medicine within the last 48 hours?"

I wait for them to shake their heads. No. They haven't, they're not.

"Fine. I need to test the iron content of your blood. Just a prick. There we go. See how it drops to the bottom? That's really good. You have strong blood."

I smile, direct them to the bleeding area. Wait for the next donor.

At 10:15, Emilie grudgingly lets me go for coffee.

When she replaced Wanda who retired, I knew she'd be trouble. All platinum blonde hair and pale white skin, efficient and a bitch of an R.N., except around the doctors and especially around Ron. I hated her from the first moment I saw her. She was too pretty, too sharp. My hands slipped that week, and I had a serious cut from a tin.

"How did you do that?" Ron asked when I caught him at coffee. Luckily, I found him alone.

"I was slicing carrots."

"Let me see that."

His hands were cool and firm. I hadn't covered the cut, enduring the pain of it breaking open in the hopes that he might see it, might touch me and heal it up with his doctor's hands. I could use the memory of that later, recalling the smoothness of his fingers, tanned on top and pale underneath, hot and cold. I'd study the bandage while I smoked a menthol with my left hand, the sensations of coolness and heat, gauze like see-through underwear, silk and lace against brown flesh and hidden bone. The menthol would be cool against my lips, and I'd dream of him wrapping and unwrapping, until the belly of the dawn.

"I don't see why you need to continue sitting here, Donna. The clinic's almost over, and you could help with boxing up the bags for transfer." Emilie leans over me, a stick fish of ivory and gilt. The only thing I pride myself on is that I have bigger breasts than she does. She's an eel/woman in a nurse's cap with the disposition of a barracuda.

"My hand still hurts. I'm not sure I can lift much."

"Then you shouldn't be here. I'm not happy with you handling the titrate as it is."

"Dr. Collins said it would be O.K."

She purses her lips at that. "Ron's... Dr. Collins doesn't run this clinic. I do."

"I could help somewhere else."

"Either you go to the back, or you go home."

I gather up my purse.

"I see," she says. "Well, if that's your decision, I'll advise Personnel that you've gone home on sick leave."

"Is Dr. Collins here?"

"Why should that concern you?"

"I want to tell him I'm leaving."

"Why would Ron...," she begins. "Just go home, Donna. I'll tell him. I'm seeing him later..."

I freeze. My hand starts to throb. "You're seeing him later?"

"Yes. No. I mean, I'll see him later sometime today. He'll be back in his office this afternoon."

I walk back to my apartment. Sometimes, when I open a tin with the can opener, I scroll it open very slowly and only part-way down. I like to peel the rest of it away with my fingers, to see how the magic breaks, whether it splits in a straight line or on a diagonal. If it's straight, then so am I. If it's at an angle, then I'm devious and hidden, my motives and actions known only to myself. As I expect, the lid opens with a curl. Only five oysters are visible.

The message is clear. Watch for fives.

At quarter to five, I return to the clinic's parking lot. Dr. Collins' BMW is there. At five, exactly, he and the eel bitch walk out the back door.

Almost always, oysters tell the truth. Since they're already dead, they have nothing to lose. For luck, I have slipped one down my blouse, a small brown penis patient and contrite. It snuggles in my cleavage, thankful for the moment until I prompt it to act. It will wait.

Ron and the eel stop briefly at his car to leave his attaché case in the trunk. Then they set off at a brisk walk.

In my opinion, they are walking much too closely together. Their shoulders brush as they move. I keep well behind so they will not see me. Part of me considers that this may make no difference; they wouldn't notice me at all. The Eel Queen laughs at something Dr. Collins has said and squeezes his arm. The oyster tucked between my breasts leaks in oily complaint. The meaning is clear enough. Ron hasn't been honest with me; his hands haven't been pure. He's been tainted, and I suspect a worse betrayal.

Several blocks down, they turn onto Fifth. I hurry to catch up before they disappear. I watch as they step into a restaurant, The Five Crowns. I hesitate at the door, but luckily, there's a small foyer that will hide me before I find a remote table. I wait at the 'Please Wait to Be Seated' sign. Ron and the eel sit in a sculpted booth, bordered by greenery, two scallops on a half shell.

"May I help you?" Raoul, the maitre-d', attends me. He's tall and gaunt and has a tiny black mustache. He's wearing a tuxedo. Unlike Dr. Collins', his fingers are long and thin. His hands show me he's too eager or too imperious, depending upon the situation. Oysters or no, it's important that I establish my dominance early. I look down my nose at him. "You can," I reply.

"Do you have a reservation?'

I study him carefully. "I've a lover who's cheating on me," I tell him. "That's him, sitting with his blonde bitch. Either you find a way for me to sit near them, without them noticing, or I confront them right here and now. Do you have a back way into the restaurant?"

He stares at me as if he hasn't quite seen me until this moment. I hold his gaze. I feel the oyster between my breasts split; he's deliberating. The restaurant is half full. I press my breasts together. The oil spreads into my blouse, but the effort is enough.

He nods briefly. "This way." He takes me past the coat check and through an office. Another door opens into the kitchen. We walk through, and the chef looks up but asks no questions. I notice oyster shells on ice. A good omen.

We slip from the kitchen, and Raoul seats me at a small table which is shielded by a palm. Dr. Collins and the eel cannot see me, but I have a clear view of them.

"May I get you something?" Raoul asks. I'll give him this. He's not fazed by me nor derelict in his duties. Raoul is a professional.

I do not lift my gaze from the table across the room. "Smoked oysters," I reply, "And the tin they came in."

# OYSTER LOVE

The oysters arrive about twenty minutes later while Ron and the eel are picking at their shrimp cocktails. Raoul serves me himself as if he's frightened to allow the waiters to do so. Of course, the oysters are set on a bed of lettuce, and the chef has arranged them in a semi-circle. I should have warned Raoul about this. In this instance, I don't want *arranged* oysters, I want them served *randomly*. I'll have to toss them myself. Between pinched fingers, Raoul hands me a brown bag as if it's something to be ashamed of, something which holds the unspeakable like little brown pieces of turd or dismembered fingers. I let it pass.

When he leaves, I cover the oysters with the empty plate opposite, and turn them upside down. I give them several good shakes.

The oysters are heaped one on top of the other, the lettuce clinging here and there like bits of clothing in dishabille. An orgy of brown thighs and vulvas and penises, beyond shame or restraint. Ron has been unfaithful for weeks, and I haven't seen! I glare at their table, and find as often happens, that the oysters have shown me more than I expect. The Eel Queen is wearing a green dress, as green as the lettuce on my plate.

She's nuzzling a foot against his calf.

I must rearrange the plate before the present moment sets. Quickly, these two apart, another three pushed to the edge. I spear an oyster in the middle and am about to pop it into my mouth when I see the unspeakable; a hair dangling from my fork. Not one of my own, but one that is short, black and slightly curled. I stare in horror at this obscenity.

This has always been the risk of ordering maverick oysters. In their tin, they are pristine, always virginal, and never handled by hands other than my own. But someone has been before me, and this has made them vulgar.

My appetite lost, I remove the offending strand. The remaining oysters, I slip into the empty tin, their waiting bed, before returning it to its bag.

Ron and the eel are leaving. It seems they've lost their appetite or have had it replaced with the desire of a different kind. I pull a twenty from my purse and leave it, with the hair, for Raoul.

They walk back to her apartment. I watch through the lobby windows as they catch the elevator up.

"What can I do?" I whimper. "What can I do?"

I fish the oyster out of my blouse. It's still holding together, despite Raoul, despite the bullying of my breasts. I hold it between my thumb and forefinger.

*Find her name on the index*, it suggests.

Emilie Nordstrom. Apartment #502.

*Press the button.*

I do.

"Yes?"

"Hi, Nurse Nordstrom? This is Donna."

*Now what?*

*Lie*, it tells me.

"I'm sorry to bother you, but is Dr. Collins with you? I'm afraid his car has been in an accident at the clinic."

"What?!" Ron's voice.

"I'm afraid so. You'll have to come and check it out."

"I'll be right down."

"Um, would you mind if I came up? I really have to go to the bathroom."

"Oh, for heaven's sake..." The eel bitch, of course.

"Please? I'm a ways from my own place, and I ran all the way from the clinic to tell you."

"Oh, all right," she huffs. "Don't be long," she adds, not to me I think, but to Ron.

I wait at the front doors and watch as Ron charges out of the elevator. He holds the door for me as I pass him by, barely giving me a nod. I hate to lie to him, but he's given me no choice.

Five floors up, Emilie watches from her doorway as I leave the elevator.

"How bad is it?" she asks. I step past her into her apartment. Unlike my own place, her suite is stark, done in Danish Modern, teak furniture throughout, and not much in the way of color except for red and white cushions on a black leather couch. To the left is a galley kitchen and to the right, a bedroom and bathroom.

"Awful," I say, considering her decorating. "A hit and run. His whole right front fender's dented in."

"What were you doing at the clinic? I thought you went home."

"I did, but I forgot my coat so I went back."

She makes a face and rubs her arms.

"The bathroom?" I prompt.

"That way." She turns from me to watch for Ron from her living room window.

I don't go into the bathroom. Instead, I quietly turn left into the kitchen. A cast iron frying pan sits on the stove. It's ugly and matches the couch. I pick it up in my right hand. My cut complains beneath its bandage, but I'll endure a little pain for love.

Emilie still watches at her window. I am quiet, as quiet as an oyster in its shell. I know eels can turn suddenly, and so I creep, creep, moving as steadily as the tide coming in, I raise my arm and bring it down, solid rock against soft shell, striking once and hard.

The eel collapses with a little 'eep', so I hit her again. She slithers at my feet, all green and nasty. Red and white, her head matches the pillows on the couch.

"Ick," I say, but I must touch her; it's necessary. I grab her by the ankles and haul her into the bedroom. Her dress hikes up and gets caught on a hall tile. She's wearing green underwear beneath. I jerk her free and hoist her onto the bed. My hand is really hurting now, but for security's sake, I wallop her once again. She doesn't look too good.

I hurry back to the window. It won't take Ron long to figure out that I lied about his car, although I know I can always claim stupidity — *but I thought your car was the gray Omni! Oh, Dr. Collins, I'm sorry! I honestly didn't mean to put you to so much trouble! I feel terrible. The last thing I'd ever want to do is cause you any grief. I feel... I think of you so highly! I feel so stupid.*

No Ron, yet. I return to the bedroom, but the eel bitch isn't stirring. She's breathing though, quite shallowly.

*You may have to do something about that.*

"I know," I reply.

Back at the window again, I see Ron coming down the street. He looks angry, my darling!

"Now what?" I inquire.

*Why ask? You're doing fine on your own.*

I suppose I am, in spite of my poor throbbing hand. I could really use a cigarette.

The intercom buzzes. That's one consolation, I suppose. Ron doesn't have his own key yet.

"Hello?" I say.

"Donna? Is that you? There doesn't seem to be a thing wrong with my car."

"What?"

"There's nothing wrong with my car."

"I was sure the Omni was yours!"

"Omni?"

"Yes...,"

"Let me speak to Emilie."

"She's in the bedroom. I don't think she's feeling well."

"What?"

"She's lying down. She thinks it was the shrimp."

"Let me in."

"How?"

"You have to push down the intercom button...,"

"Oh, I see. Like this?" I push it.

"That's it." His voice sounds distant.

"Are you coming up?" I hope he'll answer, but I already know he's on his way. My love. Soon to return to my arms.

I retrieve the frying pan from where I left it in the living room. I meet him at the door, pan in hand.

He eyes it but asks no questions. To be fair, I've given him this chance, but his concern for the Eel Queen overrides all.

"Emilie?" he calls.

"In the bedroom," I murmur, feeling his betrayal complete. How can he not see how he's hurt me?

He turns down the hall. I follow.

"What the hell?" He stands inside the bedroom doorway. Emilie is a sight with her dress hiked up, legs sprawled, and one temple bloody.

He is about to turn, but I am faster. The frying pan finds its mark a second time. He's stronger than the eel, and his arms come up. With both hands and the strength of my love to sustain me, I whack him again. He crumples at my feet in sweet surrender.

"Ron, why?" I ask, as he scrabbles at my feet. I hate to do it, but I have to hit him again. This time, he doesn't move.

A moan comes from the bed. I step out of Ron's arms and rush to the eel's side. She's going to be a problem.

I knock her quiet. Her pantyhose offer a solution, and so I wrap them around her neck but not before I use Ron's tie to bind her hands and her panties to tangle her feet. Such a good waste of underwear. Even if they *are* green.

And then a moment of brilliance overtakes me. It's magic time. I rush to the kitchen and dig the oysters and tin from my purse.

*Oh, yes, Mistress!* they cry, *We'll be good! We promise!*

I can barely hold them in my hands, they're so excited! We're so excited!

One by one, I insert them into the eel's mouth and nostrils and ears.

The body struggles a bit, but I straddle her. The oysters complain as she bites down and tries to spit them out, but I make them stay. The two in her nostrils bob up and down like seals on the waves. After awhile, she stops moving, stops breathing.

It doesn't seem right to leave Ron where he is. I haul him onto the bed with the Eel Queen and me.

"So, *this* is what you threw me over for?" I ask Ron. I reach over to my purse and fish out a menthol. I light it up and smoke it on the bed with the two of them on either side. We're oysters on the half shell. It's quite peaceful.

*Do you think her dress might fit, I wonder?*

I study the eel. I've never been partial to green, but if that's what Ron likes, then that's what we'll try. I untie her hands and wrestle the dress off her. It has buttons up the back that we'll leave undone. She has to be all of a size 5, as compared to my size 13. It's a tight squeeze, but we fit, *just.* My breasts are pushed together, and although the dress wasn't low cut on her, it is on me. I eat the remnants of the oyster I left between my cleavage. Its corpse is done, but the spirit remains. I wonder if Ron will think I look sexy. I find the eel's high heels in the front closet. They're green, too.

I wobble back to the bedroom, climb back between them on the bed. I eat a few more oysters and finger the edge of the tin. My reflection stares back at me from the dresser mirror opposite the bed. We strike a few poses, hike the dress up around my hips. Squeeze my breasts even tighter and blow kisses.

*But something is missing, Donna. We don't quite look like the eel yet. Maybe the hair?*

"Was it?" I ask Ron. "Are you partial to blondes?"

*We could be a blonde for him. Easy.*

I turn to the eel. "I'm supposed to ask you this. You haven't given blood over the last two months, have not been ill in any way, you're not allergic to anything, or have taken any medication within the last 48 hours?"

She doesn't say anything, so I take this as a 'no'.

"Fine," I say. "This won't hurt a bit. Just a prick. Here we go."

I hold the edge of the lid against her scalp. The metal is very sharp.

It takes much longer than I expect. Almost twenty minutes. I decide it's because the magic is stretched too thin. There's so much to keep track of. I have to return to Ron again, to give him another dose of the frying pan. I don't want him to wander off anywhere. He could really hurt himself, considering the state he's in. As I study myself in the bathroom, you can hardly tell that the hair is blonde, it's so wet. I wash the scalp with Herbal Essences shampoo. The bottle tells me that the chamomile and lemon will bring out the blonde highlights, and surprisingly, they *do*.

I put the scalp on my head and return to the bed. The sight of Emilie is making me ill. She looks like something that should be hanging from a hook in a fish market.

*Get rid of her.*

I push her off. She lands with a thump. The pillow her head was on is all red. I turn it over.

I consider my reflection. The blonde hair sits on my head like a sickly yellow sea urchin.

*A bad hair day?*

With the eel out of sight, we have only Ron to feast our eyes upon. It seems obscene that he's still dressed as he is, complete with shoes and socks. I slide to the bottom of the bed and pull them off.

*He has beautiful feet.*

"Doesn't he, though?" I agree. Nicely formed, and they smell faintly of foot odor, but we don't mind this at all. It reminds us of the ocean, of seaweed. We stroke his toes lovingly — *this little oyster went to market, this little oyster stayed home, and this little oyster went wee, wee, wee...!*

We giggle as he twitches, little brown oyster toes all in a row.

*Do you think he's uncomfortable in his pants, Donna? I'll bet he is.*

Off they come. He's wearing boxer shorts. Faded beige ones. This surprises us. We'd always pictured him in tight, hip-hugging jockeys in black or electric blue or maroon. But then again, he *is* a doctor. He would know that such tight shorts would cut off the circulation, make him less virile, although no less able. We swallow another oyster.

*Now, the shirt.*

He is hairless and perfect. His pectorals rise and fall with each breath he takes, although his breathing is a little erratic. We run our hands across his chest. Smooth, so smooth. His heart beats strongly. We picture his hemoglobin dropping like lead in the titrate. "That's good, baby," we tell him, our two voices combining into one. "You must have strong blood." We kiss his fingers tenderly, imagine them on our breasts and body, pulling the lettuce aside, tan hands on white, hot on cool, our nipples like limpets puckering to his touch. We lift his hands to our breasts, but they only bump against them awkwardly. How disappointing. We set them down.

After this, there isn't much to do.

Part of us wants to get on with it, to uncover the mystery, to see Ron without his shell. But another part fears the raw oyster, its hugeness and darkness and wildness. Oysters should *not* have minds of their own. Men do, and it brings them nothing but trouble. Look where it got poor Ron.

We scoop another oyster from the tin. Advice is needed. We hold it at eye level.

*How may I help you?* it asks.

"I would like something special, Raoul."

*And what might that be?*

"True love."

*Ah.*

"But it must be tame. Nothing unexpected. Nothing I can't handle."

*I'm sure you can handle anything. You've proven that time and again.*

"Well, yes, and no. Some things, I just can't deal with."

*Such as?*

"*You* know."

We sit and contemplate each other for a time.

*There's no gain without the risk.*

"I suppose."

We set Raoul in Ron's navel. Our hands are trembling as we place them on either side of Ron's waistband. Part of us feels slightly faint.

*No time to blank out now, Donna.*

Still, we close our eyes. We can't look. Not yet. Then we yank the shorts down. We swallow once, open our eyes and *see*.

Hair. Hundreds of hairs, all clinging to Ron's oyster in the most obscene way. They are short, black, and slightly curled. We stare in horror at this obscenity. The whimpering part of us knows we have seen such a thing before.

To make matters even worse, Ron's oyster lifts its head, almost involuntarily, like a sea gull startled at its nesting. Gorge rises in our throat.

"What can we do, Raoul?" we fret. "What can we do?"

*There is nothing to do but to remove the offending strands. And then tame the beast.*

We are shaking hard. Raw oysters are slimy and manipulative. They slip inside one's mouth as if they have minds of their own. We can never let that happen again. Not the way it was *before*.

We manage to hold the oyster tin between our trembling fingers. We expect we'll suffer from big red mistakes while we do it, but those are the consequences we must endure.

*It won't be so bad, Donna. Don't think about it while it's happening. Then, after you're done, we can slip it inside and kiss the lid, let our tongue stray close to the edge. You're very good at this, and in a sense, oysters are only your secondary pleasure.*

Raoul knows me well. Sometimes, I wonder how it all happened. I don't remember when he came into our life. I must have asked him to at some point. But we trust him, and we're safe. Raoul arranges everything. The set-up, the clean-up. Time and time again. We never have to worry about a thing. He's never derelict in his duties.

I'll give him this, Raoul *is* a professional.

# The Rat, Peering Out, Sees Justice Done

## by Vincent Grant Perkins

*This appears to be New Brunswick native Vincent Perkins' first professional sale since selling to U.S. science fiction magazines in the 1970s. Whatever the reason for his absence, we welcome the author's return with this darkly satiric northern Gothic concerning a country boy's employment of wild talents on some loathsomely wicked city slickers.*

Wendell McCollum was just eight years old when he discovered he could swallow handfuls of Smarties, hold them out of sight within his esophagus long enough to show that they had disappeared from his mouth, then return them to full view on his tongue without any of the candy coating dissolved. This ability was of extreme importance within the social stratum that Wendell and his adolescent peers lived and played. He was their mentor, their child-king, their god.

Wendell's pa, of course, saw little usefulness in his son's talent; but Wendell loved his pa, and wanted nothing more than his pa's respect. So he never told his pa about his talent for swallowing things even bigger than Smarties. His gullet opened to a variety of foreign objects, and Wendell secretly refined that ability to permit ever larger items to pass safely through the canal between his throat and his stomach.

Candies were easiest, of course. Jawbreakers, gobstoppers, mints — no matter how large, they all slid unhindered down his throat with a silken, sugary slickness. Coins worked well, too, although dimes proved difficult to regurgitate: their small size and thinness made their return ascent through the papillae in his esophagus a time-consuming manipulation. Table tennis balls from the county youth center were a breeze to swallow. Wendell taught himself to do four and five at a time, making a great show of sucking them in, then expelling them from his mouth in rapid succession like plastic bullets from a toy air rifle.

After the farm began losing money regularly, Wendell's pa took a job driving a semi to keep the family afloat, leaving Wendell at home with his ma and the honeybees. Though his heart wasn't set on farming, Wendell enjoyed the bees, especially at harvest time when the honey had to be taken from the hives. Then, he and his ma would suit up together in the barn, laughing and joking at each other, looking quite ridiculous in their mesh headgear, bulky suits and clunky boots. When they were ready, they would clump on out to the pasture where the hives stood like miniature Bauhaus-influenced architecture, and rob the bees of their treasure.

Wendell was twelve when word came that his pa had been killed in an accident in Ontario, after his tractor-trailer rig jack-knifed on the 401. Wendell and his ma grieved, but it was almost like saying good-bye to a stranger. Wendell's pa hadn't been home much in three years, and he had never been much of a letter writer. They missed the money he had sent home, however. Without it, the savings that Wendell's ma had managed to squirrel away dwindled rapidly.

His ma had always knit sweaters, socks and toques. Now she went at it with a vengeance, selling them at craft shows, county fairs and church bazaars. For his part, Wendell had become something of a county showman. At parties, dances and variety shows he swallowed marbles, one by one into his mouth, down his throat and back out again, easy as pie. Then he repeated the process, this time swallowing a whole handful of marbles. Then golf balls, into his stomach and out again with no problem at all. Tennis balls, while a bit of a torture to get into his mouth, were assisted in their ingestion by an ingenious method he designed to facilitate their passage: he would suck inward forcibly while pounding at his diaphragm with the ham of his fist. The noises produced during this procedure were thoroughly unpleasant, but it proved an effective incentive to swallowing whenever the items were large or eccentrically shaped. Light bulbs were ingested in this manner, as were camera films, "D" size batteries, rolls of Scotch tape and war medals. He also swallowed baseball cards, pencils, ink bottles, pocket change and goldfish. He designed a routine where he first swallowed a live goldfish, then any number of other items, after which he would systematically regurgitate the swallowed objects in a random sequence, with the goldfish returning last and still very much alive.

When Wendell was sixteen a minimalist theater troupe on tour through the county fair circuit brought their impromptu dramatics to the youth center. The manager of the troupe, a small, brash, slick-haired, chain-smoking man by the name of Tony Sepata, discovered Wendell practicing his craft in the center's rest room and immediately took him under his wing

His fulsome praise of Wendell's talent. and his exciting embellishments of Toronto's opportunities proved so alluring that Wendell, entranced by Tony's zeal, decided to have Tony accompany him to Toronto, in order to "properly guide him through the miracles and pit-falls of making it big in the big city."

"Stick with me, kid," Tony told him, lighting a cigarette and tossing the empty match-card to the floor. "I'm gonna take you to places where money just oozes from the cracks in the walls, where people will be so desperate to watch you perform they'll be clawing their way to the front of the pack just to get a close-up view of all that stuff you can put in your mouth."

Wendell had never been to the big city, but if it meant he could make more money doing what he did, he was ready and willing to give it a try.

Unfortunately, his first night in Toronto was a calamity of almost eerie proportions. Wendell was so overwhelmed by the immensity of the city, the staggering heights of the buildings and the crowds choking the sidewalks that he could scarcely even talk. And the only thing oozing from the cracks in the walls of *The Barb & Cat*, a seedy club an Yonge Street, was the accumulated sweat and smoke residue from years of intoxicated patrons and gyrating strippers. The deafening music, the stink of fried chicken from the take-out next door, and the thick pall of smoke hanging in the air like a great bubble of gaseous goo, all contributed to Wendell's increasing discomfort.

Even before he got up on stage his usually iron-clad stomach was showing signs of imminent disaster.

He should have known better than to continue. But he had never had any difficulty before, and he was urged to perform by the club's raucous crowd all of whom shouted encouragements or brandished fists and pocket knives in the air as if threatening reluctance with deadly reprisals. Tony even tossed him a leather bag filled with marbles in a great display of theatrical showmanship. The music roared, the crowd raged, the lights flashed, and Wendell downed the entire bag of marbles in one ravenous gulp.

Everyone within spitting distance must have heard Wendell's stomach bubbling its discontent; but no one was more surprised than Wendell when the entire contents of his stomach spewed from his mouth in a fusillade of glassy projectiles. The sound was like gunfire, with marbles thudding into walls, clanging off light fixtures, and slamming people in the head. Electricity crackled from somewhere, and the club plunged into darkness. Wendell felt himself yanked off the stage and dragged through a doorway. After the feverish mixture of heat and stink inside, the cool night air in the back alley of the club was a welcome change, and should have been cause for a breath of relief. But the thought that he had been pulled out here by disgruntled patrons hungry for blood roused him into a fit of fear. He threw a blind punch and felt his knuckles graze the side of someone's head.

"*Hell*, boy, are you fuckin' *crazy*? I'm tryin' to save your country ass from gettin' kicked black and blue and you gotta start *deckin'* me? I ain't got *time* for this *shit*!"

Tony's voice was not the fount of wisdom and tolerance that Wendell wanted to hear right then. Nothing he had ever done had prepared him for this moment, lying on broken pavement in a puddle of slime, his mouth reeking with the taste of vomit. He missed his ma and pa.

Tony grabbed Wendell under the arms and dragged him from the alley. Out on the street the racket of car horns, amplified music, sirens, people cursing, tires squealing, and all the other sounds of a big city slammed Wendell's senses like a thunderclap. The stink of cigarette smoke and hair grease clogged Wendell's sinuses as the little man hugged him close and helped him to walk.

## THE RAT, PEERING OUT, SEES JUSTICE DONE

Somehow they made it to a rickety staircase at the rear of an old tenement. The yard was dark, the asphalt sprouting tufts of dry, brown grass. A distant yelling and a hollow, machine-like thumping gave the still night air a peculiar vigor.

The climb up the stairs was fraught with danger. Broken banisters and rotted landings brought each misplaced step a hairsbreadth away from sending both of them crashing through to the ground below.

"Hey, what the fuck?"

Tony's whispered curse froze Wendell at the top step, the little man's stubby fingers clutching a fistful of Wendell's shirt. In the gloom, Wendell had just enough time to see a partially open door before Tony gave a blood-curdling scream and kicked at the door. It slammed open, banged back against the door-frame, then was yanked open from the inside. A furious, rushing shape surged past, one arm concealing its face, the other swinging a knife in wide, random arcs. Wendell saw the blade flash in the moonlight.

The assailant was halfway down the stairs when the lower section of framework tore loose from the main structure with a lurching squeal, and crashed in a cloud of dust and dirt to the ground below. A stocky figure crawled out from beneath the heap of debris and shuffled off into the darkness.

"Damn! We'll never get 'im now!" Tony cursed through clenched teeth.

The apartment was in wretched shape, with overturned furniture, broken glass strewn over the stained carpet, holes in the flimsy walls, and clothes scattered everywhere. Wendell stood aghast in the doorway. He had never before seen anyone's home so ruthlessly defiled, and the sight sickened him. He watched sadly as Tony picked his way through the debris and staggered into the kitchenette. He heard glass crunching underfoot, cupboard doors being opened and closed. Moments later Tony reappeared, his pudgy face drained of color.

"Well, nothing seems to be missing, anyway. *This*? Ah .... some — *friends* of mine came over to help me celebrate my .... *birthday*, I guess you could say, and we got, well, we got kinda carried away, as you can see." Tony shrugged and swiped at a fly buzzing about his head. "I never keep anything important here, anyway. This neighborhood — you just never know — " His eyes widened. "Hey! You're cut!"

171

Wendell held up his right arm. The cuff of his blue shirt was stained brown, and blood covered his wrist and hand. As he stood there, watching his wound pulse wetly, drops of blood welled up and dripped onto the carpet. A knot in his stomach began quickly to unravel, flinging shards of panic all through him. He clutched his right wrist with his left hand, clamping both tight to his chest in an effort to quell the quietly flaring pain. Tony rushed to his side, just in time to support him before a sudden dizziness made him collapse.

"Okay, okay, just take it easy there, Wendell," said Tony. "I've seen worse wounds at turkey trimmin' time, but I can see you're all screwed up about it. Tell you what. I'm gonna phone us a taxi and git us down to — *hell!* I don't got no phone! Well, not a problem. We'll just git us downstairs the front way and hail a cab. Zat sound okay, kid?"

Wendell gave a weary nod, at this point not even sure what he was agreeing to. He was pretty much a stranger to pain, and he just wanted *this* pain to stop.

The front stairwell of the building stank, and only two bare bulbs lit Wendell's and Tony's bleak descent. A numbing scream pierced the darkness. His pain, for the moment, forgotten, Wendell clutched desperately at Tony's shoulder. He could feel his teeth grinding down to nubs.

Tony's whispered response was hardly reassuring. "Don't sweat it. That kinda thing goes on here all the time. Sometimes all night long." He blinked sweat from his eyes. "They're just havin' fun."

The warped and mildewed door at the foot of the front stairs opened onto a chilly night etched by rain. Tony grabbed a handful of Wendell's shirt and dragged him down the puddled sidewalk to a taxi — its roof lights off and its windows dark and steamed — parked curbside beneath the overhanging boughs of a sycamore. Rain slopped from Tony's hair as he bent over knocked on the taxi's passenger window.

"Hey! Hey! I gotta get my pal somewhere! Finish your sandwich some other time, huh?" He opened the car's rear door and put his hand as a guide to the back of Wendell's head, prompting Wendell to duck down and climb in.

From inside the taxi came a harsh shout of surprise. "Hey! What the fuck!"

Lightning tore a strip across the sky and Wendell had only enough time to see — before Tony quickly hauled him back away from the car — the figure of a man on the rear seat, and the additional figure of a woman, crammed in between the man's legs and swallowing his penis.

For Wendell, the act he saw wasn't as fascinating as the memory it stirred within him, the memory of his own talent, and the reason why Tony Sepata had brought him to Toronto. He had come here to display his talent before the hungry eyes of thousands of people, to find his fortune and fame in the entertainment mecca of the big city. He had come here to be a star, but right about now he felt as much like a star as a rat burrowing in filth. How was it possible to feel fulfillment amongst widespread crime and depravity? Things weren't like this at home. People there cared about each other, they cared *for* each other. In the city, no one seemed to care much about anyone else. Without Tony's friendship, Wendell would have made an all-too-easy target for anyone ruthless enough to take advantage of a young boy new to the big city. Thank God he had Tony to look out for him.

"C'mon, kid," said Tony. "This ain't the only cab in town." He slammed the car's door, accidentally jarring Wendell's injured arm. Wendell cried out in pain and stumbled off the curb, but Tony managed to grab hold of him before he pitched forward into the gutter.

"Jesus! You're a hurtin' puppy, ain'tcha? Probly never been sliced before, havya?" Tony looked up and down the street. The wind and rain whirled wet debris all around them. "I can't waste any more time here. Look I got a friend lives not far from here. She usedta be a nurse or somethin'. She'll know how to fix that arm a yours."

Wendell hoped Tony was right. Although his pain seemed to be more localized now, less intense, his head felt woozy and lop-sided, as if most of its weight had shifted to one side of his skull.

Tony led them on a rough-and-tumble route through back yards and between fences until Wendell, nearly overcome with exhaustion, felt himself being carried a final few meters, and heard Tony pronounce, "We're here."

After stumbling up a dark flight of stairs, Tony knocked quietly and they were let into a small apartment smelling of scented oils and perfumed candle smoke. Wendell was fawned over by a short-haired woman with big teeth who cut off his shirt sleeve, poured something on his wound that made it hurt like blazes, and bound his wrist with gauze and tape. He remembered drinking some foul liquid that burned all the way down, but which left him glowing inside.

He slept then, and dreamed pleasantly of the farm, the bees, his pa and ma, and all of them back together again, one big happy family.

When Wendell awoke, darkness had replaced the candlelight, and the pain in his wrist had subsided to a mild throbbing. He swung his legs off the couch and sat up. With his ma's face still sharp in his mind's eye, he walked over to the telephone on a small table at the other end of the room. He didn't feel right about calling long distance on someone else's phone, but he really needed to hear his ma's voice right now.

Wendell wasn't exactly sure what time it was back home, but he reasoned there could be no more than a couple hours difference. In any case, his ma should have answered well before the thirtieth ring. He replaced the receiver slowly. The bubble of dread deep in his throat felt worse than anything he had ever swallowed.

He didn't like the big city — he knew that now. It was not the place for him. He should never have come. But even his ma had encouraged him to go and had seen him off with her blessings, knowing the time had come for Wendell to begin to make his own way in the world. She still had lots of friends and neighbors to keep her company. Wendell needn't feel guilty about leaving her alone.

But he desperately wanted to see his ma now. He wanted to see his home, the people he knew and the countryside he loved.

The cheapest and quickest way home would be by bus, but Wendell didn't have even *that* much. He had spent his last $30.00 buying gas for the trip to Toronto in Tony's dangerously rusty '71 Chevrolet, and he was *sure* he didn't have any money left in his wallet—

—His *wallet!* Where *was* his wallet?

Patting his jeans' pockets anxiously, as if that would help to make his wallet suddenly reappear, Wendell looked around the room in the hope that had had the consideration to remove his valuables and put them somewhere safe. His sneakered foot stepped on something. He bent down and picked up Tony's trousers. At that point he noticed other clothing scattered on the floor, bits of both male and female apparel that had been hastily doffed and dropped in a haphazard trail leading toward the half-open door to the bedroom. Wendell heard sounds from inside the bedroom, then, too, and the sweeping light from a passing car's headlights briefly but boldly illuminated Tony's naked figure on the bed, kneeling behind the woman who had doctored Wendell's arm, and thrusting himself upon her.

Wendell's fingers went suddenly slack and the trousers fell to the floor with a soft *thunk*. He gazed down at his wallet laying half in and half out of one of the pockets of Tony's pants. When he bent down and retrieved it a thick money clip fell out of the same pocket onto the carpet. Wendell looked back toward the bedroom, where Tony and his friend were still intimately engaged, and decided not to interrupt them. Instead, he withdrew two fifties from the clip, breathed a silent oath to his new friend that he would be back to repay him, and quietly exited the apartment.

Wendell disembarked from the bus at the crossroads and started along the dirt road leading up into the hills where the family farm was nestled. It was early in the morning, with the sun not yet showing. Clouds obscured most of the stars. The air was chilly.

In Toronto, after paying for his bus ticket, he had been accosted by a wild-eyed, knife-wielding brigand in the bus station's washroom, robbed of his remaining few dollars, gagged and bound with a filthy scarf and locked inside one of the washroom's receptacles. He was discovered an hour later by a patron either curious about the locked door or too impatient to wait. Virtually immobilized and hung up on the stall's coat hook like a sack of dirty laundry, Wendell had never been so glad to see an inquisitive face peering up at him from the space at the bottom of a public toilet's door. Fortunately, the thief had not considered Wendell's bus ticket sufficiently worthwhile for his purposes, and had left it. After being freed, Wendell had had just enough time to catch the bus he needed before it departed.

Now, as he walked, his sneakers crunched on the pebbly surface of the road, and the sound seemed to echo among the hills all about him. Birds chirped in the distance. A slow breeze swept down the slopes through the trees, and with it came the acrid tang of someone's wood-stove. No. No. It was more than just that distinctive smell of comfort. It was the stink of timber and a lot more burnt to a blackened crisp and left smoking in the morning dew.

The sun came up behind him just as he topped the rise and saw for the first time the devastation that had been wrought upon his family's home. The entire farm lay in ruins: the house, the barn, the garage, the tool-shed, the outhouse; all were smoldering piles of crisp, blackened wood, twisted metal and incinerated furniture. In his chest, Wendell felt his heart break, then a fist seemed to clutch at the fragments. His ma—

He ran, half stumbling, lurching forward impetuously, down the slope of the hill, his heart hammering inside his rib-cage now, the blood in his head near the boiling point. The driveway was a muddy, rutted mess, a chaotic jumble of tire tracks and boot prints. Tiny wisps of smoke curled up from hot spots within the charred ruins. His head ringing, his limbs frozen into near immobility, Wendell staggered forward in a zombie's leaden slouch, and stepped into a pile of blackened timbers at a spot where he thought the front door of the house had once been.

"*Maaaaaaaaaaa* — !!"

His scream rang out in the valley like a cathedral's sonorous gong, and the surrounding hills echoed terrible, tortured reverberations of his anguish. After the echoes stopped, the pounding in his temples went on and on.

"Wendell, I'm so sorry."

Wendell turned slowly. A neighbor—Joan .... something. He couldn't think of her last name. She was a friend of his ma's. Her hands were clasped tightly in front of her. She stepped carefully over the ravaged soil. Her pale face told him everything he didn't want to hear

"Your .... mother .... didn't make it out. The fire spread too quickly. Everything was destroyed by the time the volunteers arrived. We wanted to get hold of you, but no one knew where you had gone, no one had any idea." Her frown gouged deep furrows in her brow. "Who would want to do this to your mother, Wendell? She never hurt anyone in her life."

Wendell looked at her, trying to understand what she was saying. Her face blurred, her words became a mumble. Something buzzed past his ear.

"I—I have to pick up my daughter at a friend's house," said Joan. "Why don't you come with me? Are you hungry? I could take you—"

## THE RAT, PEERING OUT, SEES JUSTICE DONE

Wendell shook his head. He didn't want to leave. Not yet. He shook his head again, and Joan left quietly, alone.

He turned away from the pile of burnt rubble that had been his family's home, and started walking across the scorched grass of the yard, alongside the small vegetable garden, past the wreakage of the tool-shed, and out behind the razed remains of the barn. By this time a fair number of bees were buzzing noisily and insistently about Wendell's head. He stood near the ruins of the barn near where he and his ma used to suit up before going out to harvest the honey, and looked out toward the cluster of hives. All had been burned and knocked to the ground, but one had survived being completely destroyed. A hazy patch of air surrounding the overturned hive was actually a swarm of hundreds of bees, all of them angry, upset and confused, and dutifully trying to reorganize their habitation.

A swatch of color on the ground, in contrast to the black, browns and grays of the land, caught Wendell's eye. He bent and picked up a scorched card of matches, the outer face displaying the orange and blue logo of *The Barb & Cat.*

Something in Wendell's head clicked, and the tortured machinery of his thoughts rattled like a jack-hammer. He walked toward the hive, unprotected, realizing it didn't seem to matter much anymore. After only a few steps a cloud of bees enveloped him. Inside the cloud the noise of the bees was louder than a chainsaw's roar, the heated fanning of their tiny wings like a yellow-jacketed whirlwind sucking him into their insect realm.

It was difficult to see the condition of the hive: the bees surrounded him, crawling all over his head and eyes, blocking his vision. But they seemed to be conveying information by the frantic movements of their bodies information designed to help Wendell understand.

They had seen some things.

And they wanted to help.

Taking care not to harm any of them, Wendell lay down on his back beside the overturned hive, and opened his mouth and gullet to the bees.

At first the bees seemed hesitant about investigating Wendell's body. The foreign smells and tastes and textures and chemicals were not particularly attractive to honeybees. No bee had ever had an invitation quite like this before, and they were obviously unsure of how best to proceed.

The bees' reluctance was not lost on Wendell. A shared intimacy was at work here, and he was well aware that the colony was facing a difficulty. Realizing that, he shut down the secretion-producing processes of his body, so that digestion-promoting chemicals such as saliva and gastric juice would no longer be emitted into his alimentary canal. He did not want to eat the bees, after all; he merely wished to imbibe them, to welcome them into his body, to allow them to inhabit the fleshy grottos of his digestive tract

Then he stuck out a tongue both dry and tasteless, providing the bees with an alighting board to help them gain entrance. A few bees were enticed enough to venture into Wendell's mouth; he could feel them inspecting his tongue, the roof of his mouth and the insides of his cheeks. He offered them a silent invitation to continue further. When, finally, one of the bees brushed past his palate and moved forward to explore the darker regions of his throat, Wendell knew he had succeeded. And sure enough, no sooner did this first reconnoitering insect pronounce its satisfaction with this new chain of cavities than the swarm outside began to drop onto Wendell's tongue and follow each other into his mouth.

Wendell had swallowed many inanimate objects in the course of his life but very few living creatures. The goldfish he had ingested during his county fair shows had been taken in one at a time and almost immediately regurgitated. Now he was filled with a plethora of feverishly buzzing insects, a dense mass of vibrating life.

He rose laboriously to his feet. His abdomen was bloated with bees. He could feel all those tiny bodies inside him, crawling over each other, hectic in their need, working away inside his stomach. They clogged his esophagus and mouth, too, necessitating a Herculean effort on his part to keep his gorge from rising. Breathing seemed to be a bit of a problem, also; but by taking short, quick inhalations through his nose he appeared able to overcome that dilemma.

Wendell placed his hands delicately on his bulging belly. His stomach rolled as the ball of bees inside him turned and moved around, shifting, ever shifting, and his hands rose up and came down like driftwood.

Brimming now with intent and insurance, he started walking back toward the secondary highway where the bus had let him off. He had scarcely traveled a hundred meters, however, when he fell to his knees by the side of

## THE RAT, PEERING OUT, SEES JUSTICE DONE

the road, his guts heaving with spasms. As bees pushed into his nasal cavities and flew from his nose, Wendell realized the bees wanted *out*. He didn't *want* to let them go, but a much more explosive result was a definite possibility if he didn't comply. Reluctantly, he opened his mouth, and the bees streamed from his body in a bright yellow tide.

Wendell was desolate. Feeling strangely barren and purposeless, he watched for some minutes as the bees foraged among the wildflowers. When the bees began returning to Wendell, buzzing insistently against his lips, he realized their departure had merely signaled an urge to gather nectar. Wendell gave his bees a wide smile and welcomed them in.

The second time foraging became an issue, Wendell was better equipped to understand his inhabitants' needs. The bees flew away to perform as nature intended, and Wendell was there to accept them when they returned. He and the bees, it seemed, had formed a somewhat uneasy yet accommodating alliance.

Traffic on the secondary highway was light this early, with most cars being driven by elderly women glaring suspiciously at Wendell and his bulging belly as they drove on by. Finally, he was picked up by an overweight trucker who must have thought Wendell's lumpish figure signified an appetite for beer matching his own considerable passion. Naturally, he drove a gleaming black cab hauling a long load of Moosehead.

"Where ya headin'?" this hairy, big-armed mountain of flesh growled out around a mouthful of spit.

Wendell reached into his pants' pocket and pulled out what was left of the fire-blackened match-card. He passed it to the trucker.

"*The Barb & Cat* in Tronna? C'ain't say ah ever hearda the place, but there's gotta be a milliona those joints strung all up and down Yonge." His devilish grin lit up his greasy, fat face. "Helluva lotta pussy, ah'd say!"

Wendell took back the match-card. Outside the truck the countryside rolled past in long stretches of unfocussed greens and browns like brittle film clattering through a projector. Lulled by the view and the hypnotic rhythm of the big truck's motion, Wendell felt himself starting to doze. In some inscrutable yet eerily discernible way he knew he had to remain vigilant, and he shook himself into wakefulness, in the process burping out a mouthful of bewildered honeybees. Desperately, he clutched at the tiny cloud of insects and tried to stuff them back into his mouth, even while more bees were maneuvering themselves for an unscheduled exit. His choking drew the trucker's attention.

"Hey, *Jesus!* If you're gonna be sick, don't fuckin' do it in my *truck*, dammit! In a choreographic routine the trucker applied the brakes, downshifted, turned off the radio, signaled for a pull over, and jabbed the button to open Wendell's window. Unable to resist the bees' impetus any longer, Wendell stuck his head out the window and spewed the insects into the air in a great buzzing swath. Decelerating though the truck was, the slipstream carried the bees swiftly away. Wendell watched in dismay as they disappeared on the wind.

The trucker brought the semi-trailer expertly to a halt some distance up the highway, inflicting Wendell with a string of colorful curses the whole time he was braking. Exhausted from both his ordeal and the loss of his bees to do anything but hold his head in his hands, Wendell first realized that things had gone terribly, terribly wrong when the trucker opened the passenger door from the outside and grabbed hold of Wendell, yanking him roughly off the high seat and down onto the graveled shoulder of the highway.

"I ain't got *time* for shit like this!" the trucker yelled in Wendell's face. "*No* one—" he slammed the door shut with one hand, and clutched a fistful of Wendell's shirt with the other " — pukes in *my* truck and gets away with it!" His grimey knuckles brushed Wendell's cheek in a menacing swipe. "I know I oughtta— *huh?*"

The sound was a ratchety swell, moving like a concussion wave. The big guy turned, and a storm of honeybees plunged from the air onto Wendell's face, covering his entire head within seconds in a great, writhing mass of shifting, buzzing bodies. The trucker—dumbfounded, and still stupidly hanging onto Wendell—watched in horror as the bees pried open Wendell's lips with a squirming, wriggling insistence, and forced themselves inside.

"Fuckin' *Christ!*" he bellowed, pushing Wendell away from him.

But not in time to escape the onslaught of the bees, so frenzied by their most recent expulsion that they just wanted IN. The trucker's mouth was an open invitation and they went for it in one fitful rush, cramming themselves feverishly between his bloated, mangled lips. The big guy managed only one pitiful outcry before crumpling backwards onto the gravel. His blistered and flatulent body belched out the surviving bees like a final gaseous breath, and Wendell welcomed them home with a big, fuzzy smile.

Swelled with much more than simple retribution, Wendell had the semi back out onto the highway in minutes, and although the powerful engine lurched through the lower gears, he managed to smooth it out eventually.

It was an obliging way to travel. Whenever the bees felt the need to forage, Wendell pulled the truck onto the shoulder of the road, and waited patiently for them to rejoin him. He knew they would return: he and the bees, in the short time they had been hosting each other, seemed to have developed an almost symbiotic relationship. When they were gone he still felt tied to them somehow, as if he could sense where they were, see what they were doing. And *they*—through a similar link their intimacy had established—seemed able to correctly determine *his* location. Quite simply, their affiliation worked, to each other's advantage.

In this way Wendell made it to Toronto in a few short hours. He finally left the semi stuck in traffic after taking a wrong exit onto Bayview Avenue, and started walking from there.

Yonge Street (when he eventually found it) was long and loud and crowded even in the late hours of the night. There was music everywhere: loud raucous, cheerless music designed only to wear people down and energize their inner torments. It was the soulless breath of a soulless place, and Wendell despised it. Fortunately, he could walk along without its maniacal rhythms affecting him: his more harmonious absorption reflected the natural cadence of his tiny, buzzing passengers, who filled his body with theirs, and eased his mind with the song of the hive.

When he found it, *The Barb & Cat* was just as he remembered it: colored lights around the marquee and the perimeter of the building, neon figures of dancing girls and beer bottles in all the windows, pools of vomit and puddles of piss spotting the sidewalk. The brick building seemed almost to shake with the intensity of interior sound.

Wendell stepped into the alleyway next to the club, spent a few minutes in an anxious though eventually productive search, then returned to the sidewalk with his prize clutched securely in his pocket. He pushed open the door and walked into the noisy revelry of *The Barb & Cat.*

The place was packed. Music filled the club. Crimson laser-like beams flashed above the dance floor. Spotlights revealed half-naked women on an upraised stage, their limbs intertwined in a kind of choreographed sex show. People shouted at one another, laughing, hugging, holding hands, grabbing butts, trying to stake out little parcels of territory for themselves amongst the racket. The smell of beer and booze was rampant and sickening. Wendell let his gaze travel from one crowded table to another, examining each glistening face.

*"Wendell! Hey, WENDELL!"*

Wendell's attention needed no more summoning. He saw the little man standing behind a table near the rear of the club, waving his arm in the air and smiling as he might at a brother he hadn't seen in years. Wendell kept his teeth tightly clamped and pushed his way through the crowd to see Tony.

"Wendell! Man, ain't you a sight fer sore eyes!" Tony's own eyes gleaned with an alcoholic haze. The cigarette between his lips smoldered like a detonator. "C'mre, c'mere! Jesus! How come you took off from Beth's place so sudden-like?" He pushed greasy hair off his forehead and winked at Wendell. "Ya know, kid, I think Beth might've had a hankerin' fer ya. Ya shoulda waited around fer seconds." His gaze shifted suddenly downward and latched onto Wendell's protruding gut. "Hey, kid, ain't ya put on a helluva lotta weight awful fast? What's gotten into you, anyway?"

"Bees."

Tony sat down, his eyebrows knitting together in a heavy frown. "Huh? What the hell're ya talkin' 'bout, Wend-ell? Jesus! You don't say a fuckin' word in all the time I know ya, then ya walk in here with your gut hangin' out and ya say *bees!* Wendell, you're just not makin' any sense!"

Tightly, Wendell said, "I borrowed a hundred dollars from you when I left, and I've come to pay you back for what you did."

"Well, heyyyyy! What's a few bucks between friends? There's plenty more where that came from, kid." Tony snapped his fingers soundlessly. "Hey! You thinkin' 'bout stagin' a comeback here, kid? I could try'n line up a few dates fer ya, if I kin sweet talk the owner inta forgettin' all 'bout your *last* escapade. Whaddaya say?"

## THE RAT, PEERING OUT, SEES JUSTICE DONE

Wendell said, "I thought tonight would be a good time."

Tony shook his head and draped an arm around the bare shoulders of the woman sitting next to him. "Uh, uh. No can do tonight, kiddo. As you can see, I'm busy, and the club here's already booked. Come and see me at my office," he finished, laughing.

The bees were restless. Could they sense what Wendell had in his pocket, or was it just time to forage again? In any case, Wendell felt ready to perform, booked or not. He pulled the squirming rat from his pocket.

Tony's hearty laughter disintegrated as if crushed beneath a boot heel. The woman beside him screamed and jumped to her feet, knocking over her chair and two others. The maniacal rhythms of the music pounded into Wendell's blood and set his brain afire.

"Christ, Wendel—" growled Tony, pushing himself to his feet " — are you *crazy*, bringin' that thing in here? Give your fuckin' head a shake, you brainless twit, and get the fuck outta here!"

The rat in Wendell's fist was writhing and squealing, desperately gnashing its sharp yellow teeth. Its filthy body exuded a smell like rancid cheese. Surely, if *he* could smell it, the bees could, too. And Wendell was well aware of how much honeybees hated the stink of rodents.

His stomach was burning. He felt like a cauldron of boiling water, red hot and foaming. There were sporadic outbursts of fright from other areas of the club.

Wendell said, "Where's your acting troupe now, Tony? Out on another rampage?"

Tony pushed aside his table and staggered out from behind it to confront Wendell. "Listen, freak, I don't know what your game is, but you're dead meat!"

Yes, thought Wendell. That is exactly what I am. Dead meat. And so is my father, and so is my mother, and so are my honeybees, and so are you, Tony Sepata. *You* are dead meat, too.

Tony's thick, short fingers clamped onto Wendell's wrists, but he was too drunk to be effective. And with Wendell filled with a powerful purpose, a glorious, almost righteous ambition, there was no stopping him. Wendell raised his hand and shoved the rat head-first into his own mouth, watching the way Tony's eyes popped wide open, because this was not what Tony had been expecting at all. The little man let go of Wendell's wrists then, and started to pull away. But it was too late. Wendell opened his gullet and swallowed the rat whole.

His alimentary canal had already been filled with bees. When the rat began its descent, the bees went wild. His body rumbled, his insides twisted with contortions, and his stomach bloated like a bag of gas. Only when the rat slithered through into Wendell's stomach did the bees finally have an escape route from their trauma. In a desperate bid for freedom they exploded from Wendell's mouth, nose and ears in noisy, angry swarms, covering Tony's head first, then moving on to other men and women nearby, relentless in their frenzy, indiscriminate in their attacks. People screamed and charged for the exits, their arms and faces profusely punctured and bleeding from bee stings.

Trapped within Wendell's stomach, the rat wanted out, and it wanted out *now*. Confinement within Wendell's flesh was not a problem. By doing what it did best, the rat clawed and bit and scratched and gnawed at the membranous walls of Wendell's stomach and abdomen until it chewed its way successfully through to the outside.

At this point Wendell fell backwards to the floor, completely insensate to the pain his body had had to endure, a slash-like smile frozen on his face. He had seen what he had been dying to see: Tony's own greasy face, pierced and lacerated by hundreds of needle-sharp bee stingers, swollen by bee venom into a grotesque, inflated parody of a human head etched in crimson.

The honeybees struck person after person, again and again, repeatedly throughout the club, until there were no targets left alive, and no bees still living. A final hush fell over the club.

The rat, its initial bout of fright having evaporated while the bees' frenzy had been in high gear, now squeezed its blood-smeared body out of the hole it had clawed in Wendell's abdomen, and scrabbled for the exit, the country boy's ill-fated massacre already forgotten by the time it reached its garbage-congested heaven.

# Jane's Head

## by James Powell

*James Powell is widely recognized as one of the foremost writers of short crime fiction in the world today. For over 30 years his meticulously crafted stories in **Ellery Queen Mystery** have been amongst the most popular and critically praised in the history of that magazine, often combining elements of humor, menace, and outright fantasy. Jim once admitted that when he was a youngster, growing up in the last years of World War II in Toronto, he didn't read much mystery fiction but he did devour pulp fiction magazines like **Weird Tales**. Those early stories must have left an impression, as witness this latest Powell tale, written expressly for **Northern Frights 5**.*

"*...who clings to paranoia because it's better than its alternative,*" droned young Dr. Lehman sitting, hand over eyes, dictating into the recorder as George Muir, a spry, balding, ruddy-faced man in his mid-sixties ducked back into the office without knocking. When Lehman cracked his fingers to watch, Muir did an exaggerated tip-toe, pointing to the overnight bag he'd left beside his chair. He retrieved it and tip-toed out again, mouthing a silent apology as he eased the door shut behind him.

Muir hurried down the hall explaining himself to the security man at the desk next to the front door by raising the overnight bag head high. The man wished him a happy weekend.

Dr. Lehman encouraged his non-violent patients to spend an occasional weekend away. Until two weeks ago when a letter was forwarded to the hospital from his last address Muir thought he knew no one locally. In the handwritten note a Mrs. Jameson said his cousin Jane had asked that he be invited to her up-coming birthday party, a small celebration with a few friends.

Surprised to find Jane had retired to the Martinsville house where they'd first met over fifty years before, Muir consulted the hospital library atlas. He hadn't realized Martinsville was so close. Muir sat there with his finger on the map. Cousin Jane. She'd moved to England in the early Fifties, making something of a career for herself on the stage playing secondary roles and passing off her Canadian accent for American. She'd married several times, the last he knew to a Greek producer. Her husbands all seemed to adore her. Muir had never cared for the woman. Nevertheless blood was blood.

Dr. Lehman pressed him to go. He even offered the use of a hospital car. But Muir had his own in storage in town. This time as his devils closed in on him Muir had arranged for his doctor in Toronto to get him admitted to Meadowbrook Hospital and drove the seventy kilometers himself. There was, as he liked to tell himself, method in his madness.

So Muir called the number in the letter. Mrs. Jameson picked up the phone, her old voice coming alive at his news. "How wonderful," she said. "What a time we had finding you."

That night Muir lay in bed trying to place Mrs. Jameson whose tone had implied he should remember her. Could Jameson be Miss Fish the cook's married name? he wondered. But his memories of the Martinsville house were crowded with names and nicknames. Tin Lizzy, Mr. Jimjam, Shilly-Shally and Nonny. And Mr. Browning, of course. Muir fell asleep asking himself why "of course"?

The next morning he walked into the village to pick up his car and a small birthday present. He quickly found his gift in "Oldies But Goodies," a side street sun-porch converted into an antique shop, it's windows crammed with colored glass and china.

Reaching behind a grouping of blue "Evening in Paris" perfume bottles with tasseled stoppers Muir drew out a porcelain doll's head perhaps four inches high with shoulder holes for a fabric torso. The face and perfectly marcelled blonde porcelain hair were the image of cousin Jane the last time he saw her. That had been in Toronto in the late Sixties. She'd been touring in a Noel Coward play and had come to somebody's wedding. Muir, just back from Cyprus, had been there in his dress uniform.

His hand trembled. It was Jane to the life. She'd remembered him and looked at him as clearly then as these blue eyes were looking at him now. He turned the head away as she had quickly turned her head, found someone else to go to and moved on. Amazing. Muir had the present gift-wrapped and placed it in the glove compartment beside his army pistol.

That was yesterday. Now, Muir emerged from the hospital into the late spring day with his overnight bag. He drove off, confident he could risk this little excursion. His devils never found him right off. So he was startled when, waiting for traffic at the end of the driveway, he looked in his rear-view mirror expecting to see the hospital, two piles of red brick connected by a newer administrative wing, and saw instead a field with a stream running through it. Before he could look again the break in traffic came. He took it, blaming what he'd seen on some trick of the angle of reflection.

But he was uneasy for the first few miles. His episodes always began with the rear-view mirror. First there'd be the gray-faced man in a sedan several cars back, then the same man walking a block behind him on the street. Within the next few weeks a second gray-faced man would appear beside the driver and the sedan would inch closer. Now two men were walking behind him. Walking in step. (Dr. Lehman always found this last significant.) Later the men would increase to three, then four and the sedan would pull up directly behind him. And sometimes when he looked in the rear-view mirror they weren't men at all, but ugly alien things, each with a slot for its single eye and long anteater nose.

Meanwhile the people in the cars going the other way began laughing as though listening to the same hilarious radio station, one he could never find on his dial. But he saw how their eyes were watching him. Muir would turn away, knowing they had marked him as every kind of coward. When he forced himself to look again the car occupants would be forward facing, deadpan, lips barely moving as they whispered among themselves.

Muir never saw the fifth man but knew when he'd come. A tail-gating black van with tinted windows replaced the sedan. That's when the tunneling would start. (Muir used to joke darkly to himself that the fifth man brought the shovels in the van.) At night he would wake to the sound of digging under the bedroom floor. Just when they were about to break through he'd do something to hurt himself or run amok in a polite kind of way and get sent back to the hospital.

Muir tightened his jaw. Well, his tormentors were in for a surprise. He kept the pistol close at hand now. He had resolved to go down fighting. The next time it would be do or die.

As Muir passed a pile of black rubber lugged on the road where a six wheeler had blown a tire he checked the rear-view mirror again. Nothing in back but semis. Then in the mirror he saw the pile of rubber heave itself to life, lengthen and lumber low across the highway dragging its fat tail behind it.

Muir put the creature down to an overwrought imagination. Still it made him afraid for it was not the form his delusions usually took. And better the devils you know than those you don't. He wondered if he should tell Dr. Lehman.

Dr. Lehman believed the Cyprus business lay behind his problem. Following his father into the army, Muir had served as a officer in the Canadian contingent with the UN forces sent to the island to maintain the peace. In spite of all his care to disguise his cowardice five of his men had found him out. He knew. He heard their contempt when they called him "sir." The UN had set up a Green Line of mine fields, observation posts and road blocks to separate the Greek and Turkish cypriots. The Canadians sometimes used a winding road through one mine field as a short cut between posts on either side of the line, nosing their trucks slowly and carefully along the tire tracks. Over the next few weeks Muir practiced that road until he could take it at top speed. Then he found a reason to pile those five men into a truck with orders to follow him close behind. Muir drove off through the mine field picking up speed at every turn. Coming out of the last one he glanced in the rear-view mirror and saw their faces. Who was the coward now? As he watched the truck slid wide on a turn and exploded.

Muir never blamed himself for those deaths. The damn fools should've slowed down if they couldn't stand the heat. Oh, he'd have lined them up and cursed them as gutless wonders. That was the whole point of the drill. The military inquiry had exonerated him.

Fifty kilometers below London Muir left Highway 401. The town names were all foreign to him until he reached Jellicoe. Muir's mother had died in the spring of 1941 while his father was serving overseas in the war. "Remember to get off at Jellicoe," were the parting words of the elderly man from his father's regimental association who, avuncular and eager to be useful, had guided the ten-year-old Muir with echoing footsteps through the Union Station vastness to his train.

Both his father's aunts were waiting at Jellicoe in their little Austin. Aunt Elizabeth smelled of horehound cough drops, Aunt Sally of cigarettes. The whole ten miles to Martinsville they talked proudly about his father. Jane had nicknamed Sally Aunt Shilly-Shally because she couldn't hurt anyone's feelings. And, yes, it came back to him now, Aunt Elizabeth was Tin Lizzy because her denture made whistling sounds when she spoke. Somehow Muir had gotten it into his head that Tin Lizzy was the ballerina of brightly painted tin which stood on one foot atop a musicbox base in the glass-fronted corner cupboard filled with dolls and stuffed toys in the third floor nursery.

"That's Odette-Odile, a friend of my childhood on loan to Jane," Aunt Sally had said, noticing his interest. "Wind her up she dances to a tune about a swan.

"And the donkey's Nonny," added Aunt Elizabeth. "Used to be called Old Joe or something before that. Jane came running in with it once, crying because she'd pulled the tail off. And while I got my sewing basket Sally noticed the stuffing, a kind of excelsior that looked like hay. 'You should call it Hay-Nonny-Nonny,' she said. "And that got shortened to Nonny." Here Aunt Elizabeth got into a fit of whistling laughter.

"The cupboard's locked," Aunt Sally said. "Your cousin Jane took the key with her. She wasn't supposed to. But never mind. You don't play with dolls, right?"

Muir learned that Jane's father was overseas, too, in the RCAF and her mother was away doing war work with the Red Cross. Jane was visiting her grandmother in Halifax.

Yes, things were coming back to him. Just before Martinsville he came up on the cemetery where Aunt Elizabeth and Aunt Sally were buried, the entrance marked by two gray brick columns topped with stone balls, one draped with ivy the other bare. In the rear-view mirror they became Aunt Elizabeth in a green dress and Aunt Sally in her gray skirt and cardigan. Aunt Sally waved. It may have been another trick of the reflection but the gesture seemed one of welcome rather than farewell.

In Muir's day Martinsville's main street had been wide enough for a farmer's horse and wagon to stand at the hitching rail on either side of the street with room for traffic in between. Now this abundant middle was a small park about an old high-caliber machine gun, a relic of the First World War that used to stand next to the lawn bowling club.

The Martinsville house was at the far end of town on a street lined with old trees where the cement sidewalks looked as if some ridge-backed, underground thing had tossed the slabs about in a rush at its prey. Muir pulled into the small circle of driveway. Before he was half out of the car a white-haired, stoop-shoulder woman in a flowered dress called from the front door. "Mr. Muir? Welcome. How we've all changed."

He recognized her voice from the telephone. "A lot of time under the bridge, Mrs. Jameson."

"You've come alone?"

Muir smiled at the peculiar question. "Just me, myself and I."

After a moment she smiled back. "You'll like to clean up after your drive. I'll show you your room." She led him inside and up the stairs.

Muir found the house unsettling. What he remembered, what he'd forgotten, what had and had not changed, all left him feeling like a child trying on the glasses of its own old age. To focus himself he said, "I remember you now. You're Miss Fish."

She laughed, head tossed back. "That's rich. Fish was our name for the goggle-eyed Miss Finn, the cook. Remember?"

When they reached the third floor Mrs. Jameson opened a door and gestured him in. "The wash room's at the end of the hall, in case you've forgotten that, too. Come down when you're ready. We eat a bit late. I always say the curtain doesn't go up around here until the sun goes down." She left Muir wondering, but not wanting to ask, if this had been his old room. Then he took a towel and wash-cloth and went down to the end of the hall.

On the way back Muir stopped at the nursery's open door. Storage boxes had replaced the bookcases and the black-board on a wooden easel. A picture window overlooking the back garden had replaced the French doors opening onto a small, rotting balcony which, in Muir's day, was out-of-bounds for the children. The corner cupboard stood empty of dolls and stuffed animals. He recalled being drawn to the cupboard that first time by the vignette arrangement of the occupants, the carrot-topped Raggedy Ann doll peering down from the top shelf, the Andy grinning back up at her astride the stuffed donkey, the worn and sinister bear watching from the middle-shelf shadows, the ballerina Odette-Odile concentrated on the dance on the shelf below.

Muir remembered something and hurried back to his room. He knew a way to tell if it was the one he'd had that summer. Just inside the closet door he found a loose floor board. (Muir had always good at ferreting out hiding places.) Reaching in with two fingers he drew out something the size of his thumb wrapped in the metal-foil liner from an old cigarette box. Picking at the foil he uncovered a battered lead soldier in kilt and helmet, an officer wearing a gas mask with a breathing hose attached to a chest pack. The little figure waved a pistol on a lanyard and looked back over its shoulder, urging men forward.

Those many years ago, having led Muir to his seat in the parlor car, the man from the regimental association repeated, 'Jellicoe. Don't forget." Then he'd handed the boy a flat cardboard box and was gone.

Laid out inside the box against a printed scene of barbed wire and shell craters were six kilted lead soldiers. Not of Muir's father's regiment. Few Canadian regiments were represented in lead. But the kilt was close. Six highlanders with gas masks fighting yesterday's war, a bayonet charge through poison gas.

Muir turned the little officer in his fingers, remembering how he'd played with the soldiers in the back garden that summer, deploying them around forgotten flower beds and through the tall grass to triumph over an invisible enemy.

In August Jane had returned. Martinsville was where she went to school. Perhaps six months younger than Muir, she tossed her hair about to great effect and watched you with eyes bent on figuring you out. Jane would come out into the garden pulling the whole toy cupboard in a wagon and set them up for a tea party or some other social event. Sometimes George would join her for she had more imagination than he did. But party etiquette was strict. For example, one rule said the highland officer could attend but not the rank-and-file. Not even the sergeant, as Muir designated the soldier with a blob of lead on one foot from the molding process. (By that time he'd lost three soldiers, one down an outside drain, two more hidden somewhere and forgotten for an ambush which dinner interrupted. Muir's mother said he was careless with his toys.) Another rule made Jane the only one who could speak the voices of the dolls and stuffed animals. In fact Jane was a shrill task-master with her playthings. When one of them didn't look at her when she spoke to it, for example, she might grab the bear by a leg and beat the delinquent toy with it.

Sometimes Muir would go off by himself and play in another part of the garden. Jane's party chatter and his mouth arsenal of machine-guns and hand grenades made a strange mix to which was sometimes added growls and hee-haws when she chose to stage the epic battle between the donkey and the bear never before seen on stage or screen anywhere in the world.

Muir set the lead soldier and the memories on the bedside table and went downstairs. Mrs. Jameson was waiting for him in the living room. "Let's hunt Jane down," she said. "She's out in the garden somewhere."

They emerged from the back of the house onto a small brick patio with wrought-iron chairs and a glass-topped table. The old garden of overgrown lilac and gooseberry bushes was tended now and a small gazebo added toward the river.

"Yes, there they are." Mrs. Jameson nodded to three people starting up the slope from the gazebo, a woman in a wheelchair, another pushing her and a tall thin man walking beside the chair, hands clasped behind his back, a donut-shaped rubber pillow tucked like a cocked hat under one arm.

"Ned's bleeding piles still plague him," said Mrs. Jameson to explain the pillow.

Seeing them, the man jutted his long chin and hurried on ahead. He frowned at Mrs. Jameson and cocked an eyebrow in Muir's direction.

"Ned, you remember George Muir, Jane's cousin, whom I've been trying to reach."

Muir offered his hand. "Browning, isn't it?"

"Haines." The man spoke coolly, ignoring Muir's hand by stepping back to make way for the fragile woman in the approaching wheelchair.

After that first summer Muir had only seen Jane one other time at that wedding so long ago. Now here they were again. It made Muir think of the three groundhogs. Following the Cyprus business he'd been reassigned to a teaching job at the Royal Military College where he stayed until his father died and he could resign his commission. While there he liked to walk the woods. One spring he'd come upon a groundhog kit feeding up in a sagging mulberry sapling. He later learned that groundhog young were particularly fond of mulberry leaves. Two or three summers later close to the same spot he interrupted a groundhog in its prime with rich chocolate fur and fawn-colored forearms as it nipped off a tall wild carrot close to the ground. He watched it eat the stem inch by inch and then swallowed the flower whole before waddling off into the bushes. A few autumns later near the same place he surprised an old ratty-coated groundhog drinking at a mud puddle in the path. The creature looked up with a start, turned to run and ran head long into a stump before struggling away, sick unto death and blind. Later Muir had wondered if it hadn't been the same animal all three times. The three ages of man.

The woman in the wheelchair had large blue eyelids, withered skin over high cheek-bones and short white hair. Muir smiled at her. "Well, Jane," he said.

Mrs. Jameson and Haines laughed. The woman made a bitter, disgusted face. Smiling, Mrs. Jameson said, "Mademoiselle, this is Mr. Muir, Jane's cousin. Don't you remember him?" Making the face again, the woman turned away. "Ned," she said. Haines gave her the rubber pillow to hold in her lap and maneuvered her toward the house.

"Hello, George. What brings you here?" asked the woman who'd been pushing the wheelchair.

Jane? Muir would never have recognized her. Stiff and erect, she looked at him with incredibly tired eyes set in a face which was swollen in places, skin blue as skim milk.

Mrs. Jameson looked at Muir earnestly. "I invited him, Jane. It's time we found something out." She sat down on a chair, patting the arm of another for him to join her. "You remembers Mr. Jameson, I'm sure."

Muir made an apologetic noise. "So long ago."

"Oh, Red was hardly someone you'd forget, the steady gaze, the jaunty smile. He vanished, you know. When was it, Jane?"

Jane's attention had wandered. At the sound of her name she snapped her head around.

"When did my husband vanish, dear? I know you remember. You've reminded me about it enough times."

"On your wedding night." Jane's voice was flat but her eyes were hard and defiant.

"Yes, on my wedding night." Mrs. Jameson pursed her lips and smoothed her dress over her knees. "At the time Jane also hinted she might have hidden Red away somewhere and could bring him back whenever she felt like it. If I was very, very good. And, fool that I was I almost believed her. Until this terrible dream. I saw Red burning in a place of fire. Yet his face was smiling. 'Pray for me, Mac,' he said. 'Mac' was his pet name for me. Then he was gone.

"As you can imagine, Mr. Muir, I accused Jane of having consigned Red to the flames. That's when she changed her story and said he'd gone off with you."

Muir blinked. Then he shook his head. "I don't know what she's talking about."

Mrs Jameson nodded. "Thank you, Mr. Muir. I thought as much. Jane loves her stories. Once she even told us she'd shoved a ham bone up Red's ass and let the dog drag him off. Didn't you dear? Such language. And such anger after all these years. Yes, we'll have to work on that."

"Not for long," muttered Jane.

Mrs. Jameson didn't seem to hear. "Prayers mean he's in Purgatory," she said, marvelling, "And to think I didn't even know he was Catholic. Well, if it's prayers he wants, then prayers he shall get. Did you bring the wherewithal, Jane?"

Jane drew a handful of dried peas from a pocket, made a small pool of them on the bricks and knelt down gingerly.

"Ten 'Our Fathers' and ten 'Hail Marys' to begin, Jane. Say them carefully as you've learned them." When Muir tried to protest Jane cut him off with a look which seemed to say she could take anything Mrs. Jameson could dish out.

# JANE'S HEAD

Just then Haines called from the door. "Ann, we'll rehearse Jane's dance for tonight whenever you're done with her."

Mrs. Jameson didn't take her eyes from Jane. "Thanks, Ned," she said, a lilt of pleasure in her voice.

Muir looked from Jane praying to Mrs. Jameson listening to her pray. He shook his head and stood up. "All right, then, maybe I'll take a walk before dinner." No one answered.

Muir headed toward the gazebo, happy to get away. It was more than just their odd behavior. Memories were nibbling in around the edges, events becoming clearer. He needed to get them straight in his mind. He took the rough path down to the flood plain where it joined a narrower, more fluid path like the trail of some purposeful crawling thing following the river through shoulder-high, silver green touch-me-not.

That summer had ended in a rush as Aunt Elizabeth and Aunt Sally outfitted him for boarding school according to the Principal's hectographed list of boarder necessities, so many of these, so many pairs of that. Then Jane announced that they would celebrate his last full day at the house with the social event of the doll season, the marriage of Mr. Jimjam and Miss MacNaughty as she called the Raggedy Ann and Andy dolls.

Muir had come up to the nursery to help carry things down and found the French doors open onto the little balcony. Jane, pretending to hunt for something to use as the bridal veil, asked him to bring Odette-Odile in from out on the balcony railing. He knew at once that she was testing him. He knew Jane had gotten the ballerina out there by working her way along the still solid wood beneath the railing. But the thought of repeating what she'd done made his calves tremble. He shook his head firmly. "I promised Aunt Sally I'd stay off out there. A promise is a promise." Jane nodded as if she'd expected his answer.

The wedding ceremony that afternoon was quite a production with Nonny as minister, the bear as best man and Muir's officer, by that time the only lead soldier left, as father of the bride. With Odette-Odile condemned to watch from afar Jane would hum the music as well as doing all the voices. The cast-iron Boston bull terrier door-stop and the three ivory monkeys, see-no-evil, speak-no evil and hear-no-evil were recruited to beef up the congregation.

Jane started late and dragged the ceremony out, while making it clear she might at any moment cancel the whole affair. When at last they reached the part where Jane playing Nonny's voice asking who shall give the bride away. She answered herself in the officer's voice, "I, Captain Cowardly Custard, shall." (Muir had known for a long time what he was. That was just the first time he'd heard the word for it.) Then came the exchange of vows and of rings and the recessional with Jane humming and throwing confetti. Muir remembered the two red circles of excited happiness on the bride's cheeks.

That night he found the hiding place for the officer in the closet. He didn't want to take it with him or leave it for Jane to find. Early the next morning they drove him in the rain to the train. People from the school met him at the other end.

In the dormitory that night he found Mr. Jimjam in his tin foot-locker. He never knew why Jane put it there. He was happy enough that none of the other boys noticed. When he could he'd sneaked into the furnace room and pitched the rag doll into the flames. In her first letter Aunt Sally wrote among other things that Jane had accused him of taking away a doll and of leaving Odette-Odile out in the rain.

Why worry over ancient history? Those unpleasant people were Jane's delusions, not his. Or was that what bothered him? Muir smiled at the thought and himself for thinking it.

The air off the river had grown cold. Deciding he'd come far enough, Muir stopped in the path for a moment to look around. The river and the sky above it, the high, nodding trees and the sky behind them, one day when he died he would tuck these things around him in the grave. They would all disappear. It was time to return to the house where he was not wanted.

Muir came through the front door determined to drive back to Meadowbrook. He found everyone having a cocktail before dinner and listening to Haines' competent piano. Going upstairs, he packed and took his overnight bag out to the car. Then he got Jane's birthday present from the glove compartment and went back inside to make his excuses.

A newcomer, a large man with a flat nose and a head of curly brown hair was freshening his drink at the trolley of bottles and glasses just inside the living room door.

"I'm Jane's cousin, George Muir."

"I remember," said the man.

This inspired Muir to ask, "Browning, isn't it?"

The man shook his head. "Must have been two other guys. I'm Pinsky. Rhymes with buttinski." The man walked away abruptly, exhibited a pronounced limp, one leg swinging out in a loose arc as he crossed the room to sit on an arm of the birthday girl's chair. Mademoiselle sat on her other side. Muir poured himself a stiff one for the road and stood off a bit, meaning to take his leave as soon as Haines gave the piano a rest.

At the end of a long Victor Herbert medley Mrs. Jameson looked in from the kitchen to call everyone to the table. They gave Jane the place of honor with Mademoiselle and Haines on her left and Mrs. Jameson and Pinsky on her right.

Why not eat, Muir thought, and drive straight through? Then he saw no place had been set for him. Mrs. Jameson brought him a plate and silverware without apology.

The mealtime banter was about people or events Muir did not know. He ate in silence. Toward the end of the meal during a pause in the conversation he opened his mouth to tell Jane the groundhog story when out of the blue she looked around the table and said, "When I moved back here after Marcus died I found myself with time on my hands and used to walk a lot along the Sydenham. One spring I happened upon a groundhog kit feeding up in a sagging mulberry sapling. I later learned groundhog young were particularly fond of mulberry leaves."

Listening to his thoughts coming out of Jane's mouth, Muir felt bafflement and a kind of stage fright like a leading actor who finds his soliloquies stolen by some bit players. Yes, Dr. Lehman would love all this.

"....the three ages of man," Jane was saying. "How lonely that made me feel. Well, it was my birthday. So why not do the cake and candles and make a wish, I told myself. And so I did." She smiled. "And one by one my friends came back to me. But now it's time for me to wish again."

Muir hadn't seen Mrs. Jameson leave the table. Suddenly she was backing out the kitchen door with a birthday cake and candles. Someone started "Happy Birthday to You" and Muir sang along with the rest.

"Remember, Jane, no wish unless you blow the candles out," warned Mrs Jameson. The others leaned forward as if they had an interest in the outcome. Jane closed her eyes for a moment, smiled confidently and took a deep breath.

"One," said Pinsky.

Jane added to the breath. "Two," said Haines.

At the instant Jane leaned forward she was startled by the telephone. "Three," said Mademoiselle. Jane blew badly. Hardly a third of the candles went out. Everyone groaned with mock disappointment.

"Why do wrong numbers always come at meal time?" asked Mrs. Jameson, coming back from answering the phone. "Someone for a Mr. Browning." When she saw the cake she added, "Even worse than last year, Jane. No wish for you."

Everyone adjourned to the living room with cake and coffee. As Haines drifted back to the piano with his pillow Muir said, "Jane, I just remembered something that requires my attention tomorrow morning early. I won't be staying the night." No one protested. "But before I go I want to give you this."

Jane accepted the present with a puzzled smile. When she pulled out the bisque head she seemed delighted, holding it at eye level on her palm. Then she recognized herself and gasped.

Before she could close her hand over the head Mrs. Jameson pounced and snatched it from her. "It's Jane's head!" she cried, happy as if it was a new toy. "Catch!" she called when she saw Jane coming toward her and tossed the head to Pinsky who had to limp backward to catch it. He threw the head across the room to Haines. Jane was tottering after her present on tired legs. Haines waited and then lobbed it over her head to Mrs. Jameson who handed it off to Mademoiselle. Mademoiselle let Jane get close before tapping the head on the chrome where it curved up to the arm-rest of her wheelchair as if shelling a hard-boiled egg. Jane clutched her temples in pain and stumbled. Mademoiselle made an unhand toss back to Pinsky who pretended to fumble the head.

"If it breaks I'll die," shouted Jane. "And you'll all disappear."

"Was that your wish, Jane, to die?" asked Mrs. Jameson, catching the head and slipping it into her pocket. "Or for us to disappear? Well, enough for now. Oh, we shall have so much fun with this."

Jane looked accusingly at Muir. "So that's why you came."

"Hey," said Pinsky from over by the window, "We got people in the garden. Women."

Mrs. Jameson turned to Muir and with contempt in her voice said, "Run off to your low-life lady-friends, Mr. Muir. I regret I ever invited you."

Muir turned red and headed for the front door. Behind him he heard Mrs. Jameson say, "There's a mosquito on your cheek, Jane. Here, I'll get it." Muir turned at the sound of the hard slap. A drop of blood stood thick and red at the corner of Jane's mouth. "Look, everybody," laughed Mrs Jameson. "I've knocked a bit of Jane's stuffing out. Here, I'll push it back in again." When she jabbed at the place with a balled up handkerchief Jane cried out in pain.

"Let me help," said Haines.

"You're hurting her," said Muir indignantly, starting toward them. But Mademoiselle wheeled herself into his path. "You had your chance to be a hero a long time ago, Mr. Muir. You didn't take it. This doesn't concern you."

When Jane cried out again Muir manoeuvred around the wheelchair and tried to force himself in between Haines and Pinsky. "Stop it. You're hurting her." Without a backward glance Pinsky swung a powerful arm that drove Muir into the wall.

"You're hysterical, Jane," said Mrs. Jameson in a calm voice. "I know the cure for that."

The slap came again. Muir shouted, "Who the hell do you people think you are? What are you doing?" When they ignored him he rushed to the front door. He'd get the pistol, drive them all away and rescue Jane.

Muir hurried over to his car. He slid behind the wheel and sat there breathing heavily. His rescue resolution vanished in the night air. Had it ever been more than an excuse to get outside? That house was madness. But it was Jane's madness, not his. He imagined Dr. Lehman's furrowed brow over all of this.

If Muir started now he'd be back at the hospital near midnight. He picked up the car phone to call ahead so they'd alert night security to let him in. But a recorded message insisted the number he dialed wasn't in service. When he asked an operator to put him through she could find no listing for a Meadowbrook Hospital. Muir sat with the phone to his ear, imagining a pleasant meadow beside a quiet brook. Well, anywhere was better than here.

He turned the key in the ignition. But when he glanced in the mirror he saw women stood in the tail-light glow. Now a head loomed large in the driver's side window, a head with a slot for an eye and an anteater nose. Muir fumbled to lock the door. Then the terrible head peeled away and became a face, a younger version of the avuncular man from the regimental association. A hand made a small cranking motion until Muir lowered the window.

The man's voice was not unkind. "I think it's time, sir. We're all here." Four more soldiers in kilts, helmets and gas masks were standing behind the car.

"Yes, of course, you're right," agreed Muir in a calm voice. He started to get out of the car.

"Did you remember to bring Mr. Browning, sir?"

Muir laughed at himself. "I'd forget my head if it wasn't bolted on." He leaned across the seat and took the pistol from the glove compartment. Then he got out of the car.

"We thought across the road in the pasture would be best, sir," said the soldier, his companions nodding and staring through their gas masks.

"Couldn't have chosen better myself," said Muir. As they marched down the driveway he noticed the soldier-spokesman's limp and added, "Sorry about the club-foot."

"Not your fault, sir. It's between me and my Maker."

When they reached the road Muir raised his hand and they all stopped. Looking left and right he motioned again and they crossed the road. On the other side of the split-rail fence the men halted. Muir knew they would go no further. "You men stay here," he ordered. "Goodbye, it's been a privilege to lead you."

"Goodbye, Captain Custard, sir," said their spokesman.

Muir marched fifteen yards further into the field, stopped and planted his feet legs apart. Ahead in the darkness a touch of mist hung over the creek bed.

Muir raised the pistol. Then he remembered something and looked back over his shoulder. The soldiers had taken off their masks. Three were smoking. Another scraped mud from his boot with his bayonet. The one with the club-foot was watching Muir.

"When I pull this trigger you'll all disappear," Muir warned them.

"Do what you have to do, sir," he said. "It's all the same to us."

Muir blinked. Now the soldiers were gone. He was alone in the pasture. Above him when he raised his head was a sky of stars. And he remembered what Dr. Lehman had been saying into the recorder that very morning, how paranoia was better than the alternative.

That must mean that he was cured. For he knew now that no one was conspiring against him. More than that, he knew with complete certitude that neither here on earth nor anywhere in this galaxy or in the many universes beyond it was there one single creature that cared whether George Muir lived or died.

He heard the piano from the house, music as sad and beautiful as a swan. He imagined Jane up on one leg with the other stretched out behind her turning her old aching bones while Mrs. Jameson, Mademoiselle, Haines and Pinsky enjoyed her pain. Poor Jane.

Yet as Muir raised the pistol to his temple there was a moment when he envied the woman her madness.

# Doing Drugs
## by Sally McBride

*The author writes: "'Doing Drugs' stemmed from an idea my husband Dale Sproule had that wasn't working for him. With his encouragement I melded it with a feeling I had that certain kinds of horrific experiences contain a sort of terrible beauty that, while perhaps being incomprehensible (and even deadly) to humans, exert a pull that is not cerebral at all, but entirely of the gut. Or the heart. How far might a person go to glimpse that strange and frightful beauty? Or to try and control it? How far might they force someone else to go?"*

C.K. Wallis, on the gurney beside mine, raised his head and looked at me. "Hey, you ever see that movie, *Mariachi?*" he asked. "The one about the crime-fighting Mexican guitar player?"

I turned toward him. "Yeah. Pretty good movie."

"The director, guy named Robert Rodriguez — he financed that movie doing drugs." C.K. let his head fall back on the pillow, smiling. The tube trailing from his arm up to a drip-bag glistened in the overhead fluorescents. "Doing drugs."

"Just like us."

He laughed. "Yeah, just like us." His pillow wore a mint-green cotton case, mine daffodil yellow.

C.K. was a little guy, skinny and intense, with a well-trimmed Vandyke beard and an old case of acne that had left his skin pocked and rough. He had charm, though; I'd seen it work on women where my own brand of nice-guy, smooth-cheeked friendliness bombed out. I didn't hold it against him. We were in the same business, after all.

We had been given our doses of Drug X about five minutes ago. If C.K. were anything like me, he'd be preoccupied with monitoring his body's reactions. If any. The big bonus in this sort of thing was being in the control group; though, as guinea pigs — even high-priced ones — we weren't told at the outset.

There were four others in the test with us: a couple of clean-cut guys, probably students from Calgary's University, a depressed-looking middle aged woman with long brown hair in a braid, and a native who looked barely out of his teens. We all ignored each other after the initial, perfunctory, introductions.

I knew C.K. because we'd done this before. I'd met him here in Calgary at another outfit, Krane Pharmaceuticals, two years ago when he'd looked about a decade younger. He'd needed money for an amplifier. I'd needed money because... well, just because. I always need money. I liked him; he was weird in an interesting way, the kind of guy who reads everything and really thinks about it. And likes to talk. We'd talked about life after death, telepathy, aliens, women (perhaps the same thing), what we wanted to do after we made our pile. Late-night stuff. I always got the feeling, though, that he was holding something back. Perhaps he felt that I couldn't keep up (I'd grant him that), or that I'd think he was nuts. Well, yeah, I thought he was nuts, but I wouldn't tell him so, and it didn't matter. Call him intuitive maybe, even a little psychic.

I learned that C.K. stood for Chester Kyrome, but I knew better than to challenge him with it. My own name is just as stupid, but in a boring way: Ken Dill. Anyone who used to call me Pickle is long in my past now, and C.K. wouldn't dream of it. We reckless souls who barter our bodies' chemical integrity for the drug trade know better than to tease one another.

But then, we don't do it for the money, do we? No sirree. We do it to better humankind.

It was nice to meet up with C.K. again; always good to get reacquainted with people in the business. Often they have leads for trials that pay big and have attractive odds for minimal side effects.

I wanted to talk movies with him, but as my own IV tube dripped fluid clear as a mountain stream into the vein of my left arm, I began to taste mint. It was quite distinct, filling my mouth, and I wondered if the taste had been influenced by the color of C.K.'s pillowcase. Probably something I should report. Or maybe I should tell them it was butterscotch, throw a skew into the stats.

Just then the clinic's background noise — ventilation, subdued beeping from monitors, distant traffic — changed, just a bit, and since counting things is one of my little tics I started tracking the seconds, arriving at 35 before realizing just what had changed. C.K.'s breathing, which had whistled softly through his nose before, had stopped.

He looked okay, just lying quietly staring up and blinking. He started breathing again after 74 seconds, something I'm sure of because I take all this quite seriously (mint, definitely mint).

He opened his mouth wide and took a slow hard gasp as if his airway was constricted. There were two nurses in attendance for the six of us in the room, but they were by the door talking and had noticed nothing.

"This... this reminds me of drugs I had to pay for," C.K. remarked. His voice was sludgy and slow, and his fingers were flexing as if he were playing a very relaxed riff on his guitar.

"You okay?" I asked.

"Sure am." He was staring dreamily at the ceiling. "Kind of... disconnected. Possibilities... poss..i..."

Then his eyes snapped open, suddenly alert. He turned his head as if he were following something with his eyes. He looked surprised, even intrigued.

"Hey, what're you —" I stopped as he went rigid on the gurney.

He gasped and his hands clenched so hard his knuckles went white. I could hear the tendons pop. His back arched, and he began a series of short, hard shrieks as if he were being stabbed. The mouthwash taste on my tongue went sour, things turned white in my vision as I tried to struggle up.

He flipped over the edge of his gurney and hit the linoleum floor in a crash of metal as the IV pole came down with him. He started to strobe, white, grey, white. Whatever we were on was hitting me too, but in a different way.

Still shrieking, he snatched the tube from his arm, ripped off the adhesive tape and began to tear at the shunt imbedded on the back of his wrist.

The nurses ran over and pulled his hands back, one of them shouting for the researcher in charge. C.K.'s arm leaked blood as he sprawled on the floor, dazed and panting. The nurses began to hoist him back onto his gurney.

Doctor Lamb, "call me Sue", a pretty, thirty-something woman with short blonde hair and a soothing demeanor, was in charge of this test. She had introduced herself and the company to us at the start of the trials, explaining that her job at Psilan Limited was to develop a bonding agent to deliver several of the new line of anti-psychotics the company was pushing. She had three groups throughout the facility testing different variants, and was a busy woman.

Oh, I shouldn't use that word. *Pushing*. That definitely sends the wrong signal. You've got to toe the party line if you expect to be employed in this biz.

The first test I was involved in, for a drug that left me perky and obsessively detail-oriented for several days, was for a successful drug that's now on the market under the name Morvrit. The one we were testing now was obviously in the early stages of human trials, and if it kept doing stuff like this might not make it past them. But you couldn't bet on that.

There was some disjointed murmuring from the other subjects, who were looking much the way I probably did: bleary and apprehensive. The native man was sitting cross-legged with his sheet pulled up to his chin, watching the rest of us as we blinked and fretted. Mr. Lucky, the control dude.

Doctor Lamb arrived then, at a brisk walk. Her legs were very good, rounded calves and slim ankles strobing and twinkling, white-white, black-white.

She oversaw a quick blood-pressure check, peered into his eyes with a tiny flashlight, then they all retreated to a huddle and began to argue ferociously. I couldn't hear their words. To hell with them.

"Hey, man," I called quietly to C.K. "You okay?"

He turned his head very slowly and looked at me, his eyes full of some far-off vision that I didn't really want to ask about. He licked his lips. The strobing was still at it; his tongue seemed to be flickering very fast in and out, like a lizard's. "Yeah."

"What a kick, huh? You oughta get a bonus for this one." I tried to give him an encouraging smile.

"Yeah." He looked away again. After a while he said, "You didn't see it, did you?"

"Didn't see what?"

"The scorpion."

"Scorpion. No. No, I didn't." He seemed very serious. "What do you mean, exactly?"

"Well, I guess it was a scorpion. Looked like one, only bigger. A lot bigger, size of a, a Doberman." He fingered his IV shunt, and didn't smile. "Some kind of bug, anyway. It tried to sting me."

"That's when you jumped off your gurney?"

"Hey, wouldn't you?"

I suppose I would have. "Listen, C.K., that was some hallucination. You planning on telling anyone about it?"

"I'm telling you, aren't I?"

"Lotta good that'll do. I'm as crazy as you are."

He heaved himself up on one elbow and glared at me. "I'm not crazy," he hissed. "You got that? Whatever I saw, it looked fucking real to me, and no one can say otherwise."

"Okay, okay, you're fine. Whatever."

Dr. Lamb came over again and C.K. subsided, the whites of his eyes showing all around. I could see his hands gripping the thin mattress under his skinny hips.

"You boys all right? Kenny?" Doctor Sue eyed me first, quickly, and seeing that I was my usual meek, puppy-dog self, turned her attention to C.K. "Mr. Wallis — C.K. — you gave us quite a scare. How are you feeling now?" She took his wrist between her thumb and first two fingers, feeling for his pulse, then replaced the pressure cuff around his upper arm, pumped it and whipped out her stethoscope for another check. "Hmmm. You're fine physically, a little tense maybe, but I'm interested in your mental state. I trust you'll tell me if you experienced any visual anomalies — anything odd at all." She flashed a concerned smile at him. He didn't smile back.

"Nothing I can put into words," he said tightly. I said nothing.

She tucked her stethoscope back under her jacket and eyed him seriously. "Do you wish to drop out of this test? It's perfectly all right to —"

"Hell, no." He barked a laugh. "I've got the money spent already."

"You'll still be paid."

This stopped him for a second; it stopped me. It told me that Psilan had serious doubts about this trial, and was probably regretting taking a couple of hard-case habitual drug-test abusers on board. Better to use death-row inmates, or chimps. But chimps are expensive, and they have groups of activists to care about them. Ditto death row inmates.

C.K. looked at me for a second, licking his lips. His eyes gleamed and he seemed about to say something, then Doctor Lamb laid her hand on his forehead, the way a mother will test her child for fever. At once C.K.'s eyes snapped away from me to focus on her. His mouth fell open, but he didn't say a word.

"I think you'll be all right," said Doctor Lamb, her voice as gentle as a summer breeze. "The reaction you had tells us a lot, and we'll be monitoring you more closely now. You're one subject in a thousand, C.K." She gave him a tender, glowing smile and ran her hand down from his forehead along his cheek and across his lips. His head turned to follow her hand as a baby's will in search of a nipple.

"You'll stick it out, won't you?"

After a while C.K. nodded. He was breathing hard, and damned if I couldn't see a rise in the sheet over his groin.

She looked at me with that same warm expression, but made no move to touch me. I felt somehow slighted, but also relieved. I don't know if I could have withstood that honey voice.

She'd never intended for him to leave. Her offer was a nod to legality, that was all. But what about me?

Maybe I should give a call to my sister in Vancouver, see if she could stand to put me up for a couple of weeks. I could catch a bus and be there overnight. It seemed like a good option, as long as I really could keep the money.

After a few words with the nurses she twinkled her way out again, white-black-white, the door sighing after her like a nerveless lover.

"Hey," I said in a low voice to C.K. "How about bailing with me? You heard what she said."

But he just looked at me, smiled wanly, and then fell asleep. Or maybe he was just feigning sleep to avoid talking.

I could feel myself coming out of the drug, and there was a general lessening of tension in the ward. The two students started chatting, the middle-aged woman fell asleep, and the native boy pulled a paperback book out of the pocket of his robe and dove in. Looked like a science fiction novel, lots of yellow and red on the cover.

During the time he read thirteen pages, I decided to stay. If this sounds crazy, then consider the career options open to a thirty-year-old dyslexic drifter such as myself. Drug testing is generally an easy living, and I wasn't about to jeopardize my chances of future work by jamming on this gig.

One of the students took Dr. Sue up on her offer to leave. The look she gave me when I said I'd stick it out, just like C.K., made me glow for hours; even though I knew that C.K. was her golden boy I basked. Shit, my own mother never looked at me like that.

We were split up that evening and put in private rooms, which made life pretty boring. The meals featured measured amounts of each of Canada's official food groups, none of which, unfortunately, includes chocolate. I swear this life is what keeps me healthy; I'd never take this kind of care of myself on my own.

I'd contracted for a week, but after four days I was thoroughly sick of the food, the nurses, daytime TV, and most especially the goddamn drug. I spent my hours in a minty haze, my vision bleached out and flat, my ears ringing. It was hard to say how the others were doing; I rarely saw anyone, and the doctors and staff were typically evasive. Perhaps it's hard for them to understand that I'm not as dumb as I look, and just might be interested, college degree or not.

But I suppose whether or not medication X was coming through the test satisfactorily was none of my business. After all, I only let it into my veins. I would have been interested particularly in what C.K. had to say about it, but the two times I tried to visit his room, Doc Sue was there hovering over him and it was pretty apparent no one else was welcome.

The time went by, the dosage was varied, and for some reason citrus fruits vanished from the meal menu, but I never experienced anything like what C.K. had gone through.

Then around nine on the evening of the fifth day I ran into him in the men's communal washroom. He smiled and gave me a toothbrush salute.

"Hey, how's it going?" I asked, expecting the usual okay-I-guess answer. The skin around the taped-on shunt on his wrist was vivid purple and puffy looking, not good, and his eyes were bloodshot and jumpy. Maybe *could-be-better*, or *it's-a-living*.

Instead of the noncommittal reply I'd expected he started talking—chattering really—about how terrific it was to be part of something larger than himself, how fulfilling to be a valued team-member on the cutting edge of medicine, and so on. All complete bullshit, unlike anything he'd ever said in the time I'd known him.

He looked deeply into my eyes as he rattled on, then seemed to get distracted by something just to the left of my head. I turned fast, but saw nothing. The back of my neck started to itch.

He turned to the mirror and began to brush his teeth like a robot, up-down up-down extremely fast. Then he spat pink froth and stared silently at his own face, mouth open. He looked like hell.

"Listen, man," I said, watching him, "they've got you on something way outside the scope of a few hundred bucks. You should call it quits. To hell with it, just — "

He shook his head, my druggy eyes making him strobe like a jerky film of a man saying no. In the mirror his lips spasmed and his tongue did that flickering lizard-thing again.

"I can't. They need me. Sorry, Ken, but you and the others just don't have what it takes to participate fully in this test. Not your fault, don't get me wrong."

I held up my hands. "Hey, suits me fine. I —"

"Susan is almost there. So far I'm the only one who can see them, but she's been getting readings —"

"See them? See what?" I was afraid I knew what the poor bastard was going to say.

But he just gave me that wan little smile again, now tinged with an air of sad superiority, an expression like what I'd imagine a saint would wear during a photo op. "I shouldn't be talking about it," he said.

I didn't know what to say. I could only hope that when the test was over, C.K. would regain his normal outlook on life and we could laugh about all this over a few beers.

I had turned to the washroom door ready to leave when he reached out and caught my arm. "Ken, I want you to get out of here. Don't tell anyone, just get out. Go to Vancouver like you wanted to."

I looked back. His hand was very hot on my skin. "What? It's you that should be quitting, damn it! I don't know what they've got you on, but it's sure nothing like what I'm getting." He shook his head. Just what *did* it take to 'participate fully' in this test? "Come on, we can leave together, just get our stuff and go."

He wasn't listening to me. His left arm was swollen all the way up to his elbow now, a truly nasty grey-purple. He was looking over my shoulder again, his expression alert, expectant, and I couldn't prevent myself from looking too, towards the wall behind me.

Nothing. But there was a feeling... a sound maybe. I frowned and looked back at C.K., whose expression hadn't changed. As if he was waiting for something. There. My ears pricked. Yes, a sound; a chitinous rubbing, dry and whispery, gone as I focused on it. Nothing. The mirror behind C.K.'s head rippled like heat waves over pavement. He let go of my arm.

The door behind me opened, making me jump, and in came one of the orderlies, a tubby man named Brian with pale skin and a large gold earring in his left ear. A nice guy, friendly, always ready with a joke.

"I'm just leaving, Brian," I said to him, my voice sounding angrier than I'd intended. "Maybe you should check C.K.'s arm or something. Looks bad to me, but what the hell do I know?" I left, fed up with the whole situation.

Behind me I could hear Brian say something to C.K., I don't know what. To hell with him, I thought. He's managed to brainwash himself, it's no business of mine. Let the forefront of modern medicine take care of him.

I went to the common room and watched TV until 11:00, our lights-out, and hit the sack.

I had a hard time staying asleep though. I felt bad about C.K., and about myself too. What if we all went nuts from this drug? I'd been through some rough tests — nausea, heart flutters, muscle spasms — but nothing like this focused delusion of C.K.'s. It worried me.

My eyes persisted in popping open, and I started to get thirsty. The only option was sneaking water from the tap in the washroom, as our food and liquid intake was strictly monitored; drinking extra water was against the rules in the contract I'd signed, but at this point I'd lost interest in caring. I slipped out of bed and padded down the hall.

In the washroom was Brian, sprawled flat out on the floor and looking very dead indeed, his head at an angle against the wall, gold earring gleaming. His pale flesh had gone dark, and was so swollen it had burst the seams of his white polyester uniform in places; the skin bulged out shiny as a ripe eggplant.

"Hey," I heard myself say weakly. "Hey, someone!" No one could hear me. I put my hand over my mouth. The air smelled acrid, vinegary and thick, and the shiny white tiles behind Brian's head strobed in time with my heartbeat.

The body moved, turning slowly as if he was preparing to get up.

I backed hard into the door before realizing it was just his flesh still swelling, rolling him to one side as the body's balance shifted. He wasn't really moving.

I got out of the washroom somehow and stood in the corridor for a moment gathering my wits, trying to get my stomach back in place, then I walked carefully to the nurse's station. No one was there. I had to wait for her, a redhead named Beverly, to return from wherever she'd gone to tell her what had happened. She frowned and made me get back in my room before she'd even check the washroom, damn her; probably thought I was making a joke. Some joke.

The next morning Doctor Sue came into my room ahead of schedule. I was sitting on my bed pretending to scan a magazine, though at the best of times the words elude me. She walked over and sat on the edge of the bed, smiling at me. Not a happy or cheery smile, mind you; a sad smile. A smile much like the one C.K. had worn last night in the washroom.

"I understand you were the one who found Brian last night," she said. She paused and sighed deeply. "A very unfortunate thing to happen. As a representative of Psilan, I apologize for any distress it may have caused you." She smiled a little harder, dimpling charmingly. "As a human being, Ken, I feel shocked, and very sorry of course for Brian. And for you."

She patted my knee. I drew myself up to sit cross-legged, pulling away from her hand. "Ken," she said, "Brian was a man suffering from an allergic condition much more serious than he—or anyone here—was aware of. Apparently he was bitten by an insect or spider and had a severe reaction. Nothing could have been done to save him."

She watched me. Would I buy it?

Why sure, Doctor Sue. Would you lie to me?

After a while I realized she wouldn't look away until I replied. I swallowed and said, "Uh, Brian was an okay guy. It's too bad he had that, that condition."

Her dimples deepened, and she stood briskly. "I'm sure you'll be glad to know that the test is working out extremely well. It's people like you and your friend Mr. Wallis who make things happen—for the betterment of all."

Jesus Christ. Were they all brainwashed? Or was I simply too much of a cynic? I tipped an imaginary hat to her as she left, feeling a shiver crawl up my back. She never spent more than a couple of minutes with me anyway, and now I was sure she was headed for C.K.'s room to practice her bedside manner on him. Her golden test-boy, her key to... what? What did she want, and what the hell was she giving him?

Two more days. Should I stay or should I go?

Well, hell. What was two days? What was the death of Brian? Maybe he really had been allergic to spider bites. Just possibly I was a panicky idiot under the influence of a slightly hallucinogenic drug, and I should just take it easy.

So. Mint, and boredom, and the nagging sensation of something flickering just outside my vision. Soft dry rubbing sounds behind my head. *Nothing.*

I looked at pictures in magazines, making up stories about them, but all the stories ended in something swollen and purple and dead on the floor. *Take it easy.*

The IV dripped on schedule, I gave up my blood and shit and piss, I asked no questions and told no lies. All in the cause of science. Doctor Sue smiled at me and made it all worthwhile. Almost.

The last day. Five o'clock was checkout time, when we'd get our clothes back, our payment and our sincere fare-thee-well. Goodbye Psilan Limited.

I hadn't seen C.K. since that time in the washroom, but I wanted to either say goodbye to him now, or ideally, team up with him and head the hell out. I dressed, tucked my release form, insurance waiver, and cheque into my wallet and ambled back along the beige corridor one last time.

The place was deserted. C.K.'s room was at the north end; we'd all been scattered around the essentially empty second floor of the modern, glass-and-concrete facility, and I guess none of us had much felt like socializing. The idea is just to get through these things and resume life with money in pocket. Until you line up the next test.

C.K.'s room was empty, but it didn't look like he'd checked out yet. His jeans and a grey sweatshirt were folded neatly on the bedside chair, and a knapsack sat open on the bed, personal items scattered among the rumpled pastel sheets. I didn't see an envelope of the kind I'd received, with papers and payment in it; I assumed he was still winding things up. Rather than wait, I left his room to check around.

I found them outside.

Psilan's building, on the northern outskirts of Calgary, sported a rooftop sundeck from which you could see the Rockies to the west, and which might have been a great place to bask in warmer weather. But this was late October, and the sun was disappearing behind the mountains. We'd never used the deck, and its few metal chairs and tables were covered and stacked against a wall for winter. It was cold, the clear air darkening fast, yet C.K. was standing by the western parapet in his hospital pyjamas. The IV drip was in his arm, the chrome-plated apparatus holding the bag beside him. Doc Sue had her arms around him.

I'd seen C.K. charm the ladies before, sometimes getting women I'd thought were way out of his league, but I knew this contact had nothing to do with sex. C.K.'s slumped, dejected attitude radiated fear and despair. Maybe I can't read, but I'm good at body language. He might even have been crying, I couldn't tell from 20 feet away. I crept closer. They didn't see me.

She was talking very fast, a pleading note in her voice. — *work together, we have to work together for this*—

I don't know what I thought I could do; break up a scene, calm them down. I don't know. Before I got close enough to make out more words C.K. tore away from her and stumbled sideways along the waist-high barrier at the edge of the roof, the IV pole rocking behind him. I stopped behind a small naked birch tree in a tub, unsure of what to do.

She followed him, grabbed his good arm. He shook her off and she made angry fists, thrusting her neck out snake-like at him. Suddenly he fell to his knees clutching his head, and began to wail eerily. The IV pole fell, and he shuddered as the tube ripped out of the shunt and twisted away. I stepped forward then, but stopped as something large whipped past my ear.

I ducked and flailed the air, but there was nothing to see. The wind had picked up, and was scattering dust in my eyes.

Another harsh whir of air close by, a dim flash of gold in the corner of my eye, and acid in my nostrils. The wind pushed me sideways.

I shouted, "C.K.! Hey, are you all right —" but my voice was buried under a sudden hot roar of wind.

It was full of sand, stinging my skin, needle-sharp and burning, and I could barely breathe or see. I held my hands protectively before my face and groped my way forward to where I remembered C.K. and the doctor being. My eyes were streaming and my skin crawled and itched. The hot air seared my lungs. I would have turned and run then, had I been able to find my way back into the building.

"C.K.!" Something landed with a heavy thump on the deck beside me. Through my tears I saw it, a thing that looked very much like a huge scorpion, stinger raised. It had wings, though, stiff and transparent, and a blunt eyeless head that turned on its ropy neck, mantis-like and quick. Another landed beside it, and another. Heavy and golden-brown, glowing as if lit by some other sun than ours. A toxic desert sun.

I stood perfectly still, unable to move, perhaps instinctively knowing that if I tried to flee they'd be on me in an instant.

Through bleary eyes I looked up, cringing against the pitiful shelter of the little tree in its pot. The sky was beautiful, as if a master painter had laid a gilded wash across the air itself and made every molecule shimmer. The air was full of life, things like scorpions but not like: winged and gleaming, hard-shelled and fast as they swarmed overhead. The sky was like burnished brass.

I forced myself to take one step, then another, towards C.K. and the doctor, who clung together against the parapet.

The creatures were converging on them, crawling along the sundeck floor, diving from above, whirring and clacking. C.K. waved his arms feebly as two of them gripped him with their pincers and curled their stingers ready.

Doctor Sue lunged for them, trying I think to save C.K., but one of them drove its stinger deep into her shoulder. She spun around from the force of the attack, her mouth open as if in surprise, but she didn't scream. C.K.'s pointed beard stood out black against his skin. The doctor was struck again, and started to convulse spastically. C.K. pulled himself to his feet. He looked directly at me then, his eyes black pits, his face a bloodless mask.

"It's me," he cried over the acid wind, the pelting golden wings. "I'm doing it. God help me."

Then he turned, threw a leg over the parapet and with a quick twist dove over the edge, vanishing before I could do or say a thing.

I found myself sitting on the roof deck, my ears ringing. The cold Calgary evening was back huge and empty around me, blue pricked with a few white stars. The air had the flat dead smell of winter.

By the time I got to the edge and looked over, I was shivering uncontrollably. C.K. was a pale blob on the pavement below, unmoving.

There was no sign of the things I'd seen, not a stray broken wing nor shard of stinger; just Doctor Susan Lamb crumpled and twitching on the deck. She died as I bent over her in the falling dark. I didn't know what to do. *Nothing.* Get out.

Get out and don't look back.

There's nothing you can do.

There was no one around. I got my stuff and headed for the bus station.

# Night of the Tar Baby
## by David Nickle

*Each volume in our series has featured work by David Nickle. His novella "The Sloan Men" (**Northern Frights 2**) was reprinted in **The Year's Best Fantasy and Horror** (St. Martin's Press 1995) and was also produced as an episode in a major television anthology series. In 1998 he and Edo van Belkom — another **Northern Frights** stalwart — were co-recipients of the Horror Writers Association's prestigious Bram Stoker Award, the world's top honor in the dark fantasy field.*

*Despite its title, David points out that his latest story has little to do with Disney's racially stereotyped **Song of the South** film, based on Joel Chandler Harris' famous Uncle Remus stories, other than his own fascination with one of the tales. "All I was thinking about," he writes "was the folly of dumb little Bre'er Rabbit, who one day stokes his anger so hot he lays into Bre'er Fox's tar baby trap with both fists flailing, and survives to regret it — but only barely."*

A nasty breeze caught the fumes off the still-bubbling tar pot and brought them along the shortest route it could find into Shelly's nostrils. It was the foulest thing that Shelly had ever smelled; tar fumes stank like distilled pain, a kick in the gut or a smack across the ear, and they made her cough when they reached down into her lungs. At the sound she made, her brother Blaine punched her hard in the side.

"Shut up!" he hissed. "We're gonna get caught!"

"You shut up!" said Shelly. It was a struggle to keep her voice from quavering — Blaine was thirteen, three years older than her, and he was starting to get his man-arm. He'd hit her harder than he knew, maybe, and her ribs ached from it.

"Quiet, both of you." Their Dad crouched beside them, behind the highway sign that announced a new Petro-Canada service centre was coming here by October. His arms were crossed on the wash-basin he'd brought with them. The trowel dangling in his hand cut through the air to emphasize what he said. "This is just what I was talking about back at the house. This is why we're here tonight. Time to stop all the fighting."

"Whatever," said Blaine. "This won't land you back in jail, will it?"

"This," said Dad, "will keep all of us from jail, for the rest of our lives."

"Then why are you stealing tar, not paying for it down at the hardware?"

"Got to be filched," said Dad. "That's part of the magic."

"Whatever." Blaine rolled his eyes.

It was pretty clear that Blaine didn't buy any of this—and Shelly knew she should probably defer to her brother's judgment. After all, the last time their dad had been home for any length of time, Shelly was just five years old; Blaine, at eight, had known their father that much longer—lived through five more years of dad's promises and schemes, aftermaths of his barroom fights and late-night visits from angry OPP patrol-men; Lord knew how many three-day benders with his former buddy Mark Hollins; and maybe one or two more solemn pledges to improve himself, and turn all their lives around.

Maybe Mom was right, and their Dad was just full of shit.

Dad started down from the sign, and into the midst of the construction site. The workers had laid foundations for the garage in a huge cinder block rectangle; there were more bricks stacked over by the trees, along with some lumber, and there was a yellow digging machine that Dad figured was to hollow out a place for the big tanks underneath the pumps.

But Dad didn't care about the digging machine, or where the tanks would go or anything else. He was after the tar-pot, which had been left simmering through the night. Dad figured they had about half an hour from the time the work crew left, to the time the night watchman arrived—and that would be plenty of time to do what they needed to do.

Dad set the basin down beside the tar pot, making the bent-up twigs and wire rattle.

"Get the turpentine ready," he said. "Blaine, you listening?"

"I'm listening." Blaine reached into his pack, and pulled out the shoe-box-sized tin of turpentine they'd brought along. "It's here," he said.

"All right." Dad set the trowel down a moment and rubbed his hands together. He reached into the breast pocket of his jean jacket, and pulled out a little brown plastic bottle Shelly recognized as one of Mom's old painkiller prescriptions. He pushed on the safety lid, twisted it open, and held it over the pot. After a couple of seconds, something thick and white like condensed milk dripped out, made a long, snotty line between bottle and pot. Dad held it there until the last was poured out, then threw the empty bottle behind him.

"Shelly," he said, "hand me the skeleton."

"Don't call it that," said Shelly quietly.

"That's what it is," said Dad, sounding puzzled. "But I won't call it that. Just give it to me careful."

Shelly reached down and lifted the thing from the basin. It wasn't more than two feet long—bigger than a newborn, to be sure; but not so big she should be scared of it. She shouldn't be scared; but when a still-green twig bent like an arm flopped against Shelly's knee as she lifted it, she nearly dropped the thing. Dad was right—this was a skeleton, and it was crazy to call it anything else. When she handed the skeleton off to Dad, she was trembling.

"I hate this," she said.

"I know." Dad smiled down at her with what seemed like real love—but it didn't make her feel better. He cradled the little wooden skeleton with nearly as much affection as he lowered it to the stinking tar.

"This is going to help us all," he said, as he dipped it head-first into the boiling tar. "Everything's better from now on."


"Dad?" said Shelly as they worked. "What do we need a tar baby for anyway?"

Dad was watching the tar. "You remember what I told you about Mr. Baldwin, don't you honey?"

Shelly remembered the story, all right; Dad had told it his first night back, while everyone sat around the kitchen table not looking at each other and picking at their food.

Mr. Baldwin was Dad's prison buddy—his cell-mate for years. And Mr. Baldwin swore by his tar baby; a little man he kept under his bunk.

Mr. Baldwin's tar baby was made from a pot on the roof of the pen's south wing when it was under construction back in the 1970s and Mr. Baldwin had drawn work duty there. According to Dad, Mr. Baldwin was a puny fellow, more like a boy than a man in those days, and although Dad wouldn't say why, small size and smooth skin was always a problem in a jail house. "Particularly when you're like Mr. Baldwin, and won't stand for nothing," he said.

Mr. Baldwin had explained how he'd made the tar baby when he and Dad were cell-mates for a few months before Dad's release, and Dad had paid close attention. After all, Dad explained—Mr. Baldwin was still alive after all these years, and although he wasn't any bigger, and his skin wasn't smooth anymore, it wasn't scarred much either. Mr. Baldwin said he'd never been forced to do anything he didn't care for, and over time since that day on the roof when the tar baby got born, everyone got to calling him Mister.

"It was a good time, when I was in with Mr. Baldwin," Dad said, eyes focused far away and voice gone wistful. "No threats, no fights—nothing bad, nothing harmful. Men were respectful. The tar baby taught *everyone* a lesson."

"Sounds boring," said Blaine, watching the tar boil and bubble, the brambly skeleton now vanished beneath its surface.

"Hush," said Dad. "You don't know what you're talking about, boy." He leaned forward, peering through the thick fumes into the pot. "We need a tar baby, little girl, because your brother thinks peacefulness and respect are *boring*."

Shelly still didn't understand why Dad wanted a tar baby now that he was outside of jail, but she figured it was better not to press the point. Dad was concentrating.

"Is it done?" she asked instead.

"I think so. Lord, I wish Mr. Baldwin were here now. He'd know for sure."

"Maybe we should wait," said Shelly.

Dad thought about this, and shook his head. "No. It's time now. Blaine?" Without looking up, Dad held his hand out. Blaine rolled his eyes at Shelly, and hefted the can of turpentine. Dad took it, unscrewed the top and held it over the pot.

"Hold your nose," said Dad. He mumbled a verse about hair and salt and lizards, and began to pour. The turpentine in the hot tar made an awful dark vapor where it etched out the tar baby from the rest of it, and even though Shelly's nose was held tight, she could taste it on her tongue and feel it in her eyes as it rose up around them and blotted out the dim light of the evening. She shut her eyes against it, sealed her lips, but it was still around her; she felt it sticking to her like the tar it'd come from, and the substance of it stayed on her even when the smoke cleared and Dad, arms tar-black to the elbow and grinning like a little boy, pronounced them done for the night.

"Come on," said Blaine. "Get up off the ground, stupid, and let's go."

Shelly flinched back — expecting another punch maybe. But Blaine stood against the darkening sky with Dad, his hands tucked safely into his armpits.

"Before the cops come," said Blaine.

Mom was watching an old episode of *Frasier* on TV when they got back, and when Dad came through the door after Shelly and Blaine, she glared at him like he was trespassing. In a way, he was. This was, strictly speaking, Mom's house; she'd inherited it from her own mother, free and clear back before Shelly'd been born. The house was miles outside town, on an ugly flat scratch of land where the grass grew too high and you saw the neighbors by the smoke from their wood stoves in the winter. But it was theirs, free and clear.

Mom called it their haven; for without the security of a paid-off house in a jurisdiction where the taxes were low, who knew where their awful circumstances would take them? She couldn't work anymore, not since the accident at the restaurant three years back where she'd bunged her knee; a mortgage or even regular rent on a place like this would ruin them. She couldn't carry it on workers' compensation alone.

"Keep that thing in the shed," she said, as Dad brought the basin inside. Mom probably wouldn't have sounded angry to anyone but Shelly, and maybe Blaine.

If Dad understood her tone, he didn't let on. "Won't do in the shed," he said. "Got to be here, or there wasn't any point."

Mom rolled her eyes. "*There wasn't any point*. You got that right." She picked up the remote from the side of the couch and pointed at the TV.

Frasier's dad and the little dog vanished, and the room darkened a bit. With a grunt, Mom shifted her feet from the couch to the floor, and lifted herself on her cane. It was no mean feat; Mom had gotten *heavy* since she'd taken off work. "You going to catch a rabbit with that?" she asked.

Dad didn't get it, and Mom laughed unkindly.

"Mom's talking about Bre'er Rabbit," said Shelly, trying to help. "From *Song of the South*." She'd seen the movie over at her friend's house at Thanksgiving, and there was a tar baby in it. Bre'er Fox had used it to catch Bre'er Rabbit — and it'd nearly worked.

"Jail didn't teach you much, did it now?" she said.

Dad sucked in his breath, like he was about to say something — and he looked down at the basin in his arms.

"Oh no," he said. "We're not starting this again. Not now." He looked up, and his eyes had a calm about them.

"I'm putting this in the basement," he said. "You won't have to smell it, or even look at it if you don't want to. So it won't be any trouble for you — all right?"

"Whatever you say, *dear*," said Mom, then turned to address Shelly. "Lord, now, isn't it good to have a man around here? See, I wouldn't have any idea how to put a bucket of tar in the basement and not stink up my house with it. Stupid little me wouldn't know how to keep those fumes out of the vents, and before you know it, all the sheets'd start stinking like a blacktop highway in July!"

She was looking at Shelly, but she was moving towards Dad, stumping sideways on her cane like some kind of crab. Shelly tried not to glare at her: it seemed like Mom just couldn't give Dad a chance.

"And why, I'd *never* think to take my two children out to steal tar from a construction site! On a night just two days I'd been out of jail!"

Dad was grinning now. He held out the basin in front of him as Mom came nearer. The metal of it made a bonging sound as he lifted it an inch or so.

"Good thing," she said, raising her free hand and touching the rim of the basin, "my husband's come home to set things *right!*"

"Careful, Dornie," Dad said. "Don't want to get yourself into a state."

Mom still wasn't looking at Dad — she didn't stop looking at Shelly, and

# NIGHT OF THE TAR BABY

Shelly could see by her narrow eyes that Mom was working herself into quite a state indeed. If that state had been directed at Shelly, she would have been frightened for herself — but tonight, Shelly was just a channel, a way for five years and a day of bottled-up rage to get to Dad.

So Shelly just watched as events unfolded.

Mom's fist tightened around the edge of the basin, and she shifted her weight so she didn't need the cane under her and could lift it into the air so as to swing it. "I'll give you a *fuckin'* state," she said in a low and terrible voice, finally turning her angry eyes to focus right on Dad. The basin began to tip toward her under her weight. Dad smiled, and the metal bonged again.

There was a third bong, and it seemed as though Mom's already-unsteady footing slipped, and the basin overturned. Mom yelped, and tried to yank her hand away. Dad's grin opened up into a toothy smile, and he let the basin fall to the floor. Shelly shut her eyes as it hit — thinking about all the tar inside it, and how it'd be to clean up tar, how long it would take and what kinds of solvents she'd need to do the job to Mom's standards.

But when she opened her eyes again, she saw there'd be no need — the old shag carpet didn't have a drop of tar on it, because the tar baby was all over Mom.

It had taken hold of her hand first — two twig-boned fists grasped her fingers, and it must have used her fingers to swing on because all of a sudden its skinny tar-black legs were wrapped around her elbow. Mom was wearing a bright yellow tank-top, no sleeves, so it hadn't gotten on her clothes right at first. But as Mom reached over with her free hand to try and yank the tar baby off, she pushed the thing's back against her chest, and that did it. She was a mess.

Mom looked like a big bat as she lifted both arms away from her, strands of tar making a web between them and her chest — where the tar baby seemed to have fixed itself. "*Get it off!*" she hollered. "*Get this fuckin' thing off me!*"

Dad was laughing so you could hear it now. He bent over and slapped his blue-jeaned knee, and fell down to his knees and laughed some more, shaking his head.

"Look at that," he said. "Damn me if it's not suckling off you, Mama!" And he howled.

Sure enough, thought Shelly, it did look like the tar baby was suckling.

Somehow, it had managed to get turned around and now its face—or at least the front of it's head; the tar baby didn't really have a face—mashed into Mom's left breast, like it was taking milk.

With nothing there to hold it up, the tar baby started to peel away from Mom's tank-top; and for a second, as it turned first to face the ceiling and then forward, Shelly thought she could make out a little grinning face on the thing—mouth open, thin snot-strands of tar between upper and lower jaw, and tiny little button-eyes, staring up at Mom's tit. But the face went away as the tar baby turned, and it was just a mound of hardening tar again. Mom'd stopped hollering, and she'd started to sob. Dad picked up the basin from where it'd fallen on the floor, and held it under the tar baby. It fell into it with a bong.

Everyone stood silent. Mom was covered in tar—somehow, it'd gotten on her face and into her hair; it smeared down her shoulders and onto her hands like lines of thick, black finger-paint. Mom looked up at Blaine, and cleared her throat.

"Blaine honey," she said, voice calm and reasonable. "Fetch your Mom her cane."

Blaine did as he was told, but when it came time to hand the cane over, he didn't get to close to Mom. Shelly didn't blame him. Mom took the cane, propped it against the floor and pushed herself to her feet.

"I'll just put the baby in the basement then," said Dad, to no one in particular. He whistled as he carried the basin into the kitchen and down the stairs.

"You mean the *tar* baby," said Shelly, but Dad was beyond hearing.

Dad drank beer from a bottle at the kitchen table, and Shelly sat with him, sipping her Coke from the can. They didn't speak at all while the shower ran; Dad had just stared out the window into the dark yard, drank his beer, and occasionally reached over to pat Shelly on the hand.

For her part, Shelly just watched him. She hadn't seen Dad since she was just five—not properly anyway, not outside of a prison visitation—and he was for all practical purposes a complete mystery to her. He had last gone to jail for armed robbery—he'd used a hunting rifle to rob a grocery store in Huntsville with his buddy Mark Hollins, who'd gotten off as an accomplice and did hardly any time in jail at all. Shelly tried to imagine her father doing such a thing, and found again that she couldn't. When she'd gone to see him with Mom and Blaine, he was always laughing and gentle—even when Mom egged him on. It wasn't that there was any doubt he'd done the robbery; Dad had confessed to it and pleaded guilty when it came time to go to court. It was just that Shelly couldn't see how he'd done it, pulling out a gun and telling someone to hand over their money or they'd get it. Dad just seemed... too nice. Compared to the rest of the family, that was.

Finally, the shower shut off, and Dad squinted at the ceiling, like he was gauging something there.

"Out of hot water," he said.

"Maybe she's clean now," said Shelly.

Dad just shook his head. "Soap and water won't do a thing to tar. Your mother should know better."

Shelly nodded as though she understood, and swallowed the last of her Coke.

"She'll know better now," said Dad, staring back out the window.

They sat quiet again, as Mom stomped wet-footed on the floor upstairs and the vestiges of water drained from the bathtub through the old pipes under her feet, over their heads. Shelly squeezed her Coke can as if to crush it, but she didn't have the strength and the side just popped. Dad started at the sound, then smiled, and reached over to put his big hand over Shelly's. "Let's both squeeze," he said. Dad's thick fingers pushed on Shelly's, and for a minute she felt like he was crushing her against the can. But the metal crumpled easily under their combined grip, and Shelly laughed when Dad let go of her.

"Team work," said Dad. "That's what this family's going to be about, from now on little girl."

"Team work?"

Dad nodded sagely. "Most families do it, you know—ours is just peculiar that way. Or it has been. We've been like a bad cell block in a bad jail; we're always fighting and squabbling and hurting each other. Won't be the case any more."

Shelly looked up at her father, who was staring back out the window. It was true what he said; they were like a bad cell block in a bad jail, or at least they were always hurting each other. Dad had a point.

"Mom's wrong about you," she whispered.

Dad blinked, and smiled down into the dregs of his beer. He gave Shelly a squeeze around the shoulders.

"You better go to bed, little girl," said Dad. "It's late."

The bathroom door opened upstairs, and Mom made her way noisily to her own bedroom. A minute later, the mist of her shower wafted down — carrying with it the combined scent of perfumed soaps, old angry sweat, and tar-fume.

It was, Shelly realized, the first time she'd smelled tar since Dad had shut the basement door and Mom had gotten in the shower. For whatever reason, the tar baby's smell had just stayed put. Shelly laughed to herself: Mom had been wrong on that score too.

Dad stood up, and patted Shelly on the back. "Come on, little girl," he said. "Daddy's going out for a walk — you get on up to bed."

Blaine was already in the top bunk when she came into the bedroom. He had his reading light on, and was propped up on an elbow over some kind of magazine — Shelly couldn't see what because of the angle, but she suspected it was one of his mountain biking magazines.

"I'm not turning out the light," said Blaine.

"Who said I want you to?"

"You always want to go to sleep early."

"I'm not the one in *bed* already."

Blaine glared at her, picked up his magazine, and rolled over so he was facing the wall. Paper rustled angrily as he positioned the magazine out of his own shadow.

"You're lucky," he muttered.

Shelly supposed he was right. Normally, after a little exchange like that one, Blaine would swing down from the bunk, grab Shelly in a headlock and take the last word in the argument by sheer might. Shelly would have to apologize — no, she would have to *beg*, and if she were lucky, that would be all it took.

Tonight, Shelly guessed she was really lucky.

She sat down on the bottom bunk and pulled off her T-shirt. The springs over her head creaked as Blaine shifted his weight.

"Lucky," he said again, his voice low and kind of scary. "I could come down and pound you right now. You know I'd do it."

Shelly unbuttoned her jeans, pulled them off and slid under the covers.

"You know that—don't you, shitty Shelly?"

"Stop it, Blaine."

"*Shitty Shelly*," said Blaine, and he started to sing it: "*Shitty Shelly shitty Shelly.*"

"Stop it," she repeated, but of course he wouldn't.

"Shitty Shelly shitty Shelly. What are you gonna do, shitty Shelly? Get mad like Mom did?"

"This is *stupid*," she said. "This is what Dad was talking about."

She rolled back on her haunches, and lifted her feet to the mattress of the top bunk. Part of her screamed a warning: *Suicide! Don't even try it!* But the taunt was getting under her skin—Blaine knew how to get under her skin better than almost anyone—and she couldn't help herself. She bucked back on her shoulders, and pushed hard against the mattress with her feet—not too hard, just enough to send him a message.

She felt Blaine's weight roll to one side, and heard a crack! sound like snapping wood, and she felt the bed-frame tremble even as Blaine shouted. If she'd been even a little angry a second ago, it was all gone now; Shelly was just scared.

"You dumb bitch!" Blaine sounded an inch from tears. "You dumb goddamn bitch! That was my *head!*"

Before she could even answer, Blaine was half-way down the ladder from the top bunk. His head. She guessed she'd rolled him against one of the bed-posts, given him a good bang on the skull. Blaine was going to pound her all right. Shelly screwed her eyes shut and curled herself into a ball—waiting for the rain of fists that would follow, and hoping they'd just fall on her back and shoulders. She knew from bitter experience that if she let Blaine get to her stomach and face, there'd be no end to the pain...

But the punching didn't come.

Blaine made a strangling sound, and she heard the sound of his bare feet moving across the floor—and then she heard the door open and close.

"You're dead!" He yelled it from the hall, like he was chasing her, then repeated it from the bottom of the stairs:

"You're dead!"

Cautiously, Shelly opened her eyes.

"B-Blaine?" she whispered.

But of course he didn't answer: she was alone in the bedroom. Distantly, she heard the sound of a door downstairs opening and closing again. Shelly wasn't sure, but it might have been the basement door in the kitchen. She curled more tightly around herself, and shut her eyes again.

Shelly didn't sleep. Part of it was the Coke she'd had with Dad, but mostly she stayed awake thinking about the tar baby, and what it'd done to Mom. This, she guessed, was how it was when Mr. Baldwin got in trouble with the other men in prison back in the early days. She tried to imagine how it would have been—Mr. Baldwin's first night with the tar baby. Maybe the guy who had the top bunk there was looking for some trouble like Blaine had been, holding it and stoking it and building his meanness through the evening until it was something he could use, in the small hours of the night.

Behind her closed eyes, she could almost see the two of them, skinny little Mr. Baldwin lying still like a rabbit underneath his blanket, and the other prisoner—probably he was a lot bigger, and had been in a lot of fights, just like Blaine—him jumping down like he wants a piece, saying "*Shitty Baldwin, shitty Baldwin, shitty Baldwin*" over and over again. And because Mr. Baldwin wouldn't answer him, and wouldn't do what he said, and maybe earlier that day lipped off to him like Shelly had lipped off to Blaine, that other prisoner reached down to grab onto his shoulder, and give him a beating.

Only it wasn't Mr. Baldwin's shoulder he grabbed. He reached down to the bucket by his bunk, and that prisoner had his hand stuck deep in the tar baby's shoulder. Before he could think, he hit that tar baby again, and one more time, and that was it—he was stuck. Just like Bre'er Rabbit in the movie. Just like Mom tonight.

Shelly wondered if Mr. Baldwin laughed that first time, the way Dad had laughed when Mom had gotten herself tangled up in their tar baby.

## NIGHT OF THE TAR BABY

Or, she thought with a shiver, *maybe Mr. Baldwin just lay in his bunk, all curled up trying to go to sleep, while his cell-mate choked on tar on the floor beside him.*

Blaine had been downstairs a long time. And Dad was still out walking, and Mom hadn't budged from her bedroom.

And hadn't Dad said something about team work?

Shelly got out of bed and pulled on her T-shirt. "Mom!" she shouted, pushing her feet through the legs of her jeans. "Hey Mom!"

She walked barefoot across the floor of the bedroom and opened the door to the hallway. She took a breath to yell —

— and coughed.

The air in the hallway was sticky with the stink of tar, and she had a lung-full of it. Shelly reeled back, covering her face with her hand, but of course her fingers were no filter and the damage had already been done. She coughed again, and gasped, and managed, finally, to yell — "*Mom!*"

Shelly stumbled forward, holding onto the banister around the stairwell as she did. The air seemed to get worse the further she went, and by the time she pushed Mom's bedroom door open, she was barely taking half-breaths. The door swung open, and Shelly ran past the bed — not even looking to see if Mom was there — and fell against the windowsill. Her lungs had hitched a final time, and now she couldn't breathe at all. With the last of her strength, she grabbed onto the base of the window and hefted it up.

Shelly pressed her face against the screen, coughed one more time, and sucked deep of the clean summer night air, looked at the empty driveway, the dark land around the house. In the distance, over the low treetops, she could see the lights from the highway.

"Mom," she said, not turning back, "we got to go downstairs and help out Blaine. I think he got messed up with the tar baby. He — he was picking on me, and he turned around and went downstairs, and I think he's in the basement..."

Shelly paused. In the distance, she could hear a car engine straining up a hill; crickets rubbed their legs together in the long grass of their front yard, and the thin breeze made the leaves of the birch-tree around the side rustle like paper. From inside the house, she heard a sound that must have been the refrigerator, a rattling whine as the compressors got going.

From Mom, she didn't hear a thing.

Shelly took another breath, turned around to face the bed and made her way slowly to the still, dark form laying atop the sheets. Shelly swallowed hard. The tar smell was pretty awful as she got closer, but she was expecting it now and she knew better than to breathe too deep.

Shelly stopped by her bedside, and looked down at her mother, Mom lay flat on her back, buck naked, on top of the bedspread still wet with shower-water. Her feet were apart, and her hands were spread from her torso so no limb touched another. The tar had tinted her flesh from head to foot; it matted her hair, and gathered in globs around her shoulders and across her wide breasts, like tiny birth-marks. Mom's eyes were open, and they looked at Shelly steadily. Her chest swelled as she drew a breath to speak.

"Mom's not—" she paused, shut her eyes, and continued, her voice rough and deep, like she had a cold " —not feeling good now, honey. You go to bed."

Shelly shook her head. "No Mom, I was telling you: Blaine's gone to the basement I think." She stomped her foot, and heard her voice go whiny. "You got to *come!*"

"No good," said Mom. "Knee's acting up again."

"I think Blaine's in trouble, Mom. You got to come help him."

Mom licked her lips, then made a face like she'd bit a lemon.

"Tar's everywhere," she said. "Even on m' mouth."

"*Mom —*"

"Hey!" Mom's voice took some energy. "Don't you take that tone with me! This is *my* house, Missy!"

Mom lifted her hand up, as if to cuff Shelly, but she didn't get far: whether it took strength or will to pull away from her bed, Mom didn't seem to have enough of either.

"Your Daddy," she said, "is a very bad man."

Shelly opened her mouth to argue some more—to point out that Dad wasn't the one who wouldn't get out of bed to help his son; that Dad had paid for his crimes, if he'd even done them in the first place; that Mom wasn't always the nicest lady in town either. But she remembered why she was here: Blaine, she feared, had gotten himself into some pretty immediate trouble; and Mom was in some kind of trouble, too. She didn't like to move around much as a rule since her knee had gotten hurt, but tonight, it seemed like she was *drained*. It was like when that tar baby had latched onto her breast, it had sucked something vital out of her.

"Don't know why I married him," said Mom, shutting her eyes.

"Maybe," said Shelly, "Dad would be better if you didn't keep being so mean."

Mom's brow crinkled.

"You don't know what you're saying, Shelly," she said.

"I know what I see." Shelly stepped away from the bed. "Dad trying to fix things, and you lying in that bed."

Mom's eyes opened now, and Shelly could see they were wet with tears. Now she did lift her hand, and brushed the air near Shelly's arm. Shelly flinched away—she didn't want those sticky-black fingers anywhere near her.

"You don't know him," said Mom, her voice nearly a whisper.

"He's my *Dad*," said Shelly. "Never mind about Blaine. I'll just help him myself."

Shelly stepped back into the hallway. A taste of salt came into her mouth as she closed the door on her Mom, but she swallowed it and made her way downstairs.

Dad had left the light on in the kitchen, and he'd left his empty beer out and Shelly's empty Coke-can out too. The smell was better down here, because he'd also left the kitchen door open, and a breeze washed through the screen door and through all the rooms on the first floor.

And of course the door to the basement was shut tight.

Shelly knocked on the door. "Blaine?" she called. "You all right?"

"Shelly!" Blaine sounded like he was muffled by something, talking through the hood of his snowsuit. "Shelly! I'm sorry I called you names!"

Shelly stepped back from the door. Now it was her turn to be speechless; in all her life, Blaine had never once apologized for anything.

"Shelly? You still there, Shelly?"

"I'm here," she said, cautiously.

"I'm sorry, Shelly!"

Shelly took a breath. "You're forgiven."

"Great," said Blaine, and his voice returned nearer to normal. "Give me a hand down here, will you? Bring down a towel, and —"

" — some turpentine?" Shelly finished for him.

Blaine laughed nervously.

"Yeah," he said.

Shelly laughed as well. It was like a weight had been lifted from her. All the way down the stairs, she was sure whatever happened with Mom had also happened with Blaine; the tar baby would suck the life out of him like it did from Mom. But he sounded okay, even improved by the experience.

Shelly went over to the counter, where Dad had put the can of turpentine, and lifted it down. She grabbed a tea-towel from the handle to the stove. "I'm —"

She was about to say *coming*, but she stopped, as a set of headlights appeared at the end of the driveway, and the sound of a truck engine broke the quiet. Bright headlights washed across the kitchen shuffling shadows from one end of the room to another.

The truck rolled to a stop beside the kitchen—it was a big pickup truck, painted bright red, and Dad sat in the driver's seat. In the passenger seat, Shelly saw, was a long-haired, bearded man she hadn't seen in a couple of years: since when she was really small, and dad hadn't been to prison for his second time.

It was Mark Hollins.

The man Dad had robbed the grocery store with—the one who'd gotten off with hardly any time in jail at all. He was laughing at something Dad was saying, and then he stopped and looked in through the window—straight at Shelly. He was still smiling, at least with his mouth—but his eyes had a different kind of look to them. If Shelly had been thinking of enlisting Dad's help in cleaning up her brother, pulling him out of whatever he'd tangled himself up in downstairs, the look in Mark Hollins' eyes dissuaded her.

"Shelly!" Blaine's voice was plaintive. "Come on!"

Shelly looked away from Hollins, and opened the basement door.

"I'm coming," she said. By the time Dad and Mark Hollins were out of the new truck, Shelly had closed the door behind her and was making her way down to where Blaine had gotten himself stuck.

The air had been okay on the first floor, but it was bad again in the basement. Shelly wasn't caught by surprise by it this time, though; even before she turned on the light, she expected the tar baby's stink would be the worst where it lived.

When she turned on the light, Shelly thought she might never breathe right again.

The basement was filled with tar.

It looked like two pages of a book, with a wad of black chewing gum squished between and stretched out as the book came open. Jump-rope-thick strands of tar stretched from wall to wall, ceiling to floor, casting shadows as black as itself. The strands twitched now and then, and before long, Shelly's eye was drawn to the likely cause of that twitching—two shapes suspended in the middle.

Her brother Blaine and the tar baby were locked together there, hanging about five feet off the cement floor, directly over the floor-drain, and the now-empty washbasin the tar baby had come in.

The tar baby had come in the washbasin, but Shelly figured it would never leave in it. The tar baby had stretched and fattened to the point where it was almost as big as Blaine; bigger, she realized with a chill, than she was. Its legs were wrapped around Blaine's waist, and its arms, long and spindly, hugged Blaine around the chest. Its head—once the size of a softball, now about as big as the Nerf football Blaine kept on his desk upstairs—pressed against Blaine's cheek.

Blaine struggled to look up the stairs at her. His face was blackened with tar, and as he moved one of the tar baby's hands slithered up his neck, to the back of his scalp. His eyes screwed shut and he sobbed, as the hand fell away again, pulling a small clump of tarry hair out with it.

"*Oh, Blaine.*"

Shelly whispered it—she was pretty sure Blaine couldn't hear her she was talking so quiet, but it seemed as though the tar baby could. Its head fell back from Blaine, like it had from Mom earlier in the night, and it cricked back on its skinny neck, so it was looking straight at Shelly. Last time she'd seen it, the tar baby seemed to open its mouth. Now, there was no doubt about it: the cut in the tar of its chin was fully formed, into a jagged grin like a jack-o-lantern.

"I'm sorry, Shelly. I'm sorry, Shelly. I'm sorry Shelly." Blaine's eyes were still closed, and his voice was strangled with tears now as he repeated the apology again and again. It was like he was apologizing for every *shitty Shelly* he'd said upstairs. As Shelly thought about it, she started to feel the heat of anger come up in her again.

"Do you *mean* it?" she said, her voice low.

"I'm sorry, Shelly."

One of the tar baby's arms unfastened itself from Blaine, and the creature started to dangle. There was a sucking sound, as a strand of tar snapped away from Blaine's ankle, and he kicked his foot free of the other two still there.

"Do you *really* mean it? Or are you just saying nice to get in my good books? So I'll help you down?"

"Dad was right," said Blaine. The tears had stopped, and he was able to look at Shelly with a directness that made her want to cringe. There was a twang, and a couple of strands came loose of his shoulder, even as the tar baby's legs started to unwrap from around his waist. "We got to be better to each other."

*Dad was right.* Shelly felt her own anger melt away at that. Mom may not have understood, but at least Blaine did.

"Dad was right," she said. "That's right—team work."

"What?"

"Something Dad said," said Shelly.

Gingerly, avoiding the strings of tar along the way, Shelly made her way down the rest of the stairs to where Blaine still dangled. She held the tea-towel under her arm, and unscrewed the top of the turpentine, and soaked a corner of the towel with it. The tar baby's free arm dangled gnarly fingers near her cheek, but Shelly pulled away and the tar baby didn't follow. She handed the towel up to Blaine, making herself think kind thoughts.

"I hope you learned your lesson," she said, as Blaine touched the turpentine to the tar baby's other hand. Shelly stepped back as that arm came free. The tar baby was completely disentangled from Blaine, but it didn't fall to the ground—as it came free it swung up among the tar strands nearer the ceiling—like a big, sticky spider, in a web spun of its own substance.

Blaine fell to the floor as he came loose of that web—and it seemed as though he landed all right. But he winced as he stood, and his legs trembled under him.

"Dad was right," he said. "I wanted to hit you upstairs, and when I went to, I took a swing—and then I was down here! Hitting the tar baby, getting all stuck up like Mom."

Shelly nodded. "That's how it worked for Mr. Baldwin at prison, I bet," she said. "The tar baby smells the mad, and it doesn't matter who it's directed at; it draws the mad to itself."

"So why didn't you wind up down here? When you kicked the bed?"

Shelly thought about that. "I didn't mean to hurt you," she said. "I just wanted you to quit it—I didn't think you'd hit your head."

Blaine looked down. He really was a sad mess, Shelly thought—hair all black and sticky, and his pajamas just as bad. And he looked weaker, too—the tar baby had taken it out of him, like it had from Mom. The only reason he was standing, Shelly thought, was because maybe Blaine had had more in him to begin with. "I guess it was because *I* wanted to hurt *you* then."

"I guess that's how it works," said Shelly.

"I'm sorry," he said.

"Stop apologizing."

"Okay." Blaine started scrubbing at himself, but it was clear even with the turpentine, it was going to be a harder job than he had the strength for right now.

"Come on," said Shelly—and she took his arm, sticky as it was. They started up the stairs together.

"What in fuck you get into, kid?"

Mark Hollins was sitting at the kitchen table, a bottle of bourbon open and half-empty in front of him, when they came out of the door. The sleeves of his denim jacket were rolled up, and Shelly could see a dark green shape that had been tattooed underneath the thick black hair on his forearm. There was no telling what it represented. Dad sat across the table from Mark Hollins, and there was a paper bag on the table between them.

Dad didn't even look back.

"Don't curse in front of the children," said Dad.

"Ah, fuck you," said Mark Hollins. "Gonna learn it somewhere."

Now Dad did turn around, and he looked Blaine up and down. He nodded slowly.

"Learn your lesson, son?" Dad was smiling ever-so-slightly.

"Yes sir," said Blaine.

"Good. Take that turpentine upstairs to the bathroom, and start washing yourself. I'll be up to help in a minute."

Mark Hollins finished a long pull from his bottle, and slammed it down again onto the tabletop. He spoke directly to Blaine.

"You take your time, son. Your daddy and me got some business."

As Mark Hollins spoke, Shelly saw Dad reach up and put his hand on the paper bag. Mark Hollins saw it too, because his eyes darted immediately to Dad's hands. They had that same discouraging look to them they had when he'd smiled at Shelly, and now even the smile was gone.

"Ah, shit, Scott—don't try this crap on me. We're splitting it like always."

"No," said Dad, his voice as level and calm as could be, "not like always. Not like when I did time for you. I'm keeping all the cash. And the truck. You *owe* me."

Shelly felt Blaine's hand on her shoulder—he was squeezing too tight, but she could tell he wasn't trying to hurt her. He was just scared—like she was starting to get. She was piecing things together, or maybe just admitting things to herself: like, where did that truck come from? Dad didn't even have a valid driver's license anymore, and the family hadn't owned a car for years. And cash? She wondered if the cash was in that bag on the table; and if so, just how they'd managed to get it.

"I owe you shit," said Mark Hollins.

"That's your opinion."

She and Blaine backed out of the kitchen and into the living room. Blaine's hand was trembling, and she could hear him sniffling as he pulled her further into the living room, around behind Mom's television chair. He crouched down, and Shelly crouched beside him, her arm over his filthy shoulders.

In the kitchen, the conversation escalated—at least on Mark Hollins' side.

He slammed his bottle down on the table, not hard enough to shatter, but enough to send a gout of booze up through the neck and splash on his white-knuckled fist.

"Give me the Goddamn money!" Hollins stood up, and put his arms under the table. Dad lifted his beer and the bag, and swung back as the table fell over onto its side, empty beer bottles and Shelly's old pop can scattering across the linoleum floor. "I risked my *fuckin'* neck tonight!"

Dad got up from his chair and stood with his arms crossed — beer in one fist, bag in the other — and he chuckled, shaking his head.

Shelly pinched her nose as the smell of tar grew stronger — it seemed like she could actually see the fumes, coming out of the half-open door to the basement in a thin grey cloud. Blaine didn't cover his nose — he probably smelled enough tar his nose wouldn't even tell it — but his hands were up over his ears, and his eyes were shut.

In the kitchen, Hollins reached around to his hip pocket, and he pulled something out that flashed metal in the kitchen light. Dad stopped chuckling as Mark Hollins held it in front of him, and even Shelly could see what it was: an X-acto knife.

"That's it, you fucker," said Mark Hollins. "You're right we're not splitting this money. You're going to give it all to me — isn't that right?"

Dad looked straight at his old buddy Mark Hollins, and shook his head. "Get out of here," he said, "if you know what's good for you."

And that set him off. Hollins shouted something Shelly couldn't hear properly, and he lunged with the X-acto blade —

— straight at Dad, he must have thought —

— but in fact, straight through the door to the basement.

Mark Hollins made a painful-sounding clatter as he tumbled over the first few steps, but the falling-down sounds ended quickly. There was nothing afterwards but a series of shouts — first surprised, then angry and finally just frightened. Dad walked over to the doorway and leaned over, both arms outstretched against the door frame. He laughed like he laughed when Mom got it earlier on. "What were you saying, Mark?" Dad stopped to cough — the tar-fumes were pretty thick — and went on: "You want all the money? Truck too? You want this house, Mark?"

Mark shouted something back, and now Shelly was sure it wasn't just bad hearing on her part — he was making no sound anyone could understand.

"I'll leave you to figure your way out of that one," said Dad. "Then we can talk about how to divide things up, from now on."

He pushed himself off the door, and swung it shut, then looked to the living room.

"Blaine?" he said.

"Y-yes sir?" Blaine stuck his head up from behind the chair.

"Get on upstairs like I told you to. I'll be along in a minute."

"Yes sir," said Blaine. He got up and went to the stairs. Shelly followed, but Dad told her to wait behind a minute. He had some things, he said, to say to her.

Shelly went to her Dad. He picked up the table and set it right, and pulled the chairs back in place.

"You're in pretty good shape tonight, little girl," he said. "Didn't feel the need to hit the tar baby?"

"No," she said.

Dad nodded. "That's good. Not everyone needs to learn from their own mistakes. What did you learn tonight?"

Shelly opened her mouth, and closed it again. There was a noise from behind the basement door — like a big cushion hitting against the stairs. She had been about to say team work, but that sound stopped her.

"Little girl?"

"It's..." She looked down at her relatively clean hands. "... it's gotten bigger," she said. "There's tar everywhere now."

Dad nodded. "That's what Mr. Baldwin said might happen. His tar baby got pretty big in its time, although it didn't stay that way forever. Just while it soaked it up... all that anger ... aggression ..." Dad's face went sour "...mis-placed authority."

"What does mis-placed authority mean?" asked Shelly.

Dad patted her back. "Something you'll never have to find out about," he said. "Let's just say, the other prisoners aren't the only ones a fellow has

# NIGHT OF THE TAR BABY

to fear in jail. There's also the damn guards..."

The thumping from below stopped — but there was another sound now: distant sirens, wafting across the scrub from the direction of the highway. Shelly looked out the window at the red truck Dad had driven home from his walk, and at the brown paper bag Mark Hollins had wanted so badly he'd pulled out a knife and knocked over a table.

"Go upstairs now," Dad said. "Tell your brother I'll just be another minute."

Shelly did as she was told — but she stopped on the stairs, and peered over the banister to the kitchen.

Dad sat slouched back a bit in the chair, as peaceful and quiet as ever, as the sirens grew louder, and Shelly marveled: she *still* couldn't imagine her Dad taking a gun and pointing it at a grocery store man, and saying he'd kill him if he didn't give over some cash. Any more than she could imagine him breaking the window of a shiny red pickup truck that belonged to someone else, and taking it for himself.

Mom was wrong, so wrong: Dad wasn't a bad man at all. In spite of what everyone thought about him. As Shelly continued up the stairs, she hoped the police who were running that siren could see the goodness in Dad too; she hoped they wouldn't be too mad about everything that had happened tonight.

The basement, after all, was only so big.

# Plato's Mirror

## by Robert Charles Wilson

*Philip K. Dick Award-winning author Robert Charles Wilson was recently described as being "a damned good writer regardless of the genre." We couldn't agree more. Wilson's recent critically praised novel,* **Darwinia***, is, among other things, part wilderness fantasy, decades-spanning tragic romance, and Lovecraftian cosmic mystery, blended smoothly by the author's typically elegant prose. Bob's first* **Northern Frights** *story, "The Perseids," was nominated for a World Fantasy Award and won the 1997 Aurora Award as "best short fiction." His second, "The Inner Inner City," was also a World Fantasy Award nominee. This, his latest, requires no introduction. Enjoy.*

### 1

"You don't know me," she said, eyes wide. "But I got this for you." It was a package about the size of a coffee-table book, flat, wrapped in brown paper and tied with butcher's twine. "You're right," I said, blocking the doorway. "I don't know you."

She smiled. "I'm Faye," she said. "Faye Constance."

She stood as tall as my collar, wide mouth, small nose, eyes a stunning shade of green — sunny clover, summer lawn. *(Beware all green-eyed girls,* my father used to say. A drunk's advice.) She was, she told me later, all of twenty-two years old.

"I don't know you, Faye Constance, so I have to ask: what do you want? And what's in the package?"

"Oh my God!" She put a hand to her mouth, mock-horrified. "You must think it's like a *letter bomb* or something! Oh God! No — what happened is, I read your book. The back cover said you lived in town. So when I came across *this* I knew I had to look you up and give it to you. It's not as weird as it sounds...don't look at me like I'm from another planet or whatever."

"I'm not sure I follow."

She thrust the package at me. "It's a present, that's all. From an admirer."

The package was heavier than it looked. Downright hefty. She turned away.

"Wait," I said. "I can't accept this." Adding, against my own better judgment, "Not from a stranger."

"You know who I am."

"I know your name. That's different." I checked my watch. "You can have fifteen minutes of my time."

"I'm not buying time."

"My time you can't buy. Come in. If you want."

Her smile broadened. The glare was blinding.

Faye gazed at my apartment, which Helen had once called my "seduceatorium." The walls were lined with books, many of which I had read. The bay window was tall and relatively sunny, for a fifth-story one-bedroom buried in a canyon of condo towers. Two potted cacti braced the window and cast faintly green reflections across the ceiling. The room was done in green: in sea foam, ochre, and mist. The sofa was large and inviting if somewhat checkered with coffee stains.

Not that I meant to seduce Faye Constance. I was still a little afraid of her.

My work attracts the emotionally damaged. I had met them at "psychic fairs" and at ABA functions, clutching copies of *Plato's Mirror* and peering at me through smudged lenses murky as millponds. They believed, these people, believed with all their stilted hearts and inadequate minds, that I had tapped the wisdom of the ancients and was dispensing it one volume *per annum* through an American paperback press. A loyal crowd, but not necessarily stable.

So I laid it out for her. Counting my fingers: "One. Everything I know about history I learned while auditing a classics course at the University. Two. The book is fiction. I made it up. For money. Three. Meeting me won't make you a better person. Probably the opposite. I drink and I smoke dope and I have a lot of shitty friends."

"That's supposed to discourage me, right?"

"Only if you're smart."

She laughed, which was disarming. "Look, I don't want to marry you. I just like your writing. I was rummaging around the thrift shops and I found...well, something that made me think of you. So I was a little impulsive. It's no big deal. Anyway," checking her watch, "you can have your time back. I have to be somewhere."

As suddenly as that, I didn't want her to leave.

"Look, I'm sorry if I was harsh. Give me a number, Faye Constance. In case I want to say thanks."

"You don't have to thank me. The number is in the package."

She smiled goodbye and headed for the door. From behind she looked like some Boticelli angel who had just discovered the possibilities of gender. The seduce-atorium was sorry to see her go.

I opened the package — wouldn't you?

It was, of course, a mirror. An "antique" mirror, the sort you find in shops where any object sufficiently motheaten and older than Sarah Michelle Gellar is deemed to be an antique. (By which definition, wasn't I one?)

The frame was pinholed Victorian gingerbread with flakes of gilding still clinging to it, held together with blackened finishing nails and backed with brittle brown paper. The glass itself was perhaps older than the frame, and where the silvering had corroded there were patches of quivery distortion, the effect you get passing a magnet in front of a TV tube. The mirror reflected my own homely face, no more and no less. (Had Faye been disappointed by the face behind the book? But I create illusions and dispel them: that's what I do.)

Tucked between glass and frame was a note in Faye's childish handwriting.

*PLATO'S MIRROR? You never know!!*
Signed, *Your admirer.* Plus name, address, telephone number.

"But it's ugly," Conrad said.

"Is that a problem? I like *you,* don't I?"

"Mm. But you don't hang me on the wall, notice."

"Not that I haven't thought of it."

Conrad, my neighbor-three-doors-down, grimaced at his reflection. I had put Faye's mirror in the hallway adjacent to the bathroom. The light was dim here, making the mirror (I hoped) more decorative and less obviously trashy. Conrad disagreed. His image moved in the surface of the glass like a dolphin about to surface. "Your taste is unfailing, Donald. Everything you own, it's all so — *rec room.*"

"Ugly but fun?"

"Ugly, anyhow." He bent closer to my ear. The noise of the party had already reached deafening and was approaching traumatic. "By the way. Word of caution. Watch out for Helen. She's *not* a happy camper."

"Fuck," I said.

"Judging by her mood, not tonight."

Fifteen people in my apartment was a crowd; twenty was practically coitus. Maybe twenty-five had arrived for the weekly zoo. Oh, we were a motley crowd: five writers, three contract programmers, a dozen unemployed intellectuals and aging students, a couple of hookers, my dentist, my drug dealer, and my girlfriend. Helen. Girlfriend, I suspected, for not much longer. She was allergic to tobacco smoke, pot smoke, perfume, and red wine, which begged the question: what was she doing here?

At the moment she was engaged in a raging argument with Conrad's partner William, a writer of small-press fiction. The subject had been literary to begin with but the conversation had deteriorated when William, waxing impatient, described T.S. Eliot as "a closet queen, sewn up so tight he couldn't fart authentically." Helen's graduate thesis had been a feminist defense of T.S. Eliot. Eliot was her red flag. I had learned to wince at the sound of his name.

I put my hand on her shoulder. "William's baiting you, Hel. Ignore him."

She whirled on me. Her eyes — brown — flashed. "Stop defending me!"

"I don't think that's what I'm doing."

"Then stop defending your asshole *friends!*"

Things had been going bad for weeks. Helen was, as they say, conflicted. She liked me, we got along well (when we got along at all), but underneath all that me-too bohemianism was a fragile Bishop Strachan debutante still yearning for cashmere and clean forks.

Or else — looking at it from her point of view — she had fallen in with a crowd whose appetites and poverty had turned out to be more dismal than stylish.

In other words, we embarrassed her.

Later, she took me into the bedroom and closed the door against a crush of bodies. For reprimands, not a quick fuck. Times change. "I'm leaving," she said. "I mean it. I'm tired of beer on the rug and puke in the kitchen sink and I'm tired, frankly, of you, Donald, and your self-loathing and your pussy-chasing and the crappy way you treat people."

"About covers it," I said.

"*And* that self-serving ironic *tone* you take whenever you feel *threatened.*"

"Anything else?"

"Yes. This. For every time you stood me up while you diddled some young ignoramus."

She raked her nails across my cheek and wrestled her way down the hallway to the door. Helen slammed doors for punctuation. Slam: period. Full stop.

The new/old mirror was full of restless shapes. I headed for the kitchen. On the way I turned up the music. Polyrythmic, agressive, dangerous. Like me.

What I had neglected to tell her was how much I loved her.


The crowd faded around three, spilling out into the empty street. Conrad and William stayed behind, sharing a spliff. They were practically home already. Conrad was a city-bred white boy and William was a Nova Scotia black, but they had developed, in tandem, similar voices, similar mannerisms. At ease, they draped their arms across each other's shoulders and inclined together like lazy willows. I envied them.

I had told them the story of the mirror. (Stroking my wounded vanity with images of Faye.) Conrad said sleepily, "Well, what if she's right?"

"Right about what?"

"The mirror."

"The *mirror?*"

"Sure the mirror. How do you know it doesn't show, ah — what was it you called them in your book? Architects?"

"Archons. Archons and Essences."

William stirred from his nestling place at Conrad's shoulder. "What are Archons?"

"Shush. It's a Greek word."

"Right," I said. "It's a Greek word for 'bullshit.' Come on, Conrad, I get enough of that crap from the public at large."

"Donald, hon, I know you're a fraud; you don't have to remind me. But, heck, magic mirrors, can't we even play?"

"Busman's holiday. You play with it if you want. Just don't break it."

"You really do like the ugly thing!"

"No. I like the pretty young thing who brought it to me."

"I see. And how exactly did it work in your little book?"

In my "little book," Plato's Mirror was the long-forgotten secret of the Eleusinian rites — the ancient Greek Demeter cult that survived, in one form or another, for almost two thousand years. The Eleusinian mysteries remain shrouded in secrecy, but according to most scholars they involved an annual pageant at an underground spring: "Happy is he who, having seen these rites, goes below the hollow earth; for he knows the end of life and its beginning." Pindar.

The mirror was my own invention. It was the mirror, I claimed, that had inspired Plato's fable of the cave. You know the story? If we lived out our lives in a cave with only the narrowest of pinhole openings and no way in or out, we would experience the world as shadows projected on a wall. And if this hypothetical cavedweller were to be transported outside for the first time, the experience would be overwhelming, instant immersion in a madly hyperreal universe of colors and shapes and textures.

# PLATO'S MIRROR

Plato's Mirror, I claimed, provided that glimpse of an unmediated world. Created by Greek alchemists, the mirror had been banished to the lightless underground, where it became the secret icon of the Eleusinian Mysteries, to be experienced only by devotees and even then only briefly. The human mind, after all, can bear only so much reality.

I had adduced my evidence from Gnostic manuscripts and freshly-discovered Dead Sea scrolls which only I had seen. Documents, in other words, that didn't exist. The book was punctuated with pseudo-scholarly footnotes but all the references were blind, unavailable in any real-world library.

Fold in a little Atlantis lore, a bit of Masonic paranoia, and a *soupçon* of New Age millenarianism; yield: one not-quite-beststelling addition to the crackpot rack of your local bookstore. I had contracted for three more volumes. Carlos Castaneda, rest in peace.

Conrad wouldn't leave it alone. "It works," he said, "the mirror I mean, only in the dark, right?"

"Conrad, if you want to turn off the lights and look at your absence of a reflection, be my guest."

"Vampires," William chimed in. "Vampires have a mirror thing, don't they?"

"Vampires you *can't* see in a mirror. I think what Donald is talking about are monsters you can *only* see in a mirror."

"Are there such things?"

"No," I said, "for Christ's sake, it's pretend, all right?"

"Shall we prove it?" Conrad wouldn't let this go; he was off on some coy, stoned trajectory of his own.

"If it'll shut you up, I'll turn off the lights and dance nude."

"I am," he said haughtily, "not tempted. Jeez, Donald, did Helen leave with your sense of humor in her purse?"

So I turned off the lights and sat back down.

"This is," William announced, "already spooky."

"Draw the blinds," Conrad said. "The streetlights are glaring."

"Draw them yourself."

He did, eliminating everything but a dim green glow. I couldn't see my hand in front of my face — couldn't see anything but the faint silhouettes of the cacti, each tall as a man. There was a brief flare as Conrad toked once more before setting off for the hallway. We had all smoked enough to make it seem like a long trip. And yes, there was some of that giggly thrill about the occasion: just us kids, up past our bedtime, smoking Mom's cigarettes and telling ghost stories.

"Donald!"

Conrad's voice sounded hollow and small, as if he had gone much too far away. "What?"

"Your mirror is broken!"

"Broken?"

"Must be! I can't see a thing!"

"Stop torturing me, Conrad. Shouldn't you and William be asleep by now?"

"Spoilsport." I heard his shoes scuffling along the linoleum, his small laugh. "All right, we'll — ah — "

Long pause.

"Conrad?"

Nothing.

Annoyed, I switched on the lamp next to the sofa. William sat up, still playing along but faintly uneasy. Conrad was out of sight around the corner, all of three feet down the hall. He stumbled back into the living room, frowning. "Not funny, Donald...."

"What's not funny?"

"Practical jokes." He seemed genuinely hurt. "You set me up, didn't you? So what is it really — some kind of computer display back of the glass? One of those LCD things?"

"Who's setting who up, exactly?"

"Ah, well...I don't grudge a joke at my expense. Kudos, Donald, and good night. Thank you for a lovely party. Sorry about Helen."

"Don't kid a kidder," I said to the closing door.

Helen called in the morning — far too early. Her voice on the phone was wistful. "Maybe," she said, "I was out of line last night. I meant what I said. But I didn't have to say it like that."

"Don't apologize. You were right."

"I was right? Is this a first? Donald Wilcox admits he might have acted like a jerk from time to time?"

"Right about us, I mean. Maybe we're not, as they say, a viable option."

"You don't like hearing the truth about yourself, do you?"

"I did kind of hope we'd finished that part of the conversation."

"What's her name this time?"

"Pardon me?"

"I swear to God, Donald, when I met you I thought I saw something fundamentally good about you. Was it all an act? A little seductive innocence, just enough to get you laid? Like some, I don't know, *spider,* spinning out those psycho books and devouring any woman you happen to catch...."

"You must have the wrong number, Hel. This isn't the Verbal Abuse Club."

And she was gone, as quick as that. I didn't know whether to cheer or weep.

I made a pot of coffee. Then I called Faye Constance.

2

"Of *course* it works," Faye said.

"Didn't we make a rule? No feng shui, no crop circles, and no magic mirrors?"

"What are you so afraid of?"

Two months had passed, during which time I had learned some things about Faye Constance. Under that lovely oxymoron of a name was a young woman of fierce enthusiasms and grave gullibility; a believer, but not a fanatic; not a virgin, but enthusiastically and youthfully adventurous in bed; a self-proclaimed poet, apt to leap up at midnight full of odes and couplets, unpublishable; by day, a transcriptionist at some dreary Provincial Ministry or other. "You never *leave* this place," she had complained, so we'd been doing dinners out, sentimental movies, head-cracking concerts. Tonight, however, we dined in. Faye had rented *Emma.* But she seemed more interested in the mirror.

"I'm not afraid of anything," I said, "except maybe your obsession with that slab of glass."

"Obsession, great, thank you very much. But, Donald — it *does* work. I tried it last night, when you went out for roti."

"I wish you could hear yourself. Faye, it *works?* What's that even mean?"

"I'm not saying it's necessarily the Plato's Mirror in your book. Just that it does the same thing."

"The book is crap, my love, and there's no such thing as a magic mirror."

"Or Archons, or Essences? You didn't make those up."

"No. I borrowed them from the Gnostic writers. Who *did* make them up."

"There's some truth in every religion, I think."

"Faye. Come on. What are you saying here?"

"Let me show you."

"No. No games. I'm not in the mood."

"Just let me *show* you!"

And I agreed, because I remembered Conrad's performance, and that made me a little afraid, and I was mad at myself for being afraid and I didn't want Faye even to suspect I took any of this seriously. Helen was gone for good and Faye had become the significant female presence in my life, and without Faye's adulation what would I be? A lonely con artist, a writer without a text, a congenital liar.

Faye was afraid of nothing. I think she was born without the fear gene. She got a double dose of puppydog enthusiasm instead. Uneasy as I felt, it was a joy to watch her fuss around the apartment, pulling curtains, even switching off the air conditioner because it might emit hostile technological vibrations. She brough the mirror into the bedroom. "Now we take off our clothes," she said. "We have to be pristine."

Could she have been *more* pristine, stripped to pure pale geometry, nipples royally erect? She braced the mirror on a dresser and against the wall, angled slightly up. From where I stood I could see her reflection, knees to crown, muzzy in the age-frosted glass. And she could see mine. My hairy-legged and somewhat paunchy male nudity. "Now turn off the light," she said.

I flipped the switch.

I looked toward Faye and saw nothing but whirly retinal static. I looked in the direction of the mirror and saw —

Must I say this?

I would much rather lie.

Saw an angel.

Hyperbole in the service of truth isn't my strong suite. No, I don't know what an angel looks like. But her reflection in the mirror was awe-inspiring. I drew a quick, frightened breath. Frightened, because how can there be a reflection in a dark mirror? And how can a reflection make its own light, especially this cool mother-of-pearl radiance fractured to rainbows in the still air?

Seconds ticked away in the silence. Faye said breathlessly, "Donald?" In the mirror, an angel-mouth moved. "What do you see?"

The distilled liquor of a thousand stained-glass windows. The glow of a cloudless summer day, compacted into human form. Sum of all the wide-eyed, wide-legged girls I had ever convinced to take off their clothes, their innocence flaring into soft night breezes. Starlight in amber. "I see," I said, "I think, it's *you,* Faye, only, only...."

"Yes," she said, meaning *I know.* "And I see you."

Instantly, I turned my face away.

"Donald?"

I switched on the light.

Her face was bright with tears. "But you're so — so fucking *beautiful!* Oh, Donald! Donald!"

"You know what we saw," she said as we lay together in bed.

I had turned the mirror to the wall. "Trick of the light."

"You can't be serious."

"What else?"

"That's a lie," Faye said, turning her back to me. "A *cruel* lie."

I'm a liar by trade. The cruelty is just a bad habit.

That summer Faye took me to the shop where she'd bought the mirror — not an antique store but a cramped second-hand bookstore on Harbord Street called Finders. The mirror had been taking up space along a side wall; the pale silhouette where it had hung was still etched against the yellowed paint.

Faye said she had asked the owner if the mirror was for sale and he had shrugged and accepted ten dollars for it. The woman behind the cash counter claimed to know nothing about the deal, and the owner, she said bleakly, "doesn't like to be disturbed."

Apart from that, I didn't discuss the mirror with Faye. She knew what she had seen; she smiled obliquely whenever I dodged the subject.

But I knew what I had seen, too.

I just didn't like to think about it.

I ran into Helen at the Starbucks near my building.

She was amiable, if a little wary, when I joined her at the table. She was seeing someone, she announced. And so, of course, was I. With these admissions we relaxed into the past tense of "us," a surprisingly comfortable space.

"Yeah," Helen said, "Conrad told me about your current. A little young, he seems to think."

"Not as young as she looks. And Conrad is a gossip."

"You think it'll last?"

I shrugged.

"In other words, no."

"I didn't say that, Helen."

"Poor Donald." She looked genuinely sympathetic. "It never goes away, does it? That picture in the back of your head. Daddy drunk and mom all bruises. The nightmares."

The trouble with women is that sometimes I confide in them. "I'm not sure this is something I want to talk about in Starbucks on a Saturday morning."

Helen scrunched up her foam cup. "Somebody ought to warn that girl, Donald. Maybe even you."

Turned out Conrad had befriended Faye; the two of them had gone thrift-shop trawling together. Conrad collected vintage Barbie dolls and accessories. Faye liked to pick up any old piece of colored glass: bottles, paperweights, vases. Sunlight through a prism could keep her fascinated for hours. She had magpie instincts.

I went with them on one of these weekend flea-market expeditions. Had no idea there were so many Thrift Villas and Salvation Army shops in the city. And they all smelled the same: of old clothes and rust, Lysol and mildew. Faye and Conrad shopped knowingly, pawing through trash for gems while I scanned the book racks, the literary equivalent of the Elephant's Graveyard, last stop for Edgar Cayce, Carl G. Soziere, Lobsang Rampa, and someday, perhaps, my humble self. Sun-faded spines all uniform yellow. This, too, a sort of mirror.

We lunched at a suburban fried-chicken factory. Faye was off at the washroom when Conrad said, "You ought to keep this girl, Donald."

"You think?"

"I'm serious. She's a sweet, bright, gentle little thing. She doesn't deserve the usual Donald treatment — six months fucking and a fare-thee-well."

"I'll treasure your advice."

"There is," he said meaningfully, "a little magic about that girl."

"Magic?"

"Well? She gave you the mirror, didn't she?"

"Ah — the *magic* mirror."

"I've seen it, remember? Plus we looked at it again one night. Last week. When you were out."

"Did you."

"A little functional magic in your life at last, and all you can do is grind your teeth."

"There's no such thing as magic, Conrad."

"Oh, I don't imagine there's anything special about that old mirror, but the magic, *that's* authentic. Comes by way of Faye, I suspect. Is that why it scares you so much? There's nothing *bad* in the mirror, you know."

"Let's talk about something else, shall we?"

He rolled his eyes. "Too late to slam that barn door, Donald. Those horses are *out*."


The experience of making love to Faye, the nights she stayed over, was indescribably sweet, subtle, and gratifying. No impatience marred the act and the only selfishness was mutual and guiltless. In bed, she set me free. How then to describe, how even to admit to myself the occasional impulse, at the height of our passion, to take her guileless head into my hands and twist it until something snapped?

"Who is it," Helen used to ask, "who is it, Donald, who lives inside you, who knows how to do or say exactly the thing that hurts the most? What kind of monster has instincts like that?"

No monster. I speak from the heart.

Faye says I write from the heart, too: that's how I know things I don't think I know.

3

The sequel to *Plato's Mirror* was called *The Book of Lies*. Due in September, and it wasn't going well. Which made me irritable. Which made me say things to Faye I shouldn't have said. Which she forgave, with bravery and wounded eyes. Which led me to think our days together were numbered.

Hot summer that year. Late asphalt-scented nights, fan-cooled sheets, long showers. August storms rolled out of the west in gray-tumbled waves. For four nights in a row dry lightning flickered over the lake.

It was storming when our last August Friday party broke up, leaving behind the usual overturned bottles, aggrieved neighbors, and Conrad and William and Faye to appreciate the four a.m. calm.

Four *anne meridian,* and the night cool enough that I turned off the air conditioner and threw open the windows, letting gusts of damp air flush away memory and smoke. We were all four of us beyond sleep, our private clocks lurching toward sunrise. There was no rain but plenty of distant lightning and fitful thunder. In the dark street outside, window awnings flapped like captive birds.

We didn't mention the mirror — Faye and Conrad were too much in awe of it to raise the subject lightly; William remained gently agnostic, and I despised the thing — until a great flash of lightning filled the apartment with purple light and thunder rattled the casements. Nearby strike. A transformer or hydroelectric substation had taken the hit, I guessed, because the lamplight dimmed and died and didn't come back.

The darkness made our shared space smaller. Faye, Conrad and William huddled on the sofa; I rummaged for a tea candle in the kitchen drawer. The thought of the mirror had struck them simultaneously while I was out of the room.

"Mirrors are funny things," William was saying, gossamer-eyed by candlelight. "When I was little there was a game we played. Like a dare-you thing: who's brave enough? You go into the bathroom and you turn off the light and you stare into the mirror, and there was this little chant, like *I want to see the ghost of Lizzie Borden* or some shit. So you think, hey, I'm not that stupid, and you do it, but you know what? Not five minutes go by before there's old Lizzie Borden staring back at you with her crazy eyes all lit up. It's imagination and bullshit, and you know that, but...there she is."

"Who's Lizzie Borden?" Faye asked.

"Axe murderess," Conrad said. "Before your time."

"Hey," I said. "Ghost stories. Shouldn't we roast a marshmallow or something?"

"Donald is reinforcing his little wall of rationality. I think he wants us to help."

Maybe. I had played that game too, the mirror game, when I was young, and William was right. Try as you might not to see it, the monster would always show up, raise your hackles, scare you into the light. I dislike mirrors. I dream about them from time to time. The notion for *Plato's Mirror* had come straight from a nightmare, and that was a factoid I had neglected to share with Helen or Faye.

"But it's a perfect opportunity!" Faye said fervently. "Look, Donald, the whole *city* is dark."

And so it was. The blackout had quenched every light for blocks around. There were only occasional headlights down along Bathurst Street, and not many of those. In the apartment tower across the alley, one or two flashlights flickered behind the windows. Otherwise, dark. But so what?

"The mirror!" Faye said. "We can see the whole city — I mean the *essence* of the city."

"If we hurry," Conrad added. "They usually fix these things pretty quick."

"Gimme the candle," Faye said. "I'll fetch the mirror."

I said, "You can't be serious."
"Yes!" A chorus. "We can!"

I burned my indignation in a joint and watched them go about their little game. Faye took the mirror out onto the miniscule balcony that adjoins the kitchen and balanced it on the Adirondack chair. Their voices were nervous and enthusiastic: children's voices. Faye had found the Christmas candles and they each carried one, like monks with gaudy votive candles, red green white, initiates into the Mystery. But no Dionysian underground, only this fifth-story pigeon perch.

The hush of the four a.m. city was shocking. Live in a city long enough, you forget about quiet. Stepping out onto the balcony (reluctantly, with a candle of my own) I heard all the sounds normally lost under the pressure of daylight: dripping eaves and drawn breath and even a train whistle, some CN freight crossing the Don. Tag ends of lightning flickered far away.

"Now blow out the candles," Faye said solemnly.

Out they went.

"Yours too, Donald."

"I like the light. Helps keep me from falling down."

"Don't be a pig! You'll ruin it."

So I blew out the candle.

But I didn't look at the mirror. In the dark, would Faye see this small act of cowardice?

I should have covered my ears, too. There was, at first, nothing to hear, only the steady drip of rainwater and a breath of wind. Then, finally, their voices, hushed with awe: *So beautiful* and *It can't be* and *oh God!*

So I looked, despite my best intentions.

At first the mirror seemed merely opaque, the same fogged-silver Victorian grotesque that might have been salvaged from any condemned Toronto boarding house or crumbling semi-detached — junk, in other words. But then the surface misted and roiled like fog on a lake, and images emerged, faintly at first, then suddenly crisp. From where I stood the mirror reflected the city skyline, towers immersed in cloud made bright and intricate as cowry shells in clear water, and every brick a prism.

"It's," William stuttered, *"heartbreaking...."*

And it was. In the absence of light every object glowed with its own essence, radiated purer colors than any rainbow. How can a color you've never seen be so achingly familiar?

"And the people," Faye whispered.

People?

"Look hard," she urged me. "Let it in."

Yes. Behind stone walls, brick walls, and forests of rusted rebar: people. People sleeping, mainly. People like small galaxies, constellations suspended in the night. "So beautiful," Faye sighed again. No two alike, yet all the same, as if souls had fallen from the clouds and drifted through open windows, the banked windrift of humanity.

Conrad and William had found each other's reflections. I saw them, too. They were in love, and love has its own spectrum, its own unearthly color. Something bright and gauzy (ectoplasm? passion?) floated between them, delicate as lace. Their bodies had been unclothed by the mirror. They had become bright vortices of energy, knots of life on a rope of spine. Bones like pastel coral.

Now Faye stepped into view. I felt the heat of her attention on my skin. She said, "Oh, Donald!" Words rippled the air. Her eyes were at once fierce and gentle, lenses focusing the light of distant suns. "Look at yourself!"

I meant to. I swear I did. But something else caught my attention.

"Faye?" I said.

"...yes...?"

"Some of those people out there — they're not — "

I felt her frown. "Not what? I don't know what you mean."

Not *essences*. Oh, I saw the essences, jewel-bright in their beds and sleeping the sleep of children. But also — *look harder* — the others. The ugly, intelligent ones. Call them Archons. They float *(look harder, Faye, look as hard as you can)* between the buildings, patrolling the night in clockwork formation, skeletal, big-headed, hairy and malevolent as spiders....

I backed up a step,

You look at them, they look at you. Their attention is caustic and demanding.

"Donald, what is it?"

"Can't you see them?"

Maybe she couldn't. Bless her green eyes: maybe only the good light got through. She started to say, "Look at *yourself*, Donald, and then — " But I lashed out, kicked the slats of the Adirondack chair, which collapsed spectacularly, the mirror shattering against the concrete floor of the balcony, each fragment flashing briefly bright as lightning before it chimed into darkness.

4

Conrad and William went home — shocked, dazed, breathless. They had shared a memory they might never discuss — it really did beggar language — but it would always be there between them, for better or worse, a mystery that would echo whenever they touched.

Faye stayed behind — for a while.

She didn't say much. I did the talking.

I won't repeat the obscenities here. I cursed her at length for finding the mirror and for bringing it into my home and for mind-fucking my friends with it. When she began to cry I didn't let that stop me; I called her brainless, gullible, illiterate, an eager slut.

I was aware of hurting her. The urge to hurt her, to humiliate her, ultimately to drive her away, was palpable, a weight in my throat, a buzz behind my eyes. I watched her sink to her knees, sobbing, and felt gratified.

She said she would leave. I said, "About fucking time."

But before she left she went to the balcony and gathered what she could of the broken mirror, harvesting broken glass by candlelight. Came back with sharp silvered fragments and splintered wood and bloodied fingers. Taking back her gift, I thought, but then she did the unexpected.

She held up the largest fragment of the mirror, and blew out the candle, and said into the expanding darkness, "If only you could *see*, Donald!"

She wanted me to see that I was an angel — an Essence — as bright and full of color as the rest of them; to see my goodness, I suppose.

And I did see that. (I'm not blind.)

But I saw the *other*, too. I saw what Faye could not: the Archon, the one

## PLATO'S MIRROR

who had been with me all along, spindly arms close to mine, black-mandibled skull bobbing in back of my own. I'm not alone. I know this too well, Faye: I think I've always known it, glimpsed this image in too many dream-mirrors. The Archon is every day a little closer, close as a shadow now, close as a lover, and it will have me soon enough; and if it has me then it will have Faye or whoever replaces Faye. And the voice shouting obscenities, the shrill voice accusing her of whoring and idiocy, the voice trying so fervently to drive her away, now, now before it's too late —

It's the voice of the angel.


She left, at last, in tears, for good.

I waited for sunrise. But the room was dark. Angels wept. And I was not alone.

Québec, Canada
1999